The Fifty Most
Erotic
Films
of All Time

The Fifty Most

Erotic Films

of All Time

From *Pandora's Box* to *Basic Instinct*

Maitland McDonagh

A Citadel Press Book

Published by Carol Publishing Group

To Frank, as always

Copyright © 1996 by Maitland McDonagh

A Citadel Press Book
Published by Carol Publishing Group
Citadel Press is a registered trademark of Carol
    Communications, Inc.
Editorial Offices: 600 Madison Avenue, New York, N.Y.
    10022
Sales and Distribution Offices: 120 Enterprise Avenue,
    Secaucus, N.J. 07094
In Canada: Canadian Manda Group, One Atlantic Avenue,
    Suite 105, Toronto, Ontario M6K 3E7
Queries regarding rights and permissions should be
addressed to Carol Publishing Group, 600 Madison Avenue,
New York, N.Y. 10022

Carol Publishing Group books are available at special discounts for bulk purchases, sales promotion, fund-raising, or educational purposes. Special editions can be created to specifications. For details, contact: Special Sales Department, Carol Publishing Group, 120 Enterprise Avenue, Secaucus, N.J. 07094

Designed by Andrew B. Gardner

Manufactured in the United States of America

10 9 8 7 6 5 4 3 2 1

Library of Congress Cataloging-in-Publication Data

    McDonagh, Maitland
The 50 most erotic films of all time / Maitland McDonagh.
        p.   cm.
    "A Citadel Press book.
    ISBN 0-8065-1697-6 (pbk.)
    1. Erotic films—History and criticism.   I. Title.
PN1995.9.S45M34   1995
791.43′6538—dc20   95-19764
                                                    CIP

Contents

Acknowledgments

Many people helped make this book possible in many ways, from locating stills to confirming obscure facts and locating hard-to-find tapes.

First, I'd like to thank my agent, Chris Calhoun, and my editor, Kevin McDonough, for their unfailing support and encouragement.

Compiling the list of fifty most erotic films and the thirty-one sidebars was a formidable—though endlessly entertaining—task. I'm particularly indebted to the following people for their suggestions and assistance in this and other aspects of the book's evolution: Mark Ashworth, David Cox, Greg Day, Darcy and Sean Fernald, Gary Hertz, Alexander Horwath, Donald Hutera, Michael Isbell, Alan Jones, Jussi Kantonen, Karen Krizanovich, Kevin Lally, Rebecca Lieb, Tim Lucas, Jennifer McDonagh, Jamie Pallot, Tom Phillips, Alan Robertson, Steven Schaefer, Regina Schlagnitweit, Gavin Smith, Kent Jones,

Patrick Tappe, and many others to whom I spoke at parties, screenings, libraries, film festivals, and all the other places movie enthusiasts gather. Frank Lovece merits special mention for his selfless and unflagging help in all phases of the book's preparation.

The staff of The Movie Place—especially Ron Kopp, David Vigdor, Ken Tramell, and Gary Dennis—were particularly helpful, once they set aside their initial skepticism that all those salacious movies were being rented because of a book. "Gee, *everybody* on the West Side [of Manhattan] must be writing a book about erotic movies," one remarked, before suggesting titles worth exploring.

Finally, the research collections of the New York Public Library, particularly the Library for the Performing Arts at Lincoln Center, were an invaluable resource. Without them I would never have been able to complete this project.

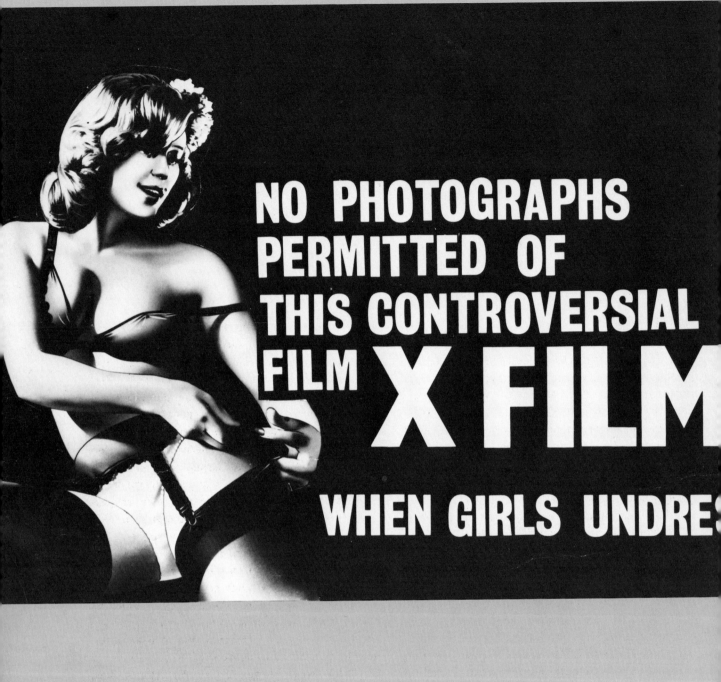

NO PHOTOGRAPHS
PERMITTED OF
THIS CONTROVERSIAL
FILM X FILM

WHEN GIRLS UNDRE

Introduction

Voyeurs get their thrills from watching, and the cinema makes voyeurs of us all. As many a Peeping Tom has discovered, even ordinary scenes become perversely interesting when watched under cover of secrecy. When you wonder how early audiences could possibly have been enthralled by all those movies about trains arriving in stations and workers leaving factories, just remember the way neighbors cooking, reading, and talking on the telephone takes on a new and beguiling sheen when glimpsed between the slats of venetian blinds.

Movies offer a panoply of exotic sights, but few of these sights have more lasting appeal than undraped flesh—luscious, enticing, and forever tantalizingly out of reach.

It's been ages since the American cinema has been constrained by a production code that proscribed the mere mention of "seduction [and] sex perversion." The idea that within living memory Otto Preminger's innocuous *The Moon Is Blue* caused a scandal by using the word *virgin* is nothing short of surreal. For all the endless skirmishes over erotic language and behavior that pit filmmakers against the Motion Picture Association of America (MPAA), which rates movies for theatrical release, the lurid sexual extremes of contemporary movies would have been unimaginable to earlier generations of moviegoers. Consider Michelle Pfeiffer as the ultimate kitten with a whip in *Batman Returns* (a children's movie, no less!) or Madonna's much-anticipated (and roundly ridiculed) *Body of Evidence*, the film with a premise like a locker-room joke: The queen of *Sex* (her book of sexy photos) and *Erotica* (her album of dirty songs) is put on trial for

screwing her lover to death. The live-action/cartoon hybrid *Cool World* proceeded from the startlingly vulgar premise that real-life cartoonist Gabriel Byrne's manly emissions could transform cartoon sexpot Holli Would into a flesh-and-blood babe. Actresses with pretensions to real careers once went tastefully nude only in the name of redeeming social value. Now women who could easily say no say yes to the most astonishing exhibitions: Sharon Stone flashing in *Basic Instinct*, Laura Dern doing Nicolas Cage every which way in *Wild at Heart*, Susan Sarandon and Jennifer Jason Leigh demonstrating oral-sex techniques in *White Palace* and *Single White Female*, respectively. The reverse is also true: Pornographic movies used to be the great inescapable ghetto for actors and actresses, but XXX-stars Traci Lords and Ginger Lynn Allen have actually landed roles in nonpornographic pictures, further blurring the line between cinema and smokers. That said, popular magazines and newspapers in search of an eye-catching trend piece can always rely on "Hollywood Movies Today Are Hotter Than Ever!" followed by the inevitable "New Puritanism Sweeps Tinseltown" as the pendulum swings back. As always, the movies are the mirror of America's deeply contradictory sexual attitudes, all hot and bothered hedonism on the one hand, righteous rectitude on the other.

Two decades ago, Marlon Brando had to go to Europe to hump butt naked for the camera in *Last Tango in Paris*, and the aftershocks rumbled for years. Compare the case of Michael Douglas's bony buns: Within months of *Basic Instinct*'s release, they made sniping *Spy* magazine's annual list of one hundred

the film has already receded into the fog of projects that didn't deliver, everyone remembers *that scene*, accompanied by the faint sound of another barrier falling. Even if she *didn't* (and she did—freeze frame doesn't lie), it was grist for cocktail-party conversation for weeks, a mainstream actress giving up the goods like a beaver babe, the unimaginable made unimpeachable flesh. And yet, though *Basic Instinct* may be—as has been claimed—the closest thing to pornography ever made by Hollywood, it's not close. Look at Nagisa Oshima's notorious *In the Realm of the Senses*, alternately lauded for its unflinching examination of obsessive sexual desire and lambasted as highbrow filth, and *Basic Instinct* slips right back into perspective: It's a big, glossy tease, too American to really get down and dirty. What was it Alfred Hitchcock once said? That the difference between English and American girls is that American girls all look as though they will, but they won't, and English girls look as though they won't, but they will. Only the specifics are new; the dichotomy remains the same.

And then there's the sex and violence thing. One media alarmist fretted that *Basic Instinct* kicked off a

things irritating and overrated. Douglas was wise not to bare them in 1994's *Disclosure*; the audience might have sued for sexual harassment. And on the subject of *Basic Instinct*, don't forget *that scene*, the one Stone says she was tricked into doing, in which possible ice-pick killer and all-around pantiless bitch Catherine Trammell crosses and uncrosses her legs while a roomful of men devolve before her as they contemplate getting a glimpse of what's between her thighs. Did she or didn't she flash a snatch of pink? While the rest of

Warner Bros. starlets baring a lot of lovely skin for 1933's *Footlight Parade*.

Beach baby Bardot works on her Saint-Tropez tan.

pressed sexual energy was displaced into violence. If only the chastity belts were tossed away, the thinking went, no one would need to rock and roll with a Tek-9. But it hasn't worked out that way. There are limits, but contemporary American filmmakers can explore virtually any sexual relationship imaginable, and most of them would still rather make war than love. Patriarchal perversion? Capitalistic devaluation of non–profit-making activity? Puritan heritage? General gynephobia? Sure, and other things besides. As a group, American filmmakers don't consider romance, relationships, and the many faces of sensuality subjects worth exploring on their own. In the immortal words of *The Fabulous*

The Pink Pussy: Where Sin Lives (1966): early '60s sexploitation or early '60s underground cinema?

murderous new era of high-voltage coupling with its depiction of "murder as a sexual aid," but 1949's *Gun Crazy* got there first—"hot as a pistol" indeed. Some of the sexiest films of Hollywood's repressed years were the noir thrillers of the 1940s and 1950s, with their femmes fatales, mother-fixated gangsters, fetishistic gunsels, and couples quite literally mad with sublimated lust. Sex and violence go together in American movies like stars and stripes, a tradition that defies easy logic. One used to be able to argue that in libertine Europe, freedom of sexual expression (in life as well as the movies) had generated an aura of open sensuality, while in the puritanical U.S.A., re-

Written and directed by "noted sexual authority" Oswalt Kolle, *The Miracle of Love* (1969) bared all in the name of helping couples deal with "bedroom problems."

Baker Boys' Susie Diamond, they're the parsley, the garnish you can always toss away. But there are always filmmakers swimming against the current, and films dedicated in whole or in part to the evocation of desire.

It started, as ever, with a kiss. *The Kiss* (1896, also called *The Irwin-Rice Kiss*) is by any name a dreary short in which two dumpy thespians, May Irwin and John C. Rice—then starring in a play called *The Widow Jones*—buss for the camera. Contemporary bluestockings reached for words like *disgusting* to describe what they'd seen, but then—as now—audiences thrilled to the hint of the forbidden, the erotic, the carnal. Romance sells, but sex sells more, and as far back as the silent era, canny filmmakers knew that a little flesh or the ghastly intimation of a fate worse than death pulled in the crowds. Decade after decade, the bad and the beautiful have shimmied and coiled around one another like rare and ravishing idols of sex so perfect it couldn't possibly be real, and movie audiences have stared in rapt fascination.

In the silent era, sleek Louise Brooks and Alice Roberts did a sultry sapphic tango in *Pandora's Box*. When platinum blonde Jean Harlow spoke in 1930's *Hell's Angels*, it was to excuse herself so she could slip into something more comfortable. Bare breasts in biblical epics and barely clad starlets flirting their way through 1933's *Footlight Parade*. Until the puritanical

Production Code went into effect in 1934, even mainstream Hollywood pictures were marbled with surprisingly frank images and attitudes. Needless to say, the Code didn't kill eroticism. It just drove filmmakers to new heights of displacement and repressed suggestiveness: Rita Hayworth smoking and slinking and only incidentally singing her way through "Put the Blame on Mame" in *Gilda* (1946) and Marilyn Monroe cooling her panties in the freezer in *The Seven Year Itch* (1955). Meanwhile, independently financed nudie-cutie pictures—often set in naturist camps or other wholesome milieux—catered to the primal need to see topless pretty girls.

Marcello Mastroianni and voluptuous Anita Ekberg's midnight dip in the Trevi fountain in *La Dolce Vita* ushered in the '60s and a new era of increasing permissiveness. Mainstream filmmakers pushed for more flesh and less frothy fantasy, while exploitation moviemakers and underground auteurs went all the way. You can't entirely dismiss the shocked viewers who couldn't tell the difference between Andy Warhol's *My Hustler* (or Jack Smith's *Flaming Creatures* or the Kuchar brothers' *Sins of the Fleshapoids* or Gregory Markopoulos's *The Illiac Passion*) and a sleazy sexploitation picture like *The Pink Pussy: Where Sin Lives*; sometimes there wasn't much. And there was even more explicit material on the horizon: White-coaters* like *The Miracle of Love* (1969) brought straightforward sex, in the guise of "marital instruction," to America theater screens.

By the '70s, the stag movie had come up from underground. The hard-core revolution started with Bill Osco's *Mona* and quickly yielded such porno chic as Gerard Damiano's *Deep Throat* and the Mitchell brothers' *Behind the Green Door*. Hard-core stars like Harry Reems, Jamie Gillis, Georgina Spelvin, Marilyn Chambers, Marc Stevens, and Linda Lovelace became household names. In fact, one of the great delusions of the '70s was that movie audiences wanted to see upscale hard-core movies with plots and production

I touch myself . . . sex-ploitation and European art-cinema variations on a theme: *The Rape (right)* and *Teorema (above)* (1968).

values; the home-video revolution of the '80s dispelled that notion. People who really want to see sex fast-forward past anything that smacks of narrative, and one of the hottest things going is amateur smut, real people sweating and grunting and grappling; it's as far as you can get from the Teflon sheen of Hollywood pictures.

In any event, the '70s also brought Mick Jagger, Anita Pallenberg, and James Fox defining polymorphous perversity in *Performance* (1970); their peculiarly enervated brand of androgyny gave way to corn-fed Tom Cruise and Rebecca De Mornay's conducting their *Risky Business* (1983) aboard a Chicago train. They were in turn supplanted by adolescent Jane March and Tony Leung's entwining their slender limbs in 1992's *The Lover*. Decade after decade, the faces change, but the frissons remain the same; the bodies and gestures and sensations melt into a shimmering collage of desire. So much can be erotic, and so little: skin and sweat and impassioned moans, or a fleeting touch, a hungry glance, a whisper of silk against skin. Almost any movie can be arousing, with-

out showing carnal acts or even revealing much flesh.

When you talk about erotic cinema, you're talking about all kinds of things, and you can't pare away all the excess until you reach a pure and integrated definition. Writer-director-critic Paul Schrader, who remade

---

*The term white-coaters was coined for porno movies in which the presence of "medical professionals" justified the salacious goings-on as educational.

xiii

Jacques Tourneur's poetically restrained *Cat People*, with considerably less temperance, nevertheless claims that the key to it all is realizing that audiences don't really want to see sex on screen: They want to *almost* see it. But *almost* is a nebulous concept; one viewer's nearly enough is another person's way too much. Only the most lemon-lipped puritan would call *Nine ½ Weeks* and *Wanda Whips Wall Street* the same thing: If *Taxi Driver*'s Travis Bickle had taken Betsy to *The Story of O* instead of to a nasty smut movie on their first date, everything might have turned out differently. So where are the lines?

Romantic movies, erotic movies, pornographic movies—they're all about the same thing: sex. It's the emphasis that's different. Romantic movies and hard-core pornography are polar opposites on the spectrum of silver-screen concupiscence: One is all veiled promise and consummations left to the viewer's fancy,

Bulle Ogier and her captive audience offer kinky, clinical thrills in Barbet Schroeder's *Maitresse* (1976).

the other pure raunchy delivery. Both have their places and their fans. But in between the two extremes is a world of erotic films, sexy pictures that titillate and illuminate far beyond the wildest dreams of movie romances but stop short of the nuts-and-bolts frankness of blue movies. While the occasional *Emmanuelle* straddles (if you will) the line, the outer edge of eroticism is pretty clear: Pornographic pictures go directly to the close-ups of organs, orifices, and ooze, while erotic movies cloak them in soft-focus photography, artfully arranged clothing, and tasteful editing. Italian semiotician Umberto Eco claims you can tell a porn movie not by its nasty bits but by its boring ones. Sex, he argues in the essay "How to Recognize a Porn Movie," however graphic, thrills only by contrast with the mundane, so there has to be lots of dreariness to make the hot and horny money shots pay off. Of course, his may just be an intellectualized but peculiarly male position. Couples films, hard-core movies

Too darned hot: Kathleen Turner.

intended for and often made by women, like former porn star Candida Royale, aim to eroticize the whole film by making the in-between parts romantic. Eco argues for what sounds like the clichéd model of male sexual experience—short, fast, and explosive—while Royale's films exemplify the typical model of female sex: lots of foreplay segueing seamlessly into rippling orgasm.

Much has been written and said about the difference between what men and women find as a turn-on in nonporno movies, most of it resolving itself in sweeping generalizations: As a group, men prefer more explicit eroticism, while women respond to intimations of romance. Women feel that less is more while men, hormonally driven Neanderthals to the core, pant "more is more" as they throw the juicy scenes into slow motion, the better to observe every salient detail. It's hard to imagine a woman buying *The Bare Facts*, Craig Hosoda's frame-by-frame video guide to nakedness in the movies, let alone writing it, even though it faithfully lists male nudity as well as female. A 1994 *New York Times* analysis—cutely titled ♀ = *Coy Banter*, ♂ = *Naked Blonds*—rehashed the argument for the '90s and came up with the same conclusions. When men were asked about scenes in recent movies they found erotic, they cited things like Stone's leg-crossing display, Annette Bening's naked-under-her-raincoat seduction

Elizabeth Berkeley and Gina Gershon in *Showgirls*.

of John Cusack in *The Grifters* (1990), Michael Douglas and Glenn Close humping on the kitchen sink in *Fatal Attraction* (1987), and voyeur Craig Wasson's watching his comely neighbor strip in *Body Double* (1984). Women went for Daniel Day-Lewis embracing Madeleine Stowe in *The Last of the Mohicans* (1992), Kevin Costner painting Susan Sarandon's toenails in *Bull Durham* (1988), and Harvey Keitel poking his finger through a hole in Holly Hunter's stocking in *The Piano* (1993). On the other hand, *Body Heat* (1981), *Dangerous Liaisons* (1988), and *Bram Stoker's Dracula* (1992) made it onto both lists, though for different scenes. Perhaps the proper position to take is, it all depends.

When you ask people to open up the closets of their erotic-movie memories, the strangest skeletons tumble out: *Persona* and *Chained Heat*, *Beyond the Valley of the Ultravixens*, *The Conformist*, and *Maitresse*. Tell one person that someone else found *Bad Lieutenant* sexy, and he or she will snort derisively, then offer Ken Russell's

Women watch and men do: the props say it all. Mick Jagger with a gun and Michele Breton with stereopticon in *Performance* (1970).

Quintessential chick movies *Ghost* (1990) *(left)* and *Thelma & Louise* (1991) *(right)*: eroticism the way women like it.

outrageous *Lair of the White Worm* and an equally outrageous justification. Eroticism is a very personal thing, a matter of gender, upbringing, sexual persuasion, and, sometimes above all, circumstance. Just as a silly song can recall a wave of potent memories in a breathless rush, a scene in a superficially mundane movie can bring back a seminal erotic revelation with shocking intensity. It doesn't matter what anyone else thinks: If you got your first hard-on watching Raquel Welch in a white bikini taunting Tom Courtenay in *Fathom* or squirmed deliciously as Robert Mitchum oozed sexual menace in *Cape Fear*, then those films are forever in your personal erotic pantheon.

Movie eroticism can be at odds with what we're attracted to or do in real life. Straight women lust for Ellen Barkin and vampires of both sexes. Staunchly heterosexual men thrill to *Top Gun* (if its homoerotic subtext were any closer to the surface, it would be playing Times Square) and can tell you exactly where Catherine Deneuve and Susan Sarandon's sex scene is in *The Hunger*. Gay men who swoon over the moment when Brad Pitt and Antonio Banderas almost kiss in *Interview With the Vampire: The Vampire Chronicles* might also be fantasizing about Julie Christie. Lesbians support sexually correct movies from *Desert Hearts* to the cheerfully funky *Go Fish*, but rocker Melissa Etheridge, whose

lesbian bona fides couldn't be more in order (this is the woman who called an album *Yes I Am*), tells a national magazine that Brad Pitt is enough to make a gay woman reconsider her position. No wonder, then, that one man's unbearably arousing movie is another's total turn-off.

The history of erotic movies is the history of violating the limits of propriety. Twenty years ago, Bernardo Bertolucci's notorious *Last Tango in Paris* amazed and offended viewers in equal proportions, offering the shocking spectacle of Brando groping and

Hot-as-a-pistol Anne Parillaud in *La Femme Nikita* (1990): who cares that she's a killer when she looks so do-able?

shagging nubile ragamuffin Maria Schneider. Brutal and antiromantic in the extreme, *Tango* offered only its continental cachet as shelter from the storm of protest; today it's in college film textbooks. Only a decade ago, *An Officer and a Gentleman* was so hot that director Taylor Hackford was forced to cool down the scene in which Debra Winger straddles a supine Richard Gere, who has his own place in libidinous history as the first Hollywood male star to bare all at the snap of a clapper board. Artiness—and the deletion of the heroine's tender age from Jeanne Moreau's absinthe-and-cigarettes voice-over—saved Jean-Jacques Annaud's *The Lover* from censure. In a less swank setting than "adaptation of Marguerite Duras's famous novel," the spectacle of nymphet Jane March wrapping her coltish limbs around smoothly exotic Tony Leung, her budlike mouth quivering with desire, would almost certainly have been dismissed as prurient trash.

Hard experience has taught audiences what to make of the ritual of hot movie hype. First we read in gossip columns and in-the-know magazines that there's all kinds of chatter from the set of *Sizzling Blockbuster*, then that preview audiences are leaving screenings in a lather. The stars give interviews about the emotional honesty of the sex scenes, coyly remarking that the really embarrassing stuff is on the cutting-room floor—thank heavens! There's trouble with the MPAA, rumors of an NC-17 rating or an unrated release, before some last-minute trimming—mere seconds—yields an R. Then the critics check in, buzzing about the most erotic scenes put on screen since the last sizzling blockbuster. Everyone knows better, but we go to see anyway, just in case. And we can usually be seduced into renting the unrated director's cut on video, to see all that stuff that was too strong for the theatrical market. The appeal of the erotic conquers all.

What men want: hot and horny humping, as seen in *Jamon Jamon (above)* and *Golden Balls* (both 1994).

The 50 Most Erotic Films of All Time isn't an all-inclusive examination of arousing cinema, but it's a far-reaching one. In an attempt to embrace the shifting shape of desire, it covers the waterfront and the back alleys besides, from the classical elegance of *La Ronde* to the low-class raunch of Russ Meyer's *Lorna*, the sublimated sensuality of the original *Cat People* and *Gun Crazy* to the arty frankness of *Wild Orchid* and *Betty Blue*, the explicitness of *In the Realm of the Senses* and *Sebastiane* to the mainstream titillation of *Basic Instinct* and *The Big Easy*. No film, no book, no theory of eroticism can truly offer something for everyone, but between *And God Created Woman* and *Women In Love*, most of us can find something.

And God Created Woman / Et Dieu Créa La Femme (1956)

Directed by Roger Vadim. Produced by Raoul J. Levy. Screenplay by Vadim and Levy. Cinematography by Armand Thirard. Edited by Victoria Mercanton. Music by Paul Misraki.

Brigitte Bardot (Juliette), Curt Jürgens (Eric), Jean-Louis Trintignant (Michel Tardieu), Christian Marquand (Antoine Tardieu), Marie Glory (Madame Tardieu).

The U.S. posters for Roger Vadim's notorious film declared: "And God Created Woman ... but the devil created Brigitte Bardot." It's easy to say no, Vadim created Bardot, but it wouldn't be exactly fair.

Bardot—born Camille Javal—was on her way to a distinctly minor career before *And God Created Woman*. She studied ballet (despite her wholly inappropriate curves), modeled, appeared in minor roles in a variety of pictures, and turned down a lucrative Warner Bros. contract because she didn't want to leave France. Her credits included René Clair's *Les Grandes manoeuvres* (1955), a romantic melodrama widely considered one of his finest films, and the British comedy *Doctor at Sea* (1956), whose director, Ralph Thomas, found her "an excessively frank girl" who scandalized the crew by sauntering naked across the set to play a coy, comic shower scene. She was a pretty starlet, nothing more.

After *And God Created Woman*, Bardot was an international phenomenon, sex kitten *extraordinaire*, subject of Simone de Beauvoir's famous essay "Brigitte Bardot and the Lolita Syndrome," a carnal phenomenon waiting for the '60s to bring everyone else up to speed. Her husband, writer-director Vadim, built the altar that invited the world to come and worship, but Bardot was a goddess of sensuality whose light entirely eclipsed him.

And God's Juliette is a beautiful orphan living in the sleepy resort town of Saint-Tropez with stern foster parents who don't understand her free-spirited hedonism. They're not the only ones: The whole town thinks she's a whore when she's just ahead of her time, sexually confident and forthright. She loves animals and children, giggles, flirts, sulks, and kicks off her shoes to dance the cha-cha-cha whenever the spirit moves her. She dallies with brutal Antoine Tardieu, then marries his shy brother Michel, who gets up the nerve to propose because if Juliette doesn't marry *someone*, she'll be returned to the orphanage. Her childish desire to be a good, conventional wife is doomed from the start; it's not in her nature to be modest, deferential, and faithful. But Michel's belief in her essential goodness is stronger than both her weakness and the hostility of his lustful brother—with whom she sleeps while her husband's away on business—and bitter mother. Despite her fling with Antoine and the public display she makes by drunkenly dancing a sizzling mambo with a group of black musicians, Juliette and Michel remain together.

And God Created Woman was a youthful lark that succeeded beyond anyone's wildest dreams. First-time director Vadim began his career as a screenwriter and assistant to noted filmmaker Marc Allégret.* But more

The "excessively frank" Bardot on the set.

---

*Vadim worked on Allégret's *Juliette* (1953), which may have given Bardot's character her name.

than anything he wanted to direct, and he knew he'd never get the chance from mainstream French producers. At the time, he later observed morosely, "youth was not a marketable commodity." It was Allégret who sent Vadim to audition Bardot, then a teenage model, for a small part; the two fell madly in love and married at the first possible opportunity, two years later. In 1955, the twenty-six-year-old Vadim met youthful producer Raoul Levy, who shared his frustration with the stuffy French movie establishment. Together they fashioned a careless, vigorous picture set in Saint-Tropez before it became the glamor capitol of Europe, shot in color, widescreen (considered vulgar by most French filmmakers), and designed to showcase the twenty-two-year-old Bardot. The plot is barely there, loosely woven around something to do with a wealthy real estate magnate, Eric, who wants to build a casino and has to buy up the Tardieu family land. But it's all about lusting for Bardot: The audience and the film's characters are united in desire for her supple flesh, tousled, honey-colored mane, and ripe, sensual manner.

And God Created Woman was a predictable scandal. In France it was lambasted as bad filmmaking, in the United States it was a revelation. In an era when Marilyn Monroe was the reigning sex goddess, Bardot was a breath of fresh air. Made only a year earlier, Monroe's *The Seven Year Itch* is a masterpiece of cinematic cockteasing; her breathy, nameless girl upstairs is a tantalizing innocent so frothy and carefully coiffed that you can't picture her getting

Quintessential Bardot: bold and bare.

sweaty between the sheets; all the film's naughtiness springs from frustrated husband Tom Ewell's lustful imagination. Bardot—the same age as Monroe's character, though eight years younger than Monroe herself—is an innocent as well, but she delivers the goods with a smile. Bardot's candid nakedness is light years beyond Monroe's hypocritical modesty, and it heralded the wave of the future. "She has the courage of doing whatever she pleases. And when she pleases," says Eric of Bardot's wayward waif, and that was her career-long appeal.

Juliette rejects all traditional virtues: She doesn't care about Eric's money; she doesn't care that the townspeople think she's a rude tramp; she does a steamy interracial mambo, shimmying bare-legged with her skirt unbuttoned to the waist; and she sleeps with Antoine because passion overwhelms her. She's not really sorry she did it, either—she's just sorry everyone is so mean to her afterward. Bardot could, in fact, act, but no one ever really cared, which may have contributed to her later bitterness about her career, which included such provocative pictures as *Mademoiselle Striptease* (1958), *A Woman Like Satan / La Femme et le patin* (1958), *A Very Private Affair / La Vie privée* (1962), Jean-Luc Godard's *Contempt / Le Mépris* (1963), *Ravishing Idiot* (1964), *The Women / Les Femmes* (1969), and *Don Juan, or, If Don Juan Were a Woman / Don Juan 1973, ou si Don Juan était une femme* (1973).

In addition to making Bardot a star, *And God Created Woman* anticipated Jean-Luc Godard and François Truffaut's *Breathless* (1959) in its loose, improvised feel; entire scenes seem contrived to take advantage of a fortuitous strip of beach or a picturesque street and you can feel the presence of the crew, almost hear the whir of the camera. The film's resounding commercial success broke the older generation's stranglehold on French filmmaking and helped pave the way for the *nouvelle vague*.

Vadim's promising career quickly degenerated artistically, and he made a series of shallow, handsome films whose chief

The wayward Juliette and her brother-in-law (Christian Marquand) make love *au naturel*

appeal was a sophisticated prurience that became steadily less relevant as cinematic sexual mores marched on, leaving him behind. Vadim was the Zalman King of his day. His later sexy romps include an adaptation of *Les Liaisons dangereuses* (1959), the erotic vampire picture *Blood and Roses | Et mourir de plaisir* (1960), and a version of *La Ronde* (1964). He married Jane Fonda—then an American sex kitten—and cast her in the "Metzengerstein" section of *Spirits of the Dead | Histoires extraordinaires* (1967), a three-part anthology of Poe stories on which he shared credit with Federico Fellini and Louis Malle (ironically directing Bardot), opposite her brother Peter (they played incestuous lovers). He also put her in the outer space sex frolic *Barbarella* (1968), in which she is best remembered for her zero-gravity strip tease. Vadim made a sad, pointless remake of *And God Created Woman* in 1987, retaining a few ideas and the figure of a feral, wanton woman, in this case Rebecca De Mornay. It was an utter failure, and he remains best known for his provocative Galateas: Bardot, Fonda, and Catherine Deneuve.

3

Brigitte Bardot: The original sex kitten; no one has yet surpassed her.

Marlon Brando: Sensitive brute Brando brooded and mumbled through two decades of sexy films, from *A Streetcar Named Desire* (1951) to *Last Tango in Paris* (1972); his black-leather-jacketed rebel from *The Wild One* (1953) is an icon of lust for both sexes.

William Holden: Holden's moment came in *Picnic* (1956), as a smoothly muscular hunk with a hint of wariness in his eyes. He'd been in movies since the late '30s but lent solid sexiness to *Sabrina* (1954), *The Proud and the Profane* (1956), *The World of Suzie Wong* (1960), and, of course, *Sunset Boulevard* (1950).

James Dean: Patron saint of angst-ridden teens of all ages, neurotic sex symbol Dean was already dead when his cult flowered. It endures despite tawdry revelations about his drinking, masochism, hidden homosexuality, and coarse misbehavior. His few film credits include *East of Eden* and *Rebel Without a Cause* (both 1955) and *Giant* (1956).

Audrey Hepburn: An anomalous waif in the pneumatic '50s, Hepburn personified suave sex appeal.

Chic, graceful, and perpetually elegant, Hepburn floated through sophisticated romances from *Sabrina* (1954) to *Breakfast at Tiffany's* (1961). She teased audiences with the promise of letting her hair down, but she never did.

Rock Hudson: Born Roy Scherer, beefcake Hudson (the Rock of Gibraltar + the Hudson River) was the '50s manly man personified—no wonder the revelation that he was gay came as such a shock. Equally at home in Douglas Sirk melodramas like *Written on the Wind* (1956) and bubbly comedies like Michael Gordon's *Pillow Talk* (1959), with Doris Day, he was the consummate studio sex symbol.

Burt Lancaster: A former circus acrobat, his athletic appeal was tempered by brooding insecurity. His sandy embrace with Deborah Kerr in *From Here to Eternity* (1953) alone guarantees him a place in erotic immortality. Lancaster was often paired with equally brawny **Kirk Douglas**, whose palpable self-absorption kept him from being truly sexy.

Jeanne Moreau: Unconventionally beautiful Moreau projected a cool, quintessentially European sexiness that seduced Americans in such films as *The Lovers* (1958), *Les Liaisons dangereuses* and *The 400 Blows* (both 1959), and *Jules et Jim* (1961). She continues to embody the eternal feminine for French filmmakers, as *Nikita* (1990) and *The Lover* (1992) attest (she supplied the smoky voice-over for the latter).

Marilyn Monroe: She was a fragile, doomed blonde with the heart of a child and a body that drives men wild. Monroe's life was her greatest performance. It culminated in mysterious death, preserving her forever at the height of her sexiness, never to grow blowsy and pathetic like Anita Ekberg, Diana Dors, and the other big blondes.

Elizabeth Taylor: Taylor grew up on screen, from adolescent horse lover in *National Velvet* (1944) to aging beauty in *Ash Wednesday* (1974). But her glory days were the '50s, when her creamy bosom and violet eyes graced *Elephant Walk* (1954), *Giant* (1956), and *Cat on a Hot Tin Roof* (1958). Her white swimsuit in *Suddenly, Last Summer* (1959) launched a thousand fantasies.

Baby Doll
(1956)

Directed and Produced by Elia Kazan. Screenplay by Tennessee Williams. Cinematography by Boris Kaufman. Edited by Gene Milford. Music by Kenyon Hopkins.

Carroll Baker (Baby Doll Carson McCorkle Meigham), Karl Malden (Archie Lee Meigham), Eli Wallach (Silva Vacarro), Mildred Dunnock (Aunt Rose Comfort).

Sexual provocateur Tennessee Williams often suffered in the transition from stage to screen. While his plays, which explore rape, homosexuality, and various forms of sexual dissolution, were considered frank, they were aimed at a relatively small and sophisticated audience of theatergoers. For American movies in the 1950s, it was all just too much, though that didn't stop the adaptations: There was *A Streetcar Named Desire* in 1951, then *Baby Doll*, followed by *Cat on a Hot Tin Roof* (1958) and *Suddenly, Last Summer* (1959). They were all sanitized to a greater or lesser degree, though it doesn't take much to see beneath the surface to the original provocative elements. *Baby Doll*, which Williams expanded from his one-act play *27 Wagonloads of Cotton*, may not be the best of the bunch. But it's certainly the most salacious, a blackly funny picture that's all about sexual deprivation and gets away with some astonishing acts of displacement and oblique—but hardly obscure—talking around the subject. *Time* magazine called it "possibly the dirtiest American picture ever legally exhibited," and hyperbole aside, it remains an astonishingly lewd piece of filmmaking with an impeccably cultured surface. What separates *Baby Doll* from *Streetcar*, *Cat*, and even the overwrought *Suddenly, Last Summer* is that while they're about sexual repression and hypocrisy

and the ways in which they warp the mind and the soul, *Baby Doll* is one long sexual shaggy dog story. It's a high-class farmer's-daughter joke masquerading as an exposé of unsophisticated social mores.

The film's first image of nymphet Baby Doll just about says it all: blond and creamy and delicately lush, she's napping in an infant's crib with the slats let down provocatively to the floor, one of her slender legs draped off the end. She's wearing baby doll pajamas and sucking her thumb with sleepy abandon. It's enough to make a Peeping Tom out of a better man than her husband, the venal Archie Lee. He's a pathetic figure of a man on every count, further reduced by thwarted desire to boring a hole in the wall so he can watch his alluring wife doze (there's a dog by his side, in case we miss the point). Archie Lee drinks and sweats and suffers from "nerves." His doctor prescribes sedatives, but the starchy nurse observes knowingly that drugs aren't what Archie needs. The fact is, *everyone* knows what Archie Lee needs, and *everyone* knows he's not getting any. He's the town laughingstock, cooped up in a ramshackle mansion he can't afford, pining after a stuck-up slip of a girl who, more than a year after their wedding, won't even let him touch her.

Teenage Baby Doll wasn't "ready for marriage" when her dying daddy gave her away to Archie Lee, but now her twentieth birthday is fast approaching and Archie Lee is itching to claim his conjugal rights. "Oh, you'll get your birthday present," he promises with a leer, but she's not worried; his picture is next to the words *impotent buffoon* in the dictionary. She teases and sulks and flounces and browbeats, and Archie takes it

Eli Wallach seduces the childlike Carroll Baker in *Baby Doll*.

all until the simmering domestic situation is brought to a boil by Silva Vacarro, a sleek Sicilian interloper whose state-of-the-art cotton gin has taken away Archie's business. Archie burns the gin down, secure in the knowledge that no one will side with a parvenu foreigner against a local boy. But Silva realizes that willful, pretentiously refined virgin Baby Doll is the chink in Archie's hometown armor.

Slender, Actors Studio–trained Carroll Baker was twenty-five when she made *Baby Doll*, but she looked younger; it was only her second major role, following a substantial part in *Giant* that same year: She gave her beguiling all and was rewarded with an Academy Award nomination (she lost to Ingrid Bergman in *Anastasia*). Baker's Baby Doll plays with bath toys, licks an ice cream cone like a little girl, dropped out of the fourth grade because she was stymied by long division, and drinks soda pop for breakfast. She's been described as retarded (which makes the whole business even smarmier), but she's really the incarnation of the white-trash Madonna, another of those unlikely fetishes spawned by America's puritan heritage. Baby Doll is all guileless insinuation and no action, a child-

ish tease who's so bizarrely innocent she doesn't know what she's doing to the men around her. "There ain't much of you, but what there is is choice," Vacarro leers, and who could disagree?

Alternately seductive and brutally domineering, Eli Wallach—in his movie debut—is surprisingly effective (if not convincingly Italian) as Vacarro, and his scenes with Baker are *Baby Doll*'s insinuating heart. Vacarro interrogates her in a rusted porch swing, inching in close and wheedling information about where Archie was when the gin burned down, terrifying Baby Doll with his enticing intimations. She may not be experienced, but she can tell he's no eunuch like her husband; she's alternately attracted and repelled. He follows her into the house, where her lamentable attempts to play a gracious Southern hostess collide with his determination to get her to sign an affidavit attesting to Archie's guilt, and their sexual cat-and-mouse games are almost painfully lascivious. The dialogue is laced with suggestive implications: When Vacarro threatens to "break this door down," he's obviously not talking about the one to the attic. But the real lewdness lies in Kazan's images: The sight of Vacarro in Baby Doll's bedroom, mounted on a toy rocking horse so tiny that only its head is visible between his thighs and gyrating to a raunchy rock song—"Shame on You"—is so vulgar it's hard to know what to say. The scene concludes with Vacarro curled up in Baby Doll's crib with his riding whip in hand; who could miss the point? The Catholic Legion of Decency, the single most powerful pressure group with which Hollywood had to contend, was outraged, as it often was in the progressively bolder '50s.

Despite its explosive sexual content, *Baby Doll* received a Production Code Seal in recognition of its serious treatment of adult material. The Legion of Decency condemned it with vigor that crossed the line into hysteria, releasing a statement calling it "morally repellent both in theme and treatment" and warning that it dwelt relentlessly "upon carnal suggestiveness in action, dialogue and costuming." In retrospect, the

Infantile eroticism: Wallach and Baker in Baby Doll's crib.

Code Authority did the right thing for the wrong reasons: What seemed sophisticated in 1956 now looks ludicrously smutty. The Legion, on the other hand, made the right call—*Baby Doll* dwells on *exactly* those things—but took the wrong action. Cardinal Francis J. Spellman, head of the Archdiocese of New York, denounced the film from the pulpit of St. Patrick's Cathedral, warning his flock not to see *Baby Doll* "under pain of sin." This was a bit much even for other men of the cloth, and Protestant Bishop James A. Pike struck back from the Cathedral of St. John the Divine, declaring that "those who do not want the sexual aspect of life included in the portrayal of real-life situations had better burn their Bibles as well as abstain from the movies."

Whether or not anyone went to hell for seeing *Baby Doll*, we'll never know. The film did solid business but was no blockbuster, in part because many theaters canceled their bookings in light of the fuss—it took *And God Created Woman* to prove that a condemned film could break box-office records. The *Baby Doll* brouhaha was the beginning of the end of the Legion of Decency's influence; its excessive fulminations sounded suspiciously like outdated, silly ravings. And Carroll Baker spawned a generation of seductive

baby dolls, including Tuesday Weld (*Sex Kittens Go to College*), Sue Lyon (*Lolita*), and Carol Lynley (*Blue Jeans*). Thank heaven for little girls.

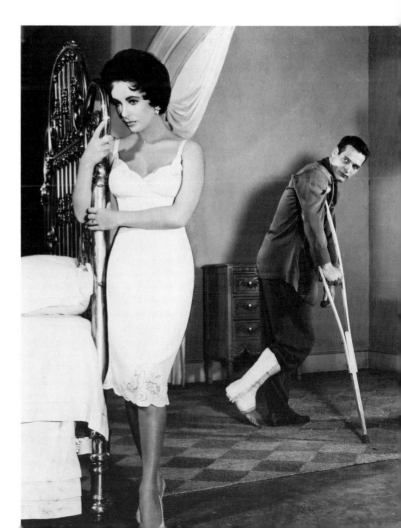

More Southern gothic: Elizabeth Taylor and Paul Newman in Tennessee Williams's *Cat on a Hot Tin Roof* (1958).

Bad Timing:
A Sensual Obsession
(1980)

Directed by Nicolas Roeg. Produced by Jeremy Thomas. Associate Produced by Tim Van Rellim. Screenplay by Yale Udoff, based on the novel *Ho Tentato Divvers*, by Constanzo Constantin. Cinematography by Anthony Richmond. Art Direction by David Brockhurst. Edited by Tony Lawson. Music by Richard Hartley.

Theresa Russell (Milena Flaherty Vognic), Art Garfunkel (Dr. Alex Linden), Denholm Elliott (Stefan Vognic), Harvey Keitel (Inspector Netusil).

A story of mad love gone inevitably wrong, *Bad Timing: A Sensual Obsession* is haunting and, yes, sensual. It opens with a brief sequence in a museum, in which the camera caresses the glittering surfaces of Gustav Klimt paintings of lovers whose bodies seem to melt into one another, resting occasionally on their mysteriously ecstatic faces. *Bad Timing* then gets down to business, and the story unfolds in the form of a mystery.

Beautiful young American Milena is brought to a Viennese emergency room in the middle of the night, near death from an overdose of drugs. She's accompanied by her former lover, Alex Linden, also an American. The hospital staff is suspicious of his account of events; his timing doesn't match her condition, and they suspect foul play. The police send insinuating Inspector Netusil to investigate. Why did Alex wait so long before calling an ambulance? He says Milena called him—but when? Was he with her when she took the pills, or did he arrive at her apartment later, as he claims? What did he do once he was there? Netusil knows Alex did something wrong; he alternately bullies

Theresa Russell.

and cajoles, tries to get Alex to admit that he ravished Milena, promising that he only wants to know, that Alex's confession will have no ramifications.

In a series of flashbacks intercut with grisly scenes of Milena's battle for life on the operating table, the story of her affair with Alex unfolds. Alex is a rule-bound academic, teaching psychology and living in an apartment whose excessive neatness says all that needs to be said about his flexibility and openness. Milena is an unpolished hedonist whose life is spiraling out of control. She's separated from her much older Czecho-slovakian husband, Stefan. She drinks too much, parties too hard, dispenses her favors too freely. She boldly propositions Alex at a party, and their relationship begins in a whirl of great sex and manic fun. But things begin to crumble when Alex becomes jealous and possessive; Milena responds by really cutting loose, and their relationship degenerates into a maelstrom of screaming fights and angry sex. The breakup is acrimonious, and when Milena calls, slurring her words and threatening suicide, Alex is unsympathetic. When he finally goes to her apartment, he berates her until she passes out, then has sex with her before calling for an ambulance.

Shot under the Bergmanesque title *Illusions*, *Bad Timing* bills itself as *A Sensual Obsession* and styles itself a very literary one. Alex and Milena read Blake and admire Klimt; there's a copy of Paul Bowles's *The Sheltering Sky* on the coffee table, doubtless the inspiration for their trip to exotic Morocco, and the sight of Freud's own couch drives them into a sexual frenzy. But the MPAA saw straight through the highbrow affectations to the copious fleshy wallowing and award-

An uncharacteristically light moment in Alex and Milena's tempestuous relationship.

ed the film an X rating. Distributor World Northal appealed the rating, but it stood and the film was released unrated.

Nicolas Roeg, codirector (with Donald Cammell) of the perversely erotic *Performance* (1970) and the man behind Donald Sutherland and Julie Christie's famously erotic sex scene in *Don't Look Now* (1973), is a former cinematographer with a libertine's eye. He never shies away from the sex that is the foundation of Alex and Milena's relationship. This is a mixed blessing, because Alex is played by Art Garfunkel, not an actor who tops the average person's list of men they want to see naked. But he is flawless casting, a pale, hairless geek who dreams of lustful abandon and dangerous romance without having the slightest idea what such passions cost. *Bad Timing* is a film about voyeurism, and Alex Linden is its spy in the house of love. He's not a good one, either; he craves control with his abandon, and the conflict drives him temporarily mad. His peculiar, suggestive relationship with Netusil is charged with a weirdly erotic intensity, fueled in part by Harvey Keitel's performance. A masterpiece of insinuation (he played oddly similar roles in 1991's *Mortal Thoughts* and *Thelma & Louise*), Keitel's Netusil understands Alex all too well and knows that his neurotic

need to confess will eventually overwhelm his instinct for self-preservation.

Theresa Russell is the refreshingly vulgar antidote to *Bad Timing*'s creepier elements. She wasn't Roeg's original choice for the role of Milena: Wan, frail Sissy Spacek was, but scheduling conflicts—she was making *Coal Miner's Daughter* when *Bad Timing* was ready to shoot—led to her replacement. It's hard to imagine what *Bad Timing* would have been without Russell, who had appeared in only two previous films, Elia Kazan's *The Last Tycoon* (1976) and *Straight Time* (1978) with Dustin Hoffman. She isn't stunningly beautiful. She has a flat, affectless voice, and her body is less than perfect. But Russell is the embodiment of utter sexual abandon; she has a reckless physicality. Her voluptuousness is always in danger of seeming blowsy, her passion on the verge of being unappealingly out of control. Her Milena is a dark hippie sex fetish, a destroying angel of erotic liberation.

The film ends with Alex catching a glimpse of Milena on a New York street, her throat marred by a puckered tracheotomy scar. She's still pretty, but she's no longer a feverish dream, a fantasy of sex as escape from the demands of bourgeois society. In *Bad Timing*, the flames of passion consume everyone and everything, leaving only bitter ashes.

Milena (Theresa Russell) and Alex (Art Garfunkel) explore the sins of the flesh.

Basic Instinct (1992)

Directed by Paul Verhoeven. Produced by Alan Marshall. Screenplay by Joe Eszterhas. Cinematography by Jan De Bont. Edited by Frank J. Urioste. Production Design by Terence Marsh. Music by Jerry Goldsmith.

Michael Douglas (Detective Nick Curran), Sharon Stone (Catherine Trammell), George Dzundza (Gus), Jeanne Tripplehorn (Dr. Beth Gardner), Leilana Sarelle (Roxy), Dorothy Malone (Hazel Dobkins).

Erotic thrillers are a staple of the videocassette market, offering flashy kicks in a context that doesn't scream soft-core pornography. But *Basic Instinct* was a worldwide theatrical smash, despite—or perhaps because of—widely reported protests by gay and lesbian activists, rating trouble, and an "ambiguous" ending that's neither truly ambiguous nor dramatically satisfying. Though some people don't like their sexual frissons leavened with the threat of death, others are excited by an omnipresent atmosphere of violence-charged eroticism, and *Basic Instinct* delivers glossy thrills galore. For Americans, who have always rejected sex as a serious subject, the beauty of the erotic thriller is that the thriller justifies the sex, which is usually scattered sparingly throughout the film. Unlike most big-budget Hollywood pictures with erotic elements, *Basic Instinct* doesn't stint on the eroticism and gets surprisingly down and dirty.

The film opens on the reflection in a ceiling mirror of a couple making love, the camera caressing their bodies as they buck and writhe decoratively. The woman, a curvaceous blonde whose face is obscured by her hair, ties her lover's hands to the bed frame with a white silk scarf, then stabs him to bloody death (especially bloody in the unrated video version) with an ice pick. The scene sets the tone for all subsequent sex scenes: beautifully photographed, carefully choreographed, pushed to the outer limits of acceptable exposure for nonpornographic movies, and driven by the risk of sudden violence.

If you know Dutch-born filmmaker Paul Verhoeven only as the director of science fiction/ action-adventure hits *Robocop* (1987) and *Total Recall* (1990), then *Basic Instinct* comes as a shock—not because of the violence, though there's plenty, but because the emphasis is so firmly on the erotic. Like most European filmmakers, Verhoeven is comfortable with sensuality in all its forms; that he's uncharacteristically fond of chasing it with violence has doubtless contributed to his American success. Verhoeven's pre-*Robocop* films are a lusty lot, several well worth seeing for their steamy sex scenes.

His first European hit, *Turkish Delight* (1973), features Rutger Hauer as an artist married to a middle-class girl and is both funny and uninhibitedly sexy. Hauer, taking a more relaxed approach to frontal nudity than Michael Douglas, bares all repeatedly. *De Vierde Man / The Fourth Man* (1982) revolves around dissolute, expediently bisexual Gerard Reve (Jeroen Krabbe), a writer who has an affair with a beautiful, enigmatic woman, Christine (Renée Soutendijk), so he can sleep with her hunky boyfriend, Hermann (Thom Hoffman). Instead, he finds himself trapped in a nightmare of omens, premonitory dreams, and death. *The Fourth Man* includes a fabulously blasphemous hallucination of beefy, swimsuit-clad Hermann on the cross and a surprisingly erotic scene of Reve masturbating as he spies on Christine and Hermann through a keyhole. Verhoeven's little-seen *Flesh + Blood*—also called *The Rose and the Sword* (1985)—offers both flesh and blood

in abundance, with Hauer as a sixteenth-century rogue and frequently exposed Jennifer Jason Leigh as the carefully reared virgin he kidnaps and rapes; she loves it, and plenty of lusty sex follows. Though made in America, *Flesh + Blood* is characterized by a very continental frankness that doubtless contributed to its non-performance at the U.S. box office.

Basic Instinct is a real Hollywood movie, slick and sanitized, but Verhoeven's earthy explicitness shows through the glossy façade. Lots of nudity and plenty of copulation, exhibitionism, cunnilingus, bisexuality, voyeurism, bondage, lipstick lesbianism, and rough sex: *Basic Instinct* offers something to titillate (or offend) just about everybody. It made a sex goddess out of hitherto anonymous blonde Sharon Stone, the movie's vicious vixen, and the scene in which, by simply crossing and uncrossing her legs, the panty-free Stone reduces a roomful of powerful, bullying men to a pathetic pack of slavering supplicants at the altar of Venus ... well, it speaks volumes about the state of sexual relations in the '90s. Her Catherine Trammell is a full-fledged psychopath in a clinging white dress, an ambisexual wanton who despises men because they can't resist her and destroys them just because she can. Macho screenwriter Joe Eszterhas's notorious $3 million script doesn't have much on the smarmy direct-to-video erotic thrillers that crowd rental shelves, but top-of-the-line production values and quality casting make all the difference: *Basic Instinct* may be sleazy, but it's not cheap.

Fabulously wealthy and blond all over, smart and stacked, friend of killers, author of crime novels, Catherine is the lover of ex–rock-and-roller Johnny Boz, who's been brutally stabbed to death. Detective Nick Curran is a walking compendium of life-in-the-fast-lane vices, a former tobacco-, drug-, and alcohol-abusing cowboy with a smoking .38, kept on a short leash by the San Francisco police department because of his involvement in several fatal shootings. While investigating Boz's murder, Nick—whose doubly suggestive nickname is "Shooter"—gets involved with the boldly sensual Catherine, despite indications that she may be a stunningly clever, completely amoral, psychopathic murderer. Their affair jeopardizes Nick's career and, perhaps, his life, but he can't tear himself away from the woman he calls "the fuck of the century," even as evidence against her mounts; he's entirely in her sexual thrall. He eventually finds the ostensible

killer and anticipates a lusty future with Catherine, but just like all the other men she's seduced, he's underestimated her calculating viciousness.

Stone's flashing scene is amazingly brazen for a mainstream American actress (she later claimed disingenuously that Verhoeven tricked her into exposing herself), and Michael Douglas performs oral sex with refreshing enthusiasm, even as he avoids showing his member in any of his nude scenes. Although it would certainly have been edited out of any scene in which it might have appeared (as was Bruce Willis's two years later, in *Color of Night*), Douglas—perhaps concerned because he was dealing with a *European* director—reportedly took no chances and had it written into his contract that he would do no frontal nudity. Verhoeven himself pointed out, by way of illustrating MPAA rating eccentricities, that the only male organ on view in *Basic Instinct* belongs to Johnny Boz, and he's dead. The MPAA Classification and Rating Administration is reported to have regretted *Basic Instinct*'s R, and the film's excesses are thought to have contributed to the tightening up of MPAA standards over the next couple of years.

Michael Douglas and Sharon Stone dancing dirty in *Basic Instinct*.

Jeroen Krabbe and Renée Soutendijk in *The Fourth Man* (1979).

13

Basic Instinct's insistent phallic symbol.

Stone and Douglas doing the nasty.

14

Movie sex is great to watch. Sex chatter about stars is titillating and keeps a raft of gossip columnists off the public dole. But star-sex gossip plus sex on the screen is an unbeatable combination. Prattle about "It" girl Clara Bow and the UCLA football team (even if it was salacious exaggeration) made *The Wild Party* (1929) seem that little bit wilder. Rumors about heartthrob Tom Cruise's sexuality made the (sublimated) homoeroticism of *Interview With the Vampire: The Vampire Chronicles* (1994) a tad more risqué. Off-screen goings-on inflect the movies, giving them that something extra.

Occasionally, the something extra is devastating. Silent funny man **Roscoe "Fatty" Arbuckle**, a Mack Sennett star, was ruined by the 1921 demise of starlet Virginia Rappe, reportedly after sex with the 266-pound former plumber. Arbuckle was acquitted of rape and murder charges, but his Paramount contract was canceled, his movies were boycotted, and his thriving career dwindled. Comedienne **Mabel Normand**, also a Sennett discovery, saw her waning career sink in the wake of the unsolved 1922 murder of director William Desmond Taylor. Coverage focused on rumors about his sex life, and Mary Pickford–wannabe **Mary Miles Minter** was also tainted beyond redemption by the scandal. **Charlie Chaplin**—the little tramp indeed—escaped with his career intact, but numerous scandals surrounding his sex life helped erode his image. His 1918 marriage to sixteen-year-old Mildred Harris (Chaplin was twenty-nine) was dissolved with limited fanfare, but his divorce from Lita Gray—also sixteen when they married, in 1924—was sensational: She claimed that sexual perversion was the cornerstone of their married life. In 1940 he was in court again, charged by unstable aspiring actress Joan Barry in a paternity suit. Blood tests exonerated Chaplin, but he was maligned in the press and in 1952 left the United States for good, accompanied by his last child bride, Oona O'Neill. In general, sex scandals don't look good on comedians: Look at Woody Allen.

On the other hand, sultry **Jean Harlow** was well served by the perception that she could drive a man mad with desire. Her husband, producer Paul Bern, killed himself shortly after their 1932 marriage amidst rumors that he wasn't man enough for the platinum temptress, giving new meaning to *Blonde Bombshell* and *Hold Your Man* (1933).

Marlene Dietrich's bisexual allure owed much to director Joseph Von Sternberg's meticulous lighting and composition, but career-long rumors about her lovers—men and women—didn't hurt; as early as *Morocco* (1930) and as late as *Just a Gigolo* (1979), her very presence smacked of sophisticated decadence.

Macho ladykiller **Errol Flynn**'s 1942 trial for statutory rape generated lurid headlines, but Flynn was vindicated in the courts and in public opinion. "In like Flynn" became a popular catch phrase, ribald but affectionate.

Adorable **Elizabeth Taylor**'s childhood charms were eclipsed by her adult voluptuousness, and her tempestuous off-screen liaisons—particularly with Eddie Fisher, whom she lured away from professional virgin Debbie Reynolds.

Polish director **Roman Polanski**'s arrest in 1979 for having sex with a thirteen-year-old girl was the last straw in his unhappy Hollywood sojourn. He fled the United States and promptly made *Tess*, based on the novel by Thomas Hardy. It was saved from Merchant/Ivory respectability by provocative teenage star Nastassja Kinski, who appeared everywhere on Polanski's arm.

The bloom was off brat-packer **Rob Lowe**'s career, but his name was back on everyone's lips when word got out about the videotape of him having sex in a hotel room with a young admirer. How fortuitous that Steven Soderbergh's *sex, lies, and videotape* (1989) gave instant headlines to the endless coverage, and that Lowe's next film, *Bad Influence* (1990), included a sex-tapes scene that everyone *swore* was in the movie before the scandal ever erupted.

As an erotic thriller, *Sliver* (1994) fizzled; what little sizzle it mustered came from the behind-the-scenes goings-on. Neo–sex bomb **Sharon Stone** took up with newly married coproducer Bill MacDonald. His jilted bride, Naomi Baka, moved on to become pregnant by married screenwriter **Joe Eszterhas** (who also scripted *Basic Instinct*, which made Stone a star), who left his wife for her. But none of these shenanigans made the film a hit, and Stone moved on to an assistant director on her next picture, *The Quick and the Dead*.

Belle de Jour
(1967)

Directed by Luis Buñuel. Produced by Robert Hakim and Raymond Hakim. Screenplay by Buñuel and Jean-Claude Carrière, based on the novel by Joseph Kessel. Cinematography by Sacha Vierny. Edited by Walter Spohr. Art Direction by Robert Clavel.

Catherine Deneuve (Séverine), Jean Sorel (Pierre), Michel Piccoli (Henri Husson), Geneviève Page (Madame Anaïs), Francisco Rabal (Hyppolite), Pierre Clémenti (Marcel), Georges Marchal (The Duke).

Belle de Jour is a seductive fantasy in the form of a film, but whose fantasy is it? It opens with jingling bells, as aristocratically beautiful Séverine rides through the woods in an open carriage with her husband, Pierre. He declares his love for her, and she responds coolly. He wishes aloud that she were less cold, and she rebuffs him. He tells the coachmen to stop and, with their help, drags her to the ground, ties her to a tree, and supervises her abuse by them. She awakens in her bedroom, telling her husband about the dream.

Séverine loves her husband, a handsome, successful doctor, but she's frigid. A gossiping friend tells her that a woman they know, the refined and elegant Henriette, works in a bordello; Séverine is both repelled and intrigued. Another friend, Henri Husson, senses her repressed fascination and tells her about the discreet, upscale brothel owned by Madame Anaïs. Séverine pays a visit and becomes one of Madame Anaïs's girls, servicing men between 2:00 P.M. and 5:00 P.M. under the name Belle de Jour—Beauty of the Afternoon. Her clients include a crudely jovial candy

manufacturer; a famous doctor who wants to be humiliated; the duke who wants her to pretend to be his dead daughter; and Marcel, a gangster with grotesque metal teeth who becomes obsessed with her. Ironically, Séverine's love for Pierre grows deeper and more profound as her double life grows more complicated. After Husson visits the brothel, Séverine decides to quit. Marcel follows her home and shoots Pierre before being killed by the police. Pierre is paralyzed and blinded; Séverine cares for him faithfully, until Husson appears and tells him everything about Séverine's sordid exploits. She returns to the room, and Pierre rises from his wheelchair, able to walk and see. Was everything just a dream?

Despite the New York *Daily News* review headlined 'BELLE DE JOUR' SORDID PORNO, *Belle de Jour* isn't pornographic, but it is genuinely, if coolly, erotic—a seductive labyrinth of dreams and fantasies linked by the icy presence of Catherine Deneuve. Her beauty is remote, glacially perfect, and she looks most beautiful when she transforms herself into a pale object of desire for an incestuous necrophile: Wearing nothing but a floor-length transparent black veil suspended from a crown of flowers, she's a vision of untouchable loveliness, crying out to be despoiled. This was the sequence that gave director Luis Buñuel trouble with French censors; it originally included the celebration of a Mass "under a splendid copy of one of Grünewald's Christs," and Buñuel regretted that "the suppression of the Mass completely changes the character of this scene."* One could hardly expect a glee-

A pensive Catherine Deneuve.

---

*From Buñel's autobiography, *My Last Breath* (New York: Alfred A. Knopf, 1983), p. 245.

guise of a cinematic poem. Much critical energy has been expended unraveling its dense texture of hallucinatory images and arguing about what was a dream and what wasn't, without ever alluding to its aloof, dreamy eroticism. Intricate exegesis is all very well and good, but unrepentant sensualist Buñuel would have been the last to ignore the film's earthier appeal, which helped make it one of his biggest hits. Proving that he was a surrealist and a gentleman, Buñuel graciously attributed the picture's success to its "marvelous whores"—Françoise Fabian, Geneviève Page, Maria Latour, and, of course, Deneuve, each more chicly French than the one before—rather than to his fine filmmaking.

fully despoiled Catholic such as Buñuel to think otherwise.

A surrealist educated by Jesuits, Spanish director Buñuel made his first film, *Un Chien Andalou*, in 1928, in collaboration with Salvador Dali. Its avant-garde, nonlinear narrative puzzled many viewers, but *Un Chien Andalou*'s notoriety came from its frank use of sexual imagery, much of it perverse, which scandalized contemporary audiences. Throughout his long career, no matter what the subject matter of his films, eroticism was seldom far from Buñuel's heart. Prior to making *Belle de Jour*, Buñuel had adapted Octave Mirabeau's fetishistic *Diary of a Chambermaid*, a celebration of Jeanne Moreau in high heels; it had next been his intention to film Matthew Gregory Lewis's notorious anticlerical novel *The Monk*, about a pious abbot who, once sexually corrupted by the Devil (in the form of a woman disguised as a young, beardless Brother), embraces debauchery wholeheartedly. But Buñuel abandoned the project and instead made *Belle de Jour*, which he adapted from a 1929 novel and embraced as an opportunity to indulge himself "in the faithful description of some interesting sexual perversions." It was his first color film, and he told reporters it would be his last movie. It wasn't.

Belle de Jour is sophisticated naughtiness in the

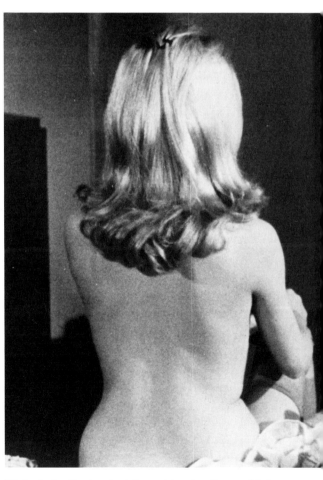

"Belle de Jour" at her day job, servicing the clients at Madame Anaïs's upscale brothel.

The Ten Sexiest Stars of the 1960s

Ann-Margret: The red-haired Swede sang and smoldered her way to stardom in musicals like *Bye Bye Birdie* (1963) and Elvis Presley's *Viva Las Vegas* (1954), but many fans prefer her as a reform-school vixen in *Kitten With a Whip* (1964); she proved she could act while flaunting her cleavage in 1971's *Carnal Knowledge.*

Warren Beatty: From sexy teen idol in *Splendor in the Grass* (1961) to sexual rebel in *Bonnie and Clyde* (1967) to sexual dynamo in *Shampoo* (1975), mythic satyr Beatty settled into the role of perpetual sex symbol in the '80s. He didn't even have to make movies (dating Madonna was enough), though marriage to Annette Bening seems to have dimmed the luster of his erotic reputation, and their *Love Affair* (1994) fizzled.

Richard Burton: Too handsome to have to act, Burton coasted for three decades on his looks and mellifluous voice, starting in the '50s as a juvenile lead. As Elizabeth Taylor's husband (twice) he was half of Hollywood's golden couple, blessed with too much beauty and good fortune for any lifetime. Though his movies are largely undistinguished, he was a feast for the eyes in *Look Back in Anger* (1959), *Cleopatra* (1963), and *The Sandpiper* (1965).

Julie Christie: Chic and radiantly beautiful, Christie embodied the cool, sexually liberated woman of the '60s in *Billy Liar* (1963), *Darling* (1965), and *Petulia* (1968) but was equally at home in period pieces *Dr. Zhivago* (1965), *Far From the Madding Crowd* (1967), and *The Go-Between* (1971).

Sean Connery: Virile and coarse, the first (and for some, only) James Bond was equally at home humiliating villains and sipping martinis in the company of ravishing women. Connery's candid manliness aged well: in his sixties, he could still cross swords with Harrison Ford, who played his son in *Indiana Jones and the Last Crusade* (1989), and win.

Catherine Deneuve: Icily beautiful and eternally cool, Deneuve starred in the musical *Umbrellas of Cherbourg* (1964) but was better used in films that exploited the troubled soul beneath the perfect exterior, including *Repulsion* (1965) and *Belle de Jour* (1967). She was once the official face of Marianne, the national symbol of France.

Sophia Loren: A teenage beauty-contest winner, Loren had a voluptuous figure that got her work throughout the '50s in her native Italy. In the '60s she went international and graced such films as *The Millionairess* (1960), *Yesterday, Today and Tomorrow* (1963), *Marriage Italian Style* (1964), and *Arabesque* (1966). She could act, witness *Two Women* (1960), but her fans mostly preferred that she not.

Marcello Mastroianni: Like that of Loren—his *Yesterday, Today and Tomorrow* and *Marriage Italian Style* costar—Mastroianni's Italian career started in the early '50s, but the world discovered him in Federico Fellini's *La Dolce Vita* (1959) and *8½* (1963). With his haunted eyes and suave manner, Mastroianni simultaneously incited lust and tenderness in *Divorce Italian Style* (1961), *The Tenth Victim* (1965), and others.

Paul Newman: A juvenile in the '50s, Newman settled into his striking looks in the '60s and '70s with *Hud* (1963), *Cool Hand Luke* (1967), *Butch Cassidy and the Sundance Kid* (1969), and *The Sting* (1973). His reign as a sex symbol continued through the '90s. In *Nobody's Fool* (1994) he was called the sexiest old man in movies.

Raquel Welch: A carefully groomed sex goddess, Welch emerged in animal skins in *One Million Years B.C.* (1966). She decorated *Fantastic Voyage* (1966), *Bedazzled* (1967), and *100 Rifles* (1969), then came a cropper in the satirical *Myra Breckenridge* (1970). She still looked great but by the '90s had degenerated into a smutty joke in a skin-tight dress.

Betty Blue / 37.2 Le Matin (1986)

Written and Directed by Jean-Jacques Beineix, based on the novel *37.2 Le Matin*, by Philippe Djian. Produced by Beineix and Claudie Ossard. Cinematography by Jean-François Robin. Edited by Monique Prim. Art Direction by Carlos Conti. Music by Gabriel Yared.

Jean-Hugues Anglade (Zorg) Beatrice Dalle (Betty), Consuelo de Haviland (Lisa), Gerard Darmon (Eddy), Clementine Celarie (Annie), Jacques Mathou (Bob).

Somewhere between sexy art films and arty sex films (see *Henry & June* and *Wild Orchid*, respectively) lie the pictures of French director Jean-Jacques Beineix. The flashy *Diva* (1981), a sort-of thriller about an opera-loving bicycle messenger who steals his idol's dress, made him the most talked-about new director of the year, but American critics quickly lost patience with him after *The Moon in the Gutter / La Lune dans le caniveau* (1983) and *Betty Blue*. His later films *Roselyne and the Lions* (1989) and *IP5* (1992) never even made it to U.S. shores. Beineix worships excess. Brilliant colors, stained-glass lighting, outrageous set design, behavior that verges on mad and looks that border on caricature, telling stories of lust, romance, and grand, all-encompassing love. Call him pretentious, call him stylish to a fault, call him an out-of-control sensualist with one foot in romance novels and the other in the gutter, but Beineix is committed to the cinematic worship of female flesh, and there's plenty of it on display in *Betty Blue*.

It opens with a long shot of an attractive couple making love, and as their writhings grow more impas-

Anglade and the lushly proportioned Dalle share a tender moment.

sioned, the camera *slowly* tracks in ever closer to a revealing medium shot. "I had known Betty a week . . ." says Zorg in voice-over, and we begin to get acquainted with the ardent lovers. As opening images go, *Betty Blue*'s is unquestionably arresting. Though no other single scene is quite so explicit and extended, the film is full of sex, and both Jean-Hugues Anglade and the lushly proportioned Beatrice Dalle are frequently and frontally nude. Its prurient appeal aside, *Betty Blue* is a classic French exploration of *amour fou*, everyone's favorite surrealist conceit: the mad, hopeless love that spits on convention and liberates desire, that burns too brightly not to destroy everyone who ventures near the blaze.

Betty moves in with Zorg, the exploited caretaker of a slightly seedy resort town. They quickly settle into a routine: They drink, have sex, and squabble about Zorg's lack of ambition. But everything changes when Betty finds a box filled with Zorg's notebooks and becomes convinced that he's a great undiscovered novelist. She devotes herself to furthering his career, typing his manuscript, sending it off to publishers, telling him over and over that he is a great writer and one day the world will realize it. That he himself is flattered but unconvinced doesn't faze her for a second. They drift from job to job, helped by their friends Lisa and Eddy, who owns a restaurant and, later, a piano dealership. Though Zorg grows increasingly devoted to her, the high-strung Betty is gradually driven insane by her own passions. She becomes self-destructive and is taken to an asylum, where she slips into a coma. Zorg's novel is accepted for publication as she lies, insensible, in her hospital bed. Zorg then secretly smothers Betty

hurls Zorg's possessions out the window when they fight. But she soon crosses the line between hot-tempered and scary: She burns down Zorg's house, stabs a nasty customer with a fork while waiting tables, and takes a straight razor to a book publisher who rejects Zorg's manuscript with gratuitous cruelty.

That Zorg stays with her would stretch credulity were she not played by luscious, twenty-one-year-old newcomer Beatrice Dalle, a magnificent beauty with pale, luscious skin and inky hair. She has a luxuriant, ripely curved body, with abundant thighs and a little pot belly, and she radiates unabashed sensuality tinged with something wild and a little frightening. Nude, she radiates defiant self-possession. Dalle's face is striking, defined by high cheekbones and a firm jaw, but without the impassiveness that so often accompanies beauty. Her face lights up when she smiles but slips frighteningly easily into ugliness; the hint of the monstrous beneath the flawless skin may be why she hasn't matured into a full-fledged sex symbol. Dalle's subsequent credits include *On a volé Charlie Spencer!* (1986), *The Witches' Sabbath / Le Vision del sabba* (1988), *Chimère* (1989), and *A Woman's Revenge / La Vengeance d'une femme* (1990); she made her American debut as an obnoxious blind woman in Jim Jarmusch's *Night on Earth* (1991).

Beineix also explored the erotic in *The Moon in the Gutter* and *Roselyne and the Lions*. *The Moon in the Gutter*, adapted from the novel by American pulp idol David Goodis, is a day-glo fantasy of sensual degradation in which Gerard Depardieu must navigate a poetically degenerate slum filled with ripely dangerous women, including sexpots Victoria Abril and Nastassja Kinski. Morbidly baroque and flamboyantly artificial, *The Moon in the Gutter* is a love letter to low life, a tone poem ripe with violence and degradation. *Roselyne and the Lions*, by contrast, is a sensual fairy tale about a beautiful girl (Isabelle Pasco) who finds her destiny at the circus as a wild-animal tamer. The film's final scene—in which a lion gently picks up a rose from Roselyne's body with its huge, velvety muzzle—packs a remarkably potent charge, conjuring up *Beauty and the Beast* (1946) and *Circus of Horrors* (1960) in the same cinematic breath, playing the tactile sensuality of fur on skin against the thrilling unease about those big teeth so close to that fine, soft belly.

rather than watch her degenerate further, and he finds escape in a renewed desire to write. Ironically, Betty has succeeded in making the apathetic Zorg into an author.

Betty is one of those girls, much loved by French films, who are made deranged by sexual appetite. She has a tattoo on her shoulder, eschews underwear, and favors a carelessly revealing wardrobe. Zorg can no more resist her than a moth can defy a flame. She's so attuned to sexual vibrations that she's picking up every other sound in the spectrum as well; it's no wonder that soon she's hearing voices, the kind that tell people to do bad things. At first it seems that she's just unusually frank and spirited: She pushes Zorg's leering, abusive boss off a balcony into the sand and throws paint on his car, smashes crockery when she's angry, and

The Big Easy
(1987)

Directed by Jim McBride. Produced by Stephen Friedman. Written by Daniel Petrie Jr. and Jack Baran. Cinematography by Alfonso Beato. Edited by Mia Goldman. Music by Brad Fiedel.

Dennis Quaid (Remy McSwain), Ellen Barkin (Anne Osborne), Ned Beatty (Jack Kellom), Ebbe Roe Smith (Detective Dodge), John Goodman (Detective DeSoto).

Even cities have screen personae. New York is dangerous and sophisticated. Los Angeles is the home of sun-washed noir. Miami is colorful and corrupt. Detroit is decayed and violent. Chicago is brawny and unpretentious. New Orleans, of course, is the Big Easy, the steamy city where sex and other sensual indulgences are behind everything—witness *A Streetcar Named Desire* (1951), *Pretty Baby* (1978), *Cat People* (1982), *Tightrope* (1984), *No Mercy* (1986), *Angel Heart* (1987), *Johnny Handsome* (1989), *Storyville* (1992), *Interview With the Vampire: The Vampire Chronicles* (1994), and a host of others. With its tropical climate and old-world architecture, its carnival and eccentric Catholicism, its Caribbean colors, voodoo priestesses, Cajun food, above-ground cemeteries, jazz bars, and pervasive atmosphere of luxurious decay, New Orleans is the city that offers delights for every sense and the promise of glorious damnation.

The Big Easy started life as a conventional cop thriller, but when its location was moved to New Orleans, everything changed. Hero Remy McSwain is a sharp young detective whose adorably laid-back ways include an abiding love of sex, food, and liquor. District Attorney Anne Osborne is an old maid in training, a prim, by-the-book public official who doesn't buy the Big Easy philosophy, figuring it as a front for

laziness at best and iniquity at worst; she has Remy pegged as part of the problem and is determined to bring him down. He, on the other hand, is determined to seduce her, a crusade that complicates two investigations: his, into drug-related murders, and hers, into his wicked ways. *The Big Easy* could just as well, and more accurately, be called *The Big Tease*. Despite its policier drag—complete with murder, drugs, wiseguys, and police corruption—it's all about when and how hunky Remy is going to get his Cajun sausage into repressed Miss Goody Two-Shoes's prissy panties.

The Big Easy's central sex scene is an unexpected paean to the thrill of imperfection, rampant in real life but rare on the movie screen. "The scene was unique," director Jim McBride later said, "because it was all about awkwardness in bed. Usually in the movies, you want things to look smooth." Women are particular fans, naming the scene as one of their favorite erotic moments on film. Its endearing clumsiness seems to owe as much to costar Ellen Barkin as to McBride (the man behind the pointless but sexually explicit remake of *Breathless* [1983] with Richard Gere and Valerie Zaprisky), who reportedly wanted her to do the scene nude. Though hardly shy about stripping on film, Barkin insisted that the scene would be sexier if she were half-dressed, and she was right. Together, Barkin and Quaid capture a heady sense of desire complicated by everything from moral qualms to uncooperative clothes, and as she gradually relaxes and begins to respond to his touch, the feeling of erotic surrender is palpable. Unfortunately, they have what may be the worst case of cinematic coitus interruptus of all time, and their tryst is aborted by his beeper summons to a

Steamy New Orleans works its wiles on Ellen Barkin and Dennis Quaid.

triple shotgun murder. The next time they try, some-one shoots Remy's brother Bobby, thinking it's Remy. But there's nothing like frustration to turn up lust's thermometer.

Crucial to *The Big Easy*'s substantial erotic appeal, particularly for women, is the pairing of Quaid and Barkin. An offbeat beauty, she brings a feral intelligence to her every move, while he has a hounddog grin that could melt the polar ice caps. Even though the erotic tension is resolved a third of the way through, it nevertheless colors the entire film and gives the low-budget sleeper enviable legs—a large part of its business turned out to be repeat viewers who couldn't resist one more look at the Zydeco-driven dance of attraction between Quaid and Barkin.

Her steamy appeal has been exploited in other films, though usually in a more conventional way; she's memorably wanton as an amnesiac in *Siesta* (1987), a possible lonely-hearts killer in *Sea of Love* (1989), a man reborn as a woman in *Switch* (1991), and an amoral bitch in *Bad Company* (1994). She keeps returning to New Orleans, as in *Down by Law* (1986) and *Johnny Handsome* (1989). Quaid's sunny smirk needs her untamed foil, which may be why, despite his evident sex appeal, he's still a second-string actor.

Body Heat
(1981)

Written and Directed by Lawrence Kasdan. Produced by Fred T. Gallo. Cinematography by Richard H. Kline. Edited by Carol Littleton. Music by John Barry.

Kathleen Turner (Matty Walker), John Hurt (Ned Racine), Richard Crenna (Edmund Walker), Ted Danson (Peter Lowenstein), Mickey Rourke (Teddy Lewis).

There was film noir before there was ever a name for it, and it seethed with unspeakable erotic impulses. Technically, film historians define film noir as a cycle of American films made between 1940 and 1958, loosely connected by a set of stock characters—the innocent man wrongly accused, the perverted über-villain, the poor fool, and the femme fatale—distinctive visual flourishes, including an exaggerated use of light and shadow, and an overwhelming mood of voluptuous, cynical despair. Spawned by pulp novels and German Expressionism and, shaped by postwar malaise, noir films were nasty, brutish, and short but were among the few places women had license to be unabashedly carnal.

Granted, they were bad women, but that didn't make them any the less blood-stirring. They were treacherous, enticing sirens who lured men to corruption and ruin. Foremost among them: the alluring Phyllis Dietrichson (Barbara Stanwyck), who captivates and betrays insurance agent Walter Neff (Fred MacMurray) in *Double Indemnity* (1945). Kitty March (Joan Bennett), alias Lazy Legs, is *Scarlet Street*'s (1945) shiny, polished erotic fetish of a girl too indolent to realize she's poisonous. Perpetual good girl Mary Astor took a turn for the wicked as Brigid O'Shaughnessy in *The Maltese Falcon* (1941). She may be the coolest lethal woman in noir history, while Ann Savage's Vera, the unhinged hitchhiker of *Detour*

(1944), is a likely candidate for the most harpyish. And Jane Greer makes Kathy Moffett, who lies to, steals from, seduces, and betrays the unfortunate Jeff Bailey (Robert Mitchum) in *Out of the Past* (1947), one of the iciest, most unselfconscious bitches in motion-picture history; Rachel Ward plays her in the 1984 remake, *Against All Odds*, and can't hold a candle to Greer.

By the 1980s the sexual revolution had come and gone, and you'd think the femme fatale would have been well and truly dead, banished to the attic of outdated stereotypes alongside the sissy (think Franklin Pangborn) and Stepin Fetchit. But *Body Heat* gave the lie to that idea; Kathleen Turner's husky-voiced Matty Walker was born to be bad, and audiences loved her for it. The appeal of the black widow spider, who kills her mate when she's done with him, is eternal.

Florida lawyer Ned Racine is a small-town cocksman who meets his match in beguiling Matty, who sums him up in a flick of her mascaraed eye. Dressed in crisp white, the breeze ruffling her hair, she observes coolly, "You're not too smart, are you? I like that in a man." He's hooked. She's a consummate tease, a brainy schemer married to an older millionaire; Ned thinks he's pursuing her, but she's really leading him around by his most private of parts. Where classic noir films had to rein in the eroticism, suggest irresistible passion with shadows and glances and languid curls of cigarette smoke, *Body Heat* dives between the sheets. Stars Kathleen Turner and William Hurt moan and twine and sweat firmly within the confines of mainstream filmmaking, but with an intensity that's unusually convincing. Much of the heat is in the details—like her hand stroking him after they've had sex—and it's not hard to believe that they're so torrid

lives in pursuit of sexual ecstasy. As quickly as the plan comes together, it begins to unravel. The local police aren't convinced by the setup, and when the will is read, Ned discovers that Matty has altered it to make herself sole heir and signed his name to the new version. The web begins to tighten: Ned becomes a suspect, Matty tells him she's being blackmailed, and the seeds of suspicion are sown too late. Before he knows what hit him, Ned is in jail and Matty is gone.

Body Heat, a knowing and reverent pastiche of classic noir style, themes, and atmosphere, jump-started the neo-noir cycle. Throughout the '60s and '70s, there were occasional, mostly low-budget films that drew from the noir well. But it took movie buff Lawrence Kasdan, fresh off the success of scripting *Raiders of the Lost Ark* (1981), to revitalize a set of mannerisms and attitudes that proved to have lost none of their luster after years on the back shelf of mass consciousness. *Body Heat*, not the original noir thrillers by which it was inspired, gave birth to the erotic thriller; it took all the repressed sexual energy that was implicit in noir and made it explicit. By and large, the new generation of erotic thrillers aren't even designed for theatrical release (the recent *China Moon* [1994], with Madeleine Stowe and Ed Harris, and *The Last Seduction* [1994], starring Linda Fiorentino as a spider woman of

together that they have to cool off in a bathtub full of ice water. Women regularly cite the scene in which Ned, crazed with lust for the tormentingly enticing Matty, kicks in a glass door to get to her (she, of course, is biding her time, confident that he can't stay away) as one of the most erotic moments in recent cinema. Men prefer the scene in which Ned ravishes Matty in the boathouse, but *Body Heat* is the rare film that appeals pretty equally to both sexes.

Needless to say, it's not long before the plot is hatched. Ned will murder Matty's husband, and the two of them will make it look like an accident; she'll inherit half his money—the other half is earmarked for his small niece—and she'll hire Ned to handle the estate. They'll get married and spend the rest of their

Turner's femme fatale clinches her hold on William Hurt's poor sap.

Body Heat's lovers hatch their murderous plot.

truly awesome viciousness, are exceptions); they're meant to be viewed in the privacy of one's own home. Once a genre powered by the brittle engine of despair and cynicism (the sad fate of the disappointed roman-

tic), neo-noir has largely degenerated into a stock set of characters, stylistic clichés, and fashionable attitudes. And you know what? It's still hot.

Burning Desire

Sex as a force of nature, exploding, pounding, burning, raging like the most tempestuous of storms—it may be romance-novel cliché, but it's very visual. If you've taken Psychology 101, you know that arsonists are sexually repressed and get an orgasmic thrill out of setting fires. You're prepared for *Endless Love* (1981), about juvenile pyromaniac Martin Hewitt's obsession with Brooke Shields; *Body Heat* (1981), in which William Hurt and Kathleen Turner's blazing desire contrasts with the hot work of firebug Mickey Rourke; and David Lynch's wildly overstated *Wild at Heart* (1990), in which arson plus screen-filling close-ups of match heads exploding into flame remind us that Laura Dern and Nicolas Cage are consumed by their mutual lust.

Nice Girls Don't Explode (1987), *Pyrates* (1991), and *Wilder Napalm* (1993) pass through the looking glass into worlds in which passion itself starts fires.

Nice Girls Don't Explode plays the idea for silly comedy, filled with jokes about hot dates, while *Pyrates* takes matters slightly more seriously—twentysomething lovers Kevin Bacon and Kyra Sedgwick are meant for each other but worry about the fires that seem to start whenever they make love. Is it just coincidence (plus faulting wiring, untended candles, etc.), or does their desire literally create sparks? *Wilder Napalm* is a firestarting three-ring circus: brothers Dennis Quaid and Arliss Howard can start fires with their minds, and they're both in love with nymphomaniac Debra Winger, who's also an arsonist—hold the "Is it getting hot in here, or is it just me?" jokes, please. And finally, there's the eerie *Bail Jumper* (1990), in which Ezter Balint and B. J. Spalding's sexual fervor causes lightning, tornadoes, meteor showers, and a solar eclipse.

Boxing Helena
(1993)

Directed by Jennifer Chambers Lynch. Produced by Carl Mazzocone and Philippe Caland. Screenplay by Lynch, from a story by Caland. Cinematography by Frank Byers. Edited by David Finfer. Art Direction by Paul Huggins. Music by Graeme Revell.

Sherilyn Fenn (Helena), Julian Sands (Dr. Nick Cavanaugh), Bill Paxton (Ray), Kurtwood Smith (Dr. Harrison), Betsy Clark (Anne), Art Garfunkel (Dr. Lawrence Augustine), Nicolette Scorsese (China).

Jennifer Chambers Lynch: proof positive that when it comes to erotica, women can be as lurid, voyeuristic, and really cruel to sexually emancipated heroines as men, and a whole lot more peculiar to boot. Exhibit A: *Boxing Helena*, a titillating movie for the perverted smarty-pants, dedicated to making viewers lust for a sex bomb who's gradually shorn of her luscious limbs. And it's not especially circumspect about its perv appeal; in fact, the film comes in, weirdness waving, and dares you to be shocked.

Boxing Helena is an erotic fable about love and dependence that dares to be as freakish as a Grimm fairy tale, and far more frank. Nick Cavanaugh is a brilliant but disturbed surgeon (warped, we learn in the obligatory flashback, by his cold and beautiful mother) tormented by his insane lust for ravishing, sexually enticing Helena, the certified grade-A bitch with whom he has a one-night stand.

He spies on her as she has sex with her brutish boyfriend, throws a party in her honor and watches

The ballad of sexual dependence: Fenn and Sands in *Boxing Helena*.

agape as she takes a *Dolce Vita*–esque dip in his fountain and leaves with another man, and endures an endless stream of insults and humiliations until fate delivers his love into his hands. Helena is run down by a car, and Cavanaugh spirits her into his mansion and amputates first her legs, then her arms. He dresses her in filmy clothes, carefully does her makeup and combs her hair, enshrines her on a flower-trimmed throne, and pledges his abject, eternal devotion. To stir her desires, he brings home a beautiful prostitute and makes love to her while Helena watches. It's all absurd, offensive, fabulously serious—in a smugly clever sort of way—and perversely effective until the "Thank God it was just a dreadful dream" finale. *Boxing Helena*'s sex scenes were hot enough to earn an initial NC-17 rating, though it was eventually released with an R after thirty seconds of sex were trimmed.

Boxing Helena managed to generate even more controversy off screen than on, mostly by way of its widely publicized casting tribulations. Written in 1987 by the then–nineteen-year-old daughter of professional oddball David Lynch (*Eraserhead*, *Blue Velvet*, *Wild at Heart*), *Boxing Helena* was first announced to star Madonna, who withdrew for "personal reasons"; her departure brought production to a halt. She was replaced by Kim Basinger, who, reports have it, suddenly began demanding that Helena be softened, made less of a bitch. Basinger pulled out and was replaced at the eleventh hour by Sherilyn Fenn; litigious producer Carl Mazzacone—who later took on the MPAA, appealing the finished film's rating) filed a $5 million breach of (oral) contract suit against Basinger. In 1993 the suit was settled against her to the tune of

The teasing temptress (Sherilyn Fenn) who finds herself when she loses her extraneous parts.

Helena triumphant: no arms, no legs, and still more than Julian Sands can handle.

$8.92 million, but the verdict was overturned on appeal the following year. In the meantime, the original Dr. Cavanaugh, Ed Harris—who hung on through eighteen months of turmoil—abandoned the project in 1991; he was replaced by Julian Sands.

Sexpot Fenn is the major reason to see the picture. Even turned into a living Venus de Milo—a connection we're encouraged to make by endless shots of the statue itself—she oozes sultriness, whether flouncing around in Victoria's Secret lingerie or doing an Anita Ekberg in her curve-skimming evening gown. On a double bill with horror sex-fantasy *Meridian* (1990), *Boxing Helena* is a Fenn fan's wet nightmare.

Bizarre Couplings

As though sex between two people weren't complicated enough (even without, say, an age difference like the one between Bud Cort and Ruth Gordon in cult favorite *Harold and Maude*), movies have entertained us with all sorts of peculiar combinations, mostly of the beauty-and-the-beast variety. Consider Vanity (billed as D. D. Winters) and an ape in *Tanya's Island* (1981), Sirpa Lane and *The Beast* (1974), and Charlotte Rampling and a chimpanzee in *Max, Mon Amour* (1986). Or Jane Fonda and angel John Phillip Law in *Barbarella* (1968), Julie Christie and a computer in *Demon Seed* (1977), Mia Farrow and Satan in *Rosemary's Baby* (1968), Barbara Hershey and an incubus in *The Entity* (1983)—because the incubus is invisible, the sex scenes involve Hershey's writhing alone while her flesh dimples to an unseen touch—and Isabelle Adjani and some sort of octopus thing in *Possession* (1981).

Sex with aliens is a particular favorite, though a bit of a cheat, because they tend to look just like us; witness Karen Allen and Jeff Bridges in *Starman* (1984), Geena Davis and Jeff Goldblum in *Earth Girls Are Easy* (1989), Anne Carlisle et al. in *Liquid Sky* (1983), Candy Clark and David Bowie in *The Man Who Fell to Earth* (1976), and Dan Aykroyd and Kim Basinger in *My Stepmother Is an Alien* (1988). It's tough out there on the singles scene.

Boy on a Dolphin
(1957)

Directed by Jean Negulesco. Produced by Samuel G. Engel. Screenplay by Ivan Moffat and Dwight Taylor, from the novel by David Divine. Cinematography by Milton Krasner. Edited by William Mace.
Music by Hugo Friedhofer.

Alan Ladd (James Calder), Sophia Loren (Phaedra), Clifton Webb (Victor Parmalee), Jorge Mistral (Rhif), Laurence Naismith (Dr. Hawkins).

It's safe to say that no one ever watched the silly *Boy on a Dolphin*, a film nominally about antiquities, diving, and the glories of the Greek landscape, because of an interest in any of those things. *Boy on a Dolphin* has one, and only one, thing to recommend it. But it's a big thing: the youthful Sophia Loren in a wet dress, skirt tucked up between her thighs, fabric outlining every inch of her luscious curves. Magazine articles have always lauded Loren's fabulous face: the almond-shaped eyes, the slanted cheekbones, the generous mouth; how odd that the camera's eye always seemed to slip farther south.

In *Boy on a Dolphin*, which was hyped as the Italian bombshell's first English-language role, Loren plays Phaedra, a poor, earthy Greek girl who dives for sponges off the picturesque coast of Hydra. Loren's profession is a convenient excuse to get her wet and tousled, her simple poverty an excuse to parade her about barefoot and in fetching rags. Filmed in Deluxe color and CinemaScope, the film has a travelogue aspect that's ostensibly defined by the magnificent Aegean sea coast, but it's really all about Loren's hills and dales.

While diving, Phaedra discovers a golden statue of a boy astride a dolphin. Though at first she doesn't realize the significance of her find, a local doctor tells her that the nail she got embedded in her knee on the same dive is thousands of years old, and she shrewdly recognizes that if the statue is equally ancient, it's valuable. She goes looking for a suitable buyer, and her choices are Victor Parmalee, a rich, selfish collector, and James Calder, an archeologist who's dedicated himself to restoring antiquities to their rightful owners. Calder wants to claim the statue for the nation of Greece; Parmalee wants to decorate with it and enlists the aid of Phaedra's roguish Albanian fiancé Rhif in getting the statue. Naturally, Phaedra eventually does the right thing, and her reward is the charming Calder.

Loren was larger than life from the start: A 1962 *Time* magazine cover story began: "Her feet are too big. Her nose is too long. Her teeth are uneven. She has the neck, as one of her rivals has put it, of 'a Neapolitan giraffe.' Her waist seems to begin in the middle of her thighs, and she has big, half-bushel hips. She runs like a fullback. Her hands are huge. Her forehead is low. Her mouth is too large. And, *mamma mia*, she is absolutely gorgeous." At five-foot-eight she was so much taller than *Dolphin* costar Alan Ladd (but then, who wasn't?) that a trench had to be dug for scenes in which they walked side by side, and it was well worth every bit of effort. As generously proportioned as America's big blondes, Loren was never mannered, artificial, or self-parodying, as they often were. She once confided, "Everything I have, I owe to spaghetti," and lived to regret it as she tried to establish herself as an actress rather than as a sex goddess. But while no more than a handful of her many movies bears watching, she's an enduring icon of sensuality, and there are worse things to be.

Sophia Loren, hands-down winner of the "wet housedress" contest.

unkindly described as half her height and twice her age; when Cary Grant—then her costar in *The Pride and the Passion* (1956)—proposed to Loren, Ponti quickly went to Mexico and arranged a bizarre divorce–marriage by proxy (lawyers stood in for Loren). The Vatican refused to recognize the ceremony, charged Ponti with bigamy, and branded Loren "the concubine." She beat Natalie Wood, Audrey Hepburn, Piper Laurie, and Geraldine Page for 1961's Best Actress Oscar, winning for *Two Women* at the age of twenty-six; the following year her marriage to Ponti was annulled, and in 1966, the couple became French citizens and remarried. It was a grand romance despite the dumpy Ponti. Ironically, the ur–Earth mother later told the press she had had trouble bearing children (she has two sons) because of a hormone deficiency.

Loren is only one in a long line of bounteous, down-to-earth Italian sex goddesses with otherworldly endowments. Remember Silvana Mangano, whose lush thighs overwhelmed the populist message of *Bitter Rice* (1948)? Or the wanton, curvy Lollobrigida, the former beauty queen who decorated *Solomon and Sheba* (1959)? Claudia Cardinale made waves in *Rocco and His Brothers* (1960),

Like all bona fide idols, Loren overcame melodramatic odds to achieve stardom. Born Sofia Scicolone in a charity ward to an unwed mother, she planned to be a schoolteacher until her burgeoning curves redirected her dreams. As a teenaged sometime movie extra, she entered a beauty contest in Rome and met producer Carlo Ponti, who told her he'd discovered Gina Lollobrigida and invited her for a screen test, which was a disaster. She began dating the married Ponti,

Virna Lisi wowed Jack Lemmon in *How to Murder Your Wife* (1965), and Monica Vitti graced the artily alienated landscapes of Antonioni's *L'Avventura* (1959), *La Notte* (1961), *L'Eclisse* (1962), and *Red Desert* (1964). But Loren outshone them all, and at nearly sixty, she was still stunning in *Ready-to-Wear / Prêt-à-Porter* (1994).

Loren demonstrating what she owes to spaghetti.

We've all seen them: movies that friends promise are really sexy but then admit have only one *really* hot scene, like the films listed here.

From Here to Eternity (1953): A raw tale of army life, *Eternity* lives on through one brief, unforgettable (and much imitated) scene: hunky Burt Lancaster and genteel Deborah Kerr in white bathing suits, locked in a carnal full-body clinch in the surf.

Yesterday, Today, and Tomorrow (1963): An Italian sex romp that's neither as funny nor as sexy as one might expect, but worth seeing for the moment when Sophia Loren and Marcello Mastroianni change places in her Rolls Royce—the sight of her sliding oh-so-casually over his lap is enough to make anyone sweat.

The Servant (1964): Amidst a brooding drama of class and psychological domination, aristocratic James Fox is seduced by common-as-dirt Sarah Miles. From the moment she swings her legs up onto the table, he's doomed by lust.

The Nightcomers (1971): A bad reworking of Henry James's *The Turn of the Screw*, but make time for Marlon Brando and Stephanie Beacham's S&M-tinged sex scene.

Altered States (1980): Ignore the psychobabble and go straight to the scene in which William Hurt and Blair Brown hit the couch. Sizzling!

Risky Business (1983): High school good boy Tom Cruise and high-class call girl Rebecca De Mornay have steamy sex on a train. The Chicago Transit Authority couldn't ask for better advertising.

Breathless (1983): The remake of the Jean-Paul Belmondo–Jean Seberg classic doesn't live up to the original, but the sex is way hotter, including a sequence that begins with perpetually bare-assed Richard Gere and nubile newcomer Valerie Kaprisky in the shower, and ends with them rumpling the sheets in a bare-all long shot.

No Way Out (1987): Sean Young and Kevin Costner take a break from political skullduggery for some very hot action in the back of a limousine. Lifestyles of the privileged and lusty.

Bull Durham (1988): Susan Sarandon and Kevin Costner tear up the screen (and her house) when they finally consummate their smoldering attraction, and the rest of the picture is a witty, literate look at love, lust, and baseball.

The Fabulous Baker Boys (1989): An old-fashioned romance at heart, but the memory of Michelle Pfeiffer wriggling seductively atop Jeff Bridges's piano and singing "Makin' Whoopee" eclipses every other scene.

The Grifters (1990): Dark, cynical, and smartly depressing, but Annette Bening—wearing a raincoat with nothing underneath—seducing John Cusack is a winner.

Thelma & Louise (1991): A feminist road movie celebrating the friendship of buddies Susan Sarandon and Geena Davis, it briefly sizzles when Davis gets a lesson in doing the wild thing from cowboy stud Brad Pitt.

The Rapture (1991): Discontented phone operator Mimi Rogers and Eurosleaze Patrick Bauchau pick up a young couple for a swinging orgy à quatre that ignites an otherwise odd and unerotic picture about faith and the Apocalypse.

Caligula
(1978)

Produced by Bob Guccione and Franco Rossellini. Principal Photography by Tinto Brass. Additional Scenes Directed and Photographed by Giancarlo Lui and Bob Guccione. Adapted from an Original Screenplay by Gore Vidal. Cinematography by Silvano Ippoliti. Edited by Nino Baragli. Editing by the Production. Art Direction by Danilo Donati. Music by Paul Clemente.

Malcolm McDowell (Caligula), Teresa Ann Savoy (Drusilla), Helen Mirren (Caesonia), Peter O'Toole (Tiberius Caesar), John Steiner (Longinus), Adriana Asti (Ennia), Guido Mannari (Macrone), Giancarlo Badessi (Claudius), Paolo Bonacelli (Cherea), Mirella Dangelo (Livia), John Gielgud (Nerva).

*C*aligula was, of course, a sensation, a $16 million hard-core film with stars of the magnitude of Malcolm McDowell, Peter O'Toole, and John Gielgud and production values to rival those of *Cleopatra* (1963), until then the ne plus ultra of lavish historical epics. No wonder people lined up around the block to see it at the newly renamed Penthouse East Theater (formerly the Trans-Lux East in Manhattan), rented by producer and *Penthouse* magazine publisher Bob Guccione for the duration of the film's run. Even at $7.50 a ticket—at a time when other movies cost $3.00—and even though the film was just about universally critically reviled. Chicago critic Roger Ebert summed up the party line by calling it "sickening, utterly worthless, shameful trash," and going on to complain, "*Caligula* is not good art, it is not good cinema, and it is not good porn." It's not good art, but it's pretty great spectacle—one definition of cinema—and, at least in places, it certainly is good porn.

Caligula chronicles the short and vicious reign of mad Roman emperor Caligula, who assumes power after the murder of his sick, debauched grandfather, Tiberius Caesar. Caligula carries on an incestuous affair with his sister Drusilla and indulges in every form of sexual gratification with the men and women who live in increasing fear of his whims. He viciously slaughters anyone who poses a threat to him, including Macrone, his longtime supporter, and humiliates and murders members of the Senate who dare question his actions. He orders the budget balanced by turning his palace into an imperial brothel staffed with the senators' wives and neglects even the most fundamental duties of state in favor of decadent orgies. He and his wife, Caesonia, are murdered in a coup, and the idiot Claudius is hailed as the new Caesar.

Variety called *Caligula* "the biggest genitalia costumer ever made," while the *London Times* described it as "a cavalcade of most known sexual perversions and a few hitherto unsuspected," all true enough. Producer and partial director Guccione resented the implication that all he'd done in *Caligula* was make the most expensive porno movie ever and pointed out to the press that he could have made the most expensive porno movie ever at a fraction of the cost. His claim that *Caligula* was a serious exploration of the notion that power corrupts and absolute power corrupts absolutely, however, must be taken with a grain of salt.

Caligula is, at heart, an opulent Hollywood Roman epic, all grand soap opera amidst togas and pillars and classical statuary. The difference is that while Hollywood pictures set in decadent Rome had to content themselves with the merest suggestion of perversion, *Caligula* went all the way: The orgy scenes are hard-core celebrations of bare breasts and butts and

Malcolm McDowell and Teresa Ann Savoy (in the role Maria Schneider walked out on) as *Caligula*'s incestuous siblings.

Franco Rossellini (nephew of neo-realist director Roberto Rossellini) to make it in Italy, where—the debacle of *Cleopatra* notwithstanding—shooting was generally cheaper than in the United States. They hired Italian exploitation director Tinto Brass, whose most famous credit is the *Night Porter* rip-off *Salon Kitty* (1976), to film at Dear Studios in Rome, where a series of extravagant sets were constructed. According to assistant director Pier Nico Solinas (who in 1981 wrote a tell-all book called *Ultimate Porno: The Making of a Sex Colossal*), his first job was to hire "disgusting dwarves" for the orgy scenes. His next was to audition sex-show girls, like the one who fed a hawk from her vaginal lips.

The trouble began almost immediately. The prickly, patrician Vidal feuded with Brass, who barred him from the set in an attempt to preserve his artistic vision; the two sniped at each other in the press. Vidal's declaration that the sets looked like Miami's riotously tasteless Fountainbleau Hotel were met by Rossellini's retort, "Have you ever been inside *his* house?" Original costar Maria Schneider, of *Last Tango in Paris* (1973), also warred with Brass, reportedly over the amount of nudity her part required. She was fired after shooting started and replaced as Drusilla by unknown Teresa Ann Savoy. Brass accused Rossellini of stealing Guccione's money and was fired "when he refused to comply with the artistic demands of the production company." Guccione and Giancarlo Lui filmed additional footage—including, reportedly, all of the hard-core sex scenes, none of which involved the top-line stars—and reedited the picture. The finished film carries no director's name—"Principal Photography" is credited to Brass, alongside "Additional Scenes Directed and

penises. The girls are wet-lipped and endlessly willing. The men appear to have been cast for the size of their organs, and the decor is a riot of phallic objects and tiger skins. If you like your sex done up in historical drag, it's all pretty hot, like a faux-Roman orgy photo spread from, oh, *Penthouse* magazine, perhaps.

Much of *Caligula*'s fame comes from the controversy surrounding production. It began life as *Gore Vidal's Caligula*, during that brief period in the '70s when it was fashionable to believe that there was common ground between hard-core sex and emancipated intellectual notions. Guccione intended to produce a $3.5 million picture (the budget ballooned during production) and joined forces with Italian producer

36

Not a Hollywood orgy scene.

Photographed by Giancarlo Lui and Bob Guccione"—and no screenplay credit beyond "Adapted from an Original Screenplay by Gore Vidal."

Caligula was completed in 1976, and in 1977 Brass sued, claiming he had right of final cut; the Italian courts declared that the film couldn't be released until the matter was settled. It was first shown in Italy in 1978 and quickly banned, then made its way to the United States in 1980, though not before a squall with Customs officials, who seized the film in August 1979. Guccione never submitted *Caligula* to the MPAA but released it with the provision that minors were not to be admitted. Conservative watchdog group Morality in Media filed a class-action suit against the U.S. Attorney General and the U.S. Attorney for the Eastern Division of New York for not instituting legal

proceedings against *Caligula* when it was seized by Customs. The film was briefly banned in some locations but found not obscene using the Supreme Court's *Miller* standard: whether "the average person, applying contemporary community standards," would find the work prurient, obviously offensive in its depiction or description of sexual acts specifically defined by applicable state law, and overall lacking in serious literary, political or scientific value. With its firm historical basis and respectable cast, *Caligula* wiggled out from under all the groping and screwing. Morality in Media did, however, manage to bully theater owners in places like Fairlawn, Ohio, and St. Louis, Missouri, into not showing the film. In 1981, *Caligula* was trimmed for an R and released to an additional 170 theaters; it reportedly lost about six minutes of footage.

Throughout everything, the feuding continued unabated. Vidal appeared on television, calling the film a turkey. Guccione rejoined that Vidal was just in a snit because he hadn't gotten along with Brass. Guccione badmouthed most of those involved with the picture: He claimed that Peter O'Toole was never sober, Malcolm McDowell was cheap, and Brass cast the film's small roles from "a pool of ex-convicts, thieves and political anarchists that he happened to keep in touch with." Guccione was later successfully sued by actress Marjorie Thorsen, a former *Penthouse* pet who appeared in *Caligula* as Anneka Di Lorenzo, who claimed that Guccione had encouraged her to do hard-core lesbian scenes in the film, thereby ruining her career.

Guccione also said that he had a second historical sex epic, set in the sixteenth century (some contradictory reports said it was a film about Catherine the

Fellini Satyricon, another hedonistic Roman spectacle.

Peter O'Toole has his way with a nubile slave.

Great), in the works; it never materialized. "I see [*Caligula*] as the most controversial film since Howard Hughes made *The Outlaw*," Guccione concluded. "I feel this film will attract from 10 to 15 imitators in its first year and I don't think films will ever be the same." You be the judge.

Hollywood is full of behind-the-scenes types who started out in porno movies, but you'd never know it from their resumés—pseudonyms are de rigueur when working in sex films. Actors with the sense God gave them stay out of porno if they want mainstream careers, because there's no hiding behind a false name when it's your flesh out front. Porn stars Marilyn Chambers and Jamie Gillis have had minor roles in minor films, but no one ever really believed Brian DePalma's fulminations about type casting Annette Haven as a porn actress in *Body Double* (1984), and he didn't—he went with Melanie Griffith instead. For hard-core superstar Traci Lords, a part in the remake of Roger Corman's *Not of This Earth* (1988) was like marrying royalty—she may be near the bottom of the acting hierarchy, mostly making direct-to-video thrillers, but at least she's on the ladder, not down in the mud.

When Demi Moore tries her best to pretend she never made a 3D *Alien* rip-off called *Parasite* (1982) and Oliver Stone regularly omits the low-budget horror picture *Seizure* (1974) from his filmography, it's no wonder that actors and filmmakers try to sweep even the mildly pornographic movies in their pasts under the nearest hand-knotted rug. But **Francis Ford Coppola** directed all or part of several early nudie-cutie pictures, including *The Wide Open Spaces* (1961), *Tonight for Sure*, and *The Playgirls and the Bellboy* (both 1962), all tame by today's standards but naughty back then. A decade later, **John** (*Rocky*) **Avildsen** got his start directing and shooting soft-core pictures like *Turn On to Love* (1969), *Guess What We Learned in School Today?* (1970), and *Cry Uncle!* (1971), while Wes Craven, creator of the *Nightmare on Elm Street* series, started out editing *It Happened in Hollywood*—produced by *Screw* magazine—and *Together* (both 1972). Craven also associate produced *Together*, an early white-coater, with longtime associate **Sean S. Cunningham**, the director-producer who later launched the phenomenally successful *Friday the 13th* series. Cunningham produced the adult comedy-mystery *The Case of the*

Full Moon Murders (1974)—also called *The Case of the Smiling Stiffs* and *Sex on the Groove Tube*—starring porn star Harry Reems. Less mainstream directors like **William Lustig** (*Maniac, Maniac Cop*), **Gregory Hippolyte** (*Animal Instincts*), **Tom DeSimone** (*Reform School Girls*), and **David DeCoteau** (*Sorority Babes in the Slimeball Bowl-a-Rama*) worked extensively in the adult-film industry, but they too are mostly pretty closed-mouthed. Only DeCoteau admits freely, "I learned everything working in adult films . . . when I started out I had *no idea* what I was doing. . . . But in adult movies, I learned."

In front of the camera, **Spalding Gray**, now typed as a patrician prig (*The Paper*), bared all, as "Spaulding Spray," in *Farmer's Daughters* (1975). **Sylvester Stallone** made his motion picture debut in 1970's *A Party at Kitty and Stud's* (buck naked, though there's no hard-core action), and art dilettante and future John Lennon spouse **Yoko Ono** appeared in *Satan's Bed* (1965), made by pioneering husband-and-wife pornographers Roberta and Michael Findlay. *Satan's Bed* features simulated sex with an S&M bent. Youthful bad judgment, in all cases.

On the other hand, pity poor **Farley Granger**, star of Hitchcock's *Rope* (1948) and *Strangers on a Train* (1951) and apparent star of the hard-core *Penetration* (1976). He actually made a sleazy but non-porno Italian thriller called *The Slasher / The Slasher Is the Sex Maniac* (1971), playing a cop hunting a killer of unfaithful women. The film's U.S. distributor spiced up *The Slasher* with hard-core footage of such porn luminaries as Harry Reems, Kim Pope, and Tina Russell, upon whom Granger then appeared to spy during his investigation. This kind of sleight of hand is exploitation business as usual; the same manner of dishonest fiddling produced *Snuff*, a few minutes of faked murder footage grafted onto a mean-spirited Manson family–style picture shot by the ubiquitous Findlays. The result: carefully nurtured scandal and gratifying box office.

Cat People
(1982)

Directed by Paul Schrader. Produced by Charles Fries. Screenplay by Alan Ormsby, based on a story by DeWitt Bodeen. Cinematography by John Bailey. Edited by Jacqueline Cambas. Art Direction by Edward Richardson. Music by Giorgio Moroder.

Nastassja Kinski (Irena Gallier), Malcolm McDowell (Paul Gallier), John Heard (Oliver Yates), Annette O'Toole (Alice Perrin), Ed Begley Jr. (Joe Creigh), Ruby Dee (Female).

(1942)
Directed by Jacques Tourneur. Produced by Val Lewton. Written by DeWitt Bodeen. Cinematography by Nicholas Musuraca. Edited by Mark Robson. Music by Roy Webb.

Simone Simon (Irena Dubrovna), Kent Smith (Oliver Reed), Tom Conway (Dr. Judd), Jane Randolph (Alice Holt).

The metaphor is a little slippery, androgynously linked up with pussy on the one hand and the traditionally masculine werewolf on the other. But it's startlingly potent, defying both common sense and the enlightened belief that sex is healthy and natural. Though it's fashionable to laud Jacques Tourneur's *Cat People* and hate the later version by screenwriter-turned-director Paul Schrader (he scripted Martin Scorsese's *Taxi Driver* and directed *American Gigolo*), both interpretations of the story about a woman who becomes a lethal cat when sexually aroused have their charms. For all-out sensuality, however, Schrader's film, starring nubile Nastassja Kinski (so young she was still Nastass*i*a) as the feline femme fatale, is the one to see.

Arriving in New Orleans, orphaned Irena Gallier

Slippery when wet: Nastassja Kinski.

is met by Paul, the older brother she has never known. He quickly disappears, and Irena, feeling rejected and confused, wanders into the zoo after a day of lonely sightseeing. It's a fateful visit. She becomes fascinated by the savage black leopard that was captured the previous night—under very mysterious circumstances—in a sleazy hotel. And she gets a job at the gift shop and meets cheerful, friendly zookeeper Alice and handsome Oliver, the zoo's curator. Naturally, Oliver and the virginal Irena fall in love.

The leopard kills a zookeeper and disappears, while Paul returns under cover of darkness and terrifies Irena with stories about their past and their future. They were conceived in incest. Their parents committed suicide. They're not even human, he says; when they have sex with anyone other than family, they turn into vicious black leopards and can't resume human form until they kill. Their lovers are doomed, and they are damned to solitary, furtive lives. But he and Irena can spend those lives together; that's why he's dedicated years to finding her. Because *Cat People* is, despite Schrader's protests to the contrary, a horror film, everything Paul says is the truth.

A distaff take on werewolf films, *Cat People* takes the timeworn image of monstrous transformation and gives it grace and ambiguity. No one wants to turn into a hairy, lumbering wolfman, but a sleek, savage cat—that sounds much more appealing. Cats are elegant and mysterious, full of secrets; they've always been the consorts of witches and the most seductive of monsters . . . consider the sphinx. Who watched *Batman Returns* (1992) and didn't prefer Michelle Pfeiffer in her Catwoman drag, even if it was only a rubber catsuit?

The aftermath of unbridled lust: Kinski in *Cat People* (1982).

And remember her predecessors, Lee Meriwether, Eartha Kitt, and Julie Newmar, the catwomen who set pulses racing even amidst the kitschy atmosphere of the '60s "Batman." Tourneur's film doesn't even *entertain* the idea of cat men; it's only the women of Irena's Serbian village who change.

It's *Cat People*'s strength that Schrader is, beneath his intellectual tough-guy exterior, an intense romantic and a tortured sensualist. He wants to believe in *amour fou*, mad love so irresistible that it's stronger than sense, stronger than social taboo, stronger than nature or religion or will. And raised as a puritan, he can't entirely banish the notion that sex is forbidden, which always ups the erotic ante. His *Cat People*, its pagan opening sequence notwithstanding, is not a paean to the natural beauty of unbridled lust. It's a hymn to the allure of the proscribed and the dirty thrill of doing the nasty.

As the panther siblings, Malcolm McDowell and Kinski are very nearly the actors he needs to pull off his jambalaya of incest, bondage, and sexual murder (there's even a hint of bestiality) in the bayous. In her dowdy skirt and sensible shoes, Kinski is all seething, repressed sexuality waiting to be set free; no one with lips so full could possibly be such a priss—not really—and when the inner cat begins to creep, Kinski stalks around naked as she was born to. When she passes a crude cardboard stand-up of Marilyn Monroe in *The Seven Year Itch* the contrast is obvious: Monroe is a sex doll, while Kinski is the living embodiment of untamed carnality. McDowell radiates a bestial sensu-

ality, graceful and dangerous. When Kinski pretends to accede to his advances and begins rubbing her face on his neck like—yes—a cat, the effect is thrilling.

By contrast, Tourneur's *Cat People* is an exercise in subtle menace. Simone Simon's Irena is kittenish, perky but oddly menacing; she exudes only the faintest hint of the claw within the velvet paw. When she toys with her canary until it dies, she looks delicately wicked, but it's hard to imagine her savaging her stolid husband in the throes of passion. As befits producer Val Lewton's intentions, this *Cat People* is a far more subtle and ambiguous film than Schrader's. For all the disturbing shadows and hair-raising panther screams from the zoo, it's entirely possible to believe that this Irena's problem is in her head, not her loins, and that psychiatry doesn't help because her psychiatrist (a role Schrader eliminates) is an unethical lecher. "So little . . . so soft," purrs Dr. Judd (played by Tom Conway, the poor man's George Sanders) as he prepares to overstep the bounds of the doctor-patient relationship.* If Schrader's cat people are a menace to society, it's Tourneur's society that's a menace to his friendless cat woman.

In both films, the hero's erotic dilemma is between down-to-earth Alice, with her forthright sexiness, and exotic Irena, whose mysterious exterior promises delights beyond the imaginings of healthy American boys. Tourneur's Oliver opts for Alice; he's too regular a guy to want Irena when he realizes what she is. Schrader's, naturally, would rather have Irena. But he's not quite romantic enough to want to die for love, so when he makes love to Irena for the last time, he ties her firmly to the bedposts—romance is one thing, sexual suicide another. Schrader's film ends on the startlingly touching image of Oliver visiting Irena-the-leopard at the zoo. This is how his wild, exotic, forbidden love ends: she pines behind bars and he stops by to scratch her under the chin. How cruel love is!

---

*Among them, screenwriter DeWitt Bodeen, Tourneur, and Conway do quite a job on the image of the psychiatrist. Judd preens and postures with his phallic sword stick, ridicules Irena's fears as the foolish products of childhood trauma, and importunes her, all the while discussing her case with her husband *and* his friend Alice and plotting with them to have her committed. It's even Judd who suggests that Oliver might like to divorce Irena *first*, since one can't divorce a person who's been declared legally insane. In all, not a portrayal the American Psychiatric Association is likely to endorse.

Damage
(1992)

Produced and Directed by Louis Malle. Coproduced by Vincent Malle and Simon Relph. Screenplay by David Hare, based on the novel by Josephine Hart. Cinematography by Peter Biziou. Edited by John Bloom. Production Design by Brian Morris. Music by Zbigniew Preisner.

Jeremy Irons (Stephen Fleming), Miranda Richardson (Ingrid Fleming), Juliette Binoche (Anna Barton), Rupert Graves (Martin Fleming), Leslie Caron (Anna's Mother).

Damage isn't a sexy art movie per se—it's no *Henry & June*. But *Damage* is a very erotic movie, a movie about sexual obsession, a mad love so all-consuming that it destroys everything with which it comes into contact.

Stephen Fleming is a respectable British cabinet minister, with a loving wife, Ingrid, and two children, fledgling journalist Martin and adolescent Sally. His staid life is shaken to the foundations when he meets Anna Barton, Martin's girlfriend. They begin a torrid, tortured affair that leaves him haggard and haunted. She warns him that it will end badly, tells him that her brother Arsin committed suicide out of incestuous love for her, and cautions that "Damaged people are dangerous—they know they can survive." He tells her he plans to leave his wife, and she talks him out of it; he accidentally meets her old lover, Peter, and is discomfited by their conversation. The night after Anna and Martin announce their engagement, during a weekend visit to Ingrid's family estate, she and Stephen meet secretly. She rents an apartment where they can continue to rendezvous after her marriage, but during their first afternoon together, Martin walks in on them. In shock, he falls over a bannister and dies. The scandal ruins Stephen's career and destroys his marriage. He retreats into seclusion, to a room dominated by a vast photograph of Anna and Martin, and sees her again only once, by accident, in an airport. She's with her husband, Peter, and their child, and she looks just like anybody else.

Josephine Hart's novel was a more-lettered-than-average potboiler, a steamy page-turner with literary pretensions. Surprisingly, the film is mostly cold, cold, cold, a grim examination of the grave consequences of lust unmediated by reason. It is, to use an overworked phrase, very French—sophisticated, mannered, analytical, and sexually irreverent. Americans expect no less from Louis Malle, whose extensive career—almost two dozen films since 1957—can be summed up in three scandalous titles: *The Lovers* (1959), about adulterers Jeanne Moreau and Jean-Marc Bory; *Murmur of the Heart* (1971), in which mother/son incest is treated with comic matter-of-factness; and *Pretty Baby* (1978), which cast the barely pubescent Brooke Shields as a child prostitute in decadent old New Orleans. They're all good films, and serious ones, and they were all greeted in the United States with cries of scandal and outpourings of prurient interest. Malle played the press like a master, declaring of *Murmur of the Heart*, for example, that he thought it was much better to sleep with your mother than to spend years thinking about it. Such a *continental* attitude.

But for all its somber moral, the tragedy of *Damage* is punctuated with sex scenes that range from merely titillating to positively steamy. That Malle could pull it off using exquisite Juliette Binoche and terminally desiccated Jeremy Irons makes his accomplishment all

the more impressive. Irons, who was generally very serious during interviews, admitted to one writer that his least favorite part of shooting the movie involved the scene in which he had to run naked down stairs, complaining, "Everything was jiggling around. I ran down those damned stairs naked for two whole days to get the shot right." What makes *Damage*'s sex scenes sizzle is everything *but* the sex itself. Yes, the naked Binoche is beautiful, and Irons is attractive in a stringy sort of way, but it's not the sight of their flesh together that titillates—it's the knowledge of what's at stake every time they defy good sense, reason, and common decency to fling themselves

Jeremy Irons, haggard with desire, and the irresistible Juliette Binoche doing damage.

Binoche and Irons violate common decency and love it.

into each other. *Damage* evokes a really frightening sense of lust so overpowering that Stephen and Anna will do anything to slake it; they're willing to sacrifice everything, every time. We don't know why, and neither do they—they just *have* to, and that sense of naked need is powerfully erotic.

The original version of the film received an NC-17 rating; distributor New Line was emphatic about wanting an R, and Malle had to snip a few seconds of footage and rearrange some shots of Irons and Binoche.

The furor sent the director—who was recovering from heart surgery—into a rage, directed at the MPAA. Malle invoked the usual argument—that the MPAA regularly gives R's to horribly violent films but awards NC-17s to films involving sex—and pointed out that *Damage* reminded him a bit of "a French film, a while back, not very good, about a man who was having an affair with his son's fiancée. It was a comedy . . . you know the French!" More to the point, you know Malle.

Alec Baldwin: Baldwin's sleek, darkly handsome good looks and dangerous air make him the perfect demon lover, and he lives up to the role in *Miami Blues* (1990), *Malice* (1993), and the remake of *The Getaway* (1994). Several Baldwin brothers act, but only the brooding Billy shares Alec's erotic charge.

Antonio Banderas: Madonna's lust object in *Truth or Dare*, Spanish heartthrob Banderas is best known for his roles in Pedro Almodóvar's films, including *Matador* (1986), *Law of Desire* (1987), *Women on the Verge of a Nervous Breakdown* (1988), and *Tie Me Up! Tie Me Down!* (1990). He invaded the American market with *The Mambo Kings* (1992), followed by *Interview With the Vampire: The Vampire Chronicles* (1994), *Miami Rhapsody*, and *Desperado* (both 1995).

Daniel Day-Lewis: The thinking woman's heartthrob first attracted notice in the '80s when *My Beautiful Launderette* and *A Room With a View* played the United States simultaneously: He was a gay punk in the former and a nineteenth-century straight boy (in all senses of the word) in the latter, covering the erotic waterfront. From *The Unbearable Lightness of Being* (1988) and *The Last of the Mohicans* (1992) to *The Age of Innocence* (1993), he oozes highbrow sensuality.

Johnny Depp: Latest in a long line of sensitive fine-boned boys for poetic girls to swoon over, Depp first became a TV teen idol, then jumped ship to play a series of fragile loners in *Edward Scissorhands* (1990), *What's Eating Gilbert Grape?* (1993), *Ed Wood* (1994), and *Don Juan DeMarco* (1995).

Sherilyn Fenn: Lushly ripe and tantalizing, Fenn seduced TV viewers by tying a cherry stem into a knot with her tongue on *Twin Peaks*. Her movie credits range from the sexploitation *Meridian* (1990) to the just-plain-odd *Boxing Helena* (1993) and include *Threesome* (1992) and *Ruby* (1992), in which she plays famous stripper Candy Barr. She was a natural to play the lead in the 1995 TV movie *Liz: The Elizabeth Taylor Story*.

Brad Pitt: His role in *Thelma & Louise* (1991) was tiny, but once audiences got a look at his washboard stomach and genial grin, Pitt's career as a sex symbol was launched. Romantics of both sexes swooned over his soulful bloodsucker in *Interview With the Vampire: The Vampire Chronicles* and fell for him in *Legends of the Fall* (both 1994).

Michelle Pfeiffer: Delicately beautiful Pfeiffer started her career as a generic babe in films like *Grease 2* (1982) but displayed surprising reserves of intelligent passion in *The Witches of Eastwick* (1987), *Dangerous Liaisons* and *Tequila Sunrise* (both 1988), *The Fabulous Baker Boys* (1989), and *The Age of Innocence* (1993).

Susan Sarandon: A paragon of mature sensuality, Sarandon is a powerful erotic presence at an age when most American actresses are mothering men the same age they are. She first won cult favor in *The Rocky Horror Picture Show* (1975), *Atlantic City* (1980), and *The Hunger* (1983) and went on to seduce audiences in *The Witches of Eastwick* (1987), *Bull Durham* (1988), *White Palace* (1990), *Thelma & Louise* (1991), and *The Client* (1994).

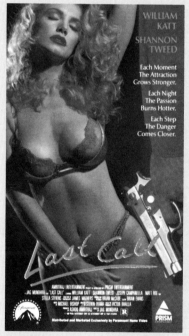

Sharon Stone: She was just another blonde until *Basic Instinct* (1992) catapulted her to stardom as the ultimate devouring bitch, but Stone's later roles are attempts to break the one-film mold. She's stalked by a voyeur in *Sliver* (1993), dumped for Lena Olin in *Intersection* (1994), and goes West in *The Quick and the Dead* (1995).

Shannon Tweed: Tall and blond, Shannon Tweed is the quintessential video sex bomb, a *Playboy* Playmate who parlayed her looks into a sort of stardom, feeding lustful fantasies in a series of direct-to-video erotic thrillers and sex melodramas, including *Surrogate* (1988), *Twisted Justice* (1989), *Last Call* (1990), *The Last Hour* (1991), and *Sexual Response* (1992).

Devil in the Flesh / Diavolo in Corpo (1987)

Directed by Marco Bellocchio. Produced by Leo Pescarolo. Screenplay by Bellocchio, with Ennio De Concini, with the collaboration of Enrico Palandri. Cinematography by Guiseppe Lanci. Edited by Mirco Garrone. Art Direction by Andrea Crisanti. Music by Carlo Crivelli.

Maruschka Detmers (Giulia Dozza), Federico Pitzalis (Andréa Raimondi), Anita Laurenzi (Mrs. Pulcini), Alberto DiStasio (Dr. Raimondi), Riccardo De Torrebruna (Giacomo Pulcini), Catherine Diamant (Mrs. Raimondi), Anna Orso (Mrs. Dozza).

A reworking of precocious Raymond Radiguet's 1923 novel of adolescent love, Marco Bellocchio's *Devil in the Flesh* is in the great European tradition of philosophical-political pornography, following in the footsteps of such films as Bernardo Bertolucci's *Last Tango in Paris* (1973) and Liliana Cavani's *The Night Porter* (1974). In fact, after *Devil in the Flesh* received its inevitable X rating, distributor Orion Classics fell back on the time-honored frank-and-fearless art defense, à la *Last Tango*, to lure highbrow viewers into the theaters.

Giulia Dozza is an emotional young woman whose fiancé, Giacomo Pulcini, is a terrorist on trial in Rome. She meets Andréa Raimondi, a student, in the courtroom, and the two of them embark upon a sizzling affair. There are many complications, including Giulia's apparent mental instability and the fact that Andréa's father was both her psychiatrist and her lover; Andréa's overly protective mother and his need to concentrate on his studies; Giulia's betrothal; her nosy relatives; and her fear of bourgeois suffocation. Pulcini, who has renounced his terrorist ways, goes on television to announce his conversion to Christianity. Giulia and Andréa meet in secret and enjoy ecstatic bouts of lovemaking, but under the pressure of their relationship, Giulia inches increasingly close to madness as Andréa shows up late for class and neglects to prepare for his upcoming exams. The film ends as he takes his oral examination, analyzing the issue of free will as Giulia, who has blown off her marriage, watches from the back of the classroom.

Radiguet's novel, a cult favorite on the order of *Catcher in the Rye* among romantic European youth, is a passionate examination of the affair between a student, François, and a woman, Marthe, whose husband is away at war. Marthe is ultimately destroyed by their secret, fervent affair—she becomes pregnant and dies in childbirth—while François is tempered and matured, sadly plucking mature wisdom from the ashes of his youth. The autobiographical novel was started in 1920, when Radiguet, a protégé of Jean Cocteau, was seventeen. It was published in 1923, the year Radiguet died of typhoid fever. The persistent rumor that the young writer committed remorseful suicide is just the icing on the *gâteau*, even better than J. D. Salinger's retreat into ascetic seclusion. It was filmed by French director Claude Autant-Lara in 1947, starring Micheline Presle and Gérard Philippe, and widely acclaimed, except by critics who disliked its antiwar stance. The film's sexual frankness was, according to the standards of 1949 (the year it was released in the United States), considerable, and it was, naturally, condemned by the Legion of Decency. But Autant-Lara's *Devil in the Flesh* was suggestive rather than explicit. This lapse in judgment was rectified by Bellocchio.

His *Devil in the Flesh* is updated and stripped of its vision of wartime as a sort of limbo in which suspended

Mad with desire: Maruschka Detmers and Federico Pitzalis in *Devil in the Flesh* (1987).

lives blossom in strange and sometimes destructive ways. The conflict between propriety and passion is blurred—the propriety of Giulia, whose father was killed by the Red Army Brigade, marrying Pulcini is highly questionable—and without the tragic ending, it doesn't really amount to much. It's all about sex as metaphor: for freedom from family, responsibility, and middle-class morals, and for rebellion against government, the educational system, and middle-class aspirations. Where but in such a film could this perfectly indicative scene exist: In the courtroom where terrorists are on trial, the defendants are confined in a huge open cage. Two of them begin to make love, partly shielded from view by the others, and court officers who try to break them up are presented as forces of bourgeois repression.

Giulia is the daughter of twin traditions: She's the (barely) older woman who initiates a naïve young man into the glorious mysteries of sex and, like Betty Blue, she's a sensualist of such pure intensity that she hovers on the brink of madness. Unlike Betty, Giulia resists acts of self-mutilation and so escapes the grim fate of most such sacred sluts: martyrdom. Dutch actress Maruschka Detmers was already notorious for her sexy

performance in Jean-Luc Godard's *First Name: Carmen* (1983), and in *Devil in the Flesh* she is frequently naked and apparently unselfconscious about her many sex scenes. The film is particularly famous for a lengthy and instructive fellatio scene, though some viewers found it less erotic than slightly unpalatable. The *Village Voice*'s David Edelstein described Detmers's demeanor with unappetizing accuracy as "the concentration of a feline cleaning a rodent prior to devouring it."

Devil in the Flesh carries a personal dedication to Bellocchio's analyst, Massiomo Fagioli, a critic of the psychiatric establishment, which may explain the film's hostile depiction of Andréa's father.

Condemned by the Legion of Decency: Micheline Presle and Gerard Philippe in Claude Autant-Lara's *Devil in the Flesh* (1947).

Dirty Dancing
(1987)

Directed by Emile Ardolino. Produced by Linda Gottlieb. Screenplay by Eleanor Bergstein. Cinematogrpahy by Jeff Jur. Production Design by David Chapman. Edited by Peter C. Frank. Music by John Morris.

Jennifer Grey (Frances "Baby" Houseman), Patrick Swayze (Johnny Castle), Jerry Orbach (Jake Houseman), Cynthia Rhodes (Penny Johnson), Jack Weston (Max Kellerman), Jane Bruckner (Lisa Houseman).

In the beginning there was Rudolph Valentino, gigolo turned silver-screen ladykiller, and his notorious Tango. Not for nothing is sex called (among many other inventive things) the horizontal boogie; Valentino's Tango was sex standing up, and anyone who thinks Hollywood didn't know it is dreaming. Dancing is always halfway to sex and, like sex, is dirty if you're doing it right. No contemporary viewers saw the title *Our Dancing Daughters* (1928) and wondered why the young ladies' parents were worried. The Waltz and the Polka, the Charleston and the Blackbottom, the Mambo and the Lambada, the Twist and the Hustle and the Bump: They're all ways of getting flesh close to flesh, opportunities to touch and wiggle and sneak a little extra kiss without really violating the laws of propriety. It may not be as good as doing the wild thing, but it's the next best.

And that's why *Dirty Dancing* is here: Like the earlier—and sleazier—*Flashdance* (1983), it's a frank celebration of the sexual potency of dancing. Dancing is all about displacement, of course, but glorious displacement, more graceful and aesthetic than the thing itself.

Dancing has a long and mostly honorable history in Hollywood movies. The classic musicals are full of it, but few exploit the potential for raw sensuality inherent in scantily clad bodies swaying together in rhythm. There are, of course, exceptions: Cyd Charisse and Gene Kelly's smoldering noir number in *An American in Paris* (1951), Dorothy Dandridge's sultry gyrations in *Carmen Jones* (1954), the firecracker dance at the gym in *West Side Story* (1961), and so on. But it was Fred Astaire who set the standard for Hollywood dancing from the '30s on, and poised and graceful though he was, Astaire had the sensual appeal of a hoe. Astaire and Ginger Rogers, perhaps the most famous partnership in classic musicals, embodied romance, but the famously cynical assessment—she gave him sex, he gave her class—is off the mark simply because *no one* could give him sex.

Flashdance and *Dirty Dancing* have striking similarities: Both were low-budget sleepers ($8 million and $5.2 million, respectively). Both were also surprise hits that unabashedly exploited the inherent sensuality of dancing; relied heavily on editing, camera movement, and stylized lighting to enhance the vigor of movement (in contrast to the style preferred by Astaire and others, which favored long shots and stationary camera, allowing the dancing to speak for itself); featured dynamic popular soundtracks, and appealed strongly to adolescent fantasies of love that conquers all (especially class difference). But they're fundamentally different in one important way: *Dirty Dancing* is about *doing*, and director Emile Ardolino puts the viewer into the dancers' shoes. *Flashdance* is about *watching*, and Adrian Lyne turns his audience into a flock of voyeurs.

"Baby" (Jennifer Grey) slums in the staff quarters and learns that dancing is dirty only if you're doing it right.

(Above) Jennifer Grey and Patrick Swayze get down and dirty, but *nicely*.

Dancing proles Cynthia Gibb and Swayze, with Catskill princess Grey caught in the middle.

Dirty Dancing takes place in the prelapsarian '60s, when earnest youngsters dream of joining the Peace Corps but vacation at Catskill resorts with their parents. Frances "Baby" Houseman is a sheltered, slightly spoiled teenager with liberal ideals and no idea what social injustice really *is*. She learns when she gets to know the employees whom her peers treat as though they were part of the kitchen equipment, but that's not what *Dirty Dancing* is really about. It's about the *other* thing Baby learns when she ventures into the employees' quarters and finds a hot party going on. When that door swings open, she discovers a whole new world: the world of dirty dancing. Couples dancing pelvis to pelvis, hands all over one another, lips brushing throats, legs around waists, faces dangerously close to groins. It's sexy and sweaty, everything that doing the Mambo on the family dance floor isn't. She wants to learn, and it's no wonder: Ardolino captures the sensuality of an arm brushing a bare back, a hip slithering across a belly, the rapturous physicality of moving to the music without worrying how you look.

Dirty Dancing's sexiness comes in part from violating class boundaries: Baby is a middle-class princess; dance instructor Johnny Castle is resolutely blue collar, undomesticated enough to have rhythm. He's *Saturday Night Fever*'s (1977) Tony Manero, only he's making a living with his dancing. When Johnny tells Baby that the steps aren't enough and she has to "feel the music," it's that old thing about giving yourself over to the heart rather than the head, with the predictable results. As she learns the Mambo routine, her outfits get scantier and sexier, her flesh exposed to the light. When Baby goes to Johnny's room and asks him to dance with her, the last clothes drop and the dancing gets back to the horizontal plane. *Dirty Dancing* is about the power of dance to inflame the senses and awaken the libido; it's a coming-of-age story with a beat.

If *Dirty Dancing* is about dance as a contact sport, *Flashdance* is about dance as spectacle. *Flashdance* takes place in a world of nonstop eroticized motion that has little to do with blue-collar Pittsburgh, but everything to do with the aphrodisiac effects of suggestive movement, whether breakdancing, ice skating, stripping, classical ballet dancing, or working out in the gym.

Pretty, eighteen-year-old Alex (Jennifer Beals) works as a welder and dreams of studying ballet. In the meantime, she dances at a local strip joint, Mawby's Bar, home to a stage show that would put a Vegas strip club to shame: costumes, lights, fans . . . it's Hollywood stripping at its finest. The girls are more beautiful, the lighting more subtle, the numbers better choreographed than real life. Alex is pursued by her boss, Nick (Michael Nouri), and has to conquer her fears (Is Nick too rich to love a poor girl like her? Is she too rough to sully the hallowed halls of ballet?) to fulfill her destiny. A techno-glossy musical fantasy, *Flashdance* was mocked as an imitation *Saturday Night Fever* and danced all the way to the bank, holding its own against the megabucks blockbuster *Return of the Jedi* on the strength of its uplifting message and its decoratively sweaty buns.

Other dance pictures tried to tap into the same sweaty zeitgeist, with generally limited success. *Footloose* equated dancing and teen rebellion, but with only a touch of sex, while *Breakin'* and *Breakin' 2: Electric Boogaloo* (all 1984) were hampered by the anti-amorous contortions of breakdancing. The dismal *Staying Alive* (1983) couldn't duplicate the runaway success of *Saturday Night Fever*, despite John Travolta's new cut-and-buffed physique. *Salsa* (1988) didn't make Latin dancing's caliente rhythms move a mainstream audience, even with *Dirty Dancing* choreographer Kenny Ortega at the helm, while *Lambada* and *The Forbidden Dance* (both 1990) failed to make the dirty dance from Brazil a national trend (though it looks pretty hot in *Wild Orchid*). Carlos Saura's *Blood Wedding* (1981) and *Carmen* (1983) came with authentic fiery flamenco credentials but were too foreign—or high toned or something—for the average American, and the stagy *Tango Bar* (1988) never captured the essence of the dance that launched Valentino. Of all things, it was Australian director Baz Luhrman's debut, the goofy, stylized *Strictly Ballroom* (1993), that brought the heat back to dance movies, even if it was a camp throwback. The romance between a cocky dance-floor stud and an ugly duckling with unexpected reserves of passion is pure old Hollywood hokum, and their numbers are more glitz than grind, but oh, that *paso doble*!

La Dolce Vita
(1960)

Directed by Federico Fellini. Produced by Giuseppe Amato and Angelo Rizzoli. Screenplay by Fellini, Ennio Flaiano, Tullio Pinelli, and Brunello Rondi, based on a story by Fellini, Flaiano, and Pinelli. Cinematography by Otello Martelli. Edited by Leo Catazzo. Art Direction by Piero Gherardi. Music by Nino Rota.

Marcello Mastroianni (Marcello Rubini), Anita Ekberg (Sylvia), Anouk Aimée (Maddelena), Yvonne Furneaux (Emma), Magali Noel (Fanny), Alain Cuny (Steiner), Nadia Gray (Nadia), Annibale Nichi (Mr. Rubini), Walter Santesso (Paparazzo).

Hollow and glittering, *La Dolce Vita* is a magnificent balancing act, a film about existential despair and romantic disillusionment that's still profoundly hopeful, sexy, and passionate. The title means *the sweet life*, and the life belongs to gossip reporter Marcello. It's a nonstop carousel of swank parties, expensive restaurants, *soigné* clubs, and assignations with beautiful women, all in the name of reporting on the amoral cavortings of Rome's café society. And he covers it all. The movie opens as Marcello follows a helicopter delivering a huge statue of Jesus to the Vatican; a group of bikini-clad women working on their tans on a rooftop wave and observe, "It's Jesus," and wonder "Where's he going?" He spends a night of debauchery with Maddelena, his very rich and very bored sometime lover. Marcello returns home to find his luscious girlfriend, Emma, unconscious from an overdose of pills; he takes her to the hospital, then heads for the airport to cover the arrival of a stunning Hollywood starlet, Sylvia, who's making a film in Italy. Later, he spends an enchanted evening escorting Sylvia around Rome.

Fantasy-made-flesh: Anita Ekberg in *La Dolce Vita*.

Through a series of vignettes, we come to see the emptiness of Marcello's life: an evening with his old-fashioned father, a party at his intellectual friend Steiner's, the press circus that develops around two small siblings who claim to have seen an apparition of the Virgin Mary, a masked ball at a castle, a flirtation with a teenage waitress at a seaside café, and, finally, the horrifying discovery that Steiner—whose bonhomie hid a deep despair—has murdered his children and committed suicide. Marcello leaves Emma and tries to drown in debauchery, but he can't lose himself. We last see him standing on a windswept beach, looking for the answer in the face of a young girl.

La Dolce Vita's serious concerns—the dark results of alienation, the inability to love, and cynicism—come wrapped in an irresistible package. Federico Fellini's vision of nightlife as spectacle is carefully crafted, designed to further his vision of hedonism as the road to spiritual hell: One good, hard look at the masklike makeup and lifeless expressions of the endlessly laughing, dancing women who crowd almost every scene is enough to give the average man nightmares. And yet, it's all so *gorgeous*, and the hardness dissolves in the haze of memory. What sticks is the image of the eternally tuxedoed Marcello, wandering the empty streets of Rome with absurdly luscious movie star Sylvia, a vision in platinum blond and chiffon. Ripely built, creamy complexioned, wrapped in black gauze and white fur, Sylvia is a dream walking, a fluffy kitten perched on her fluffy head. Their midnight dip in the Trevi fountain is unforgettable, a fantasy of romance that could exist only in the movies, free of chills and guards and expensive, ruined clothes. And Fellini, who loved the movies with all his heart, invests the fragile

Marcello Mastroianni and the lush Yvonne Furneaux, as comfortable as rumpled sheets.

fantasy with such conviction that we can't help but embrace it. His Rome is a Rome of burning headlights and gleaming streets, glittering jewelry, high heels, and succulent flesh encased in chic black cocktail dresses. It's a sensual carnival of showgirls, prostitutes and bored nymphomaniacs, playboys and transvestites, gigolos, waifs, and goddesses, all drawn like moths to the glow of the eternal city.

La Dolce Vita's women are exquisite. As Emma, Yvonne Furneaux looks like a more kittenish Sophia Loren, and as Maddelena, Anouk Aimée—whose credits include Claude Lelouch's romantic classic *A Man and a Woman* (1969)—never looked more gloriously chic. But Anita Ekberg, a former Miss Sweden with a prodigious bosom and a cloud of white blond hair, steals the film from both. Her uninhibited cavorting in the piazza, her dip in the fountain, her slow dance with Marcello—everything she does is charged with an incandescent eroticism no less potent today than when the film was first released.

La Dolce Vita won the coveted Palme d'Or award at the Cannes Film Festival in France but ran into censorship trouble at home, as Fellini doubtless knew it would. Italy's Catholics were forbidden to see the film, and it was viciously denounced by the Vatican's own newspaper, *L'Osservatore Romano*, which accused Fellini of portraying Rome as an open sewer and dishonoring all Italy with his immoral motion picture. Years later, he recalled visiting Padua and seeing a sign that read, "Let us pray for the salvation of the soul of Federico Fellini, public sinner," hanging over a church door. The church's condemnation guaranteed that *La Dolce Vita* did record-setting business, because Italian cinemagoers knew as well as Americans that anything the church condemned was bound to be good. It packed theaters all over Europe, with the exception of Spain, where it was banned because it "displayed certain immoral acts without sufficiently condemning them" and, probably more important, was critical of the Catholic church; the Spanish ban lasted more than a decade, long after the film had been shown on Italian TV.

La Dolce Vita arrived in the United States a year after its European release amidst extravagant and sometimes contradictory accolades: Conservative *Time* magazine hailed it as "ambitious, sensational and controversial," while experimental filmmaker Jonas Mekas wryly called it "Cecil B. DeMille at his best-worst-best." Perhaps still chastened by *l'affaire Baby Doll*, the Legion of Decency made the startlingly reasonable (if somewhat misguided) observation that while *La Dolce Vita* contained "some highly sensational subject matter" and "shocking scenes," the film did not merit condemnation because the "shock value [was] intended to generate a salutary recognition of evil as evil, of sin as sin." *La Dolce Vita* was released in art house theaters and in exploitation grind houses; it did well in both, proving once again that the masses will put up with no end of art for a glimpse of a voluptuous siren in wet chiffon.

56

Ecstasy / Extase
(1933)

Directed by Gustav Machaty. Produced by Frantisek Horky and Moriz Grunhut. Written by Machaty, Horky, Viteslav Nezval, and Jacques A. Koerpel. Cinematography by Jan Stallich and Hans Androschin. Music by Giuseppe Becce.

Hedwig Kiesler (Eva), Zvonimir Rogoz (Emile), Aribert Mog (Adam), Leopold Kramer (Eva's Father).

Profoundly influenced by revolutionary Soviet cinema of the '20s, with its emphasis on formalist use of film language to express complex, abstract ideas, Czechoslovakian director Gustav Machaty seems an unlikely person to be at the center of a decades-long controversy provoked by a smutty movie. He was, of course, assistant to legendary libertine Eric von Stroheim in Hollywood from 1920 through 1924, the period when the flamboyant director was making *The Devil's Passkey* (1919), *Foolish Wives* (1921), and *Merry-Go-Round* (1922), films that outraged prudes with their sophisticated attitudes toward love and sex. And Machaty did write and direct the now-forgotten *Erotikon* (1929), the then-shocking story of a provincial station master's daughter and her rich lover. It was, naturally, a scandal, but nothing like the scandal that was *Ecstasy*.

Ecstasy is one of the most talked-about films of all time, a fact that has nothing to do with its quality. Shot as *Symphonie d'amour*, its plot is minimal and bears a passing resemblance to D. H. Lawrence's *Lady Chatterley's Lover*. A young woman, Eva, leaves her husband, an impotent older man whom she doesn't love. In a gesture of newfound freedom, she goes for a nude swim in the woods, imprudently leaving her clothes on the back of her horse. When it runs off, she's left naked. Fortunately, an attractive young engineer captures the horse and returns Eva's garments. She gets dressed and, as a storm brews, the two of them make their way to a nearby hut. They spend the night together and make love.

Machaty made *Ecstasy* during the turbulent early sound period, when panic about the international market was the order of the day, and tried the ingenious (though not so ingenious that it caught on) stratagem of pruning dialogue to the barest minimum and shooting what there was of it in multiple languages. The entire film contains some twenty spoken lines. In addition, Czech actor Zvonimir Rogoz was entirely replaced by Pierre Nay in the French version. This was hardly the end of the tinkering with the film, but the rest came later, when censorship troubles arose.

Ecstasy was a hit on the continent, despite its heavy-handed use of symbolic imagery to equate beautiful young Eva with the wonderful world of nature, including the storm that accompanies her lovemaking with the virile young engineer. Even more shocking than the film's nude scenes was the sex scene in the hut; though the camera remained modestly on Eva's face, her expressions made her pleasure in lovemaking clear. Gossip was stirred by Machaty's pre-Method insistence that he hated acting on film—that what he wanted was for the camera to capture reality, living the moment for the lens. Which meant, of course, that this may be the first case of widespread speculation that actors were really "doing it" on screen.

In any event, *Ecstasy* made its star, teenager Hedwig Kiesler, notorious, particularly when her new husband—reclusive Austrian millionaire munitions

Hedwig Kiesler (later Hedy Lamarr) in *Ecstasy*, naked as nature intended.

First imported in 1934, it was destroyed as obscene by the U.S. marshal on July 5, 1935. Various prints, with bits snipped here and pared down there, made their way to the States as the '30s wore on, all seen mostly by the members of various censorship boards and declared unfit for the general public. The film was finally shown in a revised form—a diary sequence was inserted in which the lovers are married before their indiscretion, and several scenes involving nudity were taken out—at New York's Ambassador Theatre in December 1940. The theater was plastered with old magazine and newspaper clippings about the film's purported salaciousness, because people had had seven years to forget about the naughty film from Czechoslovakia.

Ecstasy failed to set the world on fire. Fans of the sleek, glossy Hollywood Lamarr weren't especially interested in her younger, less-polished self. A typical review: "It's told not in wordy dialogue but in 'significant' symbols—rearing horses, bronze statues, bees and flowers, cloudy skies—the gamut of arty clichés. As the girl, Hedy Kiesler, now known as Hedy Lamarr, is a very unattractive, graceless person. . . . It struck me as a pretentious and arty bore in the making, now perverted into a peep show" (Milton Meltzer, *Daily Worker*). And still, *Ecstasy* wouldn't die. It got a Production Code Seal in 1949, after Machaty made the extraordinary move of filming new footage (accounting for about a third of the film's sixty-five-minute length) with Lamarr to replace the troublesome older footage, and retitling it *Rhapsody of Love*. In 1963, original importer Sam Cummins, who still owned the U.S. rights, talked wistfully about re-releasing it with the offending nude footage intact, because current standards were looser than they had been in decades.

A restored version of *Ecstasy*, nudity intact, now turns up occasionally in revival houses, and to modern eyes it's more quaint than pulse-pounding. The style seems stiff and dated, and in an age when international stars regularly shed their clothes, it's hard to imagine the impact Hedy Kiesler's flesh had when it was first unveiled in shimmering black and white. But she was a pioneer, and if not the first star to strip for the silver screen, she has become the most famous.

king Fritz Mandl—began spending vast sums (he later estimated nearly a quarter of a million dollars) trying futilely to buy up every print, still, and postcard of *Ecstasy* to keep the world from seeing his bride's bare behind. Ironically, Mandl wanted to meet Kiesler in the first place because he'd seen her in the film. An indisputable if unpolished beauty who was also praised by noted theater director Max Reinhardt as a talented actress, Kiesler soon abandoned Mandl in favor of advancing her career, which she felt was best done in America. She went to London and contrived to meet MGM mogul Louis B. Mayer, who reportedly discouraged her with the self-important pronouncement that "A woman's ass is for her husband, not theatregoers. You're lovely but I prefer the family point of view. I don't like what people would think about a girl who flits bare-assed around the screen." Kiesler persisted and was rewarded with an MGM contract; by the time *Ecstasy* breached American shores, she had begun transforming herself into bona fide Hollywood star Hedy Lamarr.

Ecstasy ignited nothing but trouble in America.

Hedy Lamarr in her Hollywood incarnation. No more flitting "bare-assed around the screen."

Maurice Chevalier: A holdover from the exotic '20s, Chevalier wasn't handsome, but he oozed Gallic charm. Sound served him well: He sang and spoke with that devastating accent and carried such films as *The Love Parade* (1929), *Love Me Tonight* (1932), *The Way to Love* (1933), and *The Merry Widow* (1934).

Gary Cooper: Cooper's rugged good looks and down-home manner contrasted sharply with the sleek gigolos of the '20s, and he was a star for more than thirty years. But he was never as handsome as he was in *Morocco* (1930) and spent too much of his career on horseback rather than in the boudoir.

Marlene Dietrich: The eternal, androgynous Dietrich rocketed to fame as a slutty showgirl in *The Blue Angel* (1930) and died an icon five decades later. As alluring in a tuxedo as in an evening gown, the husky-voiced Dietrich was an erotic mirage, fetishistic and ultimately unattainable.

Errol Flynn: Born in Tasmania, Flynn radiated high spirits and athletic sensuality. His strong suit was swashbuckling, and men liked him as much as women wanted him. From *Captain Blood* (1935) to *The Private Lives of Elizabeth and Essex* (1939), he was dazzling, and in *The Adventures of Robin Hood* (1938) he managed what Kevin Costner didn't even dare attempt: looking virile in green tights.

Clark Gable: Jug ears and all, Gable exuded animal sensuality, exploited in *Gone With the Wind* (1939) and still evident in *The Misfits* (1960). In the wake of the suave seducers and Latin lovers of the '20s, he and Cooper represented a whole new breed of sexy male star, aggressively manly and American.

Greta Garbo: Goddess Garbo was first cast in stereotyped foreign seductress roles like *Mata Hari* (1932) but soon proved a more mysterious erotic force. From *The Flesh and the Devil* (1927) to her last film, *Two Faced Woman* (1941), Garbo's movies inspire erotic dreams to this day.

Cary Grant: Debonair and quick-witted, British-born Grant was Mae West's protégé and perfected the art of being continental without seeming really foreign. He flourished in screwball comedies—including *Bringing Up Baby* (1938) and *His Girl Friday* (1940)—and played leading men through the '60s, when he retired from films an undefeated champion.

Jean Harlow: Platinum blonde Harlow is widely credited with shifting erotic attention from the leg to the breast: Perpetually braless, she iced her nipples to make them perky and barely draped herself in shimmering, bias cut gowns. She played whores of every stripe in *Hell's Angels* (1930), *Dinner at Eight* (1933), *The Libeled Lady* (1936), and others.

Carole Lombard: Proving that you can be funny and sexy at the same time, Lombard sparkled in a string of sophisticated comedies, including *Twentieth Century* (1934), *My Man Godfrey* (1936), and *To Be or Not to Be* (1942). Witty and earthier than her looks suggested, Lombard was more sophisticated than Harlow but no less sensual.

Mae West: Generously proportioned and not very pretty, West perfected the art of innuendo with such cheerfully smutty lines as "Is that a gun in your pocket, or are you just glad to see me?" She shocked bluestockings with monotonous regularity because she treated sex as good, dirty fun, and many of her lines are as fresh today as when she first said them.

Emmanuelle
(1974)

Directed by Just Jaeckin. Produced by Yves Rousset-Routard. Screenplay by Jean-Louis Richard, based on the book by Emmanuelle Arsan. Cinematography by Richard Suzuki. Edited by Claudine Bouché. Original Music by Pierre Bachelet.

Sylvia Kristel (Emmanuelle), Alain Cuny (Mario), Daniel Sarky (Jean), Jeanne Colletin (Ariane), Marika Green (Bee), Christine Boisson (Marie-Ange).

Though no steamier than an episode of Zalman King's wildly popular erotic cable series *Red Shoe Diaries*, which owes it an eternal debt of gratitude,* *Emmanuelle* was a sensation in 1974. It became an international hit on the strength of its appeal to the prurient interests of men and women alike. For the guys, there's lots of flesh (European and Asian) and soft-core coupling (straight and lesbian). For the girls, there's exotic romance, and in Emmanuelle—played by refreshingly uncenterfoldlike Sylvia Kristel—a heroine with some apparent personality, intelligence, and purpose, however silly. There's also a lot of talk: about freedom, fidelity, social convention, morality, and the ways and means and mysteries of love, eroticism, and sensuality. It's all *terribly* serious and terribly French, simultaneously high-minded and salacious.

Virtuous Emmanuelle is married to worldly French diplomat Jean, who's posted to decadent Thailand and claims to want his wife to be free in every sense of the word. At first she's reluctant to stray sexually, and she's understandably repulsed by the predatory amorality of the other women she meets in Bangkok; they leer and snigger about their numerous and varied infidelities like jocks counting notches in the locker room. But a lovely teenage libertine convinces Emmanuelle to shed her inhibitions, and soon she's taking her first steps toward erotic liberation. She fantasizes about sex with a stranger on an airplane, swims naked in a public pool, smooches with her bisexual squash partner, and runs off for a country weekend with Bee, an independent lesbian—the catty wives call her "an outrageous, forward slut" because she's not part of their malicious sewing circle. Emmanuelle finally graduates to the dissolute Mario (played, amazingly, by Alain Cuny, *La Dolce Vita*'s suicidal intellectual), an older man who's dedicated his life to sophisticated debauchery.

This wasn't the first film adapted from the notorious naughty novel *Emmanuelle*, whose author, Maryat Rollet-Andriane, hid behind the pseudonym Emmanuelle Arsan. It was published in France in 1967, became an underground bestseller, and was first filmed in 1968 as *Io Emmanuelle* (*I Emmanuelle*). But it took former fashion photographer Just Jaeckin to make the material palatable for a broad audience. The cliché of Europeans corrupted by depraved Asia underlies *Emmanuelle*'s plot and imagery: From massage parlors staffed by giggling, raven-haired girls to smoky opium dens and clandestine kickboxing arenas, the film's French characters are powerless to resist the allure of the hedonistic East. It must also be said that they're not trying very hard.

While most of them are just sex mad, Mario is a true philosopher in the boudoir. From Mario's lips cas-

*King has also directed several erotic films, including *Two Moon Junction* and *Wild Orchid*. See the entries on *Nine ½ Weeks* and *Wild Orchid* for details of King's career in upscale naughtiness.

Philosophical reprobate Alain Cuny lectures Sylvia Kristel on the principles of lust.

Jaeckin makes fine use of *Emmanuelle*'s exotic locales, and the manicured images are strengthened by the soundtrack, filled with the murmurs of pretty house maids and the thud of horses' hooves, the tinkling of chimes and dancing girls' finger cymbals, the patter of rain and the whisper of the wind in the trees. Only the obvious synthesizer score introduces a note of discord. The cast is uniformly attractive and pleasingly photographed; *Emmanuelle* is carefully composed, shot with gauzy care and by and large edited to downplay the raunchy mechanics of sex in favor of blissfully orgasmic faces and aesthetically presented bodily landscapes. The film distances itself from hard-core—and much soft-core—pornography by virtue of relentless *prettiness*, and throughout, the emphasis is on cleanliness—between the rainstorms, swimming pools, and waterfalls, the thought that sex is dirty is washed away

cade most of *Emmanuelle*'s ideological underpinnings: He preaches the rejection of "false moral values, foolish taboos and conformity" and exalts the law of licentiousness. "We have to make love without reason or restraint," he lectures the spellbound Emmanuelle. "Virginity is not a virtue. The couple is not sacred. And we should destroy all limitations for all time." Mario further instructs her in the art of liberation through debasement: He invites a roadside drunk to fondle her legs, takes her to an opium den where she's raped by two addicts, and gives her as a prize to a kickboxer, who takes her surrounded by the same spectators who watched him win the brutal match. The film closes on the ambiguous image of Emmanuelle before a mirror, putting on her makeup and wearing the gown and boa Mario has given her. Has she reached the brink of true self-knowledge, or has she been degraded beyond redemption?

Emmanuelle rejects "false moral values, foolish taboos, and conformity."

before it can even form.

Jaeckin went on to direct *The Story of O* (1975), based on the classic S&M novel by Pauline Réage; *The French Woman* (1979), a soft-core mix of passion and politics; and *Lady Chatterley's Lover* (1981), based on the novel by D. H. Lawrence and starring Kristel, before trying (unsuccessfully) to change his image as a solemn European pornographer with *The Perils of Gwendoline* (1984), a sex comedy adapted from a risqué French comic book. He told interviewers he really wasn't a kinky guy and revealed that he was such a cut-up his friends nicknamed him "Just Joking." Kristel was typed as a sexy star; her later credits include *Tigers in Lipstick* (1980), *Private Lessons* (1981), *Private School* (1983), *Mata Hari* (1985), and *Game of Seduction* (1986) for upscale panderer Roger Vadim, of *And God Created Woman* fame.

There were three bona fide sequels to *Emmanuelle*, all starring Kristel: *Emmanuelle, the Joys of a Woman* (1976), *Goodbye, Emmanuelle* (1979), and, finally, *Emmanuelle 4* (1984), in which Emmanuelle—still exploring the mysteries of the sensual world—has plastic surgery, and Kristel turns over the role to a younger actress, Mia Nygren. But *Emmanuelle* also became a kind of generic term for soft-core sex pictures, resulting in a competing series of *Emanuelle*-with-one-*m* movies starring Asian actress Laura Gemser*: *Emanuelle the Queen* a.k.a. *Emanuelle the Queen of Sados* (1975), *Emanuelle on Taboo Island* (1976), *Emanuelle Around the World* (1977), *Emanuelle in the Country* (1978), and *Emanuelle's Daughter* (1979)—and a bunch of knockoffs starring various brazen leading ladies, including *Black Emanuelle* (1976), *Emanuelle in Bangkok* (1978), *Emmanuelle & Joanna* (1986). *Emanuelle 5* (1987), featuring dreary scream queen Monique Gabrielle, was a real *Emmanuelle* sequel in name only. Cheap, unimaginative, and sleazy, its original director was eccentric European eroticist Walerian Borowsczyk. He was summarily fired. Producer Alain Siritzky, who'd taken over the franchise, also squeezed out an *Emmanuelle 6* (1992) with Natalie Uher. Notorious Spanish sexploita-

Emmanuelle made Kristel the queen of arty European softcore.

tion auteur Jess Franco contributed *Las Orgias Inconfesables de Emmanuelle* (1982), which is described as a soft-core parody, a sort of meta-*Emmanuelle* picture.

In the 1990s Kristel's Emmanuelle resurfaced as the star of a European erotic TV series (very like *Red Shoe Diaries*, in fact, bringing the sequence of influence full circle), recounting to George Lazenby (a one-time-only James Bond) her many erotic adventures. Segments were combined and packaged on video as features under such titles as *Emmanuelle's Loves* and *Emmanuelle's Seventh Heaven*. When in 1994 Arsan's novel was packaged on audio tape in Britain as part of a set of erotic literary classics Kristel was selected to read it.

*Video reference books often erroneously list these titles with two *m*s.

Emmanuelle: The Joys of a Woman: Less high-minded and more salacious than *Emmanuelle*.

Porno Chic

Mainstream hardcore rivals *military intelligence* in the oxymoron sweepstakes, and today most porno movies wind up in the back room at video stores; where once there were more than 800 adult theaters in America, there are now a mere 175. But there was a brief period when filmmakers thought there was an audience for upscale hardcore. Many of these films were reviewed in respectable newspapers (even the *New York Times*), attended by upwardly mobile couples (as opposed to losers in raincoats), and discussed in polite company. It all ended with the video revolution, which drove pornographic movies right back into the shadows. And despite the occasional bad-boy bluster—Brian DePalma's insisting that *Body Double* was going to be a mainstream thriller with hard-core sex, or Paul Verhoeven hyping *Showgirls* as a big studio film that deserved its NC-17—that's where they've stayed.

But remember for a moment the brief glory days of respectable hard-core films, from foreign art picture *I Am Curious, Yellow* (1967)—director Vilmot Sjöman was a protégé of Ingmar Bergman—to the homegrown *Deep Throat* (1972), which catapulted Linda Lovelace to stardom) and *The Devil in Miss Jones* (1972). The Mitchell brothers' *Behind the Green Door* (1972) turned wholesome star Marilyn Chambers—formerly a sweet young mother-next-door on Ivory soap boxes—into a household name. The perky *Debbie Does Dallas* (1978) made porn seem like good, clean fun. And Chuck Vincent's *Roommates* (1982), starring Jamie Gillis, Veronica Hart, and Samantha Fox, was released in both an R and an X version, with the X version the real, hardcore thing. And of course, gentleman pornographer Radley Metzger won many mainstream fans with his well-photographed films, including *The Lickerish Quartet* (1970). Where is the porn of yesteryear?

19
Gilda (1946)

Directed by Charles Vidor. Produced by Virginia Van Upp. Written by Marion Parsonnet, based on Jo Eisinger's adaptation of E. A. Ellington's original story. Cinematography by Rudolph Maté. Edited by Charles Nelson. Music by Hugo Friedhofer.

Rita Hayworth (Gilda), Glenn Ford (Johnny Farrell), George Macready (Ballin Mundson), Joseph Calleia (Obregon).

One of the reigning love goddesses of the '40s, wet dream of hundreds of thousands of GIs, Rita Hayworth wasn't Gilda—a selfish, amoral, heedless, promiscuous, materialistic, vengeful, cunning bitch—and more was the pity, mostly for her. "There NEVER was a woman like Gilda," teased the ads, but the film went all out to make viewers want one. Hayworth may have been teasing the first time she accused producer Virginia Van Upp of ruining her life, complaining that "Every man I've known has fallen in love with Gilda and wakened with me." But by her fifth marriage the joke had doubtless worn thin.

In Argentina, where anything goes, sleek, wealthy Ballin Mundson owns a swank casino and hires down-on-his-luck gambler Johnny Farrell to run the place. The two are inseparable, and their relationship has distinctly

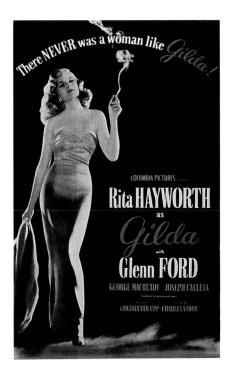

homoerotic undertones, so when Mundson returns from a brief business trip with his new wife, the breathtakingly beautiful Gilda, disaster is sure to follow. Unbeknownst to Ballin, Gilda and Johnny used to be lovers and remain a volatile combination; soon Ballin has guessed their shared past and suspects they're sleeping together. Gilda embarks on a string of affairs and Johnny covers them up so his friend won't know. Trouble at the casino forces Mundson to flee, and he's apparently killed in a plane crash. Johnny marries Gilda, intending to punish her for cheating on Ballin. The sordid situation comes to a head when Ballin returns, planning to kill them both. He's killed instead, leaving Gilda and Johnny free to realize they really do love each other.

Without Hayworth, *Gilda* would still be a perverse exercise in sublimated sexuality and eroticized violence (critic John Azzopardi called it "one of the few genuinely erotic films made in America"), but with her it's an astonishing celebration of the hellion. When Mundson, flush with the pride of a man who's just acquired the best sex toy money can buy, calls out, "Are you decent?" her needling reply says it all. "Me? Sure. I'm decent." Moments after his first encounter

All those chips and not a man looking at the table. Hayworth in *Gilda*.

with the new Mrs. Mundson, Johnny is already besieged by bad thoughts: He'd like to hit her, *and* he'd like to hit Mundson, *and* he'd like to watch them together without their knowing.

Because Gilda is *never* decent. She's an archetypal *belle dame sans merci*, stunning, sultry, conniving, rude, flirtatious, and irresistible, a glittering spider whose destiny is to screw men and suck them dry. Gilda is a riot of textures: black satin, white fur, silky skin, luxuriously curling cigarette smoke, and a cloud of fiery hair—you know it's red, even though the film is in shimmering black and white. Her voice is surprisingly

soft and clear, and you can almost smell her perfume. Gilda sways with the intuitive grace of the dancer Hayworth was in her youth (when she was still exotic Margarita Carmen Cansino) and chatters with the easy cruelty of a teenager. When she does her famous striptease, shimmying languidly as she sings "Put the Blame on Mame," she works the room into an erotic frenzy by removing a single black glove. Classy pornographer Radley Metzger, of *Harry, Cherry and Raquel* and *Camille 2000* fame, calls *Gilda* "one of the sexiest films I have ever seen" and claims there isn't a single kiss in it. In fact, there's one: "I hate you so much I think I'm going to die from it," breathes Gilda the moment before she kisses Johnny lustfully. *Gilda* is pure repression and displacement, and the effect is electrifying. There's a feeble eleventh-hour attempt made to redeem Gilda and make her an accidental femme fatale, but the scene flies in the face of everything that goes before it, and no one really believes the suggestion that she's just misunderstood.

In addition to the film's astonishing look, it's filled with brittle, provocative talk, ranging from Gilda's declaring that if she were a ranch, they'd name her the Bar *Nothing*, to Mundson's talking about his sword cane—his *friend*—the way the average man talks about his dick. Johnny chimes in with the observation that the mysterious friend must be a she, "because it looks like one thing, then, right in front of your eyes it becomes another thing," a remark so fraught with pansexual innuendo that perhaps it's better left untouched. Gilda taunts Johnny by calling him pretty; when she catches him in his bathrobe she makes sure she refers to it as his nightgown. Johnny's description of the way he'll handle Gilda's infidelities is equally revealing— even she says so: He tells her she can do anything she pleases, but he's going to take her to her assignations and he's going to pick her up, just like Ballin's laundry. Is sex dirty? Johnny's too thick to have a clue.

Gilda has no sex scenes and, with the exception of her strip that isn't a strip, nothing that even approaches one. But it's so fraught with sexual desire that you don't miss them; it keeps viewers on erotic tenterhooks from beginning to end, as glorious a tease as *Gilda* herself.

Gilda the glittering spider and her brutal lover, Johnny (Glenn Ford).

The Ten Sexiest Stars of the 1940s

Lauren Bacall: Slender and sultry, Bacall had a smoky voice and knowing manner that made her seem much older than the nineteen she was when she starred opposite Humphrey Bogart in *To Have and Have Not* (1944). The perfect noir heroine, she smoldered in *The Big Sleep* (1946), *Dark Passage* (1947), and *Key Largo* (1948).

Humphrey Bogart: Bogart wasn't handsome, but women glimpsed the sentimentalist beneath the tough façade and couldn't resist. His career began in the '30s, but *The Maltese Falcon* (1941) brought him into his own, and *Casablanca* (1942) guaranteed his place in the pantheon of wounded men waiting to be saved by pure romance.

Betty Grable: Modestly talented and plainly pretty, Grable parlayed her comely legs—insured for $1 million with Lloyd's of London—and girl-next-door wholesomeness into a stunning run as a sex symbol. She was the most popular pinup of World War II and at one time the highest-paid actress in Hollywood.

Rita Hayworth: The reluctant sex goddess, Hayworth was graceful and genuinely stunning, but she never really reveled in her own erotic appeal.

Gene Kelly: The golden boy of the golden age of Hollywood musicals, Kelly was more athletic and more handsome than Fred Astaire. He made dancing seem as natural as playing baseball and made every woman seem graceful, in such films as *An American in Paris* (1951), *Singin' in the Rain* (1952), and *Brigadoon* (1954).

Robert Mitchum: Brooding and restless, Mitchum anticipated the sexy bad boys of the '50s and outlasted them; his laid-back style still looks fresh. He was a noir regular, sidling through *Undercurrent* (1946), *Crossfire* and *Out of the Past* (both 1947), *Blood on the Moon* (1948), and *The Big Steal* (1949). Women swooned for him, even in *Night of the Hunter* (1955)—in which he played the demented preacher with LOVE and HATE tattooed on his knuckles—and the original *Cape Fear* (1962).

Laurence Olivier: Olivier played everything from the wussy Prince of Denmark to a sadistic Nazi war criminal, but as Heathcliff in *Wuthering Heights* (1939) he established himself as a romantic idol in the

Byronic mode, which he exploited in *Pride and Prejudice* and *Rebecca* (both 1940), *That Hamilton Woman* (1941), and others.

Tyrone Power: Handsome, affable Power specialized in costume roles and swashbuckled his way through a series of romantic action pictures, including *The Mark of Zorro* (1940), *Blood and Sand* (1941), and *Captain From Castile* (1947), slaying women with his rakish charm.

Jane Russell: Monumentally curvaceous Russell was discovered by eccentric millionaire Howard Hughes and groomed for stardom in *The Outlaw* (1943). She proved an appealing comedienne, and most of her notable films, including *Gentlemen Prefer Blondes* (1952), were made in the '50s, but her towering charms hung over the '40s like storm clouds.

Lana Turner: An actress of limited range, Turner did more for a tight sweater than the average girl and built her career on sultry looks and smoldering glamour. Her finest hour may have been *The Postman Always Rings Twice* (1946), but she never failed to turn up the heat in any movie in which she appeared.

20 *Goldfinger* (1964)

Directed by Guy Hamilton. Produced by Albert R. Broccoli and Harry Saltzman. Screenplay by Richard Maibaum and Paul Dehn, based on the novel by Ian Fleming. Cinematography by Ted Moore. Edited by Peter Hunt. Production Design by Ken Adam. Music by John Barry.

Sean Connery (James Bond), Honor Blackman (Pussy Galore), Gert Frobe (Goldfinger), Shirley Eaton (Jill Masterson), Tonia Mallet (Tilly Masterson), Harold Sakata (Oddjob), Bernard Lee (M).

The third in what was, until the *Star Wars* trilogy, the only A-movie series in motion-picture history (and the last before it hardened into commercial cliché), *Goldfinger* isn't the ultimate James Bond picture. No *one* film is the ultimate James Bond picture; the ultimate James Bond picture is pieced together from all of them and exists only in our minds. But *Goldfinger* is typical of the series and has that naked, gilded lady, stretched out lifelessly on Bond's bed. That counts for a lot.

The plot is thin: Goldfinger is an eccentric millionaire with interests in many businesses, not all of them legal. Superspy Bond is assigned to find out more about his illegal gold smuggling and in doing so uncovers Goldfinger's plot to detonate an atomic bomb in Fort Knox, contaminating the United

States' entire supply of gold and wreaking havoc with the world market. Bond must defeat Goldfinger's plan and win the heart of icy Pussy Galore, Goldfinger's private pilot.

What matters in Bond films is not what happens. All the plots are silly concoctions of Cold War clichés and don't bear much scrutiny. The appeal of Bond films is in the atmosphere, and much of that atmosphere reeks of sex; he lives in a bachelor pad as big as the world, complete with zebra rugs and wet bar. Bond is a womanizer in a universe in which he doesn't have to pursue women, because they hurl themselves at him. He's at play in an adolescent fantasy land of wicked villains—distinguished by physical difference, whether deformity or race—cool devices, and wanton girls who would do anything for a chance at a night with his 007. The Bond movies are the precursors of today's action-adventure pictures, all boys and their high-tech toys, but while today's action-adventure girls are an afterthought, in Bond movies—even the newer, more selfconsciously tough ones— they're the main event. Bond pictures are Bond babe pictures: Ask any fourteen-year-old boy. If prehistoric-babes-in-bikinis pictures wean kids from monsters to girls (see *When*

From Russia With Love and Paula in *Thunderball*.* The list of lovelies is prodigious: Daniela Bianchi in *From Russia With Love* (1963); Claudine Auger in *Thunderball* (1965); Mie Hama's Kissy Suzuki in *You Only Live Twice* (1967); the second *Avengers*–turned–Bond girl, Diana Rigg (the first was *Goldfinger*'s Blackman; Rigg replaced her on the show), in *On Her Majesty's Secret Service* (1969), backed up by an international bevy of beauties known only by their countries of origin, including Julie Ege (the Scandinavian Girl), Joanna Lumley (English Girl),† and Anoushka Hempel (Australian Girl); Jill St. John and Lana Wood as *Diamonds Are Forever*'s (1971) Tiffany Case and Plenty O'Toole, respectively; Jane Seymour in *Live and Let Die* (1973); Britt Ekland's Mary Goodnight in *The Man With the Golden Gun* (1974); Barbara Bach and Caroline Munro in *The Spy Who Loved Me* (1977): Lois Chiles's Holly Goodhead in *Moonraker* (1979); Carole Bouquet in *For Your Eyes Only* (1981); Kim Basinger's Domino and Barbara Carrera's Fatima Blush in *Never Say Never Again* (1983); Tanya Roberts and Grace Jones (as May Day) in *A View to a Kill* (1985); Maryam D'Abo in *The Living Daylights* (1987); and Carey Lowell and Talisa Soto (as Lupe Lamora) in *Licence to Kill* (1989).

The success of the Bond films spawned a slew of knockoffs and spoofs, of which the Matt Helm and Flint pictures deserve mention for their camp salaciousness. James Coburn played Flint, agent for Z.O.W.I.E., in two films, *Our Man Flint* (1966) and *In*

Dinosaurs Ruled the Earth), then Bond movies seduce adolescents with the promise of adventure and sex, not mushy girl romance. Bond babes are as fast as sports cars, as slick as gadgets, as hot as bullets.

There have been sixteen official Bond films to date, and two ringers: the satirical *Casino Royale* (1967) and spoiler *Never Say Never Again* (1983), in which Sean Connery, having abandoned the series after *You Only Live Twice* (1967), returned to go head to head with second-string Bond Roger Moore's *Octopussy*. They've showcased a bevy of beauties, beginning with Ursula Andress's Honey Ryder in *Dr. No* (1962). Andress returned in *Casino Royale*; she's one of only three Bond two-timers. The others were Maud Adams, who appeared in *The Man With the Golden Gun* and *Octopussy*, and Martine Beswicke, in the smaller roles of Zora in

*Beswicke was also the unidentified dancing girl in the credits sequence of *Dr. No*. Eternal Miss Moneypenny Lois Maxwell was, of course, in all the Bond films, but that doesn't make her a Bond Girl.

†After a minor film career, Lumley became a household name in the '90s. As the hellishly dissolute Patsy Stone, she was the monstrously glamorous half of TV's *Absolutely Fabulous* odd couple.

Pussy shows her claws.

Like Flint (1967). The former included an island of beautiful zombie women being trained as pleasure dolls, the latter featured a secret society of women trying to take over the world. Coburn's virile spin on the Bond persona and the wall-to-wall girls make both pictures worth seeing. The Matt Helm pictures—*The Silencers* (1966), *Murderer's Row* (1966), *The Ambushers* (1967), and *The Wrecking Crew* (1968)—featured Dean Martin as a flabby, boozing spy surrounded by luscious girls. They included Ann-Margret, Senta Berger, Elke Sommer, Stella Stevens, Tina Louise, Janice Rule, and Sharon Tate, armed with weapons ranging from bullet bras to exploding bottles of scotch. The films are unbelievably reactionary jiggle fests, awash in shots of nubiles wiggling their breasts or butts: the shots are too tight for them to wiggle both at once. They make the Bond films seem like the work of Shakespeare, but as moving pinup calendars they more than do the trick.

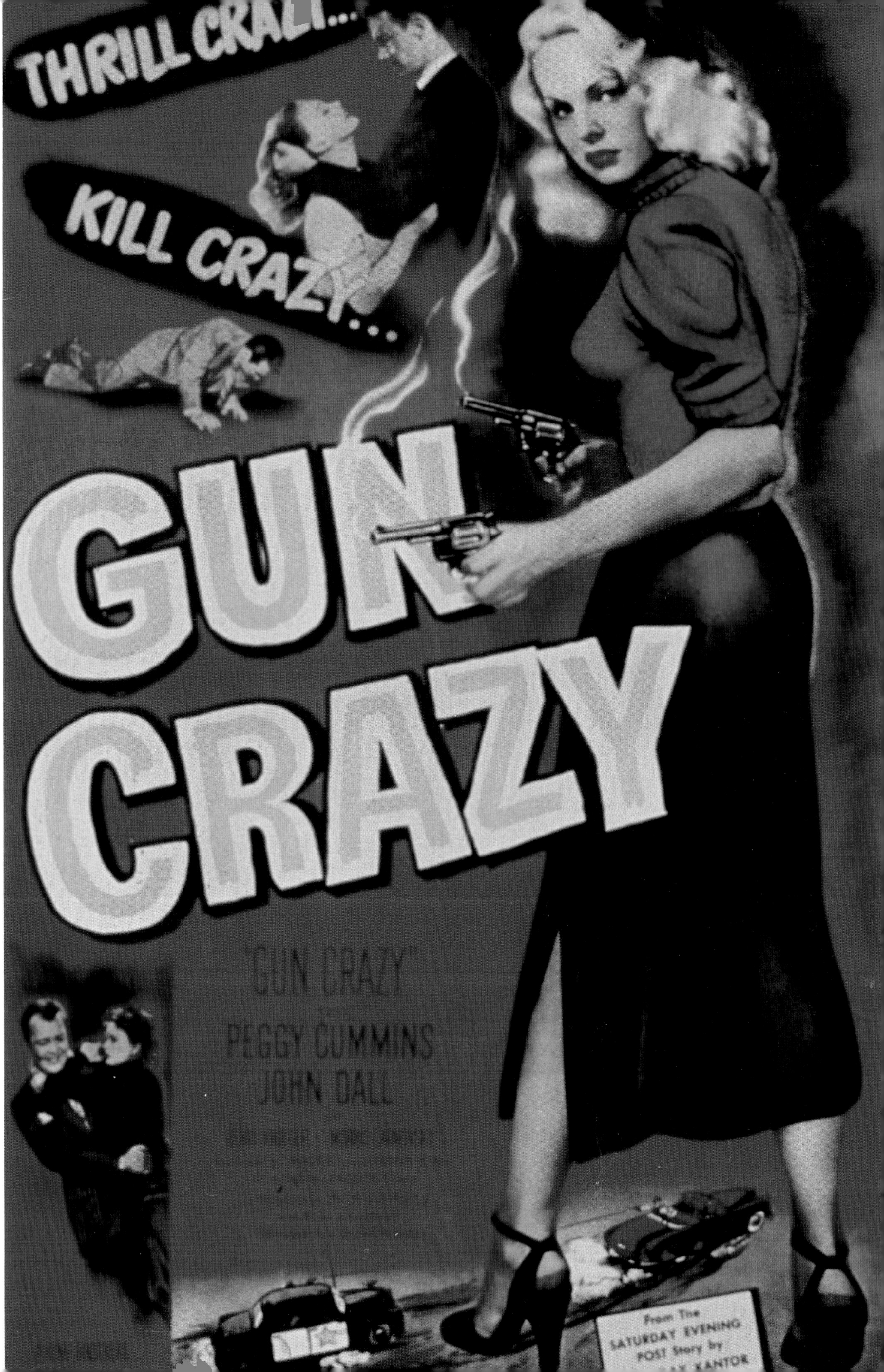
THRILL CRAZY...
KILL CRAZY...
GUN CRAZY
"GUN CRAZY"
PEGGY CUMMINS
JOHN DALL
From The
SATURDAY EVENING
POST Story by
KANTOR

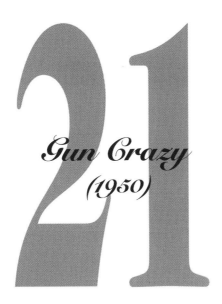

Gun Crazy
(1950)

Directed by Joseph H. Lewis. Produced by Frank and Maurice King. Screenplay by MacKinlay Kantor and Millard Kaufman, based on Kantor's *Saturday Evening Post* story. Cinematography by Russell Harlan. Edited by Harry Gerstad. Production Design by Gordon Wiles. Music by Victor Young.

Peggy Cummins (Annie Laurie Starr), John Dall (Bart Tare), Berry Kroeger (Packett), Harry Lewis (Clyde Boston), Nedrick Young (Dave Allister), Rusty (Russ) Tamblyn (Young Bart).

Movie buffs live to discover forgotten gems, and *Gun Crazy* more than fit the bill in 1967. America was in the thrall of Arthur Penn's *Bonnie and Clyde*, in which Warren Beatty and Faye Dunaway played the pistol-packing couple who inspired the notorious "They are young, they are in love, they kill people" advertising campaign. People lined up to see what everyone was talking about. Debate raged in the press over the film's violence and new-wave shifts of tone. The fashion industry saw a good thing in Bonnie's sexy, beret-topped outfits and unleashed them on a waiting world. But what about *Gun Crazy*? Made by a second-tier director, it starred virtual unknowns Peggy Cummins and John Dall. His claim to fame is as one of the homosexual killers in Alfred Hitchcock's 1948 *Rope*; hers was losing the title role in 1947's *Forever Amber*—a notoriously naughty historical romp—to Linda Darnell. But *Gun Crazy* is the quintessential couple-on-the-run movie, and it's so sexy it's hard to believe it was shot in 1949.

Gun Crazy opens with a prologue: Little Bart steals a gun from a small-town pawn shop, and his sad history of gun-related misbehavior is explored in juvenile court. He brings his gun to school (proving that there are no new problems in the world), shoots a little bird (but feels very bad), and, finally, is reduced to theft. "I've just gotta have a gun," he tells the judge pathetically. "I feel good when I'm shooting them. I feel awful good." Hmm.

Sent to reform school, Bart straightens up, joins the army, and eventually comes home. But all is lost when he and his old buddies go to the carnival and see Annie Laurie Starr, a sharpshooter, doing her sideshow act. Bart challenges her, and their match is fraught with sexual tension, as they toss the smoking pistol back and forth and light crowns of matches on each other's heads. They're so hot for each other, they're like "a couple of wild animals." Director Lewis later said his directions to the couple were straightforward: "I told John, 'Your cock's never been so hard,' and I told Peggy, 'You're a female dog in heat, and you want him.'" Dall and Cummins got it, and it shows; the whole film vibrates with pure lust.

Dall joins the carnival, and the two of them get married (just about the only concession to contemporary morality) and hit the road; soon they're down to their last dollar and turn to crime. Bart is a reluctant stickup man, fundamentally honest (though easily persuaded by Laurie's wiles) and reluctant to risk hurting others. Laurie is another story: With her cracked voice and her brittle looks, Cummins is the personification of vicious lust. Bart likes shooting, but she likes shooting people. Her face glows when she's got a gun in her hand; she tells Bart she shoots because she gets scared, but she's lying. She does it for the thrill.

They agree to go straight, but only after one last heist at a meatpacking plant (the scene is justly famous for its fluid use of moving camera). They get the cash

She's a sadist and he's pussy-whipped; together they're *Gun Crazy*.

and are supposed to split up but can't. Instead, they abandon one of the getaway cars and flee together to California. It doesn't take long for the end to start: They're identified and tracked, flee to Bart's hometown, and wind up hiding out in the woods where he used to play with his friends, while the police close in inexorably. They die together in the fog and reeds, wet and dirty and hunted, so in love that it isn't even sad. As it did with Romeo and Juliet, death unites them where life threatened to tear them apart.

Bart and Laurie "go together like guns and ammunition," and the sexual heat is palpable; if there's ever been a better film made about why people love guns, it's hard to imagine what it is. A B-movie made at the height of the original noir cycle, *Gun Crazy* is all recycled ideas—the couple on the lam, the gun fetishism, the outsider posturing—rendered with such perfection that nothing cries out to be improved. Brittle, blond Cummins oozes sex, whether she's putting on her stockings or holstering her pistol; she makes her Annie Oakley carnival getup look as provocative as a PVC bustier. Dall delivers a remarkably subtle performance as a man who's spent his life

in a kind of haze, not really aware something was missing until it drops into his lap. But once it's there, he'll do anything to keep it. *Gun Crazy* is about sex as a drug, and they're both hooked.

Tamra Davis's *Guncrazy* (1993) sure sounds like a remake, but it's not—it's a sad little story about an abused girl and her misunderstood boyfriend, who likes guns because they make him feel important. And though it stars white-trash sexpot Drew Barrymore, it isn't the slightest bit sexy. In fact, it's antisex, filled with rape, impotence, and ugly sexual exploitation. *Guncrazy* isn't a bad movie, but it's no thrill.

I Am a Camera; or, Is That a Lens in Your Pocket or Are You Just Glad to See Me?

Being photographed is erotic: When photographers say, "Give it to me baby, give me *more*," we all know what they really mean. And the camera lens is doubly eroticized: connotations of peeping on the one hand, all-too-obvious phallic stand-in on the other. So no wonder they pop up (no pun intended) in so many movies as displaced embodiments of rude desire.

In Alfred Hitchcock's *Rear Window* (1954), wheelchair-bound (read: impotent) photographer James Stewart fondles his *enormous* telephoto lens when not spying on his neighbors through it. Repressed Carl Boehm, Michael Powell's *Peeping Tom* (1960), uses his camera to photograph women as he murders them with a phallic tripod. In Michelangelo Antonioni's arty *Blow-Up* (1966), fashion photographer David Hemmings and barely clad model Veruschka engage in near-coitus during a photo session, and in Paul Bartel's *Private Parts* (1972), photography and warped desire are twisted into a bizarre psychosexual mélange. In *The Seduction* (1982) perverted photographer Andrew Stevens uses his tool to stalk and sexually harass Morgan Fairchild, but he's unmanned when she turns it on him. In Steven Soderbergh's *sex, lies, and videotape* (1990), celibate James Spader probes women's deepest sexual secrets with his video camera. Once again, he's powerless when Andie MacDowell gets her hands on the thing itself. Calling Jacques Lacan!

Henry & June (1990)

Directed by Philip Kaufman. Produced by Peter Kaufman. Written by Philip and Rose Kaufman, based on the diaries of Anaïs Nin. Cinematography by Philippe Rousselot. Edited by Vivien Hillgrove, William S. Scharf, and Dede Allen.

Fred Ward (Henry Miller), Maria De Medeiros (Anaïs Nin), Hugh E. Grant (Hugo), Uma Thurman (June Miller), Kevin Spacey (Osborn), Jean-Philippe Ecoffey (Eduardo).

Set in glamorous Paris in the fabled 1930s, *Henry & June* revolves around the writing of Henry Miller's controversial *Tropic of Cancer*, published in France in 1934 and unavailable in the United States until 1961, when it was met with a flurry of lawsuits designed to keep such obscenity out of the hands of innocent Americans. Because writers writing are dull as can be, the movie focuses on Miller's vigorous and often exotic sex life, as seen through the eyes of fellow-writer Anaïs Nin, his lover and lifelong friend.

Pretty Anaïs is the vaguely frustrated wife of devoted but clueless banker Hugo, who is astonishingly patient with her nebulous yearnings for a more daring, bohemian way of life. A friend, the nutty and amiable Osborn, introduces them to his roommate, Henry Miller, a middle-aged American living in expatriate poverty and writing his first novel, and her wish is granted.

Miller is soon joined by his crude, alluring wife, June, a bisexual taxi dancer and born whore. Anaïs excited by Henry and smitten with June, and the sexual complications quickly ensue. Henry and June fight and fornicate with equal enthusiasm, Anaïs sleeps with both and seduces her cousin Eduardo—who has adored her since childhood—the same way Henry

seduced her. June returns to Brooklyn to dally with her lesbian lover and collect money from the man who keeps her (and, by extension, Henry). Only Hugo is left on the sidelines (despite Anaïs's assertion that he's exceptionally well endowed); his wildest exploit is to go to a chic brothel with his wife to see two prostitutes put on a sexual exhibition. Anaïs selects the girls: a tall blond one like June and a short dark one like herself.

Things come to a head when June returns. Though both Anaïs and Henry have been inspired by her, she's a bitter, ungrateful muse who thinks Anaïs's writing isn't real enough, while Henry's is insufficiently flattering. The movie ends with *Tropic of Cancer* on the verge of publication and Anaïs returning to her now-famous diaries to transform matters into her own precious brand of art. Miller, the grand old man of lewd literature—grander even than D. H. Lawrence—would have approved of the film's content but would no doubt have wanted to dirty up the presentation.

Henry & June was the first film to receive the MPAA's spanking new NC-17 rating, meant to designate adult films without branding them with the scarlet X that had come to mean "sleazy, nasty porno picture." *Henry & June* is certainly not that, with its top-dollar production values, meticulous sense of period, eminently respectable cast, and unimpeachably literary subject. It is, however, teeming with fairly explicit sex scenes, all shot with impeccable care and composed within the boundaries of broad-minded good taste. Anaïs and Henry fornicate behind a scrim in a tony club, against walls, by the banks of the Seine, in cheap hotels, and even in her own bed while Hugo sits downstairs, oblivious. Anaïs and Hugo have sex on

the street at a wild *carnivale*, while Osborn has orgies with contortionists.

Henry & June's Paris is a hothouse garden of erotic experimentation, rife with elegant pornography, silk stockings, arousing films—from the repressed lesbianism of *Mädchen in Uniform* to the austere ecstasies of *The Passion of Joan of Arc* and the perversity of *Un Chien Andalou*—libidinous music, clinging dresses, provocative photographs (by Brassaï, no less), and endless smoky nights of liquor and lust. The flesh is beautiful, the lighting exquisite, the postcoital conversation literary.

American director Philip Kaufman, whose films range from the 1978 remake of *Invasion of the Body Snatchers* to Japanophobic thriller *Rising Sun* (1993), garnered much attention with the back-to-back literary erotica of *The Unbearable Lightness of Being* (1988), adapted from Czechoslovakian Milan Kundera's novel, and *Henry & June*. *Unbearable Lightness* follows the sexual exploits of an adventurous surgeon (Daniel Day-Lewis) and the two women in his life: innocent Juliette Binoche and hedonistic Lena Olin, whose nude frolics give the movie much of its appeal. Interestingly, all three stars quickly ensured their sta-

tus as erotic idols: Day-Lewis in the swooningly romantic *Last of the Mohicans* (1993), Binoche as *Damage*'s femme fatale, and Olin as the sexiest, most terrifying woman in the world in *Romeo Is Bleeding* (1994). *Unbearable Lightness's* mix of naughtiness and political commentary has a Eurotrashy tint and, taken in combination with *Henry & June*, earned the director his unkind nickname, *Philippe Kaufmann*. He is the reigning king of sexy art movies, as distinct from arty sex movies, the realm of Zalman King (see *Nine ½ Weeks* and *Wild Orchid*).

Miller's novel *Quiet Days in Clichy* was filmed in 1969 by Danish director Jens Jörgen Thorsen and created quite a stir with its full frontal nudity—male and female—and blithely frank language ("It was a time when cunt was in the air"); it was prosecuted for going "beyond customary limits of candor" but was defended under the redeeming social value criterion. It was, after all, not about just any balding lecher screwing his way around Paris; this was great writer Henry Miller. *Tropic of Cancer*, directed by Joseph L. Strick (who had already tried his hand at that other famous dirty book, James Joyce's *Ulysses*, in 1967), was released in 1970; it starred Rip Torn as Miller and Ellen Burstyn as his wife. *Tropic of Cancer*, perhaps inevitably, received an X rating but was generally treated as a respectable literary effort. Not so *The Room of Words* (1991), an opportunistic *Henry & June* knockoff by consummately sleazy Italian exploitation director Aristede Massachesi (better known by his nom d'écran Joe d'Amato). Purportedly based on the diaries of Anaïs Nin, its two hours of soft-core sleaze would try the patience of the most confirmed fan. Most recently, soft-core prince King directed *Delta of Venus* (1994), again based on Nin's writings with a narrowly erotic focus. The *Delta of Venus* link brings the arty sex–sexy art circle to a close, suggesting that there's even less difference between them than some people try to argue.

(Above) Lecherous literati.

Soft-core auteur Zalman King's *Delta of Venus*, loosely based on Nin's writings.

Hiroshima, Mon Amour (1959)

Directed by Alain Resnais. Produced by Samy Halfon. Screenplay by Marguerite Duras. Cinematography by Sacha Vierny and Michio Takahashi. Edited by Henri Colpi, Jasmine Chasney, and Anne Sarraute. Music by Georges Delerue and Giovanni Fusco.

Emmanuelle Riva (the actress), Eiji Okada (the architect), Stella Dassas (mother), Pierre Barbaud (father), Bernard Fresson (German lover).

Look up *European art movie* ('50s) in the dictionary, and you'll find a still from *Hiroshima, Mon Amour*, a deeply thoughtful, cool dissertation on love and war and race and memory, elliptical and defiantly antithetical to the filmmaking conventions polished to a high gloss by Hollywood. But that's not why Americans flocked to *Hiroshima, Mon Amour* and a host of other European films in the '50s and '60s: They came for the sex. Though discreet by today's standards, the films of Ingmar Bergman, Jean-Luc Godard, Michelangelo Antonioni, Claude Autant-Lara, Roberto Rossellini, Bernardo Bertolucci, Max Ophüls, Luchino Visconti, François Truffaut, and Federico Fellini (a fair sampling of the great names in postwar French, Italian, and Swedish cinema) were a sexual free-for-all when compared with Hollywood films of the same period. They dealt with adult sexual subjects—adultery, premarital sex, homosexuality, divorce, and sexual dysfunction—without coyness or subterfuge, and they showed pretty girls undressing, showering, and in bed with their lovers.

This was the age when exploitation distributor

Love and war, race and sex, imagination and memory are intertwined in the brief encounter of an actress and an architect.

David Friedman could release Bergman's resolutely unsensational *Monika* (1952), the story of a young woman's coming of age, to drive-ins and grind houses as *Monika—Story of a Bad Girl* and send away nothing but satisfied customers. The words *foreign film* became, for a generation coming of age before the sexual revolution of the '60s, nearly synonymous with *erotic cinema*. Foreign films offered cherished glimpses of a distinctly European approach to sex: sophisticated, risqué, unpolished, undraped. Films whose weighty philosophical underpinnings are hardly the stuff of erotic fantasy became titillating because of a single scene of nude bathing or lovemaking, convincing a generation that Americans knew nothing about sex, but Europeans, especially the French and the Scandinavians, knew *everything*.

Hiroshima, Mon Amour opens with a close-up of intertwined limbs, dusted with ash; they dissolve into the same limbs coated with glittering powder, then misted with sweat. A pair of anonymous lovers talk in ambiguous fragments about Hiroshima, the legacy of the bomb, and the persistence of memory. "You saw nothing in Hiroshima," he tells her. "I saw *everything*," she insists. By the time we finally see the faces of the French actress and the Japanese architect, we've been listening to them speak, examining their skin, for nearly twenty minutes, and director Alain Resnais and writer Marguerite Duras have pulled off an astonishing balancing trick. The beguiling images of the lovers' bodies are interspersed with shots of displays at the Atomic Dome, Hiroshima's museum of the atomic bomb, and newsreel footage of victims of the atomic blast and its radioactive aftermath. You'd think the effect would be anti-eroti-

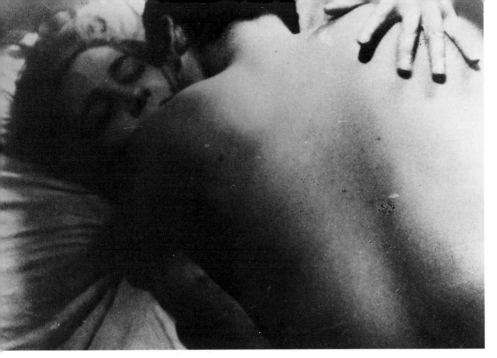

Starved for sex in movies, Americans braved subtitles to see *everything* in *Hiroshima, Mon Amour*.

cism incarnate. But it's not. The beauty of the lovers' intense, isolated relationship and the vast horror of atomic destruction coexist harmoniously, and memory soon wipes away the horror of burns and rubble in favor of recalling smooth flesh and pliant limbs.

Hiroshima, Mon Amour's two principal characters are never named. The actress is in Japan to make a film (about peace, of course); the architect meets her in a bar just before she's due to fly home, and they spend the night together. They're both married and know they have no shared future—just a night and the following day, during which they make love and share secrets. Their relationship is tinged with nostalgic sad-

Emmanuelle Riva and Eiji Okada as nameless lovers.

ness before it's even begun, and their souls—particularly hers—are far more naked than their bodies. *Hiroshima, Mon Amour* featured an original screenplay by French novelist Marguerite Duras, already famous for her spare, penetrating examinations of the intricate terrain of love, lust, and eroticism. *Hiroshima, Mon Amour* is an intensely literary film, one in which there is relatively little dialogue, but every word counts; the screenplay was published in the United States by Grove Press, long notorious as purveyors of high-toned "obscene" books.

The film is intensely sensual in a very intellectual way. In style it's light years away from the lyrical, soft-core precision of Jean-Jacques Annaud's *The Lover* (1992), which was adapted from Duras's autobiographical novel of the same title. But it's driven by all the same impulses. Though briefly accused of obscenity in Argentina (District Attorney Guillermo de la Riesta lodged a complaint in 1960; Judge Miguel A. Bueno quickly and sensibly rejected it), *Hiroshima, Mon Amour* was generally protected by its air of high seriousness. American critics focused their attention on the film's hypnotic narrative, a seductive tangle of memories and present-time action, rather than the potentially sensational details of its adulterous affair between a white woman and an Asian man. In retrospect, the official reaction (or non-reaction) to *Hiroshima, Mon Amour* smacks of a high-handed assumption that anyone smart enough to get it was smart enough not to be inflamed by the film's illicit sex, like printing the dirty bits of Havelock Ellis's *Psychopathia Sexualis* in Latin. Remember that only a couple of years earlier, Roger Vadim's less intellectually demanding but no more candid *And God Created Woman*, starring Brigitte Bardot, had been banned in certain Texas theaters as "too provocative for Negroes."

One can't speak of *Hiroshima, Mon Amour* without mentioning its jauty partner in crime, *A Bout de Souffle / Breathless* (1959), written by Truffaut and directed by Godard. A breezy, self-referential pastiche of American genre conventions, it starred French tough guy Jean Paul Belmondo and Midwestern waif Jean Seberg—only twenty-one and already seduced and abandoned by Hollywood, which failed to appreciate her gamine appeal. *Breathless* is a feature-length affront to the establishment; its junk-culture cleverness thrilled rebellious Americans looking for an excuse to embrace the throwaway movies they secretly adored. And oh those scenes of Seberg and Belmondo in bed, squirming and laughing and generally looking as though they were having a great, guilt-free time!

You Can Be My Baby, It Don't Matter If You're Black or White

Love may conquer all, but race is still an uphill battle. The Production Code, which debuted in 1930, explicitly prohibited the mere mention of miscegenation. Hollywood pretty much toed the line, except for occasional tragic mulatto girls, all played by white women: Helen Morgan and Ava Gardner as Julie in the 1936 and 1951, respectively, versions of *Show Boat*; Fredi Washington and Susan Kohner in the 1934 and 1959, respectively, versions of *Imitation of Life*; and Jeanne Crain in *Pinky* (1949). Needless to say, none could hold on to a white man once he learned her terrible secret. There were, of course, almost no films about black *men* passing for white.

In fact, as standards gradually loosened, a pattern became clear: White men might entertain thoughts about beguiling nonwhite women (especially submissive china dolls), but the reverse was seldom the case. Two of the most famous films involving black men and white women—the earnest *One Potato, Two Potato* (1964), which paired Barbara Barrie and Bernie Hamilton, and the spinelessly "controversial" *Guess Who's Coming to Dinner* (1967), with Katharine Houghton and Sidney Poitier—fall over themselves to be inoffensively sexless. The couples in *Island in the Sun* (1957)—Joan Fontaine and Harry Belafonte, James Mason and Dorothy Dandridge—which deals with racial tension on a Caribbean island, illustrate the racial double standard nicely: Dandridge and Mason get to kiss, while Fontaine and Belafonte are restricted to chaste hand holding. Inger Stevens and Belafonte in *The World, the Flesh, and the Devil* (1959) pair off only because everyone else in the whole world is dead after a nuclear accident. Mel Ferrer's arrival puts a stop to things. It is only degree that's different in 1975's con-

summately sleazy *Mandingo* (which gave offense even to people who didn't see it, by way of the poster that parodied the famous *Gone With the Wind* image of Rhett and Scarlett embracing against a backdrop of flames): Slavemaster Perry King can lust for brown sugar with impunity, but when sexpot Susan George sneaks off to the slave quarters to test out the newest big black buck, it's killing time. The sequel, *Drum* (1976), and knockoff *Mandinga* (1977) offer more of the same.

The forbidden titillation factor informs the early *Bitter Tea of General Yen* (1933), in which Barbara Stanwyck plays a white missionary consumed by lustful longing for a Chinese warlord (played, for safety's sake, by Scandinavian Nils Asther); and Jim Brown's conquest of Raquel Welch gives *100 Rifles* (1969) its punch. Black exploitation films from *Shaft* (1971) to *Truck Turner* (1974) thrived on the juxtaposition of macho black stars like Brown, Isaac Hayes, Ron O'Neal, Fred Williamson, and Richard Roundtree paired off with insatiable white women, and blaxploitation babes like Pam Grier and Tamara Dobson seduced fans across racial barriers. More recently, Annabella Sciorra and Wesley Snipes were teamed in *Jungle Fever* (1991), whose title says it all. Among the more interesting interracial pairings in recent films have been Cathy Tyson and Bob Hoskins in *Mona Lisa* (1986) and Stephen Rea and Jaye Davidson in *The Crying Game* (1993), both directed by Neil Jordan; in both cases, race turns out to be the *least* of the barriers to their complicated relationships. On the other hand, interracial sex scenes between Ellen Barkin and Laurence Fishburne caused such a stir that the release of *Bad Company* (1995) was delayed while changes were made. The more things change . . .

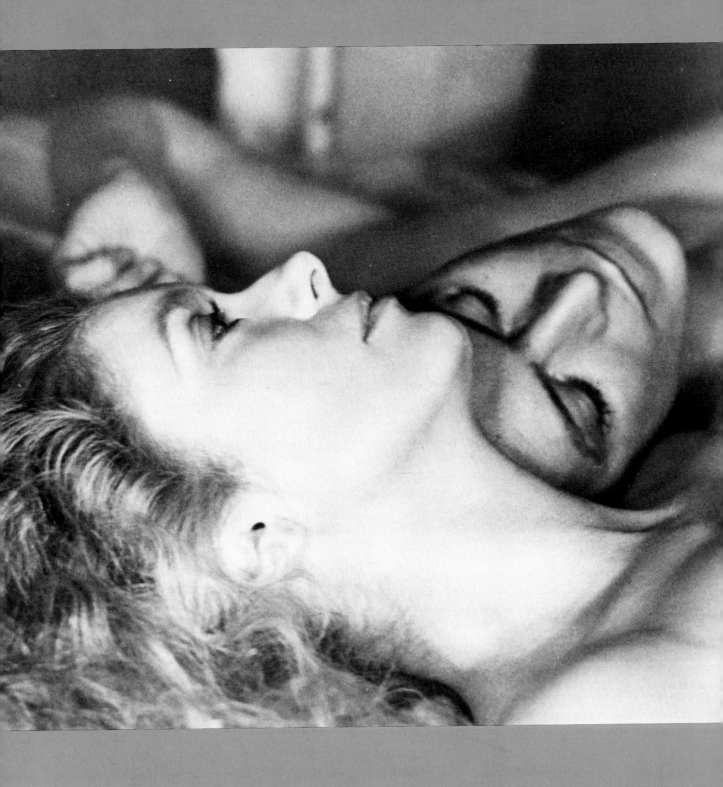

The Hunger
(1983)

Directed by Tony Scott. Produced by Richard A. Shepherd. Screenplay by Ivan Davis and Michael Thomas, based on the novel by Whitley Streiber. Cinematography by Stephen Goldblatt. Edited by Pamela Power. Production Design by Howard Blake. Music by Michael Rubini and Denny Jaeger.

Catherine Deneuve (Miriam Blaylock), Susan Sarandon (Sarah Roberts), David Bowie (John), Cliff DeYoung (Tom Haver), Beth Ehlers (Alice), Dan Hedaya (Lieutenant Allegrezza).

Pallid art-rock androgyne Peter Murphy, caged and writhing, drives a dance floor packed with leather-wrapped club kids into lustful ecstasies, while John and Miriam, the most remotely beautiful couple of the night—played by professional degenerate David Bowie and icy idol Catherine Deneuve—watch through swirls of cigarette smoke and strobing shards of light. *The Hunger* gets quickly to the point: As the music throbs, Miriam and John take home a wanton pair of would-be hedonists and, in a flurry of black-stockinged thighs and passionately torn clothing, slaughter them and drink their blood.

Centuries-old vampire Miriam Blaylock and her lover prowl the streets of New York in search of kicks, and when John succumbs to the vicious aging disease that has consumed all Miriam's lovers—only Miriam herself is truly ageless, and her promise of eternal love and youth is a cruel lie—she decides to make perky gerontologist Sarah Roberts her next paramour. She seduces Sarah to the strains of Léo Delibes's *Lakmé*, a haunting duet for two women. "It sounds like a love song," Sarah says disingenuously. "Well, then, that

must be what it is," Miriam replies coolly, and the next thing you know, their rouged lips are engaged and their flesh is bared in a surprisingly long and vivid—though consummately tasteful—sex scene. The two beauties writhe and kiss with commendable abandon; for all its much-publicized eroticism, *Bram Stoker's Dracula* (Francis Ford Coppola, 1993) can't begin to compare.

Even when no one's having any, Tony Scott's *The Hunger** oozes sex. Though it was released well into the '80s, *The Hunger*'s sexual sensibility is a decade older, bound up in fashionable androgyny and self-conscious decadence. Adolescent violin prodigy Alice, who spends hours on end with the Blaylocks in their securely sealed town house (what could her parents be thinking?), could as easily be a boy as a girl, and Bowie's pale, hairless chest is as smoothly inviting as a woman's. The club couple's murder follows sexual foreplay, and Sarah recognizes Miriam's lustful intentions while she could still reject them—"Are you making a pass at me?" she asks coyly—but doesn't. It's all divinely decadent, beautifully photographed, and swooningly sensual.

The Hunger wasn't the first vampire film to bring the sexy subtext to the surface; it wasn't even the first to exploit the men's magazine appeal of lesbian vampires. But it was the first mainstream vampire movie to go straight to the erotic heart of the vampire mythos. The film's mise-en-scène is a compendium of upscale porno magazine clichés: billowing gauze curtains, steamy showers, and fetishistic finery (spandex and silk,

The most icily beautiful couple ever to stalk the night: Catherine Deneuve and David Bowie.

*The film was based on the book by Whitley Streiber, a horror novelist whose later descent into UFO wackiness is charted in his purported nonfiction work *Communion*.

Murnau's 1922 *Nosferatu* is a conspicuous exception—have failed to exploit the erotic possibilities of the vampire myth. The vampire movies made by England's Hammer Films, starting with *Horror of Dracula* (1958), put to good use the virile appeal of actor Christopher Lee, and a host of bodacious women laced into revealing costumes, made terrifyingly sensual after their encounters with Dracula. Based loosely on J. S. LeFanu's 1872 novella *Carmilla*, Hammer's *The Vampire Lovers* (1970) and *Lust for a Vampire* (1971) feature lesbian and frequently undressed vampires, and the third *Carmilla*-inspired picture, *Twins of Evil* (1971), stars well-endowed Madeleine and Mary Collinson (*Playboy*'s first twin Playmates) as lusty vampire girls. Roger Vadim's *Et mourir de plaisir* (1960), released in the United States as *Blood and Roses*, is a dreamy reworking of the *Carmilla* story, filled with erotic suggestion.

French filmmaker Jean Rollin made a series of vaguely surrealistic sex films with vampire themes, including *Le Viol du vampire* (1967), *La Vampire nue* (1970), *Le Frisson des vampires* (1970), *Requiem pour un vampire* (1971), and *Lèvres de sang* (1976), whose titles—full of nudity, rape, and bloody lips—say it all. Belgian director Harry Kumel's *Daughters of Darkness* (1971) stars Delphine Seyrig as a lesbian vampire countess who seduces a honeymooning couple in a grand, deserted resort, and *The Velvet Vampire* (1971) tells a similar story, set in the California desert. John Badham's 1979 remake of *Dracula* stars Frank Langella as a Byronic vampire, and while Francis Ford Coppola's lavish *Bram Stoker's Dracula* pays homage to *Nosferatu* in its early scenes (burying Gary Oldman under horribly unflattering makeup), it later explores the vampire's carnal appeal, particularly in the scene in which clueless Keanu Reeves is attacked/seduced by three vampire brides. And as to *Interview With the Vampire: The Vampire Chronicles* (1994), it's not as pansexually explicit as fans of the novel would have liked. But for a mainstream, big-budget spectacle, it's amazingly to the point.

leather and lace, stockings and black panties, et al.) jostle satin sheets, crimson lipstick, and fluttering doves for space, all rendered in an orgy of soft-focus camera work and diffused lighting. Unlike most vampire movies, *The Hunger* wastes no time with the mechanics of conventional horror: There are no menacing shadows, obsessed vampire hunters, or quasi-religious symbols, no bats or wolves, no old dark houses, no cleansing sunlight burning away the evil of the undead. *The Hunger* is all about sex, and its plot is a marvel of single-minded minimalism. It really is a movie in which nothing much happens, but it doesn't happen with such sumptuous sensuality that it hardly matters.

Vampire movies have always been about sex, repressed and displaced into the piercing act of blood drinking. Bela Lugosi's *Dracula* (1931), as tame and stagey as it appears today, made the Hungarian actor a sex symbol, and few vampire pictures—F. W.

David Bowie considers Ann Magnuson's lovely throat in *The Hunger*.

In the Realm of the Senses / Ai No Corrida (1976)

Written and Directed by Nagisa Oshima. Produced by Anatole Dauman. Cinematography by Hideo Ito and Kenichi Okamoto. Edited by Keichi Uraoka. Music by Minoru Miki.

Eiko Matsuda (Sada), Tatsuya Fuji (Kichi), Aio Nakajima (Toku), Maika Seri (Maid Matsuko), Taji Tonoyama (old beggar).

Following hot on the heels of the notorious European philosophical sex films *Last Tango in Paris* (1973) and *The Night Porter* (1974), Japanese director Nagisa Oshima's *In the Realm of the Senses* proved conclusively that there were still boundaries to be tested, taboos to be shattered. *In the Realm of the Senses* went far beyond *Last Tango* and *Night Porter* in its depiction of sexual acts and organs.

Oshima was inspired by a 1936 murder case. A geisha named Sada was arrested after she was found wandering the streets of Tokyo, the severed genitals of her lover in her hands. As the story goes, she was briefly locked up and then released; she later organized a theatrical troupe and toured Japan, performing the story of her great love. After World War II, she became a prostitute and disappeared from public view. Her story, Oshima told the press, was famous in Japan; she was a pop-culture heroine.

In Oshima's film, Abe Sada is a young prostitute in an upscale brothel. Kichi is her client, an older man and a respectable merchant. They begin a relationship that quickly exceeds the boundaries of the professional and becomes an obsessive affair. They have sex morning, noon, and night, in every possible position. Kichi eats sushi dipped in Sada's vagina, and eventually she asks him to urinate inside her rather than leave their

bed and use a toilet. The maids complain they don't dare clean their room and that it smells funny; even the other prostitutes call the couple perverts.

Their lovemaking grows rougher and more intense; they experiment with bondage and other exotic practices. A sense of frenzy dominates their lovemaking. They retreat entirely from the outside world, rejecting everything about it. They have sex in front of others and refuse to bathe. Even in a house dedicated to sex, they're distracted and unable to explore their sexuality to its fullest, so Kichi and Sada flee. During sex, he encourages her to choke him with a red chiffon scarf at the height of orgasm, and she strangles him. In a strange, disconnected state, Sada cuts off Kichi's penis; a voice-over informs us that she roamed the streets of Tokyo for four days with it before being arrested.

In the Realm of the Senses is extremely explicit, if not titillating, showing erect members and frequent acts of intercourse. It was far too candid for Oshima's homeland—where dirty movies are still shown with the genital areas optically obscured—so he joined forces with French producer Anatole Daumann, whose credits include Alain Resnais's *Hiroshima, Mon Amour* (1959) and *Last Year at Marienbad* (1961), as well as Jean-Luc Godard's *Masculine-Feminine* (1966). *In the Realm of the Senses* was shot in Japan but processed in France, and was an immediate *succès de scandale*: It was shown in Japan with the customary blurs, and Japanese tourists hot to see the full version crowded charter flights to Paris.

In the Realm of the Senses was selected to be shown during the prestigious New York Film Festival and

Explicit and declared obscene by U.S. Customs authorities: *In the Realm of the Senses.*

entered the United States through Los Angeles, but U.S. Customs ordered the film seized as obscene right before its Film Festival premiere. The showings were canceled, Daumann refused to turn over the print, and controversy reigned in the press. A month later, a federal judge barred the Customs service from interfering with distribution and exhibition of the film, which went on to do boffo art-house business. *In the Realm of the Senses* was also seized as pornographic in Belgium, and Oshima found himself accused of obscenity in Japan when he published a book version of the film. He was eventually found innocent. In 1978 he made *Empire of Passion* (the French title of *In the Realm of the Senses* was *L'Empire des sens*), about a woman who plots with her lover to murder her husband. Exquisitely photographed and featuring several scenes of passionate lovemaking, it was nowhere near as graphic as the earlier film.

In the Realm of the Senses is also the obvious precursor of Ryu Murakami's *Tokyo Decadence.* A novelist turned filmmaker, Murakami tells the story of Ai (Miho Nikaido), a prostitute at an upscale agency specializing in exotica. Plain and slightly awkward in street clothes, like her demure pink suit and loose white dress, Ai is transformed when she gets into her bondage gear. Hair slicked back, mouth painted red, she's a vision in stockings, high heels, corset, and a garter belt. Though she seems strangely remote, she's transfigured by the signs of kinky sex. Ai meets a variety of perverts: the businessman who makes her crawl on the floor, the man who wants to pretend to murder then rape her in front of the image of Mt. Fuji, the masochist whose Mistress Saki makes him drink Ai's urine, and a party of deviants so scary that Ai gets one glimpse of what they're doing and flees.

The S&M goings on are pictured straightforwardly, neither romanticized nor made conspicuously grotesque, with the exception of the encounter Ai and another girl have with a drugged-up client who wants to be choked during sex—when they think they've killed him, things take a nasty turn. Murakami's point is clear: Beneath the ordered façade Japan presents to the world, there's a shocking underbelly of sexual perversion. Mistress Saki claims that her clients, rich businessmen, want to be humiliated because though Japan has wealth, it's wealth without pride. True enough, perhaps, but the appeal of *Tokyo Decadence* lies in its glossy depiction of sadomasochism, not its vague dissertation on national psychology.

Prostitute Sada (Eiko Matsuda), a "pop culture heroine" in Japan, and her doomed lover Kichi (Tatsuya Fuji).

Love leads to murder and castration.

Working Girls

Somerset Maugham's *Rain*, about the notorious Miss Sadie Thompson and the missionary man she corrupts, has been a rich source of inspiration to Hollywood. It became *Sadie Thompson* (1928), *Rain* (1932), *Dirty Gertie From Harlem U.S.A.* (1946) with an all-black cast, and *Miss Sadie Thompson* (1953), a musical. The shady ladies were, respectively, Gloria Swanson, Joan Crawford, Gertie LaRue, and Rita Hayworth. There's been no remake since, but prostitutes are a staple of movie fantasies. Movies charting the harlot's progress include:

Susan Lenox: Her Fall and Rise (1931), with the great Garbo as a cooch dancer in a carnival (a whore by another name); later she was a literary prostitute in *Anna Christie*, made in simultaneous U.S. and German versions—the German was somewhat more frank.

Waterloo Bridge (1940), in which dancer Vivien Leigh takes to the streets when she hears her fiancé is dead; the less well known 1931 version starred Mae Clark, and it was remade in 1956 with Leslie Caron.

Paisan (1946), an episodic Roberto Rossellini picture, including a segment in which whore Maria Michi picks up a drunken GI, who tells her about the pure girl he met during the war and for whom he's going to search. He doesn't recognize her and doesn't make the rendezvous her older and wiser self arranges.

Forever Amber (1947), based on the notorious popular novel about the adventures (mostly sexual) of an imaginary mistress of Charles II; the Legion of Decency campaigned vigorously against production of the film, and it made it to the screen greatly bowdlerized.

Never on Sunday (1959), the archetypal "whore with a heart of gold" picture, starring Melina Mercouri as a prostitute with charmingly pious standards.

The World of Suzie Wong (1960), a classic exploration of the lure of the exotic East, in the comely form of prostitute Nancy Kwan. *Butterfield 8*, made the same year, featured all-American Elizabeth Taylor as a high-priced call girl who pretends she isn't; she scrawls "No Sale" on men's mirrors when they offer her cash.

Breakfast at Tiffany's (1961), which skitters nervously around the obvious: Audrey Hepburn's charming Holly Golightly is a happy hooker, and the man she loves (George Peppard) is kept by an older woman. In the book, more plausibly, he's kept by an older *man*.

Walk on the Wild Side (1962) stars Capucine as a prostitute in lesbian Barbara Stanwyck's bordello; naturally, it's in naughty New Orleans.

Irma La Douce (1963), the first Hollywood film set in a brothel (and a musical comedy at that), stars saucy Shirley MacLaine as a good-natured bad girl. It paved the way for the bigger and glitzier *Best Little Whorehouse in Texas* (1982).

Midnight Cowboy (1969) tries to be daring but founders as Jon Voight's cowboy hustler protests (too much) that he does only girls. Richard Gere holds the same line in *American Gigolo* (1980), as does Billy Baldwin in *Three of Hearts* (1991).

Klute (1971) won Jane Fonda an Oscar for her portrayal of neurotic, liberated hooker Bree Daniels.

Pretty Baby (1978) breaks the age barrier with barely adolescent Brooke Shields as a whore's daughter about to take up the life herself in a New Orleans brothel filled with pretty light and prettier dresses.

Pretty Woman (1989) showcases Julia Roberts as a fledgling L.A. whore who finds her prince in Richard Gere, and it's a Disney production . . . no wonder she never actually has any johns.

Frankenhooker (1990) is the story of a bereaved mad scientist who tries to reassemble his late girlfriend from parts of Times Square whores. Never have the words "Want a date?" sounded so authentically nasty.

My Own Private Idaho (1993) is the film in which, *finally*, two hustlers—River Phoenix and Keanu Reeves—turn tricks with gay men.

Milk Money (1994) features baby-voiced Melanie Griffith as a sweet whore happy to take off her clothes for a bunch of curious adolescents to romance one boy's shy dad.

Last Tango in Paris (1973)

Directed by Bernardo Bertolucci. Produced by Alberto Grimaldi. Screenplay by Bertolucci and Franco Arcalli. Cinematography by Vittorio Storaro. Edited by Arcalli. Production Design by Ferdinando Scarfiotti. Music by Oliver Nelson.

Marlon Brando (Paul), Maria Schneider (Jeanne), Jean-Pierre Léaud (Tom), Darling Legitimus (concierge), Gitt Magrini (Jeanne's mother).

There's no denying that there's lots of sex in Bernardo Bertolucci's *Last Tango in Paris*, but for a sexy movie it can be a real bucket of cold water. The story of an affair between Jeanne, a hip young Parisienne, and Paul, a disillusioned, middle-aged American whose wife has just committed suicide, *Last Tango* is another entry in the venerable European tradition of the philosophical sex movie, in which viewers must endure extensive meditations on wide-ranging topics in order to reap the rewards: artily photographed naked writhing.

Last Tango's lovers meet accidentally and agree to rendezvous in a sparsely furnished apartment, where they abandon their identities and forget their real lives for the pleasures of uninhibited sex. It's easy to see why this arrangement appeals to Paul: He's in emotional turmoil because of his wife's suicide and uncomfortable with the evidence of his own aging. Once an actor and athlete, he's grown soft and vulnerable; sex with Jeanne allows him to hide from his own failings. She's another matter; voluptuous, independent, and sexually confident, she's dating a handsome and ardent filmmaker (he's pretentious, but that's not a liability in a Frenchman) and could easily find a more attractive and less difficult lover. Paul apparently fills

some fashionably existential void in her life, but you wouldn't know it except that virtually all European art movies of the '60s and '70s are about existential unhappiness. It all ends badly—she kills him and plans to tell the police he was a madman who followed her in off the street and tried to rape her—but before it does, Brando and Schneider couple frequently and vigorously. At least one of their sex scenes has entered into broad cultural currency: Even people who haven't seen the movie know about the scene that begins with Brando's commanding, "Get the butter . . ."

The production was surrounded by rumor and innuendo, as Bertolucci encouraged his stars to improvise dialogue (including Brando's famous and heavily autobiographical recollection of his childhood) and make the action ever more explicit. The process had a slightly incestuous edge—Schneider was the illegitimate daughter of French stage actor Daniel Gélin (one of the stars of *La Ronde*), with whom Brando had shared a Paris apartment in 1949—and Brando and Bertolucci were caught up in a bitter struggle of wills. Brando later took to deriding the director, saying he never knew what the film was supposed to be about, and that Bertolucci claimed it was about his own penis. Brando never appears frontally nude, though Schneider does; Brando's story is that on the day he was supposed to be photographed naked, "it was such a cold day that my penis shrank to the size of a peanut. It simply withered. . . . I simply couldn't play the scene that way, so [the scene] was cut." Other recollections suggest that Brando, rapidly entering corpulent middle age, wanted to cover up as much of his flesh as possible. In any case, Schneider—a '70s icon of frizzy hair

Marlon Brando set a precedent with *Last Tango in Paris*, but drew the line at exposing his shortcomings.

and slutty clothes—delivers the bulk of the film's famous nudity.

There's also no getting around the fact that *Last Tango* is a landmark in the history of sexually explicit films: For an American actor of Marlon Brando's caliber—nothing short of legendary—to appear naked; simulate sex in a variety of positions and locales; talk at length, in detail, and in the frankest possible language about sexual acts; *and* expect the end result to be taken seriously was a first. Not everyone was taken with the result, of course, but some of the naysayers emerged from surprising quarters. Veteran exploitation producer-director David Friedman, whose exploits included making grind-house gold out of a documentary double bill of bloody African tribal rituals and concentration-camp footage (*Karamoja* and *Halfway to Hell*), didn't much care for the challenge to traditional distinctions between mainstream and trashy filmmaking. "The idea of Brando, the Academy Award winner, in there putting butter up some broad's ass and jumping her and you see his ass twittering as he's on top of her, it's hard to compete with that," he complained. Other viewers were just offended and

failed to see the art in all the fornicating.

Last Tango in Paris rode into the United States on a tsunami of prerelease publicity and was the closing-night feature at the prestigious New York Film Festival. It was in trouble with the Italian censors, and U.S. distributor United Artists cannily appealed to critics to support the film, claiming that only the press stood between Bertolucci's masterpiece and mutilation by prudes. The film was seized shortly after its initial release in Italy and banned two years later. It was theatrically rereleased in 1986 after years of court wrangling, and did solid business. In the United States, *Last Tango* was initially rated X. It was trimmed for an R in 1975—the R-rated version was never shown, and the X version stayed in circulation—then resubmitted in a revised version in 1981; it received an R and was shown on cable television. Critics responded with an outpouring of praise, led by *The New Yorker*'s trendsetting Pauline Kael.* She declared *Last Tango* as impor-

---

*Ever-sour critic John Simon was one of the few dissenters, though his criticisms were undermined by their nastily personal tone, evident in such remarks as, "Maria Schneider's Jeanne is a buxom guttersnipe, with the face of a perverted cow and the acting ability of a petulant ox."

tant as Stravinsky's *Rite of Spring*, which changed the history of modern music but shocked and offended contemporary audiences. "This must be the most powerful erotic movie ever made," she wrote, "the most liberating movie ever ... a movie people will be arguing about, I think, for as long as there are movies." Distributor United Artists, recognizing the kind of publicity money can't buy, took some of the cash it saved and reprinted Kael's article whole as a two-page Sunday *New York Times* ad.

Kael was right and wrong. She's right about the arguing—people are still debating *Last Tango*'s merits. She's wrong about the eroticism; *Last Tango* is a movie about sex, but it's not an especially sexy movie.

Euro-waif Maria Schneider.

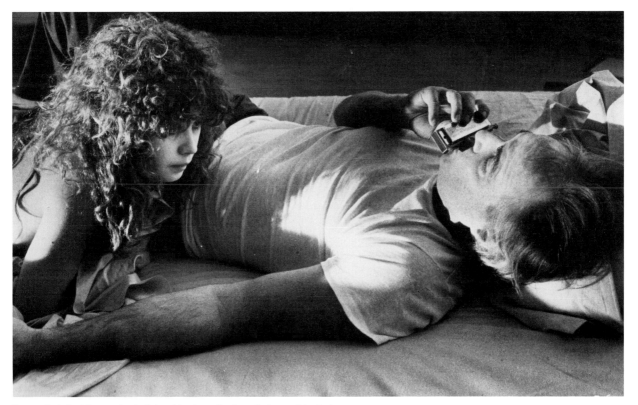

Post-coital double standard: Schneider is nude, Brando keeps his clothes on.

Bo Derek: Created by husband John Derek—who stage-managed the careers of previous wives Ursula Andress and Linda Evans—Bo's descent into the ranks of "where are they now?" was as swift as her rise. She summed up the fantasies of a decade with *10* (1979), but her later films, from *Tarzan the Ape Man* (1981) and *Bolero* (1984) to the pathetic *Ghosts Can't Do It* (1990), all flopped.

Faye Dunaway: Perhaps the last of the old-fashioned divas, Dunaway rocketed to stardom with the trendsetting *Bonnie and Clyde* (1967) and followed up with *The Thomas Crown Affair* (1968), *Chinatown* (1974), *Network* (1976), and *The Eyes of Laura Mars* (1978). By the '90s, her icy looks had frozen into an impassive mask that undermined her sex appeal.

Pam Grier: Statuesque and tough, Grier rode the blaxploitation wave to cult stardom, playing the title roles in *Black Mama, White Mama* (1972), *Coffy* (1973), *Foxy Brown* (1974), and *Friday Foster* (1975) and starring in many other films. She was hot, cool, and funky, a one-woman campaign for racial harmony: Everyone wanted to jump her bones.

Ali MacGraw: Cool and self-possessed, MacGraw was another girl of the moment, the embodiment of '70s chic. In both *Goodbye, Columbus* (1969) and *Love Story* (1970), she was the babe everyone wanted. She made few films after *The Getaway* (1972), but for those brief years her star burned brightly.

Steve McQueen: McQueen was the guy every man wanted to be and every woman wanted to tame. He became a star in the '60s with films like *Love With the Proper Stranger* (1963) and *Bullitt* and *The Thomas Crown Affair* (both 1968), but the '70s added a gritty edge to his screen image, and he shone in *The Getaway* (1970), *Junior Bonner* (1971), and *Papillon* (1973).

Ryan O'Neal: Pretty-boy Ryan O'Neal leapt from TV's *Peyton Place* to stardom with *Love Story* (1970) and charmed his way through a series of light romances, including *What's Up, Doc?* (1973), *Paper Moon* (1975), and *Nickelodeon* (1976).

Charlotte Rampling: Delicate and elusive, Rampling specialized in creepy eroticism. *The Night Porter* (1974) is the best known of her films, but she was equally alluring in Luchino Visconti's *The Damned* (1969) and continued to court censure in films like Nagisa Oshima's *Max, Mon Amour* (1986), in which her lover is a chimpanzee.

Robert Redford: Bland and blond, Redford was the impossibly perfect boy next door, a dream lover with no dark secrets. *Barefoot in the Park* (1967) and *Butch Cassidy and the Sundance Kid* (1969) launched him as a sex symbol; he followed up with *The Sting*, *The Way We Were* (both 1973) and *The Great Gatsby* (1974) and is still playing sexy roles in such films as *Havana* (1990) and *Indecent Proposal* (1993).

Burt Reynolds: The man who posed naked for *Cosmopolitan* magazine specialized in good ol' boys with a secret sensitive streak. He always got the girl, and if his films were never *about* sex, they seldom lacked it.

John Travolta: Travolta parlayed TV sitcom stardom in *Welcome Back, Kotter* into blue-collar-icon status with *Saturday Night Fever* (1977), one of the definitive movies of the decade. His star dimmed quickly, though he continued to work, and eventually reemerged bigtime in *Pulp Fiction* (1994).

Lorna
(1964)

Produced, directed, photographed, and edited by Russ Meyer. Screenplay by James Griffith, based on a story by Meyer. Music coordinated by Griffith and Hal Hopper.

Lorna Maitland (Lorna), Mark Bradley (fugitive), James Rucker (James), Hal Hopper (Luther), James Griffith (prophet).

Sexploitation legend Russ Meyer, mocked by the mainstream press as "King Leer," promises his autobiography in the form of a film called *The Breast of Russ Meyer*. And that's what his films bring to mind, from *Faster Pussycat! Kill! Kill!* (1966) to the notorious *Beyond the Valley of the Dolls* (1970) to *Supervixens* (1975): glorious, oversized, gravity-defying breasts, the kind that make you want to drop to your knees in wonder. *Lorna* isn't Meyer's most famous film, but it's one of the best, a heady mix of sharply photographed sex and violence laced with an undercurrent of psychotic evangelical disapproval.

Beautiful, sex-starved Lorna and her handsome, half-witted husband, James, live in a backwoods shack. He loves her but doesn't appreciate her sexual needs. She doesn't know how to tell him what she wants. The local half-crazed preacher man predicts there will be trouble, and there is. One day, while her husband's at work in the salt mines, Lorna goes for a walk in the woods and is raped by an escaped convict. Far from being traumatized, Lorna is delighted; she takes him back to the house and the two make love until her husband returns home. Horrified, he attacks the convict, and in the melee both Lorna and her lover are killed.

California-born Meyer got into the army as a cameraman on the strength of his amateur work—some of

his World War II documentary footage wound up in 1970's *Patton*—but as a civilian failed to get work in Hollywood. He turned to shooting pin-ups and girlie photos to pay the rent. Meyer's interests converged with *The Immoral Mr. Teas*, released in 1959. Shot in four days, the soft-core *Teas* told the silly story of man plagued by X-ray vision; its appeal lay in a bevy of naked beauties parading their assets. With *Teas*, Meyer single-handedly gave birth to the nudie-cutie film. Nudie-cuties weren't the first independent movies to exploit nudity. That honor belongs to the achingly *healthful* nudist camp pictures that showed naked people of all shapes and sizes (not all appealing) playing volleyball, picnicking, soaking up the good clean sun, and extolling the virtues of naturism at tediously well-intentioned length. Meyer offered endlessly attractive, glossily photographed female flesh woven into a comic narrative, and audiences flocked.

Meyer's films fall into three periods—nudie-cuties, 1959–63; nudie-roughies, 1964–69; and camp lampoons, 1970–79—but all have one thing in common: They're never subtle. Cleavage yawns like the Grand Canyon, lips glisten like overripe fruit, flesh ripples, thighs tremble, bodies thrash together like fish flailing in a net. No soft-focus shots of fingers trailing across skin for Meyer: His philosophy of sex scenes is to get in there and pound away until something gives. Meyer's men are mostly hunky and stupid. His women are insatiable sex machines, devouring black holes of libidinous desire; Meyer's stars include some of the most awesomely full-figured girls of all time: Uschi Digart, Candy Samples, Shari Eubanks, Kitten Natividad, Haji, Erica Gavin, Lorna Maitland, Raven De

La Croix, Edy Williams, and, of course, Tura Satana.

With *Lorna*, Meyer abandoned the innocent voyeurism of the nudie-cuties for the nastier blend of rough-and-tumble sex laced with violence that characterized *Motorpsycho* (1965), *Faster Pussycat! Kill! Kill!*

thing as a perfect motion picture, *Beyond the Valley of the Dolls* is it. In a world of Hollywood glitz it combines elements of sexploitation with experimental camera work, and narration worthy of the best educational film with the bouncy good nature of a Beach Party movie.

Lorna Maitland, star of *Lorna*, in a carefully doctored advertising montage. Note the strategically placed branches.

(1966), and *Finders Keepers, Lovers Weepers* (1968). *Lorna* is what a generation of sweaty-palmed (and bitterly disappointed) adolescents thought they'd find between the covers of Erskine Caldwell's *Tobacco Road*: lots of hot and raunchy redneck humping. *Mudhoney* (1965) and *Common Law Cabin* (1967) offer more of the same. *Vixen* (1968) takes the formula to rural Canada and features a luscious nymphomaniac whose partners range from a Mountie to her own brother.

Meyer's later films are disappointing, except on the mammary front. *Beyond the Valley of the Dolls* was his bid for respectability, with a screenplay by film critic Roger Ebert and the support of 20th Century–Fox. The story of an all-girl rock band, it purports to be a groovy satire of Hollywood mores, but its entertainment value is purely derisive. There's a so-bad-it's-good argument that goes like this: "If there is such a

It has sex and violence, rock 'n' roll, drugs, Nazis, hermaphrodites, lesbians, cripples, blacks, pathos, bathos, and a woman giving head to a .45 automatic."* But that makes it sound better than it is, and it's still better than what came next. Meyer's horribly serious adaptation of Irving Wallace's anticensorship novel *The Seven Minutes* (1971) was a disaster, and he retreated to bigger, more ridiculous rehashings of his earlier work: *Blacksnake* (1972), an attempt to cash in on blaxploitation movies; *Supervixens* (1975), *Up!* (1976), and *Beneath the Valley of the Ultravixens* (1979). The world of hardcore pornography and sleek direct-to-video erotic thrillers and raunchy sex comedies has passed Meyer by, and perhaps it's best that he never make another film.

*Jim Morton, "Russ Meyer Filmography," *Incredibly Strange Films* (San Francisco: Re/Search, 1986), p. 87.

It was once fashionable to laud Meyer as an atavistic auteur, but except as a cinematographer (his films became progressively more technically accomplished) he never developed beyond his unsophisticated beginnings. Other adult filmmakers of the '60s—including Joe Sarno (*Sin, You Sinners!*, *Moonlighting Wives*, *Warm Nights and Hot Pleasures*, *Flesh and Lace*), Doris Wishman (*Nude on the Moon*, *Bad Girls Go to Hell*), and A. C. Stephens, the psuedonym of Stephen C. Apostoloff, who directed *Suburban Confidential!*, *Motel Confidential*, *Office Love-In*, *College Girl (Confidential)*, and *The Divorcee*—have developed underground cult followings and critical reputations. But Meyer's only real competition in the classy smut racket is gentleman pornographer Radley Metzger.

Metzger began his career as an editor, then segued into distributing "daring" foreign films—including *Mademoiselle Striptease* (1956) with Brigitte Bardot—sometimes adding new footage to make them even spicier. Metzger began making

his own soft-core adult films in 1963 with *The Dirty Girls*, and *The Alley Cats* (1966), *Carmen, Baby* (1967), *Therese and Isabelle*, and *Camille 2000* (both 1969) followed. Like Meyer, Metzger had an eye for composition and lighting. Unlike Meyer, he had some gift for directing actors and took himself very seriously. Metzger was born in the Bronx but shot most of his films in Europe. Their mix of glossy art direction, discreet but vivid sex scenes, and philosophy in the boudoir have more in common with films like *Emmanuelle* than with Meyer's raunchy tit fests.

Metzger continued making movies throughout the '70s, including *The Lickerish Quartet* (1970), *Score* and *The Punishment of Anne* (both 1973), and *Naked Came the Stranger* (1974), and worked occasionally in

the '80s; he made *The Princess and the Call Girl* for the Playboy Channel in 1984. Metzger also made hardcore pornographic films under the pseudonym Henry Paris; they include *The Private Afternoons of Pamela Mann* (1975), *The Opening of Misty Beethoven* (1976), and *Barbara Broadcast* (1977), which feature all-star casts, including Jamie Gillis, Marc Stevens, Georgina Spelvin, Gloria Leonard, and Annette Haven, and have all been lauded as unusually artful examples of pornographic filmmaking. Like Meyer's, Metzger's one attempt at a mainstream film, a remake of the classic old dark house thriller *The Cat and the Canary* (1978), failed to overshadow his reputation as a smutty filmmaker.

(Right) Gender-bending hijinks in *Beyond the Valley of the Dolls* (1970), Russ Meyer's bid for the big time.

(Opposite) Bodacious Meyer babes surround the master.

The Fate Worse Than Death

Movies dealing realistically with rape are rare, wrenching, and the best thing to a lock come Oscar time: Jane Wyman, Sophia Loren, and Jodie Foster were just about guaranteed Best Actress for, respectively, *Johnny Belinda* (1948), *Two Women* (1960), and *The Accused* (1988) from the get-go. But movie rape is most often fantasy rape, the sleazy threat of the fate worse than death whose legacy stretches back to films like *Traffic in Souls* (1913), which traded on the lurid thrill of white slavery. Southern prude D. W. Griffith regularly imperiled virginal Lillian Gish, and without the threat of defilement there'd be no Tennessee Williams as we know him: In particular, the erotically charged *Baby Doll* (1956) and *A Streetcar Named Desire* (1951) would deflate entirely. Vivien Leigh swoons when brutal Clark Gable ravishes her in *Gone With the Wind* (1939), lusty half-breed Jennifer Jones really wants Gregory Peck (she only says she doesn't) in *Duel in the Sun* (1946), and Patricia Neal secretly throbs with desire for cruel Gary Cooper in *The Fountainhead* (1949), whose jackhammer symbolism is legendary.

Anatomy of a Murder* (1959) titillated audiences with torn panties; the original *Cape Fear* (1962) is propelled by the threat of ravishment, with Barrie

Chase, Polly Bergen, and little Lori Martin all menaced by Robert Mitchum; and the relentlessly salacious *The Chapman Report* (1962) reaches its low point when Claire Bloom taunts Corey Allen and his card-playing buddies into gang raping her. *Goldfinger*'s (1964) hottest scene involves real man Sean Connery wrestling dyke Honor Blackman to the floor and showing her what she's missing, and Adrienne Corri's assault by Malcolm McDowell and his "droogs" in *A Clockwork Orange* (1971) is played for maximum stimulation. Town slut Susan George gets what she wants and deserves in *Straw Dogs* (1971) from the local toughs, while the sleazy *Lipstick* (1976) has it both ways, as Margaux and Mariel Hemingway are victimized by handsome Chris Sarandon: eroticized attack plus satisfying vengeance. *Dressed to Kill* (1980) justifies Angie Dickenson's steamy shower assault by showing that it's just her fantasy, the one that gets her through boring sex with her husband.

Contemporary movies are far less cavalier about sexual assault, so count on the ever-provocative Pedro Almodóvar's *Kika* (1994) to raise a critical ruckus with its prolonged, comic rape scene involving a tireless, psychotic porn star and a brainless and free-with-her-favors bimbette.

The Lover
(1992)

Directed by Jean-Jacques Annaud. Produced by Claude Berri and Paul Rassam. Screenplay by Gérard Brach, based on the novel by Marguerite Duras. Cinematography by Robert Fraisse. Edited by Noelle Boisson. Production Design by Than At Hoang. Music by Gabriel Yared.

Jane March (the young girl), Tony Leung (the Chinese lover), Melvil Poupaud (Paul), Arvaud Giovaninetti (Pierre), Lisa Faulkner (Helene Lagonelle), Ann Schaufuss (Anne-Marie Streeter), Frederique Meininger (the girl's mother), Xiem Mang (the lover's father).

Widely dismissed as a literary Zalman King movie, an even artier dirty movie than Philip Kaufman's *Henry & June, The Lover* is a slippery film. It's based on the novel by Marguerite Duras, a longtime fixture on the French literary scene and screenwriter of, among others, *Hiroshima, Mon Amour* (1959), who's known for her highly stylized and increasingly remote novels exploring the many faces of love. Directed by Jean-Jacques Annaud, who also filmed Umberto Eco's semiotic medieval mystery novel *The Name of the Rose* (1986), it looks like another dispatch from *Emmanuelle* country with a very politically incorrect protagonist, an underage girl whose dewy flesh cries out to be despoiled in defiance of all that's proper. But it's actually a better film than it's given credit for and maintains much of the uneasy clarity of Duras's writing in the form of a voice-over by French actress Jeanne Moreau. The novel's language, its knowing, direct tone, is preserved in Moreau's whisky-and-cigarettes voice and almost succeeds in charging the exotically pretty images with the bitter complexity it takes to lift it out of the realm of pretentious soft-

The lovers.

core. And there's plenty of sex, graphically and seductively photographed.

Set in 1932 (though you would know only from the music playing in a dance hall; the mise-en-scène is conspicuously timeless) in what was then French Indochina, *The Lover* is the story of the amorous awakening of the precocious fifteen-and-and-a-half-year-old* daughter of French parents. Raised by her mother and two brothers, Pierre—an opium addict—and Paul, in grinding rural poverty, she attends a prestigious girl's school in Saigon and only occasionally visits her family. Returning from one such trip, she boards the ferry that is the first leg of her long journey back to school. Her pigtails, man's fedora, gray silk shift, and cabaret shoes studded with little sparkles are all infinitely alluring, and as a white girl she's already an arresting sight on a ferry crowded with Asian faces. She attracts the attention of a handsome, wealthy young Chinese man, who strikes up a conversation and then offers to drive her back to school.

They quickly begin an affair that scandalizes everyone: her schoolmates, her teachers, and her family, none of whom can believe that a white girl would willingly sleep with a Chinese man, except perhaps for the money. They meet in his bachelor room in the seedy part of Saigon; he gives her money for her family, who accept it even as they treat him with disrespect and revile her as a whore. It all ends sadly, and soon: At his father's behest, the lover becomes engaged to marry a Chinese girl, and she returns to

---

*When it was released in the U.S., *The Lover*'s voice-over was subtly but significantly altered. Her age, stated in the European version, goes unmentioned in the U.S. version, so viewers can choose to think she's not jail bait.

France, already wise beyond her years.

The look of *The Lover* is pure soft-core pornography: the untouched boarding-school girls lying together in bed, gossiping and caressing, dancing together in their white chemises in the broad halls. The girl and her lover in their room, their limbs intertwined in light that seeps through the bamboo curtains. The dripping jungle and the fevered dance hall. The film is all gauze and matchstick blinds, blue-lit dormitories hung with clean white sheets, colorful lanterns and the teeming, exotic streets. The girl—who, like her lover, has no name—is a wild fantasy of a nymphet, a virgin who doesn't want her lover to love her, who forges ahead and undresses him when he has qualms, who begs to be treated casually, like the many mistresses she's convinced he has. Their lovemaking is bathed in a golden glow; their bodies are lean and hairless, their skin smooth and silken. But Duras hides thorns in her bouquet of unfettered desire, and Annaud—with whom she had such a falling-out during production that she refused to work any further on the film—preserves them. The girl's casual ignorance, her youthful callousness, and her self-confident superiority, born of nothing but her white skin, are very much in evidence. Her complicated family relationships, whose crux is the fact that her mother wildly favors the brutal, dissolute

Pierre over her younger children, are carefully explored, and the film's ending is surprisingly poignant: On the ship back to France, the girl hears a pianist playing Chopin, and the music sets free the repressed thought that perhaps she did love her paramour, and that now he's gone forever.

Duras was born in Vietnam; her brothers were named Pierre and Paulo. *The Lover* was published in 1984, when she was seventy, and she made no bones about its autobiographical content. The novel was well reviewed, praised as Duras's best work in years, more direct and accessible than her other recent books, which had been marked by a chilling remoteness. *The Lover* was praised for its attention to detail, sifted sharply out of the haze of memory. Until she quarreled with Annaud, Duras was the screenwriter of *The Lover*; she was replaced by Gérard Brach and set about perversely undermining the film of her book. She published *The North Chinese Lover*, a new novel about the relationship between a young French girl and an older Chinese man (including such revelations as the girl's incestuous relationship with her younger brother), just before Annaud's *The Lover* was released. The new novel even contained camera angles and soundtrack directions; Duras claimed it was more true than Annaud's film of her previous book. They had parted ways, she said, because he was telling a story she didn't recognize, a bit of literary obfuscation of a very French sort.

The Lover is only the most recent in a long line of films exploiting the erotic appeal of young girls, from D. W. Griffith's simpering innocents, most famously Lillian Gish (twenty-three passing easily for twelve) in *Broken Blossoms* (1919), to Jodie Foster's Iris, the barely adolescent streetwalker of *Taxi Driver* (1976) and Pia Zadora's ripe, incestuously alluring Kady (after whom she named her real-life daughter) in *Butterfly* (1981). Among the earliest is the German *Mädchen in Uniform* (1931), purportedly an anti-authoritarian message pic-

Hot to trot: March and friend indulge a schoolgirl crush.

ture but cherished for its claustrophobic atmosphere of adolescent lesbianism. *Young Aphrodites* (1966), set in Greece, 200 B.C., is a faux-primitive tale of love between nomadic shepherds and the women of a fishing village. But the film's emphasis is on the romance of a barely pubescent boy and girl, fetchingly clad in impeccably historically correct scanties. The scene in which the two youngsters learn the ways of love by watching their elders copulate in a cave has a particularly dubious tone. Festival awards notwithstanding, Nikos Koundouros' film smacks of unhealthy obsession cloaked in anthropological drag. *Bilitis* (1975), directed by swank boudoir photographer David Hamilton, cloaked its salacious intent in the gauzily photographed story of a young girl's first romance. No one was fooled.

The Blue Lagoon (1949), based on the teasing Victorian novel about shipwrecked cousins growing to adolescence and sexual maturity on a deserted island, features Donald Houston and Jean Simmons as the young lovers. But it took the sumptuously photographed 1980 remake, starring Brooke Shields and Christopher Atkins, to really put the cards on the table: it's a feature-length child sex fantasy whose gloss only makes matters worse.

Shields's underage allure is, however, at its most potent in Louis Malle's *Pretty Baby* (1978), in which she plays the twelve-year-old daughter of a New Orleans prostitute, "saved" from following in her mother's footsteps by marriage to photographer Keith Carradine. Sumptuous and titillating, *Pretty Baby* is terribly tasteful in the worst possible sense of the term. Ten years later, Catherine Breillat's *36 Fillette* (it's a junior dress size) ran into the same dilemma: It may be a sensitive study of a fourteen-year-old's sexual awakening, but its principal appeal is to middle-aged heavy breathers who'd give anything to play teacher to such a nubile pupil.

But the most respected child lust movie of them all is, of course, Stanley Kubrick's *Lolita* (1962), based

101

on the novel by Vladimir Nabokov. The film was a scandal before it was ever made, though in the end much criticism was averted by raising the nymphette's age from twelve to fourteen and casting lush Sue Lyon, who looked even older. Kubrick's *Lolita*, which Nabokov scripted, is a long black joke in which James Mason's European sophisticate, Humbert Humbert, is constantly shocked by an America in which suburban couples insinuatingly describe themselves as broad-minded, sexual innuendo lies beneath the promise of cherry pie, *intellectual* means perverted, and *normal* suggests anything but. Humbert is mesmerized by Lolita as she swings her hula hoop around her hips, even though she's a gum-chewing, potato chip– and French fry–eating, soda- and malted-milk-swilling pig-in-the-making. He's undone by the combination of childish diffidence and incipient vulgarity. Though they're never seen having sex, it's clear that they are, and that she was the initiator. Still, ultimately Kubrick's *Lolita* falls flat; it's too cool to be arousing.

Naughty Nuns

High on the titillating-fantasies list is sex with nuns, which conflates a host of taboos: It's blasphemous, it's a transgression against authority, and it promises either the sweet, rare thrill of debauching a true innocent or the opportunity to expose some holy feet of clay. And, oh, those clothes! Where there's blue desire, there's a movie pandering to it, and for every perky singing nun in the cinema, there's a temptress in a scapular.

Black Narcissus (1946) is all suggestion, but what it suggests is choice. Novice nun Deborah Kerr joins a convent in the Himalayas, where the sisters are tantalized by the intoxicating influence of native life, while in Jacques Rivette's *Suzanne Simonin, La Religieuse de Denis Diderot / The Nun* (1966), a nun is driven to suicide by lesbian sex and other worldly temptations. One segment of *The Decameron* (1970), Pier Paolo Pasolini's first bawdy compendium picture, involves a gardener who seduces a whole convent full of good sisters, while in Ken Russell's *The Devils* (1971), Oliver Reed's Father Grandier is an unrepentant sensualist, frustrated Mother Superior Vanessa Redgrave's fantasies cast her as his Magdalene, and the writhing nuns aren't possessed by the devil at all: a few applications of Grandier's heavenly staff and there'd be no more vulgar displays at the convent. Unrepentant lapsed Catholic Pedro Almodóvar's *Dark Habits* (1984) involves a singer who hides out in a convent filled with debauched, druggy nuns and plays it for comedy; if Whoopi Goldberg's strangely similar *Sister Act* (1992) and *Sister Act 2* (1993) were only a little bawdier, they'd be much more fun.

Italian trash filmmakers are especially naughty nun–obsessed. Witness such shameless displays as Gianfranco Mingozzi's historical *Flavia, The Heretic* (1974), starring Florinda Bolkan and notorious for its sexual and violent excesses; Giuseppe Vari's *Sister Emanuelle* (1977), one of the Laura Gemser ersatz-*Emanuelle* series, in which she joins a convent and continues her exploration of sexual liberation; and Giulio Beruti's 1978 *Suor Omicidi / Killer Nun*, which features Anita Ekberg as a man-hating, homicidal nun whose holy sisters indulge in a range of un-nunly activities, including sex and drug taking. *Immagini di un Convento* (1979), directed by the notorious Joe d'Amato and *very* loosely based on Diderot's novel, in which nuns are possessed by a statue and indulge in an orgy of sex and violence. Spanish exploitation filmmaker Jess Franco—famous for, among other things, a virulent anticlerical inclination—made *Die Liebesbriefe einer Portugiesischen Nonne* in 1976. Based on a novel by Maria Alcoforados, it recounts the travails of an relatively innocent girl in a medieval convent full of sex-mad satanists. The novel was filmed again in 1978 by Jorge Grau.

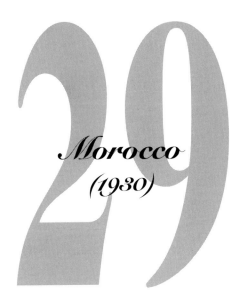

Morocco
(1930)

Directed by Josef von Sternberg. Produced by Hector Turnbull. Written by Jules Furthman, based on the novel *Amy Jolly* by Benno Vigny. Cinematography by Lee Garmes and Lucien Ballard. Edited by S. K. Winston. Art Direction by Hans Dreier. Music by Karl Hajos.

Marlene Dietrich (Amy Jolly), Gary Cooper (Tom Brown), Adolphe Menjou (La Bessière), Ulrich Haupt (Adjutant Caesar), Juliette Compton (Anna Dolores).

Morocco is a sex film without sex scenes, an erotic romance that has little to do with *amour fou* and everything to do with tingling fetishism. It was Marlene Dietrich's first American film, her follow up to the amoral *Blue Angel* (1930), in which she played untamed cabaret girl Lola-Lola, who lures a stuffy high school teacher to sexual degradation and death. Coarse and slightly plump, though undeniably alluring, Dietrich remade herself between Germany and Hollywood. With the help of svengali Josef von Sternberg—who guided her through both films—she became the sleek incarnation of sophisticated sensuality, all glossy surface and brittle gestures, flesh pared and honed to perfection. Did she really have her back teeth removed to make her cheekbones appear higher? They certainly look as though they could cut glass. Dietrich was a star, but she became something even more: an icon whose icy sexual allure is as potent today as it was in 1930. Prettier women and better actresses have faded and been forgotten; Dietrich is eternal.

In *Morocco*, Dietrich plays world-weary Amy Jolly, a casualty of love's far-flung battlefields, who's washed up in North Africa penniless and disillusioned. She takes a job as a cabaret singer and attracts the attention of two men: prosperous, middle-aged roué La Bessière and penniless Foreign Legionnaire Tom Brown. The sophisticated La Bessière promises wealth and security, Brown promises nothing at all. Naturally she takes up with the older man but gives her heart—and the key to her room—to the younger one. There are quarrels, and promises are made and broken; the Legion leaves, Amy stays behind and promises to marry La Bessière. But when the soldiers return she can't feign indifference even for the duration of her fiancé's dinner party. She spins in her chair, catches her lustrous rope of pearls on its sharp back, and watches blankly as the beads roll across the floor—her mind's eye is on her legionnaire. *Morocco* ends on the delirious image of Amy watching the Legion march once more into the desert, then impulsively flinging off her high heels and following her man. It's desperately romantic, with a bitter, world-weary edge that's chillingly sexy.

There isn't much to *Morocco* on a narrative level. The story is so thin it's barely there, and the romantic triangle too lopsided to be of much concern. What brings it all to life is sheer emotional intensity, the elusive disillusionment that colors Amy's poignant question to Tom, "Do you think you can restore my faith in men?" It's not as quotable a line as, "It took more than one man to change my name to Shanghai Lily" (*Shanghai Express*, 1932), but it's far more resonant, filled with concealed longing and all but imperceptible hope. The young Gary Cooper is as brutally attractive as Dietrich is lustrously alluring; virile and casually masculine, he's an animal in a man's skin, and they're the punctuation marks in the film's lexicon of desire.

Morocco is defiantly artificial, a dream of the exotic

East constructed of potted palms and tasseled camels, graceful arches, beaded curtains, and veiled women. It's a film about texture and surface: gauze, brick, silk, sand and tile, velvet and khaki, and satin and gleaming flesh. Dietrich, avatar of the eternal feminine, makes her most striking impression in drag, performing one of her nightclub numbers in a man's tuxedo, complete with top hat. Her appearance in black tie is startling enough: this was, remember, a time when women simply did not wear trousers. When she pauses afterward at a table of admirers and kisses one giggling woman squarely on the lips, it's a moment of amazing, thrilling transgression.

Dietrich's career was a long and successful one, but by the end of the '30s, following the increasingly expensive box-office failures of her elaborate collaborations with von Sternberg, she needed to change her image to survive. *Destry Rides Again* (1939) revitalized her career, but it changed her persona from that of a woman of infinite mystery to that of a brazen hoyden, not really as interesting a thing. The myth of Dietrich is articulated in her early American films, and it's those films that still thrill and arouse.

Dietrich's allure is pansexual, less about having sex than imagining it, and while she's actually quite lovely in her earlier films, including *Morocco*, she quickly hardened into a flawless, remote idol. It's no

Dietrich and her true love: the camera.

A thing of beauty…

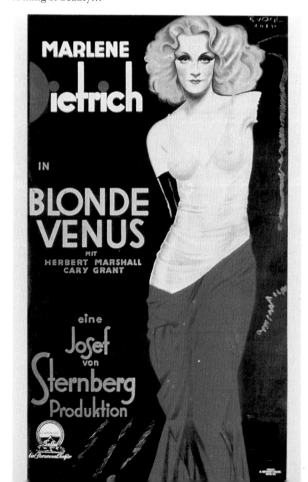

wonder that generations of transvestites modeled themselves on her image: In the films she made for von Sternberg—*The Blue Angel, Morocco, Dishonored* (1931), *Shanghai Express, Blond Venus* (1932), *The Scarlet Empress* (1934), and *The Devil Is a Woman* (1935)—she's less a woman than an incredible hallucination of one, suitable for reproduction. One can see her refracted through performances as diverse as Helmut Berger's defiant drag act in *The Damned* (1969) and Madonna's faux-expressionist *Express Yourself* (1991) video.

Lola Coca-Cola, or:
Girls Will Be Boys and Boys Will Be Girls

Oh, the gender-bending appeal of drag, the ultimate dress-up fantasy. It can go either way, of course, though most often we see men dressed up as luscious women—pictures like *Tootsie* (1982) and *Mrs. Doubtfire* (1994), in which ugly guys Dustin Hoffman and Robin Williams become even uglier women, don't count. Neither does *Switch* (1991)—the misbegotten remake of *Goodbye Charlie* (1964), in which a murdered gangster returns as Debbie Reynolds—in which Perry King plays a philandering pig who's murdered and reincarnated as Ellen Barkin. She does a fine job as a man in a woman's body but is still unarguably a woman. Drag films vary on many fronts, most importantly the level of gender confusion they're willing to abide—the more they allow, the sexier the result.

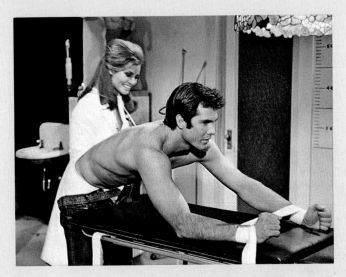

Raquel Welch as gender bender Myra Breckenridge (1970).

Guys Are Dolls

The very funny *Some Like It Hot* (1959), a remake of a 1951 German film called *Fanfaren der Liebe*, features Jack Lemmon and Tony Curtis, who never dare to look good in a dress and still make time with guys, because, after all, no one's perfect. In *The Damned* (1969), Helmut Berger's turn as a Dietrich-inspired chanteuse (who looks more like Liza Minnelli in *Cabaret*) is a sign of his decadence, while hunky Adrian Pasdar and handsome Johnny Depp simply like women's clothes in *Just Like a Woman* and *Ed Wood* (both 1994). *Last Exit to Brooklyn* (1989) offers Alexis Arquette as an unglamorous, working-class cross-dresser, while *The Adventures of Priscilla, Queen of the Desert* (1994) made a trio of female impersonators seem positively cuddly. *To Wong Foo, Thanks for Everything, Julie Newmar* (1995) is a chocolate box of drag queens, dark, white, and milk: Wesley Snipes, Patrick Swayze, and John Leguizamo. And then there's *The Crying Game* (1993), which won androgynous Jaye Davidson an Oscar nomination (occasioning frenzied speculation as to what he was going to wear) and proved to middle America that drag doesn't have to be a joke.

Dolls Are Guys

In *Sylvia Scarlett* (1935), one of the more surprising comedies of the '30s, Katharine Hepburn dresses as a quite convincing young man and has to wiggle out of being vamped by a smitten woman. *Victor/Victoria* (1982) features Julie Andrews as a nightclub singer in 1930s Paris who poses as a man in drag. Got that? It was based on a 1933 German film called *Viktor und Viktoria*, which was remade in England as *First a Girl* (1936) and again in Germany in 1957. *The Ballad of Little Jo* (1993) stars Suzy Amis as a nineteenth-century woman who passes herself off as a cowboy, while in *Salmonberries* (1994) singer k. d. lang—as a woman passing as a man—wins the heart of purportedly heterosexual Rosel Zech only after she reveals the truth. And in *Nine ½ Weeks* (1986) Kim Basinger gets duded up for a boy's night out with sadistic paramour Mickey Rourke. Then there are Linda Hunt, who plays Billy Kwan in *The Year of Living Dangerously*; Anne Carlisle, who takes the roles of both a woman and a gay man in *Liquid Sky* (what was in the air in 1983?); and perennial star Lassie, who's always been a male dog playing a bitch. Hollywood is, after all, the land of illusion.

105

The Night Porter
(1974)

Directed by Liliana Cavani. Produced by Robert Gordon Edwards. Screenplay by Liliana Cavani and Italo Moscati; story by Cavani, Barbara Alberti, and Amedeo Pagani. Cinematography by Alfio Contini. Edited by Franco Arcalli. Art Direction by Jean Marie Simon and Nedo Azzini. Music by Daniele Paris.

Dirk Bogarde (Max), Charlotte Rampling (Lucia), Philippe Leroy (Klaus, the lawyer), Ugo Cardea (Mario, the restaurateur), Gabriele Ferzetti (Dr. Hans Folger), Amadeo Amadia (Bert, the dancer), Isa Miranda (Countess Erika Stein), Geoffrey Coppleston (Kurt).

Writer-director Liliana Cavani, it's reported, claimed the seed that became *The Night Porter* was planted while she was making a documentary on Dachau in 1969. She saw a well-dressed woman lay red roses on the remains of one of the camp's buildings, which turned out to mark the spot where the Nazi the woman loved had first tortured her. Even in less nervously correct times, it took gall to spin so provocative and potentially offensive an image into a feature-length film. But Cavani forged ahead, apparently following in the footsteps of Luchino Visconti and Bernardo Bertolucci, whose *The Damned* (1969) and *The Conformist* (1971) also associated Nazi tyranny with sexual perversion. In fact, *The Night Porter* is much closer in intent to Fred Schepisi's *Plenty* (1985), adapted from David Hare's play about an English woman whose life is one long, bitter disappointment when compared with her memories of wartime, when everything—but especially sex—was made thrilling by the constant threat of death. In any

event, Cavani's film provoked and offended, and it spawned a slew of films that cashed in shamelessly on its perversely tantalizing images of sex and sadism beneath the broken cross.

The Night Porter's plot is straightforward. Shortly after the war, former Nazi commandant Max hides in Vienna, working as the night porter at an elegant hotel and meeting regularly with a circle of fellow Nazi war criminals. They're preoccupied with a bizarre form of group therapy: They seek to expiate their guilt through mock trials. Almost as an afterthought, they destroy all evidence of their crimes, including their surviving victims. As Max's day in court approaches, the exquisite, wealthy Lucia comes to stay at the hotel with her husband, a famous conductor. Lucia recognizes Max as her wartime tormentor; he fears that she plans to betray him.

But things are far more complicated than they first appear; theirs was a relationship of tormented and infinitely erotic intensity, and they begin to relive it in the present. Max hides Lucia in his apartment, even though the police—sent by her husband—are looking for her. Max's friends learn that a witness to his war crimes exists and track her down. They watch the apartment day and night and refuse to allow deliveries of food in, or the lovers out. Eventually, they spirit Max and Lucia away and shoot them on a deserted bridge.

The Night Porter's appeal is a disturbing one. As Lucia, Charlotte Rampling is exquisitely beautiful, in a delicately luminous way; Dirk Bogarde embodies a certain repressed sensuality that carries with it an inescapable hint of the unhealthy. The film is at its

Sadomasochistic thrills with a politically incorrect subtext.

107

Something to offend everyone: bondage, adultery, Nazis ... *The Night Porter* earned its controversial reputation.

most erotic in the wartime flashbacks, as fragile Lucia, her hair shorn like Falconetti's Joan of Arc, and smartly uniformed Max grope and nuzzle each other. The scene in which Lucia sings for Max and the other officers, dressed only in oversized pants and suspenders, Nazi cap, and full-length leather gloves, is truly provocative. The extremely slender Rampling looks equally like a high-fashion model (move over, Kate Moss!) and a prisoner in a concentration camp; the choreography and lighting would be perfectly at home in a depraved cabaret. No wonder her picture (discreetly cropped) graced almost every review. For all its political trappings, *The Night Porter* is yet another exploration of *amour fou*; Max and Lucia are trapped by their desire for each other, desire that can only destroy them. They surrender to it with the fatalism of doomed romantics from time immemorial.

The Night Porter, distributed in the United States by old-time showman Joseph E. Levine and released a year after *Last Tango in Paris*, was touted with the surefire "MOST CONTROVERSIAL PICTURE OF OUR TIME!" campaign and was predictably snidely re-viewed. Reviewers dubbed it *Last Tango in Auschwitz* and *Next Tango in Vienna* and hauled out the full range of disapproving adjectives, including *sick, trashy, opulent clap-trap,* and *pretentious*. Feminists disapproved of the sug-gestion that women crave sexual humili-ation and torture by men. Jews objected to the implication that victims of Nazi persecution secretly wanted to be abused and murdered. Sadomasochists protested that it didn't portray the rituals of domination and submission enticingly enough. *New York Times* critic Vincent Canby complained that Levine had taken out of context quotes from Canby's negative review (including "... a hectic love affair" and "... what a kinky turn-on!"), disregarding the open-ing sentence, "Let us now consider a piece of junk!" Levine used them in an ad that seemed to give the film Canby's seal of approval.

Controversy aside, *The Night Porter* fared much better in America than it did in its native Italy. The *New York Times* reported that the film was actually con-fiscated by the Italian censor after its opening in Rome and that Cavani, her producer, and the film's stars were brought up on crim-inal charges. Italian critics came to the film's defense, and a Milan district attorney reversed the censor.

Dirk Bogarde plays a suave Nazi and Charlotte Rampling his concen-tration camp lover.

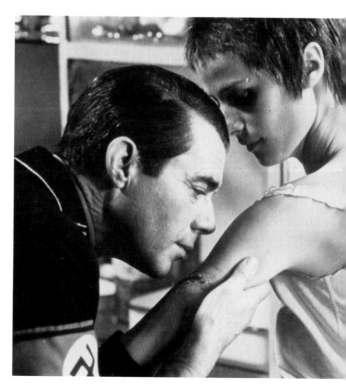

Nazi Naughtiness

The Night Porter has some things to answer for. Foremost among them is a slew of nasty Nazi sex pictures, which justified their salacious excesses by equating sexual perversion and Nazism—a lesson of sorts, one supposes. American exploitation old hands Bob Cresse and R. Lee Frost (a producer-director team) got on the joy-division bandwagon early with *Love Camp Seven* (1968), and noted Italian director Luchino Visconti explored the degeneracy—sexual and otherwise—of Nazis in *The Damned* (1969). In 1974, *The Night Porter* jockeyed for screen space with the notorious *Ilsa, She-Wolf of the SS*, starring Dyanne Thorne. Ilsa, a sex-crazed sadist, has her way with prisoners of the Nazis and escapes to repeat her vile crimes in other locations in *Ilsa, Harem Keeper of the Oil Sheiks* (1978), as well as in *Ilsa, the Tigress of Siberia* (1979). *Ilsa, the Wicked Warden* (1978) is actually *Greta, the Mad Butcher*, an *Ilsa* knockoff by shameless Spanish exploitation director Jess Franco. *Ilsa* was produced by exploitation great Dave Friedman (who also appeared in *Love Camp Seven*), who found it such an unpleasant experience that he refused screen credit. In any event, after that the flood gates were open.

Perhaps the best-known *Night Porter* knockoff is *Madame Kitty / Salon Kitty* (1976), directed by Italian sexploitation veteran Tinto Brass (*Caligula*) and starring *The Damned*'s Ingrid Thulin and Helmut Berger. Dispensing with *The Night Porter*'s psychological car-

rying on and ruminations about guilt, responsibility, and other unerotic topics, *Madame Kitty* went straight for the systematic sexual exploitation of prisoners by sleek, fetishistically dressed Nazis. The plot revolves around a Nazi brothel and the depraved things that go on there. This synopsis works equally well for virtually all the other naughty Nazi pictures, of which *Madame Kitty* is the most respectable. Lina Wertmuller's *Seven Beauties* (1976), starring Giancarlo Giannini and Shirley Stoler, puts a gender-reversal spin on the sordid situation. Nineteen seventy-six also saw no fewer than five Nazi cathouse movies, each nastier than the one before, and all Italian: *SS Girls Camp / La Casa Private per SS* and *Women's Camp 119 / KZ9—Lager di Stermino* (both by Bruno Mattei), *Liebes Lager* (Lorenzo Gicca Palli), *Love Camp #27 / La Svastica nel Ventre* (Mario Caiano), and *The Gestapo's Last Orgy / L'Ultima Orgia del III Reich* (Cesare Canevari). *The Gestapo's Last Orgy* comes closest to being a sleaze remake of *The Night Porter*, as many years after the war the ex-commandant of a Nazi love camp meets his Jewish lover. And finally, 1977 saw the release of *The Red Nights of the Gestapo / Le Lunghi Notti della Gestapo*, directed by Fabio Agostini, and featuring a small twist on the regular plot: An SS agent is assigned to uncover the sexual weaknesses of seven members of the German intelligentsia suspected of disloyalty to the Third Reich. Let's watch!

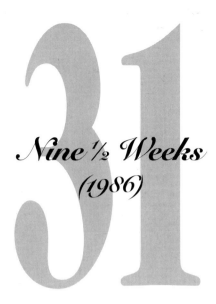

Nine ½ Weeks
(1986)

Directed by Adrian Lyne. Produced by Anthony Rufus Isaacs and Zalman King. Screenplay by Patricia Louisianna Knop, Zalman King, and Sarah Kernochan. Cinematography by Peter Biziou. Edited by Tom Rolf and Caroline Biggerstaff. Production Design by Ken Davis. Music by Jack Nitzsche.

Kim Basinger (Elizabeth), Mickey Rourke (John), Margaret Whitton (Molly), David Margulies (Harvey), Christine Baranski (Thea).

The most notorious soft-core movie of all time is based on a now-forgotten trendy book, 1978's *9½ Weeks*, by pseudonymous "Elizabeth McNeill," which purported to be the account of an actual sadomasochistic affair in the form of a novel.

Elizabeth, divorced and lonely, works at an art gallery. John is an arbitrageur with a fabulous, isolated houseboat and an even more fabulous loft. They meet at a street fair, go out on a date, and begin to get to know each other. The first half hour of the film is simply a prelude to the rest, a series of extended sex scenes involving ice cubes, silk blindfolds, the contents of the refrigerator. Elizabeth and John have sex standing up in a clock tower, and dinner while she's disguised as a man. An encounter with scary thugs leaves them so full of sexual energy that they screw against the wall of a watery basement. They also indulge on a department store display bed in the name of product testing. Elizabeth masturbates while looking at artists' slides and does a very hot strip for John, making maximum use of a set of venetian blinds. She crawls across the floor on her hands and knees, picking

Turn that thermostat down!

up money while he cracks a whip; John brings home a Latina whore, and Elizabeth flees to a porno theater. Eventually, she's had enough, and his eleventh-hour personal revelations—small-town origins, white-trash parents—aren't enough to make her stay. For all its visual polish, *Nine ½ Weeks* has a surprisingly true core. John and Elizabeth's relationship is all about control, and when she realizes that no matter how much he says he loves her, that's all there is to it, she leaves.

The screenplay was written by glossy kinkmeister Zalman King, then an actor trying to make the transition to working behind the camera, and his wife, Patricia Louisianna Knop. King intended to direct the film himself but quickly found that no one was interested in financing a movie about sadomasochism. With the addition to the mix of director Adrian Lyne, fresh off the success of *Flashdance* (1983), TriStar became interested, and committed to the project. But three days before the cameras were due to roll, financing was withdrawn. Production shut down for two weeks, then started up again with money from Producer's Sales Organization, former exploitation actor Mark (*House of Usher*) Damon's company. Lyne expended a fair amount of energy claiming that *Nine ½ Weeks* wasn't a film about sadomasochism, and the set was tense, reportedly because Rourke and Basinger hated each other and Lyne encouraged the hostility in order to add intensity to the film. Basinger reportedly said kissing Rourke was like kissing an ashtray. He's said to have militated for a sexier actress—Isabella Rossellini was among those auditioned—and this is certainly a case in which the on-screen sparks had nothing to do with off-screen hanky-panky. Or on screen, for that

Kim and Mickey's behind-the-scenes hostility didn't affect their on-screen sizzle.

matter—Rourke is widely reputed to disdain faking love scenes, and rumor had it that his sex scenes with Lisa Bonet in *Angel Heart* and girlfriend Carré Otis in *Wild Orchid* were the real thing. Lyne later called the whole *Nine ½ Weeks* experience "an ordeal."

The result was a glossy soft-core picture whose look is pure MTV, and though it's certainly not graphic, it is very intense in its depiction of sexual behavior. Though directed by Lyne, it looks very much like King's later forays into upscale smut, including features *Two Moon Junction* (1988) and *Wild Orchid* (1990) and the cable series "Red Shoe Diaries." *Nine ½ Weeks* was, of course, threatened with an X rating, and Lyne trimmed it by two and a half minutes to get an R. A more explicit version went to tape, and a still raunchier version was released in Europe (the film played for

years in Paris). Talk of a restored *four-hour* version surfaced around 1989, but it hasn't been seen yet. The initial reaction to *Nine ½ Weeks* was hostile. "We would have test screenings where there were a thousand people in the theater when it started and a hundred by the time it was over," King says. "People were so outraged they were walking out in droves. It was written off as a failure." But it performed well theatrically overseas and did excellent business on video; it's still a big rental item.

A sequel was announced in 1989, reteaming Basinger and Rourke, with a screenplay by King and Knop, and Roman Polanski directing. *Four Days in February*, however, never materialized, so for now Polanski's *Bitter Moon* (1992), a blackly comic chronicle of a sadomasochistic relationship, will have to stand in.

Kim Basinger and Mickey Rourke as lovers out on an S&M limb.

You Always Hurt the One You Love

Classical pornographers Leopold Sascher-Masoch and the Marquis de Sade have more readers in universities than dirty bookstores, but their names live in the erotic lexicon as masochism and sadism. Once, the slightest hint of leather or rubber, zippers or laces, or studs could raise eyebrows, but that was long ago: Now thigh-high boots and bustiers are busting out all over, and Michelle Pfeiffer can get dolled up in head-to-toe vinyl and cavort with a whip in the PG-13–rated *Batman Returns* (1992). Full-fledged S&M is still a bit off the, um, beaten track, but movies offer a number of opportunities to study up.

For the clinically minded, there are Alain Robbe-Grillet's *Trans-Europe Express* (1967) with Jean-Louis Trintignant and Marie-France Pisier, and Barbet Schroeder's *Maitresse* (1976), with Bulle Ogier as a professional dominatrix. Pier-Paolo Pasolini's *Salo, or the 120 Days of Sodom* (1975), based on de Sade's novel, is also extremely (and unpleasantly) explicit, linking sadism and political fascism.

The soft-core porn front includes Jess Franco's *Marquis de Sade: Justine* (1968), with Klaus Kinski as the Marquis and Eurosleaze favorite Maria Rohm as the virtuous Juliette (Franco also made *DeSade's*

Juliette in 1975; it appears to be a lost film); Massimo Dallamano's *Venus in Furs*—not to be confused with Jess Franco's 1970 *Black Angel*, retitled *Venus in Furs*—featuring Laura Antonelli; Radley Metzger's *The Punishment of Anne* (1973), an adaptation of Robbe-Grillet's novel *L'Image* (written under the pseudonym "Jean de Berg"); and Just (*Emmanuelle*) Jaekin's *The Story of O* (1975), based on the erotic classic by "Pauline Réage."

For glimpses of the S&M scene, check out *Cruising* (1980), about a killer stalking gay men; *Videodrome* (1983), in which James Woods and Deborah Harry conduct a mutually sadistic relationship; *Heart of Midnight* (1988), in which Jennifer Jason Leigh inherits a building that was once a sleazy sex club; *Bitter Moon* (1993), Roman Polanski's purportedly satirical catalogue of sexual variations; *Whispers in the Dark* (1992), which involves bondage; and *Body of Evidence* (1992), featuring Madonna dripping candle wax on Willem Dafoe. And for the oddest S&M picture ever, take a look at Garry Marshall's *Exit to Eden* (1994), a bizarre comedy–cop-thriller–sex picture adapted from Anne Rice's erotic novel. Who ever thought we'd live to see Rosie O'Donnell and Dan Aykroyd in studded leather?

An Officer and a Gentleman (1982)

Directed by Taylor Hackford. Produced by Martin Elfand. Screenplay by Douglas Day Stewart. Cinematography by Donald Thorin. Edited by Peter Zinner. Production Design by Philip Jeffries. Music by Jack Nitzsche.

Richard Gere (Zack Mayo), Debra Winger (Paula Pokrifki), David Keith (Sid Worley), Robert Loggia (Byron Mayo), Louis Gossett Jr. (Sergeant Emil Foy), Lisa Blount (Lynette Pomeroy).

Let us now discuss the girl movie. It's no secret that men and women often part ways abruptly when it comes to defining what makes a movie sexy. It's tough to admit the truth in the old clichés, but the truth is, most men like their sexy movies as explicit as possible, and most women don't. It's a gross generalization, there are exceptions, but ... when women as a group say sexy, they mean romantic: Daniel Day-Lewis kissing Michelle Pfeiffer's wrist in *The Age of Innocence* (1992), Harrison Ford and Kelly McGillis dancing together in *Witness* (1985), Mel Gibson and Sigourney Weaver kissing as they drive through roadblocks in *The Year of Living Dangerously* (1982). They love old romances filled with meaningful looks and eloquent gestures, and they swoon for the new romances, ushered in by Taylor Hackford's *An Officer and a Gentleman.*

The '60s and '70s were rough decades for romantic movies. As the Hollywood movie factories crumbled, the standard-issue romantic movie became an increasingly rare commodity. Studio-trained directors

Raunchy romance with a sentimental streak as wide as Puget Sound: Debra Winger and Richard Gere in *An Officer and a Gentleman.*

were old and getting older, trapped in the romantic clichés of their youths and by and large not up to the job of rethinking them for a new generation. Was there ever a sorrier display than *My Fair Lady* (1964), a sumptuous musical spectacle that captured viewers' hearts *despite* everything: the monstrous frou-frou costumes, the ghastly age difference between stars Audrey Hepburn and Rex Harrison and the entrenched misogyny and homoeroticism of both the story and the production—in the famous Ascot Race scene, every single woman looks like a man in drag. That it was directed by George Cukor is the coup de grace. His career was built on women's pictures, including Greta Garbo's *Camille* (1937), classic screwball comedy *The Philadelphia Story* (1940), two Katharine Hepburn–Spencer Tracy romances—*Adam's Rib* (1949) and *Pat and Mike* (1952)—the Judy Garland remake of *A Star Is Born* (1954), and Marilyn Monroe's *Let's Make Love* (1960).

Hollywood's new generation of filmmakers, many coming up though the perpetually adolescent ranks of exploitation filmmaking, was woefully short of romantics, but teeming with boys who knew their way around guns and cars and pornography, from Walter Hill to Martin Scorsese. They made films about the relationships between men, while women receded into the background, to be retrieved for some quick and dirty sex and then banished again. Virtually the only moviemaker whose films dealt consistently with the relationships between men and women was Woody Allen, and he didn't have anything especially good to say. As the decade drew to a close, relationship movies had degenerated to the antiromance of *Looking for Mr.*

Goodbar (1977), in which men are pigs, women are sluts, and sex is degrading and leads to murder.

The '80s and '90s brought a new round of romantic movies, girl movies brought up to date with a generous dollop of sex, and *An Officer and a Gentleman* is the perfect example of the form. It's unquestionably a girl movie, sexy because of the romance, but spices up the mushy stuff with enough sex and action (mostly in the form of basic-training dramas) to appeal to guys as well. A relatively low-budget film at $7 million, *An Officer and a Gentleman* became a blockbuster hit. Critics liked it, too, and few failed to mention that it was the sort of film Hollywood didn't make anymore.

Zack Mayo is the son of a common, whoring sailor, a bad boy who wants to be good and hopes to make it through officer training at Washington Naval Base. Feisty, pretty Paula and her best friend, Lynette, are "Puget Sound debs," local factory girls who hang around the base looking for flyers-in-training, hoping to

marry out of working-class poverty. Zack and Paula are made for each other—they're both feisty, ambitious, and determined to wash away the shame of their parents' failure to make anything of themselves—but it takes them a while to figure it out. Their romance is mirrored by the doomed relationship of Zack's friend Sid, who washes out of training, and the fickle Lynette, who dumps him when she realizes he's never going to wear an officer's uniform. The result is a classical Hollywood romance with lots of sex, even though the first kiss is almost forty-five minutes into the movie.

Once Zack and Paula hit the sheets, the action is pretty hot. In fact, director Taylor Hackford was forced to tone down the scene in which Winger wriggles lustily atop Gere, who has his own place in libidinous history as Hollywood's first male star to bare all at the drop of a lens cap. Hackford used a postproduction optical to turn an X-rated long shot into a less revealing medium shot. Today, the original would hardly rate a raised

116

eyebrow, but then it pushed the envelope of mainstream acceptability. Yet at the same time, the sex in *An Officer and a Gentleman* is sweet and redemptive, followed by meaningful talking in bed and cuddling: the film has it both ways, hot for the guys, sweet for the girls. A double suicide in 1983, involving high school lovebirds who both hanged themselves in apparent imitation of Sid (who commits suicide after Lynette dumps him), caused a flurry when it was widely reported that the teenagers had seen *An Officer and a Gentleman* at least five times: She hanged herself in a movie theater ladies' room during a showing.

Gere, all macho swagger and tight T-shirts, is the quintessential sex symbol of the '80s, but he's also the classic Hollywood bad boy we love: rough on the outside, wounded on the inside, talks tough but secretly believes in the transcendent power of love. *An Officer and a Gentleman* was Winger's moment in the sun

(along with 1980's *Urban Cowboy*, in which she costarred with sex symbol John Travolta): She cornered the market in dark, lusty, husky-voiced sirens with wanton hips and no-nonsense desires.

Moonstruck (1987) mined the same romantic vein, pairing Cher and the offbeat Nicolas Cage (whom women adore, despite his odd looks and nasal voice), as did *When Harry Met Sally . . .* (1989), with terminally cute Meg Ryan and Billy Crystal. Unfortunately, the sex component got smaller and smaller, making the neo–girl movies less appealing to guys. *Ghost* (1990) became a surprise smash on the strength of its story of love strong enough to transcend even the grave (and its love-at-the-potter's-wheel scene), and *Bull Durham* (1988), *The Fabulous Baker Boys* (1989), the remake of *The Last of the Mohicans* (1992), *Sleepless in Seattle* (1993), *Love Affair* (1994), and *Only You* (1994) are all unabashedly romantic.

Old-fashioned romance in modern movie packages: Demi Moore and Patrick Swayze in *Ghost* (1990) *(left)* and Madeleine Stowe and Daniel Day-Lewis in *The Last of the Mohicans* (1992).

The Ten Sexiest Stars of the 1980s

Ellen Barkin: Lean and feline, Barkin has a smoldering gaze that promises sex with a dollop of danger, and she used it to good effect as the seductress who may be a killer in *Sea of Love* (1989). She's equally provocative in *The Adventures of Buckaroo Banzai: Across the 8th Dimension* (1985), *Siesta* (1987), *Johnny Handsome* (1989), and *Bad Company* (1995), and she's both funny and alluring in *Switch* (1991) as womanizer who wakes up to find he's become a woman.

Kim Basinger: A Bond girl, pouty Basinger earned her sex-symbol stripes in *Nine ½ Weeks* (1985). Though surprisingly funny in *Nadine* (1987), she remains typecast as a sultry man-baiter.

Tom Cruise: Boyish and sleekly muscled, Cruise was Hollywood's biggest male box-office attraction in the '80s, flaunting his unthreatening charms in *Risky Business* (1983), *The Color of Money* and *Top Gun* (both 1986), and *Cocktail* (1988). He is the ultimate toy boy, and *Interview With the Vampire: The Vampire Chronicles* (1994) didn't change a thing.

Richard Gere: His sex appeal is evident in *American Gigolo* (1980), *An Officer and a Gentleman* (1982), and *Breathless* (1983); his diaper dance in *King David* (1985) is best forgotten. Gere returned in the '90s with a head of silver hair, heating up *Internal Affairs* and *Pretty Woman* (both 1990).

Mel Gibson: The Errol Flynn of the '80s, Gibson makes men cheer and women melt. His forte is action films like the *Mad Max* and *Lethal Weapon* series, but he also made a madly romantic *Hamlet* (1990), broke hearts as a handsome retarded lad in *Tim* (1979), and bared his chest with period flair in *The Bounty* (1984).

Nastassja Kinski: Lithe and feral, Kinski divides her life as a sex symbol between art-house films—*Tess* (1979), *The Moon in the Gutter* (1983), *Paris, Texas* (1984), *Crystal or Ash, Fire or Wind, As Long As It's Love* (1989)—and exploitation pictures like *Harem* (1985) and *Terminal Velocity* (1994). Kinski's judgment is questionable, but her appeal never flags.

Jack Nicholson: Young Nicholson had charisma, but his looks locked him out of romantic leads. He blossomed as an aging rake whose bad-boy reputation guarantees the girls will fall to their knees—the smirk and the insinuating voice get them every time. How else to explain *The Witches of Eastwick* (1987), in which Susan Sarandon, Michelle Pfeiffer, and Cher vie for his favors?

Dennis Quaid: An all-American roughneck with an irresistible grin and a heart of gold, Quaid knocked women dead with *The Big Easy* (1986) and lent his naughty charms to *The Right Stuff* (1983), *Innerspace* and *Suspect* (both 1987), and *Everybody's All American* (1988), as well as to the darker romance *Flesh and Bone* (1993).

Theresa Russell: Alluring and faintly mysterious, Russell debuted in *The Last Tycoon* (1976) but hit her stride with *Bad Timing* (1980). Her icy seductress in *Black Widow* (1987) was a top-notch femme fatale turn, but she made too many noncommercial films with husband Nicolas Roeg to have the career as a sex symbol she deserved.

Kathleen Turner: Star of *Body Heat* (1980), Turner blazed briefly but incandescently before degenerating into a fleshy grande dame. She sizzled in *Crimes of Passion* (1984), opted for athletic sensuality in *Romancing the Stone* (1984) and *Jewel of the Nile* (1985), voiced the unforgettably sensual Jessica Rabbit in *Who Framed Roger Rabbit?* (1988), and proved a wet tee-shirt sizzler in *The War of the Roses* (1989).

The Outlaw
(1943)

Directed and Produced by Howard Hughes. Screenplay by Jules Furthman. Cinematography by Gregg Toland. Edited by Otho Lovering and Wallace Grissell. Music Direction by Victor Young.

Jane Russell (Rio MacDonald), Jack Buetel (Billy the Kid), Walter Huston (Doc Holliday), Thomas Mitchell (Pat Garrett), Mimi Aguglia (Guadalupe).

*T*he Outlaw is a real tempest in a teapot, but what a tempest! Bankrolled by eccentric billionaire Howard Hughes, it's a psychological western before its time that embroils outlaws Doc Holliday and Billy the Kid in a tempestuous three-way relationship with Rio MacDonald, the bosomy bitch they both love. Billy blows into town and spies the horse that was stolen from him a few burgs back. It's been bought by Doc Holliday, and the two legendary badmen spar and bicker about the beast. Billy, meanwhile, is distracted by the bounteous Rio, who tries to kill him (he killed her brother) and then falls in love with him. But she's also attracted to Doc, setting the stage for a showdown between the two men.

As a western, The Outlaw is a great showcase for full-figured star Jane Russell, whose character is treated abominably badly throughout: She's traded for a horse, raped in a barn, and strung up between two trees by the vengeful Billy. Contemporary viewers can't miss the heavy homoeroticism between the two gun-toting he-men, and the whole film is melodramatically overwrought. But Russell is quite a sight, especially in a low-cut blouse, galloping on horseback. Before his eccentricities flowered into full-blown madness, Hughes cut a path through Hollywood, a garden of earthly delights for a randy young man with enough

money to bankroll a motion picture all on his own. Before The Outlaw, he'd tested the waters of scandalous movie making with Hell's Angels (1930), the film that introduced uninhibited Jean Harlow slipping into something more comfortable.* Hughes reportedly discovered Russell working in a dentist's office as a receptionist and declared she had the "most beautiful pair of knockers" he had ever seen. Her account differs somewhat, but the big picture remains the same: It wasn't Russell's talent that prompted Hughes to sign her to a contract in 1940 and build The Outlaw around her. A native Californian who'd worked as a model and, less glamorously, as a chiropodist's assistant and a box folder in a packaging plant, Russell recognized The Outlaw as the lucky break most girls would kill for, even as it took three years to make its way into theaters. Howard Hawks was hired as director, but he lasted only a week before departing and taking cinematographer Lucien Ballard with him. Hughes took over and hired Gregg Toland (best known for having shot Citizen Kane) to replace Ballard. Production dragged on for nine months, and in a now-legendary act of obsessiveness, Hughes dedicated much of his time to engineering a special brassiere that would give Russell the busty, braless look he craved. But, she insists in her autobiography, the finished product was diabolically uncomfortable, and she never wore it. Hughes also hired publicist Russell Birdwell, who orchestrated the search for Gone With the Wind's (1939) Scarlett O'Hara, to make

---

*Expatriate British director James Whale (*Frankenstein*), who's credited as the film's dialogue director, is said to have written and directed much of the film for Hughes. The fact that Hughes could afford to install himself as the director of a feature-length film didn't mean he was good at it.

(Opposite) Jane Russell and her breasts, the real stars of *The Outlaw*.

Would you like to tussle with Russell?

Russell's breasts famous. Birdwell gave the job his all, setting up a slew of photo opportunities.

The Outlaw is a monument to one man's mammary preoccupation; the judge who observed that Russell's breasts hang over the film like storm clouds was not exaggerating matters. The film couldn't get a Production Code seal because of them, and was held up for two years. Hughes's battle with the Hays Office was all-out war; they wanted a reported 108 cuts made but agreed to waive 105 of them when Hughes hired a mathematician to prove that other stars had been allowed to show more inches of cleavage than Russell. He refused to make the other three cuts and opened *The Outlaw* (which eventually cost $3,400,000, a lot of money in its day) in San Francisco in February 1943, without a seal. The advertising was even more salacious than the film itself, featuring Russell in a variety of alluring postures and posing such questions as, "What are the two reasons for Jane Russell's rise to stardom?" All the hype was for naught. The picture opened and closed; it was released again in a few cities in 1947 but wasn't widely seen until 1950.

120

52

34
Pandora's Box / Die Büchse der Pandora (1929)

Directed by G. W. Pabst. Screenplay by Ladislaus Vajda, based on the plays *Erdgeist* and *Die Büchse der Pandora* by Frank Wedekind. Produced by George C. Horsetzky. Cinematography by Gunther Krampf. Edited by Joseph T. Fliesler. Art Direction by Andrei Andreiev.

Louise Brooks (Lulu), Gustav Diessl (Jack the Ripper), Fritz Kortner (Dr. Schön), Franz Lederer (Alwa Schön), Carl Goetz (Schigolch), Alice Roberts (Countess Geschwitz).

*P*andora's Box is a morality tale with no moral, except perhaps the Freudian observation that desire denied is desire deformed, usually with undesirable consequences. Frank Wedekind's 1904 play, on which the movie is based, was so shocking in its day that it wasn't even performed in Germany until 1918. The playwright was called a pornographer, and its main character, Lulu, denounced as the product of a degenerate mind. It begins with a prologue in which an animal tamer steps out of a circus tent, cracks his whip, and invites the audience to enter his menagerie. Pabst's film dispenses with the image but holds the thought: His *Pandora's Box* is a glossy, amoral animal act in which all the beasts are driven by lust to betrayal, despair, suicide, and murder. And the embodiment of lust is Lulu, a lissome girl with pale skin and a shiny helmet of black hair: American Louise Brooks, a sassy dancer-turned-actress who in five years had appeared in supporting roles in a dozen forgettable films.

Seduced as a child by the pimp Schigolch—with

Thoroughly modern gold-digger Louise Brooks in *Pandora's Box.*

whom she continues to associate, and whom she represents variously as her father and as her old friend—pretty, captivating Lulu coasts through life on the favors of those who covet her. She seduces Herr Schön, a middle-aged newspaper magnate, and breaks up his plans to marry a more respectable girl. On their wedding day, he catches her in the arms of no fewer than three rivals: she kisses Schigolch, waltzes seductively with Countess Geschwitz, a wealthy lesbian; and embraces Schön's own son, Alwa. Schön commits suicide, and Lulu is charged with his murder.

True to form, Lulu captivates the jury and is convicted only of manslaughter; when a false cry of "fire" goes up in the courtroom, she escapes in the melee, and she, Schigolch, and Alwa flee the country. In exile, Alwa gambles away their money and Lulu is sold to an Egyptian whoremaster; before she can be taken off to his brothel, the trio escapes to London. By Christmas they're destitute, and she takes to the streets. Her first customer is Jack the Ripper, and though her allure at first makes him drop his knife, he later murders her.

The fifth movie version of Wedekind's play, *Pandora's Box* is saturated with sex, and Brooks's recollections of Berlin, where the film was shot, suggest part of the reason:

> Sex was the business of the town. At the Eden hotel . . . the café bar was lined with the higher priced trollops. The economy girls walked the street outside. On the corner stood the girls in boots, advertising flagellation. Actors' agents pimped for the ladies in luxury apartments in the Bavarian quarter.

Race-track touts at the Hoppegarten arranged orgies for groups of sportsmen. The nightclub Eldorado displayed an enticing line of homosexuals dressed as women. At the Maly, there was a choice of feminine or collar-and-tie lesbians. Collective lust roared unashamed at the theatre. In the revue *Chocolate Kiddies*, when Josephine Baker appeared naked except for a girdle of

Pabst found her "Too old [all of twenty-six] and too obvious—one sexy look and the picture would become burlesque," he was nonetheless ready to sign her when his first choice, the largely untried, twenty-one-year-old Brooks, became available. Brooks is a thoroughly modern seductress, lithe and unpredictable; she switches from the eternal feminine to an unsophisticated girl in seconds. Her photographs tell you how beautiful she was, but the first surprise of *Pandora's Box* is

Countess Geschwitz (Alice Roberts) and Lulu (Brooks) waltz at Lulu's wedding, in the mother of all lesbian dance scenes.

bananas, it was precisely as Lulu's stage entrance was described by Wedekind: "They rage there as in a menagerie when the meat appears at the cage."*

Pandora's Box was shot in the Berlin of *Cabaret*, where decadence was indeed divine and Lulu its high priestess. Marlene Dietrich (the pre–*Blue Angel* Dietrich, veteran of a slew of undistinguished German sex romps) had campaigned for the role, and though

her vivacity—she's utterly captivating. Bold and capricious, sensual and direct, Brooks knows exactly how to drape herself over a sofa, reach out her arms to be embraced, stroke a man's hair or a woman's arms. She's utterly sensual, and *Pandora's Box* is charged with her seductiveness.

Pandora's Box ultimately made a star of Brooks, though she never really got a chance to enjoy it. A silent film made on the brink of the sound era, a picture whose amorality and frank attitude about sex led to extensive cuts when it was shown abroad (in the

*Louise Brooks, *Lulu in Hollywood* (New York: Knopf, 1983), p. 97.

124

P703-152

United States, a new ending had Lulu joining the Salvation Army!), *Pandora's Box* was scarcely noticed in America until its 1955 resurrection, when Henri Langlois of the *Cinémathèque Française* and James Card of George Eastman House International Museum of Photography joined forces to restore the butchered and underappreciated film.

Brooks had long since retired from a business that didn't know what to make of her smart mouth and insolent ways. But her look and the attitude it embodied are as fresh today as they were then. It inspired two comic strips, *Dixie Dugan* (1926–66), about a clever showgirl, and Italian cartoonist Guido Crepax's sensual *Valentina*, which debuted in 1965. In Jonathan Demme's *Something Wild* (1986), modern sex kitten Melanie Griffith dons a Louise Brooks wig and calls herself Lulu when she wants to be the wild thing of the title.

Theda Bara: The original vamp got the kind of P.R. they just don't make anymore: Born in the shadow of the pyramids, trained in the secrets of love and given in supernatural marriage to the Sphinx, she had hobbies that were exotic—distilling perfume, for example—and charms that were lethal. She was the star of *A Fool There Was* (1915), *The Vixen, Camille,* and *Cleopatra* (all 1917), *Salome* (1918), *The Unchastened Woman* (1925), and many others, but her popularity waned even before the silents did.

John Barrymore: Handsome and lazy, the "Great Profile" acted because it was easy sailing through *Beau Brummell* (1924), *Don Juan* (1926), *The Beloved Rogue* (1927), and a host of other films. His career faltered in the '30s, but in his prime he was a romantic idol.

Clara Bow: Red-headed Bow, the model for Betty Boop, was the ultimate jazz baby. Novelist Eleanor Glyn chose her as the "It" girl, "It" being an irresistible allure that transcended sex appeal. Her films include *The Daring Years* (1923), *Kiss Me Again* (1925), *Mantrap* (1926), and *The Wild Party* (1929).

Louise Brooks: The star who never was, beautiful, capricious Brooks threw away a promising career that included G. W. Pabst's classic *Pandora's Box* and *Diary of a Lost Girl* (both 1929), but she gained a cult following years later. With her cap of black hair and her unaffected manner, she's the most contemporary of silent sex symbols.

John Gilbert: Romantic lead Gilbert is best remembered opposite Garbo in *Flesh and the Devil* (1927) and was considered the heir to Valentino, a homegrown lothario with flawless features; his appeal is evident in *The Merry Widow* (1925), *La Boheme* (1926), *Love* (1927), and *Queen Christina* (1933). Contrary to popular rumor, his voice was as attractive as his face, but he didn't survive the transition to sound.

Mae Murray: Vivacious Murray, the "girl with the bee-stung lips," flounced through *The Delicious Little Devil* (1919), *The Masked Bride* and *The Merry Widow* (both 1925), *Altars of Desire* (1927), and others. Like Bow, she was the quintessential jazz baby, but the sound era passed her by.

Ramon Novarro: Mexican Novarro replaced Valentino in *The Prisoner of Zenda* (1922), and a new exotic heartthrob was born. Athletic and charming, he had credits that include *Scaramouche* (1923), *Ben-Hur* (1925), *Call of the Flesh* (1930), and *Mata Hari* (1932).

Ivor Novello: When British matinee idol Novello starred in Alfred Hitchcock's *The Lodger* (1926), the ending had to be changed—Novello couldn't be Jack the Ripper, no matter what the evidence. Pale and soulful, Novello was a sex symbol for dreamy girls with poetry on their minds.

Gloria Swanson: Before she was Norma Desmond in *Sunset Boulevard* (1950), Swanson was the epitome of brazen glamor, and the daring sex comedies she made with Cecil B. DeMille before he found religion include *Don't Change Your Husband, For Better, For Worse,* and *Male and Female* (all 1919), *Why Change Your Wife?* (1920), and *The Affairs of Anatole* (1921).

Rudolph Valentino: The original Latin Lover, Italian-born Valentino shot to stardom in *The Four Horsemen of the Apocalypse* (1921) and for six years, until his untimely death, was Hollywood's reigning sex god, blazing through such films as *The Sheik* (1921), *Blood and Sand* (1922), and *Son of the Sheik* (1926).

Paris, France
(1994)

Directed by Gerard Ciccoritti. Produced by Eric Norlen and Allen Levine. Screenplay by Tom Walmsley, based on his novel. Cinematography by Barry Stone. Edited by Roushell Goldstein. Production Design by Marian Wihack. Music by John McCarthy.

Leslie Hope (Lucy Quick), Peter Outerbridge (Sloan), Victor Ertmantis (Michael), Dan Lett (William), Raoul Trujillo (Minter).

"You have to trust your own cunt" is the frank first thought shared with us by Lucy Quick, the sometime narrator of *Paris, France*. It's a sentiment worthy of Henry Miller, but delivered with such schoolgirl intent to shock that you wonder whether it's meant to be a joke and, if so, what sort of joke it's meant to be. In fact, *Paris, France* ("the most erotic place you can go") is a self-conscious hybrid of *Jules and Jim* (1961) by way of *Henry & June* (1992) with a touch of *Teorema* (1968), all seasoned with a sly ongoing *hommage* to *Breathless*. Canadian director Gerard Ciccoritti was a mere toddler when the *nouvelle vague* broke on North America's shores, but *Paris, France* is steeped in the romance of its seminal works, particularly the vision they offered young Americans of Europe—especially Paris—as a place of freedom, danger, and sophisticated excitement, all with a sexual edge. The wonder of it all is that the blackly comic *Paris, France* is actually rather clever and surprisingly candid: No one will go away complaining that for an arty sex movie there isn't enough sex.

Toronto writer Lucy hasn't put pen to paper in years, but she nurtures the fantasy that one day she'll finish her erotic novel—called *Paris, France*, of course—about an American girl who goes to 1960s Paris to sleep with gangsters. Lucy's husband, Michael, owns a small literary press. He published her one slim book of short stories, as well as the work of her best friend—and his business partner—William, a gay poet. Michael's newest discovery is Sloan, a sexy, muscular, young Charles Bukowski of a writer, whose first book, *Under My Skin*, is a tribute to Wisconsin serial murderer Ed Gein. Sloan is powerfully attracted to Lucy (during a dinner party at her home, she catches him stealing a pair of her panties.) William has the hots for Sloan, so only Michael is (temporarily) out of the sexual loop, caught up in the delusion that he's received a phone call from beyond the grave from John Lennon and has only a few days to live. Lucy and Sloan begin a torrid affair. Sloan also starts sleeping with William, who's putting him up as a favor to Michael. Though interrupted at regular intervals by the sort of pompous conversations about the nature of sex and lust and commitment and creativity that you'd expect from a pack of writers, *Paris, France* wastes no time getting between the sheets and spends a lot of time there.

The film's best sequences, though, are Lucy's *Breathless* fantasies about life as a French gangster's girl, which we gradually realize are fabricated in large part from her affair with a thug called Minter, whom she met in Paris. The late Minter also wanted to be a writer, and Michael—acting under Lennon's supposed influence—becomes obsessed with dusting off Minter's (dreadful) poetry and setting it to music. Shot in cool, gritty black and white, the Paris segments pack a powerful erotic charge, partly because they're good and raunchy, and partly because they evoke the

European art movies of the early '60s, all *soigné* hedonism decked out in fitted cocktail dresses, stiletto heels, bouffant hair, and inky eye liner. Lucy aspires to be a contemporary Anaïs Nin, and her relationship with Minter is a classic *amour fou*; it ends with his death from cancer, though she reimagines his demise as a dramatic murder at her hands—that is, after all, the more literary end.

In fact, the Canadian-made *Paris, France* is a European arty sex movie manqué, which is both the best and the worst thing about it. On the downside, there's a tendency to solemn pronouncements that really are beyond the pale—Alain Cuny's philosophical marathons in *Emmanuelle* (1974) have nothing on *Paris, France*'s ruminations about all the usual subjects. On the plus side, however, *Paris, France* is genuinely funny—not *always* by accident—and fearlessly sexy. Ciccoritti's background is in horror films, including the very stylish vampire picture *Graveyard Shift* (1986), and *Paris, France* always looks fabulous.

Paris, France was released unrated, and deservedly so. Reviewers didn't know quite what to make of it and took refuge in faux innocent amazement at the steamy goings-on. "They do it in bed, they do it against the wall—and when that gets boring, they don leather, tie each other up and do it some more," marveled Bill Hoffman of the *New York Post*. And they do.

(Above) Raunchy writers in love: She (Leslie Hope) writes about sex, he (Peter Outerbridge) writes about cannibal murder, and they can't get enough of each other.

Shades of *Teorema*: Sloan (Outerbridge) and two of his conquests (Hope and Dan Lett).

36

Performance
(1970)

Directed by Donald Cammell and Nicolas Roeg. Produced by Sanford Lieberson. Screenplay by Cammell. Cinematography by Roeg. Edited by Anthony Gibbs and Brian Smedley-Ashton. Art Direction by John Clark. Set Decoration by Peter Young. Music by Jack Nitzsche.

James Fox (Chas), Mick Jagger (Turner), Anita Pallenberg (Pherber), Michele Breton (Lucy), John Bindon (Moody), Stanley Meadows (Rosebloom), Johnny Shannon (Harry Flowers), Anthony Valentine (Joey Maddocks), Ken Colley (Tony Farrell).

Deeply druggy and divinely decadent in that very '60s way, *Performance* is all furs and groovy stereopticons, velvet drapes and Moroccan wall hangings, driven by the dichotomy between two parallel universes: the cruel, violent, but oh-so-conventional world of London gangsters, and the sensual, gender-bending cosmos that exists behind the closed doors of a shabby town house owned by a reclusive rock star.

Chas is a workaday bad boy, a vicious, petty thug in the employ of smal-time hood Harry Flowers, who threatens, intimidates and terrorizes people with casual efficiency. Chas may not be a model citizen, but he knows who he is. He likes

Vice. And Versa.

Mick Jagger.   And Mick Jagger.

James Fox.   And James Fox.

See them all in a film about fantasy. And reality. Vice. And versa.

performance.

Hear Mick Jagger sing his own song "Memo From Turner."

James Fox/Mick Jagger/Anita Pallenberg/Michele Breton

Written by Donald Cammell/Directed by Donald Cammell & Nicolas Roeg/Produced by Sanford Lieberson in Technicolor A Goodtimes Enterprises Production from Warner Bros. Hear Mick Jagger sing "Memo From Turner" in the original sound track album on Warner Bros. Records and tapes.

his girls pretty and his sex rough; his apartment is a mass of middle-class pretensions with a touch of that *Playboy* savoir faire. A brutal falling out with Flowers sends the wounded Chas scurrying for cover until he can figure out a way to flee the country, and a snippet of overheard conversation at a railway station leads him to Turner. An androgynous, reclusive rock star, Turner has withdrawn from the real world and made his own within a once-elegant town house, attended by his two girlfriends, voluptuous Pherber and boyish Lucy.

At first repelled by the aura of unbridled sensuality that surrounds Turner, Chas is gradually seduced by the ambience of mind-altering drugs and gender-bending sex that envelops Turner and his harem. They dress in one another's clothes, make love indiscriminately, and have dreamy conversations about the nature of identity. This idyll comes to an end when Harry Flowers's goons arrive at the door: Before they take Chas away, he shoots Turner. But the film's last shot, of Chas in the back seat of the gangsters' car, is a puzzle: Why does he now look exactly like Turner?

Performance, which got an

Three androgynes in a tub: Mick Jagger, Michèle Breton, and Anita Pallenberg.

X rating on its original release, is a psychedelic *Persona* whose atmosphere of druggy perversity has a touch of Kenneth Anger about it, *à la Inauguration of the Pleasure Dome*, all rich, lurid color and sensual textures. It picks up where European art films of the day left off, swaddling sex in an aura of intellectual difficulty while remaining genuinely sensual. The image of too-cool-for-words Anita Pallenberg (most famous as Rolling Stone Keith Richard's girlfriend) as Pherber, lying on a bed in a fur coat with nothing underneath and absently fondling the area over her crotch as she speaks to the nonplussed Chas, is unforgettable. *Performance* is the sort of film that makes you want to take drugs and have sex in huge beds crowded with embroidered pillows and hung with mosquito netting. Or at least, it has that effect on some people; others side with critic Richard Schickel, who declared it "the most disgusting, the most completely worth-

less film I have seen since I began reviewing."

Shot in 1968, *Performance* languished for more than a year awaiting U.S. release, while rumors flew that it was so incomprehensible that it would never be

Regular guy James Fox flanked by scruffy sensualists Pallenberg and Jagger.

shown. It finally emerged trimmed of some sex and violence to generally unfavorable reviews. The dominant note was hostile obliviousness, heralded by the word *pretentious*. *Perverted, kinky, lurid,* and *sordid* were also popular, none used in a positive sense. Critics wrote at length about the film's nearly intolerable violence; for better or worse, that aspect of the picture now looks well within the bounds of mainstream acceptability. What's still notable is the casual bisexuality and the no-big-deal drug use, neither of which would pass muster in today's oh-so-well-behaved Hollywood.

Performance is also clearly a film with a message, some of which came through loud and clear: Sex and violence are inextricably linked in Chas's life, and his experiences in Turner's house of voluptuous wonders lead him to a personal awakening. But the overall message is that we live in a sensual world, if only we're willing to embrace it, a world of color and texture and sounds and smells that are all glorious and exotic. Sex is one of those experiences, but so is eating magic mushrooms and looking at exotic, 3D images of the pyramids and the Great Sphinx. Perhaps the problem was Jagger: For all his androgyny and druggy idol bona fides, he always suggested violence. The Doors' Jim Morrison might have been a better choice, but when the film was being cast, he was already on the path to bloated extinction.

In any event, *Performance* is a nostalgic magic carpet ride through sexual mores that seem unimaginably distant; 1968 is so weirdly alien that it could be centuries gone rather than the recent past.

Beyond the Helping Hand . . .

There's always sexy lingerie, and the occasional light bondage (silk scarves and stockings) doesn't raise many eyebrows, but when it comes to any other erotic paraphernalia, the movies offer surprisingly few illustrations. Perhaps that's why these are so memorable.

Victoria Abril masturbates in her tub with the aid of a **little wind-up frogman toy** in Pedro Almodóvar's *Tie Me Up! Tie Me Down!* (1990) and amazes her less experienced lover in *Amantes* (1992) by demonstrating the erotic use to which a **knotted scarf** can be put. A **scarf** also features prominently in *In the Realm of the Senses*, but put to very different use: Courtesan Eiko Matsuda strangles her lover with it at the peak of his orgasm.

Alex Casanovas needs a **Polaroid camera** to get his jollies in *Kika* (1994), and when Marlon Brando tells Maria Schneider to fetch the **butter** in *Last Tango in Paris* (1973), he's not planning to cook, any more than the possessed Linda Blair intends to pray before her **crucifix** in *The Exorcist* (1973).

Holly Woodlawn turns to a **beer bottle** (Miller) when Joe Dallesandro can't oblige in *Trash* (1970). *Bitter Moon* (1993) is a virtual directory of sex toys, of which the most memorable is probably Peter Coyote's **pig mask**, while **handcuffs** liven up the sex lives of Melanie Griffith and Jeff Daniels in *Something Wild* (1986), as well as those of Clint Eastwood and Genvieve Bujold in *Tightrope* (1984). **Foreign languages** turn on Jamie Lee Curtis in *A Fish Called Wanda* (1988), and Debra Winger's **mechanical bull** ride in *Urban Cowboy* (1980) is still the hottest thing in that picture.

Long live the erotic imagination.

The Postman Always Rings Twice (1946)

Directed by Tay Garnett. Produced by Carey Wilson. Written by Harry Ruskin and Niven Busch, based on the novel by James M. Cain. Cinematography by Sidney Wagner. Edited by George White. Music by George Bassman.

Lana Turner (Cora Smith), John Garfield (Frank Chambers), Cecil Kellaway (Nick Smith), Hume Cronyn (Arthur Keats), Audrey Totter (Madge).

(1981)
Directed by Bob Rafelson. Screenplay by David Mamet, based on the novel by James M. Cain. Produced by Rafelson and Charles Mulvehill. Cinematography by Sven Nykvist. Edited by Graeme Clifford. Production Design by George Jenkins. Music by Michael Small.

Jessica Lange (Cora Papadakis), Jack Nicholson (Frank Chambers), John Colicos (Nick Papadakis), Michael Lerner (Katz), John P. Ryan (Kennedy), Anjelica Huston (Madge).

Romance doesn't get more hardboiled than this: Amoral drifter Frank Chambers and ambitious floozie Cora can't keep their hands off each other, but their affair is thwarted by her husband, Nick. She doesn't love Nick, but doesn't want to abandon the roadside diner they own and start over again, penniless. So Frank and Cora kill him, then turn on each other when a clever lawyer figures out the plot behind Nick's "accidental" death. Ironically, they both escape the clutches of the law, but it all ends badly anyway. Cora is killed in a genuine car accident, and Frank is sent to the electric chair for murdering her.

Based on the novel by James M. Cain, black prince of the pulp novel, *The Postman Always Rings Twice* is a flawless example of the noir credo: Nothing is what it seems, no one can be trusted, and fate is always hiding around the bend, ready to stick out its foot and trip you up when you least expect it. *Postman* has been filmed four times, first in France as *Le Dernier Tournant* (1939), directed by Pierre Chenal and starring Fernand Gravet and Corinne Luchaire, later in Italy as *Ossessione* (1942). An uncredited adaptation directed by Luchino Visconti (it was his first film), *Ossessione*—which starred Massimo Girotti and Clara Calamai—wasn't shown in the United States until 1959, when the copyright on Cain's novel had elapsed; it was still hot stuff.

The first American version of *Postman* starred sexpot of the moment Lana Turner, a lethally alluring vision in white whose entrance is preceded by her lipstick, which rolls across the floor and comes to rest at costar John Garfield's feet. He's smitten, as anyone would be; mad love once again raises its terminally seductive head,* and there's nothing anyone can do to stop the flames of lust from burning down the house. Though restrained by the time and the high-profile stars—Lana Turner never got as down and dirty as second-tier femme fatale Gloria Grahame—the 1946 *Postman* is a genuinely sexy picture. Turner is luscious, Garfield brutally handsome; together they suggest real passion within the boundaries of Hollywood propriety.

The 1981 remake is an altogether more candid story. It was announced in 1972, but it took eight years

John Garfield has the hardboiled hots for Lana Turner in the film noir classic *The Postman Always Rings Twice.*

---

*See *Betty Blue*, *The Devil in the Flesh*, and *Gun Crazy* for more on the subject of *l'amour fou.*

fact, Lana Turner obligingly labeled Lange's performance "pornographic." The second *Postman Always Rings Twice* goes heavy on the concupiscence—not a review failed to mention the scene in which Cora and Frank have sex on the kitchen table—and the rumor machine added even more spice to the mix. *Postman* benefited mightily from the heavily reported suggestion that Nicholson and Lange weren't acting.

New York's *Daily News* dedicated itself to particularly thorough coverage of the scuttlebutt about *Postman*'s sex scenes. "Sex could be posing a problem at Paramount this week when executives get their first look at Jack Nicholson's and Jessica Lange's kitchen sex scene in 'The Postman Always Rings Twice,'" read one breathless item. "Insiders say the scene is so startlingly explicit that, unless it's toned down, it will get the film an X rating." Gossip doyenne Liz Smith used her considerable influence to get the insiders to spill details: "Jack Nicholson recently ran an uncut version . . . for special pals out in Hollywood. Verdict? . . . Nicholson's 'Postman' may well be the most erotic movie ever made. One who saw it says, 'They show absolutely everything—genitals, the act, everything. It's positively pornographic!'" Wow! Still later, columnist Marilyn Beck reported that the sex scenes in the finished film were "more graphic than anything you've ever seen in a production turned out by a major studio" and wondered what you had to do to get an X these days. But it fell to the ever-brazen *New York Post*, after the film's release, to disseminate the most prurient gossip of all; it reported that Nicholson had transferred the steamy outtakes of himself and Lange to tape, the better to show them to his friends.

After all that, the movie could hardly live up to the legend, and it doesn't. But it's unquestionably libidinous, and Nicholson and Lange capture the sadomasochistic undercurrent that runs through Cain's prose. His Frank describes Cora as having lips you wanted to mash with a fork, and Nicholson hits just the right note of violent desire.

to assemble the right package of director and stars and get the cameras rolling. It finally fell to colorful Bob Rafelson, whose pre-filmmaking background included jobs as various as jazz musician and rodeo rider, to direct Jack Nicholson and Jessica Lange (then best known as the girl in the Fay Wray role in Dino DeLaurentiis's dreadful 1976 *King Kong*) in a remake that focused on all the material around which the 1946 version skirted. Despite the new version's screenplay by critically acclaimed playwright David Mamet, the difference between the two versions of *Postman* has nothing to do with plot or dialogue and everything to do with exposed flesh and lustful groping. Liberated by the increasing frankness of 1970s movies, Rafelson reportedly told his stars to pretend they were making an X-rated picture. They appear to have complied; in

Jack Nicholson and Lange in the steamy remake (1981).

Erotic Thrillers

Once *erotic thriller* was purely a movie buff's term. Now erotic thrillers (heavy on the erotic) are videostore kudzu, multiplying so fast they're crowding everything else off the shelves. The lineage is clear: Most film noir classics—from *Out of the Past* (1947) to *Kiss Me Deadly* (1955)—are erotic thrillers, with their wicked femmes fatales and their smoky aura of potential violence, and *Body Heat* (1981)—Lawrence Kasdan's updated, revisionist *hommage* to noir conventions—prepared the ground for the current crop. The genre blossomed with 1985's *Jagged Edge*, in which lawyer-in-too-tight-skirts Glenn Close falls in lust with client Jeff Bridges, who's accused of having brutally murdered his wife. From the mainstream *Whispers in the Dark* (1993) to the direct-to-video *Body Chemistry* (1990), *Stripped to Kill* (1987), and *Night Eyes* (1990) series, they're sexy pictures for people who don't want to rent *Emmanuelle*—thrillers for viewers who like their sex and violence well mixed.

The world of the erotic thriller is one of perpetual night and rain, in which men are detectives, bodyguards, surveillance experts, and vaguely menacing "businessmen," while women are professional strippers, mistresses, and sex surrogates. Deals always sour, relationships dissolve in lies and betrayal, and danger lurks behind every beautiful face and well-muscled torso. The principal danger to viewers, however, lies in renting movies they've already seen and not realizing it until the midway point. Erotic thriller box copy all sounds alike: "A steamy shocker whose twists and turns will keep you guessing until the last stunning moment" will cover everything from *Body Heat* (1981) to *The Last Seduction* (1994), and the box art is a study in sameness. Mix and match water, lingerie, windows, fog/smoke, guns, alleys, venetian blinds, and red lips/nails, and you've got a cover image that will suit *Fatal Attraction* (1987) and *Mortal Passions* (1990) equally well. And as to titles, well, any combination including such key words as *attraction*, *chemistry*, *dark*, *deadly*, *embrace*, *exposure*, *fatal*, *heat*, *illusion*, *image*, *instinct*, *intimate*, *lethal*, *lust*, *mortal*, *obsession*, *passion*, *private*, *seduction*, *temptation*, or *weapon* is fair game. Try it yourself: *Deadly Temptation, Fatal Illusion, Lethal Seduction, Private Image* . . . it's easy, and it's lucrative.

La Ronde
(1950)

Directed by Max Ophüls. Screenplay by Jacques Natanson and Ophüls, based on the play by Arthur Schnitzler. Cinematography by Christian Matras. Production Design by D'Eaubonne. Edited by Leonide Azar. Music by Oscar Strauss.

Anton Walbrook (the narrator), Simone Signoret (the prostitute), Serge Reggiani (Franz), Simone Simon (Marie), Daniel Gélin (Alfred), Danielle Darrieux (Madame Breitkopf), Fernand Gravey (Monsieur Breitkopf), Odette Joyeux (the *cocotte*), Jean-Louis Barrault (Robert), Isa Miranda (the actress), Gérard Philipe (the officer).

Max Ophüls's *La Ronde* was the first film version of Arthur Schnitzler's play *Reigen*, in which ten characters in search of love, sex, romance, or some combination of the three form an elegant daisy chain of desire, one-half of each couple breaking off and introducing the next. The film opens with a waterfront prostitute and closes as the tenth lover, an army officer rejected by a capricious actress, goes home with her for an impotent tryst. Ophüls's film is witty and sophisticated, sexually frank without being flagrantly erotic. It's highly stylized, narrated by a roué in evening clothes who introduces each vignette against the symbolic backdrop of a merry-go-round.

In Vienna in 1900, a prostitute seduces a soldier, Franz, by the river bank. Franz has a girlfriend named Marie, a maid, and they make love in the woods. He abandons her, and she takes up with Alfred, the young and inexperienced son of her employers. Emboldened by the experience, he has an affair with a married woman, Mme Breitkopf whose husband scarcely

The Poet (Jean-Louis Barrault) and the Cocotte (Odette Joyeux).

notices her. M. Breitkopf takes up with a young woman who makes him feel rakish, and he installs her as his mistress in a nice apartment. She begins an affair with a poet, who stands her up for an actress. The actress throws him over for an army officer who, after their rendezvous, gets drunk and wanders down to the waterfront and goes home with the prostitute.

There's no sex shown in *La Ronde*, though there's obviously plenty of sex going on. It was the film's cheerfully nonchalant attitude toward fornication that got it into trouble in the United States, where the New York State Board of Regents banned it as immoral in 1952. The ban was overturned by the U.S. Supreme Court in the light of that year's decision—set in motion four years earlier by the banning of Roberto Rossellini's *The Miracle* as sacrilegious—that movies are entitled to constitutional guarantees of free speech. The film was, naturally, condemned by the Legion of Decency. The carousel of desire kept on turning nonetheless, and *La Ronde* is a small masterpiece of cinematic foreplay, leading the audience through the smiles, the small talk, the discreet touches that lead up to sexual gratification, and then leaving them deliciously on the brink.

La Ronde was remade in 1964 as *Circle of Love* by oh-so-continental smutmeister Roger Vadim, who changed the setting from Vienna to Paris and the time from the turn of the century to 1914, on the eve of World War I. The stars include Vadim's then-wife, Jane Fonda, in the Danielle Darrieux role, Jean-Luc Godard's wife, Anna Karina, in the Simone Simon role, and Catherine Spaak in the Odette Joyeux role. Though the screenplay was by noted playwright Jean

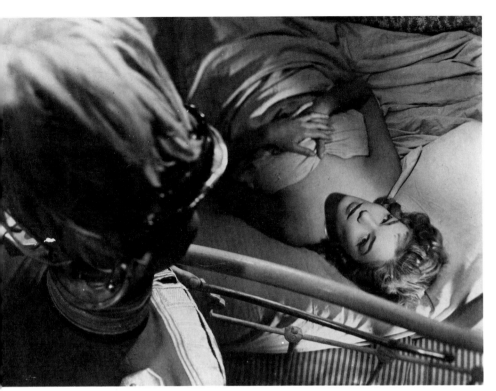

The Prostitute (Simone Signoret) and the Officer (Gerard Phillipe) complete the chain of desire in *La Ronde*.

Schnitzler's conception by including gay and bisexual pairings, and lets the ghost of AIDS hangs over all their liaisons. *Chain of Desire* is far more explicit than any of the previous versions, showing a variety of sexual acts—from gay hustling to a man and a woman masturbating at their windows, each able to see, but not touch, the other. But the domino theory of desire is familiar: A singer, Alma (Linda Fiorentino), sleeps with a workman (Elias Koteas), who goes home to his wife, a maid. She has sex with her employer, the wealthy Jerald (Patrick Bachau), who moves on to sexual adventurer Linda (Grace Zabriskie). Linda's husband, Hubert (Malcolm McDowell), a tabloid TV reporter, picks up Keith (Jamie Harrold), a crack hustler, who tricks with social worker Ken (Tim Guinee), whose bisexual lover, David (Dewey Webber), is a performance artist at the club where Alma sings. The carousel of carnality continues to turn . . . .

Anouilh, critics were cruel, finding better things to say about the set design than about the script or the performances. They were generally kinder to the women—noting that at least they all *looked* beautiful—than to the men, and Fonda's romp with young Jean Claude Brialy (in the Daniel Gélin role) was singled out for its daring.

In 1993, *La Ronde* was reworked again as *Chain of Desire*, directed by Temostocles Lopez, who restored one notion from the original play and made several changes of his own. Schnitzler's carousel of desire was haunted by the specter of syphilis, a nasty matter entirely ignored by both Ophüls and Vadim. Lopez updates his story to New York in the '90s, interrupts the symmetrical girl-boy-girl-boy alternation of

Anna Karina as a naughty French-maid fantasy come to life in *Circle of Love* (1964), Roger Vadim's smutty remake of *La Ronde*.

The Sailor Who Fell From Grace With the Sea (1976)

Directed by Lewis John Carlino. Produced by Martin Poll. Screenplay by Carlino, based on the novel by Yukio Mishima. Cinematography by Douglas Slocombe. Production Design by Ted Haworth. Edited by Audrey Gibbs. Music by John Mandel.

Sarah Miles (Mrs. Anne Osborne), Kris Kristofferson (Jim Cameron), Jonathan Kahn (Jonathan), Margo Cunningham (Mrs. Palmer), Earl Rhodes (the chief).

O h the pounding surf, displaced sound of throbbing desire; oh the deep, murky sea, as mysterious and dangerous as the darkest heart of lust! Based on the novel by philosophical libertine Yukio Mishima, *The Sailor Who Fell From Grace With the Sea* was a sensation that's been all but forgotten. Though the R-rated film was taken to task by some reviewers for its frank eroticism, the real scandal was a *Playboy* pictorial of unprecedented raunchiness for a pair of mainstream stars. The photos, in which Kris Kristofferson and Sarah Miles re-created erotic images from the film, appeared in the magazine's July 1976 issue and were far more graphic than any seen in the finished movie. The accompanying text declared *Sailor*'s sex scenes the biggest breakthrough in mainstream fornication since Donald Sutherland and Julie Christie's notorious roll in Nicolas Roeg's *Don't Look Now*, three years earlier.

Young Jonathan Osborne lives in a vast house by the sea with his mother, Anne, a young widow. She runs a profitable antiques business but is less successful dealing with her son: Just entering puberty, he's becoming defiant and sullen, increasingly secretive about what he and his little friends are up to after school. Anne has no idea how much she ought to be worrying: Jonathan and his chums are in the thrall of a charming adolescent sociopath with Nietzschian delusions. He calls himself the chief and has organized them into a secret society whose "games" are tinged with sadism and perversion. Jonathan, who has already begun spying on his mother through a peephole in her bedroom, needs a man's firm hand—though scarcely more than she does—and the man who comes into their life is Jim Cameron.

Not since *Potemkin* have so many ship's pistons plunged with such ferocity as they do on Anne and Jonathan's first visit to Cameron's ship. A weatherbeaten sailor who's secretly begun to weary of the seafaring life, Cameron falls in love with Anne and becomes the focus of all Jonathan's adolescent fantasies about manliness, strength, and the boundless power and mystery of the sea. Jonathan hangs on his every word, enthralled by Cameron's stories of storms and wrecks and exotic places, fascinated by the older man's muscles and scars. Jonathan shares his admiration for Cameron with his friends, earning the chief's scorn. He tells Jonathan that his sailor—like all adults—is secretly weak and corrupt, setting the stage for a test of loyalty that can only end badly.

Although *The Sailor Who Fell From Grace With the Sea* didn't really blur the line between pornographic and mainstream films, as some reviewers suggested, it did test the limits of what was erotically acceptable in a serious film. Kristofferson and Miles are a lusty couple, and their sex scenes are bold and lovingly photographed. Once again, literary origins provided the license to thrill, though Mishima was considerably less famous than D. H. Lawrence, and his reputation was

Sarah Miles caresses herself in *Sailor*'s notorious masturbation scene.

for it to seduce apple-cheeked Anglo-Saxon small fry.

The Sailor Who Fell From Grace With the Sea has a distinctly unwholesome air that's at odds with the idea that sex is a healthy and natural occupation. As in the book, the film's eroticism is all naughty and somehow tainted. For all the gorgeous shots of cliffs and beaches and rolling fields—nature at her most metaphorically vigorous—the sex scenes are all shrouded in tangled bedclothes and shadowed lighting. Perhaps because Jonathan's incestuous peeping hangs over the film like an unhealthy pall, the film's sex scenes—from Miles's tasteful masturbating to her energetic couplings with Kristofferson—are all undeniably titillating, but a bit smutty. The brightly lit *Playboy* photos radiate playful passion by comparison.

The U.S. Catholic Conference, the sad and largely ignored remnant of the Legion of Decency, condemned *The Sailor Who Fell From Grace With the Sea*, but nobody cared. The newspaper ads carried the pretentious warning: "Like the act of love, this film must be experienced from beginning to end. Therefore no one will be seated once the picture starts." It's a safe bet that no one cared much about that either.

always tainted with hints of depravity and indulgence. Mishima was a bisexual physical-culture buff whose right-wing politics (which culminated in his ritual suicide in 1970) had much to do with uniforms and sexually charged rites of power and submission. It's not hard to detect his voice in the chief's childish worship of masculine beauty and brutality. No wonder the thing that seemed to bother critics most was that Mishima's tale had been transposed from Yokohama to the British countryside. It's one thing for that sort of perverted nastiness to be taking root in the minds of Japanese children, but quite another

Kris Kristofferson falls from grace in the arms of sexy Miles.

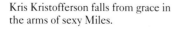

One of the sex scenes that Miles and Kristofferson later recreated for *Playboy* magazine, with scandalous results.

Sex With the One You Love

Once, solo sex was the purview of deeply serious films about disorder, sexual and otherwise; witness Ingmar Bergman's *The Silence* (1963), in which Ingrid Thulin's nervous breakdown manifests itself in alcoholism and self-abuse, and Mark Rydell's adaptation of D. H. Lawrence's *The Fox* (1968), in which ambivalent lesbian Anne Heywood masturbates circumspectly in front of a steamed-up mirror. That said, a sweet and unusual masturbation scene in Jean Vigo's *L'Atalante* (1934) defies all the stereotypes: Separated lovers Jean Dasté and Dita Parlo each pleasure themselves (discreetly, but indisputably) in their lonely beds; Vigo's cross-cutting turns it into a mutual sex scene. It is, however, a lovely exception to the rule.

Hard though it is to make sexual coupling look anywhere near as good as it feels, masturbation presents an even tougher challenge. Woody Allen defended it as "sex with someone I love," but in the movies masturbation tends to look like sex with the only one who will have you, and that's pathetic. Dennis Christopher in *Fade to Black* (1980) jerking off to a picture of Marilyn Monroe, and Jennifer Jason Leigh masturbating alone in her room in *Single White Female* (1992), are only two of the grimmer exam-

ples. Sharon Stone in her bathtub in *Sliver* (1993)—a squirm-inducing scene that was misguidedly *lengthened* for European release—was only slightly better.

Shirley MacLaine looks embarrassed in *Being There* (1979)—she's one of many who misinterpret retarded gardener Peter Sellers's mantra "I like to watch." The same can't be said for Jeroen Krabbe in *The Fourth Man* (1979), wanking frantically as he peeps through the keyhole at comely Renée Soutendjik and Thom Hoffman going at it. In fact, the '80s brought a flood (as it were) of uninhibited masturbators, including Judge Reinhold in *Fast Times at Ridgemont High* (1982); Melanie Griffith in *Body Double* (1984)—it's actually a plot point, too—Kim Basinger in *Nine ½ Weeks* (1986); Antonio Banderas (to slasher movies) in *Law of Desire* (1987); the ever-uninhibited Harvey Keitel in *Bad Lieutenant* (1992); while he terrorizes two girls in a car, and the hunky blind (or is he?) handyman in *Sirens* (1994), a cheerfully smutty fantasy with high-art trappings. *Spanking the Monkey* (1995) went so far as to announce its preoccupation with solitary vice in the title. At this rate, no one will need to teach masturbation in school.

Sebastiane
(1976)

Directed by Paul Humfress and Derek Jarman. Produced by Howard Malin and James Whaley. Screenplay by Whaley and Jarman. Cinematography by Peter Middleton. Edited by Humfress. Music by Brian Eno.

Leonardo Treviglio (Sebastiane), Barney James (Severus), Neil Kennedy (Maximus), Richard Warwick (Justin), Donald Dunham (Claudius), Ken Hicks (Adrian), Janusz Romanov (Anthony), Stefano Massari (Marius), David Finbar (Julian).

Painter and art director–turned–filmmaker Derek Jarman's first picture is unique: a lyrical, homoerotic film in Latin (it is, in fact, not only the sexiest film ever made in Latin but the *only* film ever made in Latin) that revels in religious ecstasy and physical passion. Drawing rather freely on the story of third-century martyr Saint Sebastian—patron saint of archers, athletes, soldiers, and gay men—Jarman and cowriter-director Phil Humfress fashioned an eighty-three-minute meditation on the beauty of male bodies in motion: bathing, sparring, hunting, playing ball, riding horseback, swimming, wrestling, and throwing the discus nude or nearly so. Jarman cheekily remarked that all the nudity was because "the budget wouldn't run to authentic costumes." But *Variety* struck a blow for blinding glimpses of the obvious when it reported, in GAY LADS' NUDE SEXUALITY UPS SUBTITLED ARTY TO BIG U.K. BIZ, that the film's bare asses appealed mightily to homosexual audiences. *Sebastiane* was rated X both in its native England and in the United States, where it was released in 1978.

Treviglio in a rustic variation of the soft-core favorite, the shower scene.

Shot on location in the starkly beautiful Sardinian countryside, the film is visually poetic and often genuinely sensual, but the result is nevertheless somewhat odd. In particular, it takes a while to get used to hearing Latin speech—which sounds, reasonably enough, very like Italian—translated into such subtitles as "Bugger off, Anthony ... I've told you to leave me alone," "Max! Back to the barracks and clean the armor," "Come on, motherfuckers," and "Hey Justin, you creep, take this."

Sebastiane opens in the decadent court of Roman emperor Diocleitian, where a eunuch in a red G-string and a circle of nude men wearing enormous phalluses are doing an erotic dance for the depraved nobles. Sebastiane, a member of the elite Praetorian guard, protests a particularly sordid and capricious act of violence and is stripped of his rank and exiled to a remote desert outpost, under the command of Captain Severus. Sebastiane hears the voice of the Lord and becomes a Christian, for which he's scourged, starved, staked in the sun, and reviled by Severus, who secretly loves Sebastiane and resents his faith. Sebastiane refuses to renounce his religion, and while some of his fellow exiles sympathize, others—egged on by the brutal, homophobic Maximus—grow increasingly hostile. Eventually Sebastiane is tied naked to a stake, and shot to death with arrows.

Humfress and Jarman, who began his career as a design consultant to the ever-extravagant Ken Russell on *The Devils* (1971) and *Savage Messiah* (1972), tap into a canny mix of gay obsessions in *Sebastiane*: the cult of athleticism; sexual desire sublimated into religious euphoria; baroque sadomasochism; and the Steve

of the past as a foreign country. But its characters—with the exception of the pious Sebastiane—are startlingly prosaic in their behavior and interests. When Max regales his barracksmates with stories of the good old days (when the whores were more brazen, the orgies more extravagant, the games a real spectacle, and the Colosseum a true wonder, not a sorry shadow of its former self), we hear every blowhard who ever monopolized a bar room conversation. Still, its principal appeal lies in the way the camera caresses the flesh of its attractive cast, lingering on the curves of well-toned bellies, the swell of muscular calves and biceps, and the contours of exposed genitals.

After *Sebastiane* Jarman went on to cowrite and direct a series of high-minded, frankly erotic art films whose lush visuals belie their low budgets, including *The Tempest* (1979), *Caravaggio* (1986), *Edward II* (1991), and *Wittgenstein* (1994). With independent financing and a singular clarity of vision, he rejected entirely the coded, sublimated homoeroticism that sustained earlier generations of gay movie goers. An example of such attitudes: *Gentlemen Prefer Blondes* (1953) in which Jane Russell sings "Is There Anyone Here for Love" in a room full of succulent weight lifters, a camp fest of the first order. Jarman followed instead in the footsteps of Kenneth Anger's seminal *Scorpio Rising* (1963), which exploited the fetishistic appeal of the biker only hinted at in Marlon Brando's *The Wild One* (1953) and anticipated such later films as Rainer Fassbinder's *Querelle* (1982), starring Brad Davis and based on the novel by Jean Genet; the "Homo" section of Todd Haynes's *Poison* (1991), based primarily on Genet's *Thief's Journal*; Gregg Araki's *The Living End* (1993); and Tom Kalin's *Swoon* (1993).

Reeves appeal of underdressed, overmuscled men, stripped of its wholesome manly drag. Saint Sebastian, commonly depicted in his martyrdom as a dewy youth in a scanty loincloth, is the perfect locus for these preoccupations. "The arrows have eaten into his tense, fragrant, youthful flesh and are about to consume his body from within with flames of supreme agony and ecstasy": Japanese novelist Yukio Mishima was particularly eloquent in describing, in *Confessions of a Mask*, the appeal of Guido Reni's voluptuous seventeenth-century painting of the dying Sebastian, but he wasn't alone.

Like Fellini's grotesque and sexually extravagant *Satyricon* (1969), which also explores in lustful (though not particularly attractive) detail the sexual excesses of declining Rome, Sebastiane proceeds from the notion

Camp homoeroticism in *Gentleman Prefer Blondes* (1953): These gentlemen clearly prefer one another to curvy Jane Russell.

Wagging Your Harvey

Women are always baring it all, but men have been less generous about sharing their private parts in the movies. The films of Peter Greenaway are often instructive (in that they show lots of willies) though seldom erotic. The lovers in *The Cook, The Thief, His Wife and Her Lover* find all sorts of ingenious places to have sex (confirming some of the worst things we ever imagined about what goes on behind the scenes in restaurants), but it's all too sad. And while *Prospero's Books* allows the viewer to see more penises than the average urologist, there's barely a thrill in sight, unless one counts dancer Michael Clark's bare parts, trussed into an alarming package that's the focus of all horrified attention whenever it's on screen. Among the major actors who have bared all are:

Joe Dallesandro in *Flesh* (1968), *Trash* (1970), and *Heat* (1971)

Rutger Hauer in *Turkish Delight* (1973)

Jan-Michael Vincent in *Buster and Billie* (1974)

Dennis Hopper in *Tracks* (1976)

Graham Chapman (hilariously) in *Monty Python's The Life of Brian* (1979)

Gerard Depardieu in *1900* (1977)

Peter Firth in *Equus* (1977)

Richard Gere (briefly!) in *American Gigolo* (1980)

Eric Stoltz in *Haunted Summer* (1988) and *Naked in New York* (1994)

John Malkovich in *The Sheltering Sky* (1990)

Tom Berenger (shaved and tied up with bits of foliage!) in *At Play in the Fields of the Lord* (1991)

Jaye Davidson in *The Crying Game* (1992)

Tim Robbins (under a thin sheen of mud) in *The Player* (1992)

Harvey Keitel in *Bad Lieutenant* (1992) and *The Piano* (1993)

James Woods in *The Curse of the Starving Class* (1995)

Douglas Henshall (quite semi-erectly) in *Angels and Insects* (1995)

The Seven Year Itch
(1955)

Directed by Billy Wilder. Produced by Charles K. Feldman and Wilder. Written by Wilder and George Axelrod, based on Axelrod's play. Cinematography by Milton Krasner. Edited by Hugh S. Fowler. Music by Alfred Newman.

Marilyn Monroe (the girl), Tom Ewell (Richard Sherman), Evelyn Keyes (Helen Sherman), Sonny Tufts (Tom McKenzie), Robert Strauss (Kruhulik), Oscar Homolka (Doctor Brubaker).

Millions of words have been written about the eternal Marilyn and nearly as many about her films, which are mostly a sorry bunch. *The Seven Year Itch* is one of the best, along with *Niagara* (1952), *Gentlemen Prefer Blondes* (1953), *Bus Stop* (1956), *Some Like It Hot* (1959, also directed by Billy Wilder), and *The Misfits* (1961), and it's a consummate tribute to what passed for sexual sophistication in the mainstream '50s. Made within a year of Brigitte Bardot's *And God Created Woman*, *The Seven Year Itch* epitomizes Hollywood high artifice and coy sexuality. Though it starred America's reigning sex goddess, platinum blonde Monroe, her character is so utterly without personal identity that she doesn't even have a name: The credits identify her simply as "the girl." Monroe is said to have disliked her status as a sex symbol because "a symbol becomes a thing—I hate to be a thing. But if I'm going to be a symbol of something I'd rather have it be sex." But she *is* a thing, a squeaky-clean thing, teasing sensuality personified: pale, carefully painted, and poured into a variety of pretty pastel outfits, from the chastely slinky white gown whose

Tom Ewell watches Marilyn Monroe strike the quintessential innocent tease pose over the subway grating.

straps she can't fasten without help, to the famous pleated white dress whose skirt is blown aloft by a passing subway train, and a shell-pink blouse and matador pants ensemble.

The place is Manhattan, during a sweltering summer, and the plot simplicity itself. Vaguely discontented and too-nearly-middle-aged husband Richard Sherman (Tom Ewell), editor of pulp paperbacks whose lurid covers couldn't be further from his uneventful life, vows not to be one of those philandering husbands who stray while their wives and children vacation in the country. But the first time he sees the girl (Marilyn Monroe) who's sublet the apartment upstairs, he puts his neck out trying to look up her dress as she ascends the stairs, and he collapses into a positive orgy of salacious imaginings.

After she reveals demurely that she beats the summer heat by keeping her undies in the icebox, he's smitten big time and invites her down for a drink, dreaming of a Rachmaninoff-fueled fantasy that includes her in a ludicrously lubricous, skin-tight, tiger-striped gown. Sherman flirts clumsily, and the girl remains ravishingly (perhaps deliberately) oblivious. After their nontryst, he's smitten with guilt and envisions everything from her humiliating denunciation of his wolfish behavior to his wife's holiday infidelity with a bestselling lothario. A second date takes them to the movies and then back to his air-conditioned apartment, where she chastely spends the night. In the morning, she sends him off to visit the family with a wholesome kiss and the ego-fortifying assurance that if she were his wife, she'd be very jealous in his absence.

Directed by Austrian expatriate Billy Wilder,

A bottle of Champagne, a bag of chips, and the girl: Monroe and Ewell.

A kiss is never just a kiss, and the first movie buss—the be-all and end-all of *The Kiss* (1896)—got decidedly mixed reviews: The word *disgusting* featured prominently in one assessment. It wasn't just that plump May Irwin and mustachioed John C. Rice were less-than-perfect specimens of humanity; the whole scale and intimacy of the cinema struck some neo-cinephiles as distasteful. But not for long.

The immortal (if mostly misquoted) line "Kiss me, my fool" is an intertitle from *A Fool There Was* (1915), an early Theda Bara vehicle in which she plays the prototypical vamp. Her kisses are fatal, and audiences hung on her lips' every quiver. Soon, kissing was everywhere, and among early screen idols, opinions about technique were contradictory: Virginal Lillian Gish argued for leaving the actual smooch to the imagination, while Polish-born Pola Negri held the advanced view that more was more—she had to downplay her lusty displays for American movies. Gish's inclinations ruled: Lips met, but in a stylized ritual that radiated passion without saliva, tongues, or smeared lipstick. The notorious Motion Picture Production Code, formulated in 1930 but not vigorously enforced until 1934, made special mention of kissing, discouraging the "lustful" and "open-mouthed" variety, which everyone knows is the only kind that counts.

As movies got bolder, kisses became wetter and more wide ranging, and today most stars have abandoned the classic Hollywood kiss in favor of a more realistic but generally less aesthetic exercise. Highlights of the kiss's progress include:

The Sea Beast (1925): Lothario John Barrymore's *looooong* kiss with Dolores Costello was pieced together from four takes, and Warners publicists spread the word that Costello fainted on the set.

Flesh and the Devil (1927): Greta Garbo comes between John Gilbert and Lars Hanson, and who can wonder? Garbo's kisses are a marvel, simultaneously hungry and delicate; they seem to linger long after they're gone.

Un Chien Andalou (1928): Amidst the general perverse desire, a woman kisses the big toe of a statue with greedy zest, proving—probably not for the first time, certainly not for the last—that it takes all kinds.

whose cosmopolitan sensibilities make films as disparate as *Sunset Boulevard* (1950) and *Ace in the Hole / The Big Carnival* (1951) such bracing experiences, *The Seven Year Itch* is a glossy study in impotent fantasizing, one long celebration of American sexual shame and hypocrisy embodied in weasely Tom Ewell. In addition to imagining an affair with Monroe, Ewell conjures up trysts with his buttoned-down secretary; a wanton, well-starched nurse; and even his wife's best friend (à la *From Here to Eternity*). But when the flesh and blood girl is well within his reach, he makes only the most tentative moves, which she brushes off like bothersome gnats—much to his relief. *The Seven Year Itch* features what may be the definitive Monroe performance. She slinks and shimmies, purrs and whispers, giggles and bats her lavishly mascaraed eyes, tosses back her head to reveal a milky throat that cries out to be kissed. Every carefully arranged strand of white-gold hair remains firmly in place, and not an inch of

The Bridge of San Luis Rey (1929): Don Alvorado slid his lips along the fine neck of Lili Damita in one of the last exotic kisses for years; the Production Code subsequently restricted motion-picture kisses to the lips.

Dracula (1931): Unlikely sex object Bela Lugosi brought the vampire's kiss to life in "the strangest love story ever told" and paved the way for generations of bloody embraces.

You're in the Army Now (1941): Regis Toomey and Jane Wyman set the record for longest continuous movie kiss, at three minutes and five seconds.

Notorious (1946): Ingrid Bergman and Cary Grant enjoy an obscenely long kiss, expertly staged by master of the perverse Alfred Hitchcock. As she prepares dinner, he follows her around the apartment, and their lips never stay together long enough to flout contemporary standards. But they just keep coming back for more. Hitchcock's kisses are indeed notorious: In *Spellbound* (1945), Gregory Peck and Bergman kiss as suggestive opening doors are superimposed over their faces, while in *Rear Window* (1954) Grace Kelly awakens James Stewart with a kiss so magical it's in slow motion. The following year, she takes on Grant in *To Catch a Thief* (1955), where they cause literal fireworks, and in *North by Northwest* (1959), Grant and Eva Marie Saint's kiss is followed by a shot of a train roaring through a tunnel. Could it be Freudian?

From Here to Eternity (1953): Adulterers Burt Lancaster and Deborah Kerr turn a kiss into a whole-body experience, twined together on the beach with the waves lapping at their toes.

Underwater! (1955): Novelty is everything as Jane Russell, in a fetching swimsuit, smooches . . . underwater. Wet and wild and not something to try at home.

Tea and Sympathy (1956): The ultimate compassionate kiss—Deborah Kerr plants one on the lips of "sensitive" John Kerr, just so he can rest assured he's not gay.

Some Like It Hot (1959): Guileless Marilyn Monroe, as breathless Sugar Kane, must cure pathological liar Tony Curtis—a poor playboy musician who's temporarily abandoned his drag masquerade to pose as a rich playboy with a big yacht—of his feigned indifference (impotence? homosexuality?) to women. Claims director Billy Wilder, "The scene is so sexy because we turned the roles around completely . . . *this* is the fantasy—not to seduce a sexy woman but to have a beautiful woman conquer him." And it's funny too.

Touch of Evil (1958): Janet Leigh and Charlton Heston demonstrate the dangers of miscegenation (he's, um, Mexican; she's the blonde next door) in the corrupt border town of Los Robles. As their lips meet, an offscreen explosion lights up the darkness in the opening of Orson Welles's dark masterpiece.

True Lies (1994) pays homage as Arnold Schwarzenegger and Jamie Lee Curtis—Leigh's daughter—patch up their marital discord with a kiss while a mushroom cloud swells in the background; it's bigger, but not better.

Sunday, Bloody Sunday (1971): All anyone talked about was the kiss Peter Finch planted on Murray Head's lips in this bisexual romantic triangle; the same was true of *Deathtrap* (1982), only it was Michael Caine and Christopher Reeve, and everyone talked *around* it for fear of revealing the twisty plot's final turn. Now it can be told. Twenty-five years later, it still takes a non-American actor to be careless about homosexual kissing; witness Daniel Day-Lewis in *My Beautiful Launderette* (1985), and Antonio Banderas in *Law of Desire* (1987) and other films for Pedro Almodóvar, but conspicuously not *Philadelphia* (1993).

Deep Throat (1973): If oral sex is the ultimate kiss, then *Deep Throat* is the ultimate porno movie about the ultimate kiss: Comely Linda Lovelace discovers that her clitoris is in her throat, and her search for orgasms is defiantly oral.

When the last barriers to nudity and explicit sex on screen fell in the 1970s, the art of kissing declined precipitously as the action moved south. More's the pity.

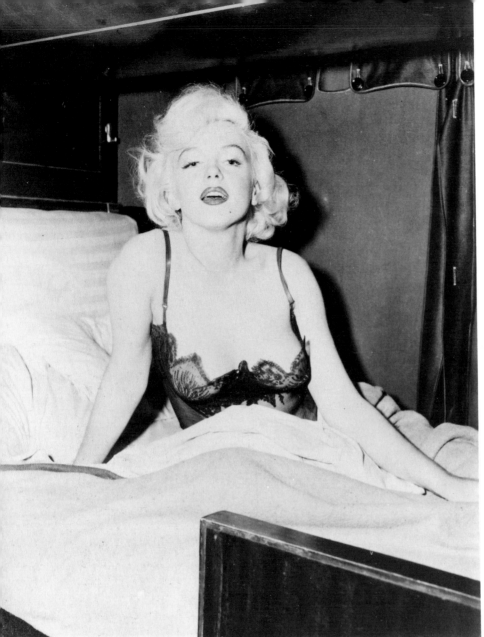

make a story about getting her toe stuck in the bathtub faucet sound positively obscene and contends she doesn't understand why men are always asking her to marry them. Her favorite term of approval is "elegant," because she wouldn't know elegance if it bit her ass. Monroe has been called the last working-class sex goddess, all breasts and thighs and butt, but that's wishful thinking on someone's part—for every Audrey Hepburn there was always a Raquel Welch, for every Kate Moss an Anna Nicole Smith.

Monroe spawned a school of blonde bombshells, all coarser, most more refreshingly vulgar, and a handful almost as well known. First and foremost there was Jayne Mansfield, whose brains were buried by her bosom. She arrived in Hollywood at the peak of Monroe's reign and proved a press agent's dream, endlessly willing to pose for caricatured publicity shots. Mansfield received some acclaim for the cartoonlike *The Girl Can't Help It* (1956) and *Will Success Spoil Rock Hunter?* (1957) and

unruly flesh slips free of her amazingly constructed clothes: Monroe is every inch the Hollywood star, buffed and teased and lipsticked to antiseptic perfection.

The girl's inviolate persona is all the more remarkable for its white-trash origins, however sugar coated. She feels sorry for the *Creature From the Black Lagoon* (he's kind of scary looking, but he just needs affection), dips potato chips in champagne, sucks her finger and frets about being seen without toenail polish, lifts her blouse to luxuriate in the air-conditioning and thrills to the breeze from a subway grating, and proudly displays her semi-nude photo in *American Camera* (the picture won honorable mention; the job paid $25 an hour and took *hours and hours*). She can

achieved immortality by way of her gruesome decapitation in a car accident. Mamie Van Doren was the knockoff, a B-movie pin-up whose sleaze appeal rests on such exploitation classics as *High School Confidential* (1958), *The Beat Generation* (1959), and *College Confidential* (1960), while the acid-tongued Diana Dors was the English answer to pneumatic blondes. Dors starred in *Lady Godiva Rides Again* (1951) and a host of forgettable features; her brief stay in Hollywood was cut short by a scandalous affair with Rod Steiger. And then there was Swedish Anita Ekberg, most grandly endowed of all. She ensured her place in movie history as Sylvia, the vacuous American starlet in *La Dolce Vita*. She's "like a doll," complains world-weary Marcello Mastroianni, who's nevertheless intoxicated.

150

The Sheik
(1921)

Directed by George Melford. Produced by George Melford. Screenplay by Monte M. Ketterjohn, based on the novel by E(dith). M(aude). Hull. Cinematography by William Marshall.

Rudolph Valentino (Sheik Ahmed), Agnes Ayres (Diane Mayo), Adolphe Menjou (Raoul de Saint Hubert), Walter Long (Omair), Lucien Littlefield (Gaston), George Waggner (Youssef).

Before Rudolph Valentino, there were football heroes and boys next door, strapping blonds with all-American good looks and healthy appetites. After Valentino, the movies were awash in Latin lovers, silver-screen gods of exotic eroticism who promised a world of forbidden delights. While he was undeniably handsome by any measure, Valentino's acting looks pretty stiff and mannered by today's standards—as does that of virtually all the stars of the silent era. But his foreign fantasy personae—Argentinean gaucho, Spanish bullfighter, Arab sheik, Indian Raja, French aristocrat, Russian swashbuckler—spoke to the repressed desires of an age. He was virile but not macho, alluring and wondrously unlike the regular guys who scuffed their toes and lowered their eyes in the presence of a beautiful woman. Valentino was lust in an incense-scented wrapper, and women ate it up.

The Sheik is pure potboiler, romantic trash whose racist vision of Arabs as lustful beasts inflamed by the glimpse of a white woman's flesh makes it at best a guilty pleasure for modern viewers. Diane Mayo, a proud English girl, is captured by Sheik Ahmed, who wants her in the worst possible way and swoops down on his horse to carry her off. "Why have you brought me here?" she wonders in his tent, amidst enough lavish pillows and draperies to set-decorate a dozen ravished-by-desert-prince photo layouts. "Are you not woman enough to know?" he leers. She refuses to submit but falls under his spell, is captured by enemy bandits and rescued, her virtue still miraculously intact but her horizons presumably broadened by this taste of spicy romance. Though coy, *The Sheik* is about nothing but carnal desire, and Valentino is a sexual predator who offers the decorously reluctant maiden with the secretly pounding heart the perfect fantasy out: He made me do it. Besotted fans sent Valentino letters, underwear, and nude photographs; the film broke all previous box-office records. Though *The Sheik* doesn't hold up especially well, the Sheik, with his patent leather hair and his deepset eyes, does.

Valentino's life and legend are inextricably linked with his film persona, and he embodied the "live fast, die young" credo decades before the James Dean generation turned it into dreary cliché. Born in Italy, Rudolpho Gugliemi came to America with little more than the clothes on his back and parlayed his attractive physique, considerable charm, and talent for dancing into a career as a gigolo. He moved to Hollywood in 1917 (fleeing a scandal involving a wealthy Chilean heiress), changed his name—first to Rudolpho di Valentina—and eked out a living playing bit parts, mostly as foreign-looking bad guys, because the taste of the time was for fresh-scrubbed heros. All that changed in 1919 when screenwriter June Mathis, who saw in him something everyone else had overlooked, got Valentino the role of an Argentinean artist in Rex Ingram's lavish *The Four Horsemen of the Apocalypse.*

Rudolph Valentino is *The Sheik*.

Women swooned, and a sex symbol was born.

Valentino's off-screen life was genuinely exotic, though more troublesome than his film roles. He married two lesbians, first minor actress Jean Acker, and then her glamorous friend Natacha Rambova (née Winifred Shaunessy, of Salt Lake City). Rambova's artistic ambitions took many forms; she nearly ruined Valentino's career with her pretensions and demands, but he wore faithfully the platinum slave bracelet she gave him. He had an affair with fellow hunk Ramon Novarro (the muscular star of the 1927 *Ben Hur*) while studio publicists worked overtime to quash rumors about his sex life. Men hated Valentino: The *Chicago Tribune* went as far as to call him a "painted pansy" and blamed him for the feminization of the red-blooded American male. Valentino challenged the writer to a duel, and women continued to flock to his films, which include the classic *Camille* (1921), and the bullfighting melodrama *Blood and Sand* (1922), which features a beefcake scene in which he's dressed for the arena. It

prompted the approving Rambova to observe that he looked best in the nude. *Son of the Sheik* (1926) was his last film, and it was a smash hit.

Valentino died in 1926 at the age of thirty-one, the victim of a perforated ulcer. There were riots as his body lay in state, and his funeral was a mob scene. He probably wouldn't have made the transition to sound, which was hard on the silent stars generally and the Latin lotharios in particular, but his premature death ensured his status as icon, a sleek sexual fetish. He was the subject of two movie biographies. The 1951 version was entirely forgettable. Ken Russell's 1977 *Valentino* isn't great cinema, but it's bold and sexy, and ballet superstar Rudolf Nureyev perfectly captures Valentino's wild, pansexual grace; his sensual same-sex tango is an erotic highlight.

Nureyev and Michelle Phillips recreate *The Sheik*'s tent seduction in *Valentino*.

Siesta
(1987)

Directed by Mary Lambert. Produced by Gary Kurfist. Executive Produced by Julio Caro and Zalman King. Screenplay by Patricia Louisianna Knop, based on the novel by Patrice Chaplin. Cinematography by Bryan Loftus. Edited by Glenn A. Morgan. Production Design by John Beard. Music by Marcus Miller.

Ellen Barkin (Claire), Gabriel Byrne (Auguste), Julian Sands (Kit), Isabella Rossellini (Marie), Martin Sheen (Del), Alexi Sayle (Cabbie), Grace Jones (Conchita), Jodie Foster (Nancy).

*S*iesta is a feature-length *Twilight Zone* episode with nudity (*lots* of nudity) and a kinky if sublimated *Devil in Miss Jones* twist. It's designed to make you lust for a dead woman (the *siesta* of the title is the big one) as she wends her erotic way through one last fling with the living. *Siesta* is high toned softcore that's always teetering perilously on the brink of self-parody (a dangerous metaphor in a film about a woman who skydives and walks a literal tightrope), a film that entices in all the conventional ways, then goes for the sucker punch.

Siesta opens as comely Claire, dressed in a skin-tight scarlet dress, awakens on the ground, unable to remember who she is or how she got there. There, as it turns out, is on an airport runway. She flees, finds a nearby stream, and strips to wash out her dress. Ominously, it's stained with blood, though Claire is uninjured. She then sunbathes nude while it dries. What more could one ask of the first few minutes of an arty sex film?

Scarlet woman Claire (Ellen Barkin) and her mysterious lover (Gabriel Byrne).

Claire is a professional daredevil who's abandoned her American husband and failed to execute a much-ballyhooed stunt that involved leaping from an airplane with no parachute. She soon learns she's in sultry Spain, home of her ex-lover and mentor, philosopher of the trapeze Auguste. And she begins to remember bits of the last few days, during which she may have murdered Auguste's wife, Marie. As Claire struggles to regain her memory, she falls in with lechers of all stripes, ranging from a monstrous cabbie with metal teeth (shades of *Belle de Jour*) to Eurotrash artists and their impeccably dressed groupies. The film proceeds with the logic of a nightmare: No matter how hard Claire tries to get back to the small town where Auguste lives, she keeps finding herself in the same place. The cabbie offers to drive her and accept sex in place of the cash she doesn't have, but Claire can't quite bring herself to accept the repulsive bargain and escapes, then throws herself on the mercy of spoiled photographer Kit. He promises to drive her the next day, but when morning comes his car's been stolen. Claire finally returns to the scene of the crime, and learns the truth of what happened: She did indeed tussle with Marie, and there was a bloody knife, but it's Claire who's dead. Heavy.

Barkin's husky voice, perpetually narrowed lynx eyes, and sleek flesh (as often out of her clingy red dress as in it) are among *Siesta*'s main attractions, and director Mary Lambert—who cut her teeth on music videos, including clips for the Eurythmics, the B-52s, and Madonna's "Material Girl" and "Like a Virgin"—puts her through the usual soft-core paces with assurance. The cast is a constant surprise, ranging from stylishly dissipated Julian Sands (who, it appears, will do absolutely *anything* he's asked; see *Boxing Helena*) to Grace Jones, Isabella Rossellini, and Jodie Foster (as English socialite Nancy, with whom Barkin shares a knowing kiss). At the end of Claire's quest lies the revelation that she's been wandering the limbo between this world and the next, making *Siesta* a superior necrophilic fantasy. While it commits all the sins of pretentious sex movies, it also delivers a great look wrapped around an entertainingly loony narrative.

Siesta was written by Patricia Louisianna Knop, wife and longtime collaborator of soft-core impresario Zalman King, who helped produce it. The original cut received an X rating, and the film had to be trimmed down to a commercially acceptable R. Because *Siesta* was both written and directed by women, a rare occurrence, it seems the perfect opportunity to introduce that old sexy movie question: Are erotic pictures directed by women really different from erotic pictures directed by men?

Well, it depends. Yes, if you're talking hardcore. The differences between hard-core pornography produced by men (which is to say, almost all of it) and hard-core pornography made by women fall into three main areas: aesthetics, narrative focus, and tone. The first two are fairly obvious: Pornography made by women tends to be prettier (nicer photography, fewer hairy men wearing grimy socks) and to pay more attention to narrative—how the bodies get into bed together rather than just what they do once they get there. The tone issue is more nebulous, but women's porn films tend to be a little softer, a little less nasty in their underlying assumptions about the relationship between sex and power.

Softcore, on the other hand, all appears to be created equal, and *Siesta* is dramatic proof. Perhaps it's something in the form itself—the tone is inherently subdued, and, deprived of erections and penetration shots, all soft-core filmmakers have to fall back on holding viewer interest through photography and story. In any event, trying to compare, say, *Siesta* and *Wild Orchid* with an eye to locating sex-based differences in erotic articulation is an exercise in futility. They're both sex obsessed and restrained by being able to show everything *but*; both sumptuous, serious, and more than slightly silly, both potentially annoying if you're in the wrong mood and kind of titillating if you're in the right one. *Wild Orchid* has more persistently intrusive philosophical underpinnings; *Siesta* has better overwrought symbolism and dream sequences. Toss a coin, or pair them on a double bill.

Carnal Appetites

Food and sex have been linked in art since time immemorial, and movies, too, have exploited the connection between the two favorite forms of oral gratification. The most famous food-related sex scene in movie history is probably in Tony Richardson's bawdy *Tom Jones* (1963), involving Albert Finney, Joyce Redman, and an aphrodisiacal feast that leads to even fleshier pleasure. Juzo Itami's *Tampopo* (1986) is an entirely obsessed comedy in which all aspects of life are viewed through food; while Marco Ferrari's *La Grande Bouffe* (1973) revolves around four sensualists who decide to eat themselves to death—victuals are not the only thing on their suicidal menu. Dusan Makavejev's *Sweet Movie* (1974) includes scenes of lovemaking in a sea of chocolate and on a mountain of sugar, while Peter Greenaway's *The Cook, the Thief, His Wife and Her Lover* (1989) features its adulterous lovers—Helen Mirren and Alan Howard—having sex amidst cheeses, vegetables, and hanging sides of beef.

One of the most famous sequences in *Nine ½ Weeks* (1986) revolves around Mickey Rourke's feeding the blindfolded Kim Basinger a variety of foods, from strawberries and honey to hot peppers. No one who saw *Fast Times at Ridgemont High* (1982) can forget Phoebe Cates teaching Jennifer Jason Leigh how to fellate a carrot, while in Pedro Almodóvar's *Kika* (1994) a slice of orange is all the sweeter after it's been between Veronica Forque's legs. The lovers in *In the Realm of the Senses* also share food that has been dipped in Eiko Matsuda's honeypot.

Jorge Arau's *Like Water for Chocolate* (1994), a mystical Mexican film that did surprisingly strong business in the United States, told a story of thwarted love and the magical power of food to incite powerful passions, including lust. One wonders what they were eating on the set, since stars Marco Leonardi and Lumi Cavazos fell in love during production. Perhaps, then, it isn't music that's the food of love after all.

Kinky Claire and her partners in erotic crime *(clockwise from left):* Gabriel Byrne, Jodie Foster, and Julian Sands.

Something Wild
(1986)

Directed by Jonathan Demme. Produced by Demme and Kenneth Utt. Screenplay by E. Max Frye. Cinematography by Tak Fujimoto. Edited by Craig McKay. Production Design by Norma Moriceau. Music by John Cale and Laurie Anderson.

Melanie Griffith (Lulu / Audrey Hankel), Jeff Daniels (Charles Driggs), Ray Liotta (Ray Sinclair), Margaret Colin (Irene), Dana Preu (Peaches).

Stuffy young tax whiz Charles Driggs gets caught walking out on his lunch check at a funky little diner one Friday afternoon. His accuser, Lulu—a vision in black and fashionable tribal accessories, all topped with scarlet lipstick and a shiny raven bob—shames him and teases him, flatters him by divining that he's a "closet rebel," then offers him a lift back to the office. Once in her car, Charlie is off for the ride of his life.

Lulu interrogates him, discovers that he's married, has two children, has just received a promotion at work, and has never done an impulsive thing in his life. So she spirits him off to a sleazy New Jersey motel, handcuffs him to the bed, and has her merry way with him. Before she's done, he's lied to his boss and his wife, done a year's worth of drinking in an afternoon, and has had the best sex of his recent life. Confused, nervous (and he doesn't even *know* that Lulu robbed a liquor store while he was making a phone call), thrilled, and intrigued all at the same time, Charlie allows Lulu to persuade him to accompany her on a visit to her mother in Pennsylvania. There she

Melanie Griffith does a Louise Brooks to seduce staid Jeff Daniels in *Something Wild*.

dyes her hair an angelic shade of blond, confesses that her name is really Audrey, and sweet-talks Charlie into escorting her to her high school reunion. She passes him off as her husband and he plays along, reluctantly realizing that he's falling in love with this wild thing who never seems to run out of surprises.

The adventure takes a nasty turn with the arrival of Ray, Audrey's husband. A lethally charming ex-con in a leather blazer and menacingly pointy boots, Ray beats up Charlie, implicates him in a brutal convenience-store robbery, and plays the fledgling lovers off against each other. His ace in the hole: He tells Audrey that Charlie isn't really a safely married man—his wife left him months earlier. But true love wins out: Charlie rescues Audrey from Ray, and when Ray follows them back to suburban Stony Brook, Charlie proves that he really has changed.

A hip, genre-bending romantic comedy plus, *Something Wild* defied easy categorization, prompting such labored comparisons as "a new wave *It Happened One Night*" and "*Bringing Up Baby* by way of Kafka." It puts a contemporary spin on the classic screwball formula, which looks like a snap and defeats just about all pretenders to the throne of Howard Hawks, Frank Capra, and Preston Sturges. Their surface preoccupation with flirting and engagements and marriage (and, frequently, *re*marriage) is the thin ice over a whirlpool of carnal concerns, mostly getting laid. Screwball comedies were movies about sex for an age when sex itself was unmentionable, and their knowing misdirections are one reason they hold up so well today.

Screwball comedies come in many forms, but the uptight man and the madcap woman who loosens him

Wild is a far raunchier romp than any of its ancestors—it could coast a long way on the image of Griffith in her black scanties straddling the deliriously helpless Jeff Daniels—but it's far more than a smutty *hommage* to a classic genre. It takes the formula and spins it, twists it up with a touch of thriller here and a dab of road movie there, and makes it all feel really fresh and new. Joel Hirschman tried to pull off the same motley mix in *Hold Me, Kiss Me, Thrill Me* (1994); he crudely dubbed the result "fuckball comedy," and it didn't amount to a thing.

Griffith is *Something Wild*'s red-hot core; alternately sultry and kittenish, she's equally at home in slinky black, a flowered sundress, and a pristine white prom gown. She's enough to bring a man back from the dead, and that's exactly what she does for Charlie. He kids himself that he's a secret nonconformist, but he's really timid and defeated, ready to let life bleed him pale and weary. Audrey jumpstarts his libido and then his life: By the time it's all over, he's ditched that safe, secure job for an uncertain but less soul-destroying future. If she nearly kills him, well then, that's the price of liberation. But she's not the whole story—Ray Liotta is scary sex incarnate, a bad boy cubed. He's the dark face of emancipation, so free from civilizing constraints that he's a menace to society. But oh, you just know he's a dervish between the sheets. Neither of them has ever been as sexy, though Griffith, of the baby doll voice and the Monroe-like curves, has had her memorable moments: She's kinkily adorable as porn star Holly Body in Brian DePalma's *Body Double* (1984) and sleazily luscious as a lesbian stripper in *Fear City* (1985).

up is a standard: Just think of ditzy heiress Katharine Hepburn and stuffy paleontologist Cary Grant in *Bringing Up Baby* (1938), wisecracking chippie Barbara Stanwyck and stodgy linguist Gary Cooper in *Ball of Fire* (1941), runaway rich girl Claudette Colbert and ambitious newspaperman Clark Gable in *It Happened One Night* (1934). Melanie Griffith's sparkling, free-spirited Lulu is sister to them all, though she's certainly the black sheep of even so strenuously unconventional a family—not for nothing does she name herself after Louise Brooks's amoral femme fatale. *Something*

160

A Streetcar Named Desire
(1951)

Directed by Elia Kazan. Produced by Charles K. Feldman.
Written by Tennessee Williams and Oscar Saul, adapted
from Williams's play. Cinematography by Harry Stradling.
Edited by David Weisbart.
Music by Alex North.

Marlon Brando (Stanley Kowalski), Vivien Leigh (Blanche
DuBois), Kim Hunter (Stella Kowalski),
Karl Malden (Mitch).

Closely adapted from Tennessee Williams's Pulitzer Prize–winning play, Elia Kazan's film of *A Streetcar Named Desire* was a triumph of adult material over the restrictions of Hollywood's prudish Production Code. It was the first general-release film that was clearly meant for adult audiences only, and it is still a startlingly sexually charged film.

Schoolteacher Blanche DuBois, a fading Southern belle, comes to New Orleans under mysterious circumstances to visit her pregnant sister, Stella. Stella's brutish husband, Stanley Kowalski, takes an instant dislike to the haughty, affected Blanche. She, in turn, makes no secret of her dismay at the Kowalskis' small apartment in a seedy neighborhood and of Stanley's unrefined manners and friends. Witty and sophisticated but perilously fragile, Blanche misses no opportunity to denigrate Stanley, who retaliates by nosing into her past. In the meantime, Blanche takes up with Stanley's coworker, Mitch, an unpolished but good-hearted man who drops her after Stanley reveals some unsavory skeletons in Blanche's closet: Before fleeing to New Orleans, she was fired by the school board for her alcoholism and inappropriate relationship with a seventeen-year-old and was thrown out of the sleaziest hotel in town for her free way with men.

Stella goes into labor, and Blanche and Stanley are left alone together. Stanley rapes his sister-in-law, who, already unhinged by losing Mitch, her last hope for marriage and a respectable life, retreats into madness and must be taken to an asylum.

The play was a Broadway smash: Sophisticated theatergoers reveled in Williams's psycho-sexual swamp, ennobled by its poetically despairing message about the fate of beauty in a harsh world. And it made an overnight star of Marlon Brando, whose brutal, déclassé lustiness anticipated the Bruce Weber look by decades. In an age when leading men wore dinner clothes, Brando made a sweaty T-shirt stink of sex. The costume designer for the stage production, reportedly inspired by a crew of Con Edison ditch diggers, distressed Brando's jeans and fitted them skin tight so they'd outline every manly curve, even taking out the interiors of the front pockets. Brando approved, saying, " . . . I think that Stanley would have liked to put his hands in his pockets and feel himself." His Stanley is a beast, the embodiment of pure, howling lust, and while his cry of "Stella!" may have become a joke, his appeal is no such thing.

From Alex North's honkytonk score to the dark, ominous cinematography, *Streetcar* is about the power of lust to invigorate and destroy. Blanche may wonder why Stella stays with Stanley, but no one else does—he pulled her off her good girl pedestal and showed her what a good time there was to be had in the gutter. From beginning to end, the play reeks of sex: When Blanche first brushes up against Stanley's muscular arm, the frisson is enough to make the hair stand up on the back of your neck. Given the volatility of the mate-

The passionate *Streetcar* ran afoul of censors because it dealt with "sex problems."

rial and the fact that movies were far less liberal than the theater, it's no wonder that *Streetcar* was shot behind closed doors ("I'm nervous," Kazan confessed to *Life* magazine near the end of 1950) and underwent certain revisions, though they were, for the most part, relatively minor. The biggest change from stage to screen was in the ending. In the movie, Stella leaves Stanley because he has to be punished somehow for his brutal violation of Blanche. In the play, she stands by her man.

Streetcar didn't run into real trouble until just before it was released, when Joseph Breen, overseer of the Production Code administration, deemed portions of the film "unacceptable" and tinged with "perversity." The Catholic Legion of Decency called the picture "immoral" and particularly objected, curiously enough, to Stella's evident passion for her husband. The Catholic War Veterans said they were considering a boycott of all Warner Bros. films. Warners caved in and began trimming, despite loud protests by both Kazan and Williams. In addition to various relatively minor changes, the Code office demanded that the entire rape scene be deleted, at which point Kazan and Williams almost dissociated themselves from the film. Williams wrote an impassioned letter to Breen, arguing that despite its sexual elements, his play was a deeply moral work. The rape scene stayed, though it was pruned. Hollis Alpert's 1951 *Variety* review suggests that Warners wasn't concerned without reason: While praising the film, it frets about the content, "the slow moral collapse of a southern schoolteacher," "nymphomania theme," "moral transgressions," and "a sex problem that is dangerous story-telling for films." Nevertheless, *A Streetcar Named Desire* was nominated for twelve Academy Awards and received four.

In 1993, it was rereleased with four minutes of restored footage, discovered by a Warner Bros. film archivist in an unmarked can in a company vault. Heard for the first time in decades were Blanche's

Psychosexual thrills in *Streetcar.*

(Opposite) Brutish but desirable: Marlon Brando in his prime.

Beauty and the beast: Brando and sister-in-law Vivien Leigh.

retort that her sister's attachment to Stanley is "brutal desire"; and her soliloquy about the young soldiers who used to gather on her lawn at night, calling for her; and Stanley's remark "Maybe you wouldn't be so bad to interfere with," which presages the climactic rape. A shot of Stella returning to Stanley after a brutal fight was also put back, and her sinuous walk down the stairs makes it clear what attracts her.

A frightening 1981 gossip column item had Sylvester Stallone ready to take on the role of Stanley Kowalski in a remake, prompting Tennessee Williams to declare, "Sylvester Stallone is a terrible actor. I would never allow him to remake 'Streetcar,'" and then later denying he'd said any such thing. In any event, it never came to pass.

Nudge, Nudge, Wink, Wink: Sex and Censorship in the Cinema

Too much versus not enough: Hollywood's ongoing battle of excesses, with defenders of common decency on one side and filmmakers with *épater le bourgeoisie* branded on their souls on the other, started in the days of the nickelodeon. Then, bluestockings complained about bathing beauties and belly dancers. Now moviemakers and the MPAA Classification and Ratings Administration skirmish regularly over sex, violence, and bad language. A short history:

1915: Nascent cinema stripped of First Amendment protection by Supreme Court ruling that "the exhibition of motion pictures is a business . . . not to be regarded . . . as part of the press of the nation or as organs of public opinion."

1919: National Association of the Motion Picture Industry formed to battle censorship legislation.

1921: Former postmaster general Will Hays hired to head the newly formed Motion Picture Producers and Distributors Association of America (MPPDA, forerunner of today's MPAA) and help clean up the image of Hollywood, pilloried as a pit of "debauchery, riotous living, drunkenness, ribaldry, dissipation [and] free love."

1927: Hays Office devises the ridiculous list of *Don'ts* and *Be Carefuls*. *Don'ts* include nudity, miscegenation, sex hygiene and venereal disease, ridicule of the clergy, childbirth, profanity, and sex perversion; *Be Carefuls* include safe cracking, dynamiting trains, rape, sedition, drug use, and excessive kissing.

1930: Motion Picture Production Code voluntarily adopted. It lists images, attitudes, language, and subject matter filmmakers are to avoid, ranging from crime and vulgar language to nudity, cruelty to animals, rape, blasphemy, dancing, and sex. Filmmakers largely ignore it.

1933: Catholic Legion of Decency formed to rate films for moral content; its *Condemned* designation directs a generation of moviegoers to titillating fare.

1934: Hollywood agrees not to distribute or exhibit films lacking a seal of approval from Hays protégé Joseph I. Breen's office; movies that flout Code guidelines don't get one. Ignoring the Code becomes harder.

1943: *The Outlaw* is released after years on the shelf, during which eccentric producer Howard Hughes waged war with censors—official and unofficial— over the salacious story line and overexposed star Jane Russell.

1951: With its high-powered credentials— Tennessee Williams, Elia Kazan, Pulitzer Prize, Broadway smash—and fundamentally smutty subject matter, *A Streetcar Named Desire* forces reinterpretation of Code guidelines concerning adult topics.

1952: After Roberto Rossellini's neo-realist *The Miracle* (1948) is banned by the New York Board of Censors as sacrilegious, the U.S. Supreme Court decides unanimously that movies *are* entitled to constitutional guarantees of free speech.

1953: Otto Preminger's innocuous *The Moon Is Blue* uses the forbidden word *virgin* and is released without a Code seal. It grosses a then-substantial $6 million, disproving the equation *no seal = no box office.*

1954: *The Garden of Eden* launches a wave of nudist camp movies in which discreetly naked men and women extol the virtues of naturism. New York Court of Appeals rules that "Nudity . . . without lewdness or dirtiness is not obscenity in law or common sense."

1958: *And God Created Woman*, paean to sex kitten Brigitte Bardot, arrives in the United States two years after wowing Europe. Banned, condemned, and fulminated against, it becomes a smash hit.

1959: Russ Meyer's *The Immoral Mr. Teas* launches the independent "nudie-cutie" picture, featuring pretty naked girls and sexually suggestive stories.

1965: Sidney Lumet's somber *The Pawnbroker* becomes the first Code-approved film to bare a woman's breast.

1967: Ingmar Bergman protégé Vilmot Sjöman's *I Am Curious, Yellow* mixes left-wing politics with candid sex scenes and frontal nudity. Seized by U.S. Customs and found obscene by a federal jury, it's shown when an appellate court rules it can't be kept out of the country. Audiences ignore its dullness and eat it up.

1968: The Production Code dies a quiet death, and the MPAA Code (since 1977, Classification) and Ratings Association is formed to rate increasingly frank movies. The first ratings: G, M (Mature), R, and X (Adults Only). MPAA fails to copyright X rating— first given to Brian De Palma's *Greetings* (1968), then to such films as *Midnight Cowboy* (1969) and *A Clockwork Orange* (1971)—and pornographic movies self-apply it with glee. M later becomes GP, and finally PG.

1972: *Deep Throat* becomes the film against which local prosecutors brought more actions than any film since *Birth of a Nation* (1915). Costar Harry Reems is the only actor ever federally prosecuted for his role in a movie, indicted as part of a nationwide conspiracy to transport an "obscene, lewd, lascivious and filthy motion picture" across state lines.

1973: Supreme Court establishes new, confusing guidelines for recognizing pornography: Whether "the average person, applying contemporary community standards," would find the work prurient, whether it's obviously offensive, and whether it overall lacks serious literary, political, or scientific value.

1980: Lavishly pornographic *Caligula* released and, after being targeted by conservative pressure group Morality in Media, is subjected to numerous legal actions designed to drive it out of theaters, to no avail.

1984 Following outcry over intense but PG-rated violence in *Indiana Jones and the Temple of Doom* and *Gremlins*, PG-13 rating is introduced.

1990: *Henry & June* receives the first NC-17 rating, devised to replace the scarlet X after media melee over Xs received by Pedro Almodóvar's *Tie Me Up! Tie Me Down!*, Zalman King's *Wild Orchid*, John McNaughton's *Henry: Portrait of a Serial Killer*, and comedian Sandra Bernhard's concert picture *Without You I'm Nothing.*

Tie Me Up! Tie Me Down! / ¡Atame! (1990)

Written and Directed by Pedro Almodóvar. Produced by Agustin Almodóvar. Cinematography by Jose Luis Alcaine. Edited by Jose Salcedo. Production Design by Esther Garcia. Music by Ennio Morricone.

Victoria Abril (Marina), Antonio Banderas (Ricki), Francisco Rabal (Maximo Espejo), Loles Leon (Lola), Julieta Serrano (Alma).

Imagine *Magnificent Obsession* (1954), *Written on the Wind* (1956), *Imitation of Life* (1959), or any other wildly overwrought Douglas Sirk film, dressed up with copious nudity and sex: Now you have the aesthetic of Spanish filmmaker Pedro Almodóvar. In *Tie Me Up! Tie Me Down!*, a drug-addicted porno star named Marina is trying to break into mainstream films by making a low-budget horror movie.* She's kidnapped by her biggest fan and one-time lover Ricki, a first-class hunk newly released from a mental institution. All he wants is to marry Marina and start a family, but she rebuffs him callously. So he ties her to her own bed (no cramped closet or damp basement for Ricki's beloved), and vows not to let her go until she falls in love with him. She resists and schemes to escape, even

*Though this may seem like just another ridiculous Almodóvar plot device and an excuse to set several scenes on a ridiculously elaborate Euro-horror movie set, this is exactly the career path of underage porno star Traci Lords. She started her career as a teenager, making over a hundred ultra-quickie hard-core pictures. Where once she would have been a pariah for life, she successfully made the transition to the mainstream with *Not of This Earth*, exploitation director Jim Wynorski's remake of Roger Corman's classic low-budget opus. Lords is now the queen of direct-to-video genre pictures (hardcore star Ginger Lynn Allen recently followed in her footsteps) and has even appeared on TV's *Melrose Place* and *Roseanne*.

Tie Me Up! Tie Me Down! is Almodóvar's politically incorrect fairy tale about desire, dependence, and bondage.

though Ricki is the most gentlemanly of captors: He never tries to molest her, buys soft ropes and nonabrasive tape, cries when she's mean to him, and, finally, to prove how much he cares, goes out to buy dope for her and gets beaten to a pulp for his trouble. As befits a melodrama, Marina *does* fall in love with Ricki, and by the time her sister Lola comes to the rescue, Marina wants nothing more than to be tied up again.

Tie Me Up! Tie Me Down!, which includes the infamous scene of Victoria Abril masturbating in her bath with the help of a little wind-up toy scuba diver, got an X from the MPAA. Almodóvar went on the warpath, complaining that he'd been humiliated, felt misunderstood, and thought that censorship in America was worse than in Franco's Spain. As to the feminists who complained that his movie was an offensive fantasy on the themes of abuse and oppression of women, Almodóvar no doubt made the recent *Kika* (1994), whose centerpiece is a long rape scene played for slapstick comedy, just for them, and got an NC-17 in thanks.

A former telephone repairman, the irrepressible Almodóvar started out as a part-time underground artist, a member of Madrid-based underground pop-cultural movement *la movida*. From the beginning, he was obsessed with sex: He sang in drag, published the steamy "memoirs" of fictitious porn star Patty Diphusa, wrote a short novel called *Fuego en Las Entranas / Fire in the Guts*, penned erotic comics, shot naughty fotonovelas, and made super-8 short films with titles like *Two Whores, or a Love Story Which Ends in Marriage* and *The Fall of Sodom* (both 1974), *Sex Comes and Goes* (1977), and *Fuck Me, Fuck Me, Fuck Me,*

Victoria Abril.

Tim (1978). Dictator Francissimo Franco's death in 1975 cut loose Spanish popular culture, which was suddenly liberated from the brutal censorship that marked his regime. By 1980 Almodóvar had launched a career in feature films with *Pepi, Luci, Bom and Other Girls on the Heap.*

With an anarchic sense of humor and a healthy dose of *épater le bourgeois* cheekiness, Almodóvar makes riotous comedies about incest and nymphomania (*Labyrinth of Passion*, 1982), junkie nuns (*Dark Habits*, 1983), amoral housewives (*What Have I Done to Deserve This?*, 1984), vengeful lovers (*Women on the Verge of a Nervous Breakdown*, 1984), and *Candide*-esque sex addicts (*Kika*, 1994). He also makes movies about the uncontrollable vagaries of passion, like *Matador* (1968), *The Law of Desire* (1987), *Tie Me Up! Tie Me Down!*, and *High Heels* (1993) and doesn't hesitate to mix the two. Almodóvar cites American comedies like *How to Marry a Millionaire* (1953) and directors such as Sirk as his inspirations; he always adored American movie stars like Ava Gardner and Rita Hayworth, and Hollywood's "world of sinning women played by Natalie Wood and Liz Taylor, and written by Tennessee Williams." When the priests of his Catholic childhood told him the stars were sinners, he created a fantasy world in which they were saints and made that world real in his films. And that world is full of sex, of every variety.

Matador, for example, opens with aspiring bullfighter Antonio Banderas masturbating to horror movies and ends with retired matador Nacho Martinez and bullfight groupie Assumpta Serna—both serial sex murderers—making love and killing each other in an erotic suicide pact. The first image of *Law of Desire* is a handsome young man being told to undress and masturbate by an off-screen voice. The film goes on to explore the tangled relationships of director Eusebio Poncela, his unrequited love Miguel Molina, his new lover Banderas (again), and his transsexual actress sister Carmen Maura, Almodóvar's longtime muse. It's all trashy, convoluted, vulgar, inventive, explicit, and oddly correct in its relentless incorrectness: Almodóvar's films take place in a world in which all deviants are created equal. Though he himself is gay, Almodóvar's films give homo- and heterosexual eros equal time. The women in his films come in all desirable sizes and shapes, from angular Rossy DePalma and winsome Carmen Maura to sultry Victoria Abril and haughty transsexual Bibi Anderssen. Foremost among the men is the hunky Banderas; in the 1991 documentary *Truth or Dare*, he's the one guy sex goddess Madonna says she wants to meet. Pronounced accent notwithstanding, he's seduced American viewers in *The Mambo Kings* (1992), *Interview With the Vampire: The Vampire Chronicles* (1994), and *Miami Rhapsody* and *Desperado* (both 1995).

For all the flesh—and there's plenty of it—on display, most of Almodóvar's films are almost too good-natured to fit the American definition of eroticism, which demands a punitive tinge of the sinful. With their candy colors, riotous décors, wildly improbable plots (there's more than a hint of the dirty soap opera), and insouciant attitudes, his pictures are driven by the idea that sex is confusing, awkward, time-consuming, and occasionally bothersome, but above all a lot of fun.

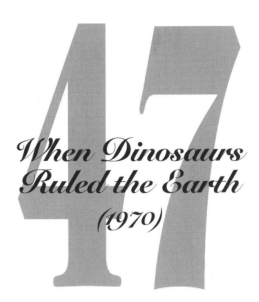

When Dinosaurs Ruled the Earth (1970)

Directed by Val Guest. Produced by Aida Young. Screenplay by Guest, from a treatment by J. G. Ballard. Cinematography by Dick Bush. Edited by Peter Curran. Special Effects by Jim Danforth. Music by Mario Nascimbene.

Victoria Vetri (Sanna), Robin Hawdon (Tara), Patrick Allen (Kingsor), Drewe Henley (Khaku), Sean Caffrey (Kane), Magda Konopka (Ulido), Imogen Hassall (Ayak).

Picture yourself an eleven- or twelve-year-old boy, into dinosaurs and monster movies and teetering on the brink of volcanic adolescence. Now, what's wrong with *Jurassic Park* (1993), which may well have the best dinosaurs ever committed to celluloid? That's right, no women in animal-skin bikinis, running for their lives. Laura Dern in Banana Republic safari duds just doesn't cut it.

Prehistoric-babe movies are the link between monsters—the graven images of the presexual years—and the lustful preoccupations that supplant them during puberty, and *When Dinosaurs Ruled the Earth* is an exemplary example of the form. Sure, it lacks the high-brow credentials of *Quest for Fire* (1981)—proto-language by Anthony (*A Clockwork Orange*) Burgess, body language by Desmond (*The Naked Ape*) Morris—and the full-body nakedness of Rae Dawn Chong, whose contributions to prehistoric society include body paint and the missionary position. It's not as silly as *Clan of the Cave Bear* (1985), in which Cro-Magnon aerobics instructor Daryl Hannah shows those Neanderthals a thing or two. It doesn't have Raquel Welch, like *One Million Years B.C.* (1966), or statuesque Julie Ege, like *Creatures the World Forgot* (1971). *When Dinosaurs Ruled the Earth* is nowhere near as sleazy as *When Women Had*

Tails (1970) and *When Women Lost Their Tails* (1975), cheap Italian knockoffs featuring Senta Berger discovering prehistoric sex. It lacks the aggressively catty appeal of *Slave Girls/Prehistoric Women* (1968), in which brunette Amazons led by Martine Beswicke enslave all their blond sisters and pimp them to the local brutes to keep peace between their tribes.

But you have to love a movie that opens with a bunch of well-fed, hairless white men in *International Male* underpants worshipping an idol that looks like Marlon Brando and preparing to sacrifice a trio of vacant bottle-blondes in scanty, white suede bikinis. And to its eternal credit, *When Dinosaurs Ruled the Earth*—which entirely ignores the fact that dinosaurs and primitive humans never shared the same slice of the evolutionary pie—fulfills its commitment to exposing acres of supple flesh.

Lovely Sanna, one of the sun-kissed sacrificial maidens, falls into the sea and is swept into the net cast by a bunch of prehistoric fishermen. They are all amazed by her beauty, especially the handsome Tara. They take her back to their village, where she makes the local brunettes—especially Tara's girlfriend—jealous. When the men leave on their next fishing expedition, the women drive Sanna away. When the men return, they organize a search party and come face to face with dinosaurs and deadly snakes, eventually coming to the conclusion that Sanna has brought them nothing but bad luck. Meanwhile, Sanna's tribe organizes its own search party to bring her back to the hill so their sacrificial ceremony can be completed.

Deeply in love with Sanna, Tara defies his tribe, which retaliates by setting him adrift on a burning raft.

(Right) Going down in history: Harrison Mark's *9 Ages of Nakedness* (1969).

(Opposite) Veronica Vetri, flanked by prehistoric brunettes, in a cheesecake publicity still from *When Dinosaurs Ruled the Earth*.

Raquel Welch demonstrating the appeal of caveman couture in *One Million Years B.C.* (1966).

He escapes and sets up housekeeping with Sanna in an isolated cave. They're discovered, and his tribesmen tie him to a wooden frame on the beach and prepare to burn him alive. They're interrupted by a tidal wave and, in the chaos, Sanna frees him. With another couple, Tara and Sanna escape to build a new life.

Prehistoric-babe movies are one long skin show—more or less graphic, depending on the factors of year made, relative celebrity of stars, and country of origin—driven by the same impulses that propel jungle movies, from Johnny Weissmuller's *Tarzan* films to Bo Derek's, and pictures like *The Blue Lagoon*, filmed three times to date, most recently in 1980 with Christopher Atkins and Brooke Shields. They're all feature-length excuses for hunky guys and curvaceous girls to frolic wholesomely in scanty, faux-primitive get-ups, and they're even better than beach-party movies, because atavistic innocents *never* have to get into regular clothes and go to school or to their part-time jobs. They

Bo Derek discovers the virtues of wild man Miles O'Keeffe in *Tarzan the Ape Man* (1981).

sometimes speak stone-age gibberish, but that's not really a liability.

When Dinosaurs Ruled the Earth features fine dinosaurs and some very scary giant crabs, alongside prehistoric luaus, dirty dancing by the fire, and cat fights in the surf. Star Vetri, under the name Angela Dorian, was *Playboy*'s 1968 Playmate of the Year and is extremely lovely to look at. Costar Robin Hawdon has fine beefcake appeal, and both of them run, writhe, and get wet regularly. It's all very stimulating, in a good clean fun sort of way, an erotic picture to which you could actually take the kids.

Cartoons don't have their squeaky clean reputation for nothing. In America, at least, animation equals Disney, and Uncle Walt was a prude. The classic Disney cartoons are rife with subtext, of course: There's Snow White shacking up in the woods with seven little men (but are they little where it counts?); those remarkable scenes in *Fantasia* in which miniature cupids turn tail and exploit the heart shape of their buttocks; the undercurrent of bestiality so strenuously unexploited in *Beauty and the Beast*; and Timon and Pumbaa, *The Lion King*'s snappy meerkat and warthog duo, Disney's first apparently gay couple. But Disney isn't the half of it, as these examples show.

Betty Boop: The wide-eyed flapper queen of cartoonland from 1915, based on "It" girl Clara Bow and forever boop-oop-a-dooping around in her strapless, thigh-high frock, Max Fleischer's Betty was always just this side of salaciousness. Evading the sexual advances of a panoply of smarms without ever suggesting that sex *itself* was the problem, Betty was an early casualty of the puritan Hays Code. Her skirt got longer and her flirty garter disappeared, and Betty censored wasn't really Betty at all.

Buried Treasure (c. 1928): Hot on the heels of *The Virgin With the Hot Pants* (1924), the first pornographic cartoon, this anonymous chronicle of the adventures of Everready—an everyman with a Brobdingnagian, detachable penis—took dirty cartoons to new heights. *Buried Treasure*'s bawdy interludes leave little to the imagination. They include sex with a woman who has an irate crab in her vagina, a donkey, and a man buried in the sand. Needless to say, such naughtiness was *not* part of the fondly remembered newsreel and cartoon combo—it stayed on the stag circuit.

Red Hot Riding Hood (1943): The first of Tex Avery's risqué cartoons for MGM turned Red into a saucy showgirl and the wolf into a tuxedoed masher. *Wild and Wolfy, Swing Shift Cinderella, Uncle Tom's Cabana*, and *Little Rural Riding Hood* followed, and 1994's *The Mask* contains a live-action recreation (assisted by computer animation) of *Red*'s famous image of the wolf, eyeballs popping and heart leaping from his chest, as he watches the object of his lustful desires perform. Smokin'!

A Thousand and One Nights (1969): From Osamu Tezuka, who created *Kimba the White Lion* and *Astro Boy*, the first full-length (two and a half hours!) erotic animated picture. This Oriental sex fantasia was erroneously advertised as the first cartoon for adults only.

Fritz the Cat (1972): Animator Ralph Bakshi, underground comic book artist R. Crumb, and the sexual revolution brought dirty cartoons above ground, and *Fritz the Cat* was still a scandal. Anthropomorphized cartoon critters swearing, drugging, and having sex appalled reviewers and spawned such subsequent shockers as Bakshi's *Heavy Traffic* (1973), *Coonskin / Street Fight* (1975), and the compilation *Heavy Metal* (1981), inspired by the sex, drugs, and rock 'n' roll comic magazine.

Shame of the Jungle (1975): An X-rated Belgian import (edited down to an R), created by cartoonist Picha and revised for 1979 release to American audiences by *Saturday Night Live* writers Anne Beatts and Michael O'Donoghue, *Shame* is a smutty spoof of Tarzan movies voiced in the United States by John Belushi, Bill Murray, Brian Doyle-Murray, and Christopher Guest.

Who Framed Roger Rabbit? (1988): *Playboy* joke cum tribute to Tex Avery, Jessica was drawn bad. Because the awesomely expensive mix of live action and animation features is aggressively innocuous, the scandal over reported pantiless frames of Jessica—discovered when the film was released on laser disc—was all the sweeter.

Cool World (1992): Ralph Bakshi again, doing *Roger Rabbit* one better with this fabulously lurid rehash of *Heavy Traffic* by way of *Pinocchio*. Cartoonist Gabriel Byrne gets sucked into his imaginary world, where seductive Holli Would has the two-dimensional hots for him because his precious bodily essences can turn her into a real girl, portrayed by Kim Basinger.

Legend of the Overfiend (1993): Contemporary Japanese animation includes a slew of erotic, grotesque films in which graphic sex is usually coupled with monstrous violence; *Overfiend*, with its notorious sequences of rape by demon, is one of the best known, but hardly one of the most extreme.

Wide Sargasso Sea (1993)

Directed by John Duigan. Produced by Jan Sharp. Screenplay by Sharp and Carole Angier, based on the novel by Jean Rhys. Cinematography by Geoff Burton. Edited by Anne Goursaud and Jimmy Sandoval. Production Design by Franckie D. Music by Stewart Copeland.

Karina Lombard (Antoinette Cosway), Nathaniel Parker (Edward Rochester), Rachel Ward (Annette Cosway), Michael York (Paul Mason), Martine Beswicke (Aunt Cora), Claudia Robinson (Christophene), Rowena King (Amalia).

The Sargasso Sea is literally "miles and miles of floating weed," but metaphorically it's the swamp of female sexuality, dark and damp and tinged with lunacy: Joseph Conrad's heart of darkness was miles up the Amazon, but in *Wide Sargasso Sea* it's no further away than between a woman's legs. A man could drown there, and tense, uncomprehending Englishman Edward Rochester nearly does. He faints dead away when he's first introduced to lovely Antoinette Cosway, the landed Creole girl his family has arranged for him to marry, and it's not just the fever he caught at sea that's to blame. Based on the 1966 novel by Jean Rhys, *Wide Sargasso Sea* is a prequel to *Jane Eyre*, the story of the first Mrs. Rochester before she passed into literary notoriety as the madwoman in the attic, the embodiment of the seething sexuality repressed by the rustling corsets of Victorian England.

The Cosway family has fallen on hard times. They're Creole, despised by the colonial English and loathed by the native Jamaicans, neither European nor

Nathaniel Parker and Karina Lombard wallow in the *Wide Sargasso Sea* of sin.

Caribbean, aristocrats nor commoners. After her despairing husband drinks himself to death, beautiful Annette marries a wealthy Englishman so she and her daughter Antoinette can keep their decaying estate in the mountains. A fire set by the vengeful plantation workers destroys the house and kills their new baby, driving Annette mad. Her husband flees to England and Antoinette is abandoned to convent schools until her distant stepfather arranges her marriage to Rochester, the landless son of a respectable English family.

Despite their inauspicious first meeting, Antoinette and Rochester are married; he's bewitched by her grace and sensuality, and she blossoms beneath his caresses. They move up to the hills, surrounded by the lush greenery and intoxicating flowers, make love, and luxuriate in the riotous beauty of the tropics. But their happiness soon withers in the oppressive heat and the poisonous atmosphere of gossip and resentment that surrounds them. Rochester grows distant and Antoinette's frantic efforts to win him back look increasingly like madness. He begins an affair with Amalia, a servant. Antoinette drinks and makes scenes. Eventually Rochester takes Antoinette to England, where the cold and grayness unhinge her mind entirely; the film ends as Antoinette hears that her husband intends to marry an English girl, and she sets fire to the vast, forbidding house as chilly as his heart.

Rhys's novel is that rarest of things, an adjunct to a great work of literature that stands on its own merits. Rhys was raised on the Caribbean island of Dominica, and her sensibilities were forged in the conflict between the order of European civilization and the

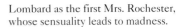

skin the color of milk with the barest hint of coffee. It takes only a venomous whisper to convince Rochester that her candid sensuality and childlike delight in living are manifestations of the corrupting touch of madness, and soon he's dreaming that he's trapped under water in the weeds, strangling as Antoinette swims by like a happy, heartless porpoise. Like Jean-Jacques Annaud's *The Lover* and other adaptations of sensual literature, *Wide Sargasso Sea* is always teetering on the brink of smuttiness. Australian director John Duigan pushes it right over the edge, prowling the bedroom— a soft-core fantasy of artfully weathered walls and gauze—as stars Karina Lombard and Nathaniel Parker strip and grope and fondle each other. They're gorgeous, as is the film, and if Duigan doesn't quite capture the bitter subtlety of Rhys's novel, he gets the look, which is more fun anyway. His *Wide Sargasso Sea* is what *Wild Orchid* (1990) would be if it had literary origins rather than literary pretensions.

sensual allure of the jungle, real and metaphorical. Just as the specter of the first Mrs. Rochester haunts *Jane Eyre*, the demons of race and class and the legacy of slavery haunt *Wide Sargasso Sea*. Rochester is too English ever to understand Jamaica; he's a benign bigot and a prude to his very bones, a man who mistrusts self-indulgence and believes so completely in the world's unshakable rationality that a glimpse of the seething emotions beneath its surface nearly drives him insane. And he's afraid of Antoinette because her wanton loveliness inflames the beast beneath his own skin, the beast he would like to deny.

Antoinette is Creole, conceived as a white man's beguiling, nightmare lover: She has the wildness of Africa in her beneath her French coquettishness and

Duigan returned in 1993 with *Sirens*, the story of a prissy clerical couple, Tara Fitzgerald and Hugh Grant, and their liberating encounter in the outback with an unconventional painter and his trio of free-spirited models, Elle MacPherson, Kate Fischer, and Portia de Rossi. The clash is once again between civilized repression and wild abandon, without *Wide Sargasso Sea*'s discomfiting allusions to racism and slavery, which may be why critics embraced it as a spirited, erotic romp with a progressive message. It's less explicit than *Wide Sargasso Sea*, and less ambitious, but the girls are lovely, and Fitzgerald's dreamlike encounter with the film's brawny, blind Adonis of a handyman is extraordinarily sensual.

Wild Orchid
(1990)

Directed by Zalman King. Produced by Mark Damon and Tony Anthony. Screenplay by Patricia Louisianna Knop and King. Cinematography by Gale Tattersall. Edited by Marc Grossman and Glenn A. Morgan. Production Design by Carlos Conti. Music by Geoff MacCormack and Simon Goldenberg.

Mickey Rourke (Wheeler), Carré Otis (Emily Reed), Jacqueline Bisset (Claudia Lirones), Assumpta Serna (Hanna Minch), Bruce Greenwood (Jerome MacFarland), Oleg Vidov (Otto Minch).

Actor-turned-writer/producer/director Zalman King's life can be divided into two eras: Before *Wild Orchid* and After *Wild Orchid*. Before *Wild Orchid*, King was a fringe character. After a well-publicized flap with the MPAA over *Wild Orchid*'s X rating and a raft of lascivious media speculation about the climactic sex scene between grungy exhibitionist Mickey Rourke and his then-girlfriend (later battered wife) Carré Otis—were they or weren't they really *doing it*?—King was officially a notorious fringe character, a swanky smutmonger dishing up guilty pleasures with a kinky twist. He's complained that now if he submitted *Bambi* to the MPAA they'd give him an X. King acted in a lot of trashy movies, including camp exploitation classics *A Trip With the Teacher* (1975) and *Blue Sunshine* (1977), but his interest as a filmmaker is upscale erotica—arty and tasteful, not violent and sleazy. *Wild Orchid* is a swooningly sumptuous ode to the joy of sex, written by King with his wife, Patricia Louisianna Knop (who also wrote Mary Lambert's *Siesta*), set in alluring Rio de Janeiro and art directed beyond *Playboy*'s wildest dreams.

Prim young lawyer Emily Reed joins a prestigious law firm and is immediately sent to Rio with ruthless banker Claudia Lirones to try to save a huge real estate venture that's about to go under. Once in Brazil, small-town girl Emily is plunged into a world of sensuality she never knew existed and is drawn into the disturbing orbit of enigmatic, libertine millionaire Wheeler. He teases and flatters her, tempts her and then retreats, admitting he can't bear to be touched and lives his erotic life through others. He persuades her to fantasize about a couple at a neighboring table in an expensive restaurant, to attend a masked orgy, to watch a couple make love in the back seat of a limousine, and, finally, to sleep with a stranger who takes her for an upscale whore. In the end, she cures Wheeler's emotional paralysis, and they engage in passionate, rapturous sexual healing.

Wild Orchid is lusty indeed and features a relatively high-profile cast. Well-bred bitch Bisset (who took on the role after Anne Archer, already on location, got cold feet) attacks business and pleasure with equal ardor. Prissy Emily—a stock character from Victorian pornography, the virgin trembling to be liberated from her morals—gets into the spirit of things after watching a pair of beautiful Brazilians coupling picturesquely in a damp alley. Beauties Brooke Shields and Cindy Crawford were both in the running for the role, but Shields backed off because of the nudity and Crawford was passed over in favor of first-timer Otis. Though the stunning former model can't act at all, she isn't really asked to and looks fabulous in and out of slinky dresses, feathered masks, and eyeglasses of the "*Miss Fenster*, I never realized how *beautiful* you are" variety.

The movie's real weak link is Mickey Rourke.

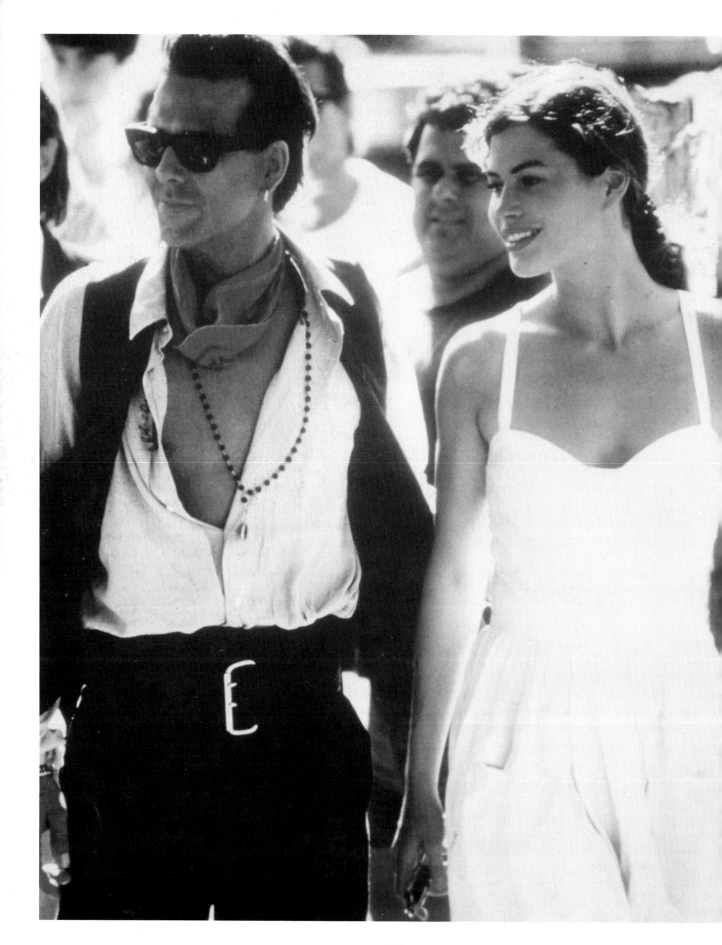

(Right) Carré Otis as Emily, the virgin trembling to be liberated from her troublesome morals.

(Opposite) Mickey Rourke and Otis lose themselves in *carnivale.*

You can see how hiring him must have seemed like a good idea: He was famous, semi-respectable, and had already proved he had what it takes as star of *Nine ½ Weeks*, which King produced and cowrote with Knop. But Rourke, who had his cheekbones surgically enhanced before shooting, looks horrible—his face is puffy and tight—and doesn't give half the performance he gives in *Nine ½ Weeks*, even though he's playing virtually the same character.

But no matter. King's lighting is exquisite, his sense of composition harmonious, and his cutting sharp, capturing the interplay between passionate individuals and the ever-present swirl of carnival in the Rio streets, hotels, and alleys. The sex is varied—various locations, various positions, various well-formed bodies in various stages of undress—and plentiful, and King's aesthetic is almost reverent. In a telling scene, Wheeler asks Emily, who's uncomfortably seated next to a copulating couple, what she sees. "Two people having sex," she replies coldly. "Making love," he corrects her, and for King that's what it's all about. His characters really do want to make love, not rut like beasts.

Critics and the sort of wits who quip that life is too short for softcore hate King's films, and it's hard to argue when people call them silly. They're not about significant social issues, they're not tough and gritty, and they're not structurally challenging. But you have to give him credit for diving head first into the subject of carnal desire, which most American filmmakers seem to regard as the horseradish of filmmaking: More than a little is too much, and you certainly never want to have it by itself. King's films—*Wildfire* (1987), *Two Moon Junction* (1988), *Wild Orchid, Wild Orchid 2: Two Shades of Blue* (1991), *Delta of Venus* (1995) and the cable telefilm *Red Shoe Diaries* (1993)—take erotic love passionately seriously. They're not thrillers or mysteries or melodramas with sex. They're movies about what people do for lust, and they have an audience: They're video and pay-per-view hits in the States, and they do great theatrical business abroad.

Because of production problems, *Wildfire* has never been released, but *Two Moon Junction* is a particular feast for Sherilyn Fenn fans (more cheerfully sexy than the arty *Boxing Helena*, on a par with the supernatural *Meridian*), who get to see her play a proper debutante whose horizons are broadened by a hunky carni-

Is It Real, or Just an Incredible Simulation?

Thinking about the mechanics of filming a steamy sex scene—the lights and camera jostling for space, the body makeup, the measuring tapes—is a grade A bucket of cold water to the libido. There's no mystery left after we're done reading about how the actors had to hit marks hidden in the sheets and the director was worried about losing the light, and just about everybody in the movie business is part of the conspiracy to make all us wonderful people out here in the dark feel grateful that they put themselves through the ordeal of shooting sexy scenes. Directors all complain they're embarrassed, stars all insist they're uncomfortable.

Perhaps in reaction to this orgy of professional distaste for the nasty business, we get a particular tingle from the thought that maybe all that heavy breathing isn't faked and watch particularly closely when we hear whispers to that effect. Among the couples who were rumored to have done it for real for the camera:

Marlon Brando and **Maria Schneider** in *Last Tango in Paris* (1973)

Julie Christie and **Donald Sutherland** in *Don't Look Now* (1973)

Jack Nicholson and **Jessica Lange** in *The Postman Always Rings Twice* (1981)

Bruce Dern and **Maud Adams** in *Tattoo* (1981)

Mickey Rourke and **Lisa Bonet** in *Angel Heart* (1987)

Mickey Rourke and **Carré Otis** in *Wild Orchid* (1990)

Jane March and **Tony Leung** in *The Lover* (1992)

Kim Basinger and **Alec Baldwin** in *The Getaway* (1993)

val worker. *Wild Orchid 2*, a sequel in name only, is largely set in a deliriously opulent brothel; the lingerie alone is worth the price of admission. *Red Shoe* (as in patent-leather, fuck-me pumps) *Diaries*, made for Showtime, explores a successful business woman's secret, reckless sexual life and initiated a cable series in which women's diaries are the hook on which assorted tales of fanciful passion are hung. Packaged three to a set, they're also released theatrically abroad and on videocassette in the United States under the *Red Shoe Diaries* umbrella. King's films are particularly popular with women because, he theorizes, "I think I write from a woman's point of view, at least some of the time. I like women. I'm fascinated by women. I became interested in writing about romance and sexual experience while working on *Nine ½ Weeks* and I think that to some degree I'm still working out those ideas."

(Opposite) Down and dirty: Rourke and Otis in the "did they or didn't they?" climax.

Bibliography

Anger, Kenneth. *Hollywood Babylon* (New York: Dell Publishing Company, 1975)

Balbo, Lucas, and Blumenstock, Peter, editors. *Obsession: The Films of Jess Franco* (Berling, Germany: Graf Haufen & Frank Trebben, 1993).

Blumenstock, Peter. *See* Balbo, Lucas.

Burchill, Julie. *Girls on Film* (New York: Pantheon Books, 1986)

De Grazia, Edward, and Newman, Roger K. *Banned Films* (New York & London: R. R. Bowker Company, 1982)

Di Lauro, Al, and Rabkin, Gerald. *Dirty Movies* (New York and London: Chelsea House, 1986)

Durgnat, Raymond. *Eros in the Cinema* (London: Calder and Boyars, 1966)

Frank, Sam. *Sex in the Movies* (Secaucus, New Jersey: Citadel Press, 1986)

Frasier, David K. *Russ Meyer—The Life and Films* (Jefferson, North Carolina, and London: McFarland & Company, 1990)

Friedman, David S. *A Youth in Babylon* (Buffalo, New York: Prometheus Books, 1990)

George, Bill. *Eroticism in the Fantasy Cinema* (Philadelphia: Imagine, Inc., 1984)

Jackson, Jean-Pierre. *Russ Meyer ou Trente Ans de Cinema Erotique Hollywood* (Paris: PAC Editions, 1982)

Jeavons, Clyde. *See* Pascal, Jeremy.

Juno, Andrea. *See* Vale, V.

Leach, Michael. *I Know It When I See It* (Philadelphia: The Westminster Press, 1975).

Lenne, Gerard. *Der Erotische Film* (Munich: Wilhelm Heyne Verlag GmbH & Co., 1986).

Lethe, Robert I. *See* Strick, Marv.

Limbacher, James L. *Sexuality in World Cinema*, two volumes (Metuchen, New Jersey and London: The Scarecrow Press, 1983).

McGillivray, David. *Doing Rude Things* (London: Sun Tavern Fields, 1992).

Newman, Roger K. *See* De Grazia, Edward.

Pascal, Jeremy, and Jeavons, Clyde. *A Pictorial History of Sex in the Movies* (London, New York, Sydney, and Toronto: Hamlyn, 1975).

Peary, Danny. *Cult Movies* (New York: Delta, 1981).

Phillips, Baxter. *Cut: The Unseen Cinema* (New York: Bounty Books, 1975).

Rabkin, Gerald. *See* Di Lauro, Al.

Russell, Jane. *Jane Russell: My Path & My Detours* (New York, London, Sydney, Toronto: Franklin Watts, Inc., 1985).

Schumach, Murray. *The Face on the Cutting Room Floor* (New York: William Morrow and Company, 1964).

Shipman, David. *Caught in the Act: Sex and Eroticism in the Movies* (London: Elm Tree Books, 1985).

Sinclair, Marianne. *Hollywood Lolita: The Nymphette Syndrome* (London: Plexus, 1988).

Smith, Adrian, editor. *Delirium: The Complete Guide to Italian Exploitation Cinema*, two volumes (London, England: Media Publications, 1990s).

Strick, Marv, with Lethe, Robert I. *The Sexy Cinema* (Los Angeles: Sherbourne Press, 1975).

Tohill, Cathal and Tombs, Pete. *Immoral Tales* (London: Primitive Press, 1994).

Tombs, Pete. *See* Tohill, Cathal.

Turan, Kenneth, and Zito, Stephen F. *Sinema* (New York and Washington: Praeger Publishers, 1974).

Tyler, Parker. *Sex in Films* (New York: Citadel Press, 1974).

Vale, V., and Juno, Andrea, editors. *Incredibly Strange Films* (San Francisco: Re / Search, 1986).

Walker, Alexander. *The Celluloid Sacrifice: Aspects of Sex in the Movies* (New York: Hawthorn Books, 1967).

Wortley, Richard. *Erotic Movies* (New York: Crescent Books, 1975).

Zito, Stephen F. *See* Turan, Kenneth.

Index